AN UNTAMED VALLEY

A STABLE LIFE SERIES

MARIA V. BADIN

CIELO VISTA
— BOOKS —

For Jarett

CONTENTS

BEFORE DAWN

Darkness cloaked the valley. The hour before dawn whispered through half-open windows, where birdsong, cricket chirps, and frog croaks drifted in on the rhythm of an oscillating fan. The stillness cracked as the overhead light flicked on, revealing a teenage boy's world built by hand and heart.

Model airplanes, trucks, and cars—each crafted with meticulous care and precision—lined hand-carved wooden shelves that Hank Miller, fifteen, built alongside Grandpa Joe's watchful eye. F-14 Tomcats, Ford pickups, and vintage Chevys stood at attention between polished junior rodeo belt buckles, faded ribbons, and dusty trophies. The air held the faint scent of sawdust and enamel paint, anchored by the earthy tones of worn wood and well-loved leather.

A half-finished 1967 Mustang Fastback sat center stage on a scarred oak desk, flanked by miniature jars of black and white paint, bristle-worn brushes, and a dented reading lamp that cast a halo over Hank's work.

"Get dressed," came a voice—firm, unceremonious.

Marshall Miller, fifty-four, tall and broad-shouldered, strode past the doorway. Sun-creased skin, jeans stained from decades of labor, and a brown pearl-snapped shirt framed a man shaped by droughts, cows, pigs, bulls, and harvest seasons. He didn't wait for a reply.

Hank blinked against the light and sat up, the coarse sheets of his twin bed bunching under him. He raked a hand through his tousled blond hair, pushing it into a passable shape. Outside, the day awaited, but inside, the ghosts of yesterday lingered.

He pulled on Jesse's old Wranglers—knees worn to softness—then shoved his feet into scuffed boots and shrugged into a flannel shirt faded from years of sun and sweat. He reached for his cowboy hat, the one his mama gave him last Christmas, and placed it with reverence on his head. In the mirror above his dresser, his piercing blue eyes searched for something unspoken—something waiting.

He stepped out onto the porch. The chill of morning clung to the boards beneath his boots. His father stood, thermos in hand, steam curling upward like breath from a horse's muzzle. Without a word, Marshall handed Hank his own. Hank took a sip, the warmth jolting him to full alertness.

"Where's Jesse?" he asked.

Marshall's steely blue gaze met his, clouded with history—of war, of hard seasons, of things left unsaid. He turned and walked toward the barn.

Hank didn't press. He tightened his grip on the thermos and followed.

Hank and Marshall stepped into the barn just as the first strokes of sunlight brushed the horizon, painting the sky in layered hues of lavender, rose, and gold. A low mist hugged the ground outside, lifting slowly as dawn broke over the valley like a slow inhale. The barn, weathered red with white trim and a tin roof that popped as it warmed, glowed faintly in the new light. Inside, the air was thick with the mingled scent of fresh hay, oiled leather, warm cowhide, and the ever-present musk of manure and feed—earthy, pungent, and alive.

The familiar clatter of cowbells echoed softly, a symphony of metal tones that signaled the start of another day. The Holsteins stirred, their breath visible in the chill, their dark eyes blinking with recognition. Each Holstein cow, identifiable by the numbered ear tags clipped to their ears, waited patiently in their milking bays. The tags, some faded and others newer, were essential for tracking milk production and health records—a testament to the meticulous care the Millers invested in their herd. Marshall moved with calm precision, grabbing a stool and metal pail, settling beside Dolly like clockwork.

"You take Penny and Nora," he said, not looking up. He didn't have to. Hank was already moving.

They worked in tandem, the sound of milk hitting metal echoing beneath the wooden rafters, joined by the creak of the barn's timber frame and the hum of fluorescent lights overhead. A transistor radio murmured faintly in the background, catching bits of classic country through the static. Hank leaned into the warmth of the cow, his hands finding the pulse and pace of milking without thought. They didn't speak of their bond—they practiced it. Learned. Inherited.

Through the barn doors, the sunrise strengthened, casting golden light across the corral and slipping through the knotholes and cracks in the barn walls. It dappled the hay-strewn floor and turned floating dust into glittering particles.

The beam of light passed over Marshall's broad back as he leaned into his work, his silhouette framed by a brilliance that softened his edges—like the sun respected his labor.

Hank caught the sight and paused, just for a moment, struck by how the light seemed to mirror the rhythm they shared: the rise and fall of days marked by effort, sweat, and duty. The sun rose for men like them—steady, uncomplaining, tethered to land and livestock.

They finished as the light climbed fully into the barn, the world outside now awash in amber. Chickens clucked awake in the coop, and a tractor engine coughed somewhere in the distance.

Then it came—the clang of the old iron bell from the farmhouse porch. Two clear strikes. June's signal.

Marshall stood and stretched, his knees cracking, and looked at his son. Their eyes met, not just in acknowledgment of a completed task, but in shared understanding. This life, this work—it didn't need explanation. It simply was.

"Feed the chickens and pigs before breakfast," Marshall said, tossing the rag over his shoulder.

"Yes, sir," Hank replied, grabbing the feed buckets.

As he crossed the yard, the sun crested the hills behind the valley, washing the barn, the pasture, and the rusted silo in molten light. The sky gleamed overhead—bright, open, full of promise. Hank felt it in his bones, in the way the earth warmed beneath his boots, in the way his father's voice still lingered in the air.

The kitchen pulsed with life—pots clanged, grease sizzled, and the warm scent of home-cooked comfort clung to the air like a loving hand on the shoulder. The sun spilled through the gingham curtains, bathing the room in a golden morning glow. Copper pans hung from a wrought-iron rack above the stove, catching the light like polished relics. The walls bore painted plates, rosaries, and weathered signs etched with sayings such as *"As for me and my house, we will serve the Lord"* and *"Bless this mess."*

June, the matriarch of the Miller family, moved with purpose, her apron smudged with flour, flipping bacon and sausage on a cast-iron skillet while calling over her shoulder to her daughter, Tegan, who grated golden potatoes into hash browns at the counter.

Tegan—ten-years-old with sun-kissed skin and honey-blonde hair that fell in loose waves past her shoulders—stood on her toes for better leverage, sleeves pushed high. She wore Hank's old jeans, baggy and rolled several times at the cuffs, cinched at the waist with a length of baling twine. An oversized flannel shirt, borrowed from June, hung untucked and flowing past her knees, fluttering with every move like a flag of rebellion and joy.

Her cheeks still glowed from gathering eggs at dawn, her eyes lit with morning mischief. Barefoot on the cool tile, she danced between stove and counter, hips swaying to the rhythm of Stevie Nicks' "Landslide" playing from the battered Panasonic radio on the windowsill. She sang in harmony with her mother, their voices rising above the clatter and sizzle like church bells on Sunday—sweet, strong, and full of soul.

Grandma Ginny entered with a woven basket brimming with sprigs of rosemary, thyme, marigolds, and fresh produce—crimson tomatoes, green beans, and a perfect yellow squash. She set it down near her corner nook, a sacred space filled with glass jars, dried bundles of herbs, mortars and pestles, and hand-labeled remedies for ailments both real and imagined.

"Smells like heaven in here," she said with a wink, brushing flour off Tegan's nose before pulling a bundle of sage from her basket.

Grandpa Joe, quiet and steady as a river stone, finished setting the table—a handcrafted white oak rectangle flanked by matching chairs he and Jesse had built together last winter. The wood still smelled faintly of varnish and sawdust. He placed down pitchers of fresh-squeezed orange juice and cold well water with a practiced grace, then smoothed the embroidered table runner stitched by June's mother long ago.

Just as the final tray of biscuits came out of the oven—golden, flakey, steaming—the screen door creaked open.

Marshall and Hank stepped in, their boots dusted with dry straw and the smell of morning chores clinging to their sleeves.

"Wash up before you sit," June said without turning. "And scrub, not splash."

"Yes, ma'am," Marshall rumbled with a grin, clapping Hank gently on the back as they detoured toward the sink.

By the time the men returned, the kitchen table had transformed into a banquet: platters piled high with crispy bacon and sausages, fluffy scrambled eggs speckled with herbs, golden hash browns, thick cream gravy in a ceramic boat, and biscuits stacked like edible bricks of gold.

Everyone found their place. Marshall took the head of the table, his calloused hands resting on either side of his plate. Grandpa Joe sat at the other end, upright and proud. Hank slid in beside Tegan, who barely suppressed her humming. June sat next to her husband, and on the other side, the empty seat Jesse usually filled stood stark and silent.

Marshall's eyes flicked to it, then to June. She met his gaze and gave a small, solemn nod.

They all joined hands.

Grandma Ginny bowed her head and spoke: "Lord, we thank You for this food, for the hands that prepared it, and for this family. Bless our labor, mend our hurts, guide our children, and remind us that every sunrise is a gift. In Jesus' name, Amen."

"Amen," they echoed.

Plates clattered, and voices rose with laughter and plans. Hank and Marshall discussed the broken irrigation line—"We'll dig it up before noon, patch it before lunch," Marshall said. Grandpa Joe mentioned he'd be out in his shop finishing the last of the ladder-back chairs for the Sullivan wedding. June reminded Hank to deliver a jar of elderberry syrup to old Mrs. Pritchard, and Tegan slipped an extra sausage onto Hank's plate when their parents weren't looking. Hank smiled, and mouthed the words, 'thanks sis', winked, and stuffed the sausage into his mouth.

Then the phone rang.

A metallic trill echoed throughout the room. Tegan jumped up before anyone else could move, skidding across the tile to the pale yellow rotary phone mounted on the wall. She plucked the receiver off its hook, twirled the cord in one hand, and covered the mouthpiece with the other.

"Daddy," she said with wide eyes, pointing the receiver at him. "It's some funny-sounding man."

Marshall raised an eyebrow. "Funny, huh?"

She grinned.

He crossed the room and plucked the phone from her, pinching her cheek on the way with mock disapproval.

"Ow," she said, laughing.

"Morning," Marshall answered. "Yes, sir... Uh-huh... Mmm." He turned away, voice low and steady. "We'll be there."

He hung up and walked back to the table.

"Well?" June asked, raising an eyebrow as she passed him a biscuit.

"A job," Marshall said, sitting back down. "Estancia Castilla. All their hands are sick. They need help moving cattle from the pasture."

June gasped, hand fluttering to her chest. "*The* Estancia Castilla? With the terracotta roof tiles and the arcade courtyard and that fountain with the lion heads?"

Tegan's face lit like fire. "Can I come? You know I'm a better cowgirl than all of y'all combined."

Marshall snorted, shook his head. "Thought I'd take Hank."

"But Daddy—"

He held up a hand, already shaking his head with a smirk. "Fine. I guess I could use the help. And someone's gotta keep your brother out of trouble."

He leaned back and mockingly added, "Maybe I'll even wake our dead eldest son, see if the spirit moves him to pitch in."

"Don't tease," June said, lightly swatting his arm. "He was out late working, and you know it."

Marshall raised an eyebrow. "Is that what's called work now?"

June pursed her lips. "Jesse contributes too, just differently."

Marshall gave her a long look, then placed his hand gently over hers. "Alright," he whispered. "You win. I'll take care of it." Marshall said with a smirk, already rising from his seat.

The wooden steps creaked beneath Marshall's weight as he climbed the narrow staircase to the loft. Morning light slanted through the slatted vents above the garage door, illuminating dust in lazy spirals. As he reached the landing, he paused in front of Jesse's door. A hand-painted sign hung crookedly from a nail, its script looping and elegant, as if plucked from a Renaissance manuscript. It read: "Enter Freely and of Your Own Will." A direct affront to the more typical teenage warning—"Stay Out."

Marshall exhaled, knocked once. A muffled groan echoed from the other side.

He pushed the door open.

Inside, Jesse's world unfurled in stark contrast to the rest of the ranch. The space was spartan and bohemian—an organized chaos of creation and defiance. Half-finished sketches littered every surface—lined notebooks, napkins, even the bare floor—charcoal horses in flight, stylized nudes, fractured portraits. Crumpled lyric sheets blanketed the foot of the bed, scrawled in black ink and coffee stains. Guitars leaned against the wall like sentries: an old acoustic with a cracked bridge, a Stratocaster missing a string, a banjo with hand-painted vines along the rim.

Posters from Rolling Stone and *Creem* magazine were taped haphazardly to the walls—Springsteen frozen mid-leap, Blondie smirking beneath a neon sign, a Van Halen tour ad curling at the edges. A cheap boom box sat on the dresser, its chrome knobs worn, a mixtape half-spooled inside. Milk crates filled with vinyls leaned crooked by the bed—The Clash, Talking Heads, Fleetwood Mac—records stacked without sleeves, some warped from sun through the window. A Polaroid of Jesse with friends at a county fair was wedged in the mirror's frame, its colors fading already.

An easel stood in the corner by the single arched window, a canvas turned away as though ashamed to be seen. A harmonica rested atop another stack of vinyls beside a portable record player. Incense ashes curled in a dish shaped like a hand. The air smelled faintly of turpentine, old wood, and cigarettes.

Jesse lay tangled in his sheets like a fallen angel, half-draped in morning shadows. He wore a white tank top clinging to his pale, perfect skin, and threadbare jeans cuffed at the ankles. His boots—scuffed, cracked, broken-in like truth—sat abandoned at the foot of the bed.

Marshall stepped in and looked around the room, his eyes scanning the sketches, the lyrics, the instruments—and then landed on his son.

He gave Jesse's foot a tap with the toe of his boot.

A grunt.

Jesse peeled open his eyes, bloodshot and rimmed in darkness, their natural gleam dulled by another late night.

"Morning, General," he rasped, voice dry as hay left too long in the sun.

Marshall didn't smirk, didn't scold. He just stared.

Jesse rolled his head toward the wall, exhaling slowly. "I know," he muttered. "I'm a disappointment. Again."

Marshall said nothing. Instead, he picked up a sketch from the nightstand—a graphite rendering of a girl with wild hair riding bareback across open land—and studied it for a breath too long. Then, without looking back, he said flatly, "Need your help moving cattle."

Jesse raised a slow, sarcastic salute. "Sure thing, General. I'll be down in ten."

Marshall turned to go, pausing in the doorway. He looked at his son again—this boy-man who bore none of his callouses, none of his certainty—and then quietly stepped out, the door creaking shut behind him.

From within the loft, Jesse watched the shadow under the door vanish. He sat up, swung his legs over the edge of the bed, and ran a hand through his ink-dark brown hair.

Then he reached for his boots.

ESTANCIA CASTILLA

The hum of tires on asphalt gave way to the steady, mechanical purr of Bess—Marshall's meticulously kept 1972 Chevy C20, her red and white two-tone paint glinting under the morning sun like polished enamel. She pulled the gooseneck trailer with ease, chrome bumpers catching the light, every bolt snug, every panel spotless. Marshall had kept her running smooth as butter for decades, tuning her carburetor by hand, greasing her hinges, waxing her fenders. Bess wasn't just a truck—she was a member of the family, his pride and joy, as dependable and unyielding as the man behind the wheel.

Tegan sat beside him, legs tucked under her, eyes glowing with excitement. She talked a mile a minute, blond braid bouncing as she gestured animatedly. "Mama said they have lavender hedges lining the paddocks and wisteria climbing the barn rafters. And a real courtyard. Like Spain-Spain, not just California-fancy."

Marshall raised an eyebrow, keeping his eyes ahead. "Hope their cattle know how to appreciate all that landscaping."

Tegan grinned. "You just wait. It's gonna be beautiful."

Hank, tucked between her and Jesse, leaned slightly forward, absorbing every word. His shoulders sagged just a touch from the morning's chores, but his curiosity overpowered his fatigue. His blue eyes darted toward the windshield, tracking the tree line ahead.

At the end of the bench seat, Jesse slouched near the passenger window, arm hanging out into the breeze. He wore his hangover like a badge of rebellion—sunglasses hiding bloodshot dark brown eyes, jaw unshaven, lips slack. The wind tangled his dark curls, and though his body slumped, his gaze never left the landscape blurring past.

Marshall downshifted and turned the wheel.

Bess rolled confidently off the county road and onto a tree-lined stone driveway, her tires crunching against the granite in a rhythm as old as ranching itself. Towering oaks arched above, their branches interlaced like fingers in prayer, dappling sunlight across the hood and windshield in moving patches of gold.

As they crested a rise, Estancia Castilla revealed itself in full glory.

The estate stretched across the hillside with commanding elegance—a Spanish colonial-style estate, low and expansive, its whitewashed stucco walls bathed in sunlight. Terracotta roof tiles glowed warm in reds and oranges, weathered and noble. Arched corridors circled a lush central courtyard, where water tumbled from a tiered stone fountain guarded by carved lion heads. Wrought iron lanterns hung beneath eaves of exposed timber beams, their scrollwork delicate, their presence stately.

Climbing bougainvillea spilled color down every corner—scarlet, fuchsia, magenta. Rosemary hedges flanked the cobblestone walkways, and the scent of lavender bloomed on the breeze. To the east, olive orchards fanned out in neat, silver-green rows, leaves fluttering softly like silk. A gentle slope led to immaculate stucco barns, their orange-tile roofs mirroring the mansion's crown. Beyond them, cattle pens bordered by low whitewashed walls cradled a small herd of glossy, well-fed stock.

Marshall exhaled slowly, eyes narrowing as he took it all in. Even he had to admit—it was something.

From across the courtyard, a man emerged on foot, long-legged and smiling, his arms spread in welcome. Don Antonio Castilla, regal in presence but warm as sunlit leather, strolled toward them. He wore tailored riding breeches, polished Argentine boots, and a linen shirt beneath a dark vest embroidered subtly with silver thread. A wide-brimmed gaucho hat shaded his dark eyes, and a burgundy silk pañuelo tied at his throat fluttered in the breeze.

"Marshall Miller!" he called out, voice rich with accent and genuine pleasure. "Qué alegría. Bring her up to the barn, mi amigo."

Marshall tipped his hat, hand patting Bess's dash like one would a loyal dog.

Tegan pressed against the window, eyes wide. "Mama won't believe this."

Hank leaned forward, gaze locked on the barn's fine lines and polished gates. Jesse, finally sitting upright, slipped off his sunglasses, squinting at the estate as if seeing something he didn't expect to care about—but did.

The moment Bess rumbled to a stop beside the pristine barn, the Miller family spilled out in a flurry of dust, denim, and sun-creased weariness. Boots thudded against the gravel; they adjusted their hat brims and suppressed yawns. Their clothes bore the creases of early chores—shirts untucked, jeans dusty, and hair tousled by wind and windows. A mismatched, road-worn band of cowboys—and one radiant cowgirl—stood in stark contrast to the manicured perfection of Estancia Castilla.

Don Antonio Castilla stepped forward with open arms and a smile that faltered—just for a heartbeat. His sharp eyes, trained to assess livestock and men alike, scanned the group. The slightest arch of his brow betrayed his surprise, maybe even mild doubt. But he masked it quickly, his gaze locking onto Tegan.

"And who," he said with affectionate curiosity, "might I ask is this?"

Tegan stepped forward, chin high, braid swinging behind her. She met his gaze with clear blue eyes and offered her hand with confidence.

"I'm Tegan Miller," she said firmly. "The best cowgirl in the county, sir."

Don Antonio's eyes lit with laughter, charmed and thoroughly disarmed. He gripped her hand with both of his and gave it a vigorous shake. "Then I am in your debt, Señorita Tegan."

Marshall, already unlatching the trailer gate, called over, "Tegan, help the boys unload the horses."

"Yes, sir," she chirped, turning smartly and heading toward the trailer where Jesse was reluctantly reaching for a lead rope and Hank was already removing the tack.

Marshall strode up to Don Antonio with the steady gait of a man who didn't waste steps. His demeanor shifted—boots grounded, shoulders squared, voice all business.

"How can we be of service?"

Don Antonio clapped a hand to his chest with dramatic flair. "Marshall, I'm so grateful you and your family came on such short notice. Of all days, my workers have chosen this one to be sick." He rolled his eyes with theatrical exasperation. "And of course, today is the day we must bring in the cattle from pasture—sort them, castrate the young bulls, and vaccinate the lot."

Marshall gave a slight nod. "We'll get it done. My boys can handle the castration. Tegan'll take care of the vaccinations. We're well-versed in animal husbandry."

Don Antonio's face broke into animated relief. He flung his arms around Marshall in a spontaneous, heartfelt hug. "Then let's not waste time, my friend. Vamos."

The herd pushed forward in a slow tide across the sun-soaked pasture, hooves thudding and tails flicking, a chorus of lowing echoing over the open hills. Dust swirled in lazy spirals, rising into the bright morning air. The Miller family rode in formation, flanking the cattle with practiced precision.

Don Antonio Castilla rode at the head on his stunning bay Criollo stallion, Patrón. The horse moved with collected power, muscles rippling beneath a coat like polished mahogany, his black mane and tail flowing like ink spilled in motion. Don Antonio sat tall in a hand-tooled leather saddle, carved and adorned in exquisite Argentine craftsmanship—silver inlays, rawhide braiding, and an engraved horn that caught the sun like fire.

To his right rode Marshall, steady in the saddle, surveying the herd with a rancher's eye. On Don Antonio's left, Hank rode with quiet focus, his gelding alert beneath him, ears flicking forward and back.

Hank nodded toward the Criollo. "That's a fine horse. And the saddle... I've never seen work like that up close."

Don Antonio's face lit with pride. "My brother bred Patrón at the original Estancia Castilla in Córdoba, Argentina. Our family breeds Criollos, yes—but also thoroughbreds, Paso Peruanos, and Pura Raza Española stallions imported directly from Spain. We breed not just for beauty, but for heart and purpose."

Hank opened his mouth to respond, but a sudden burst of motion shattered the calm.

Three calves broke from the herd, spooked by a flapping bird wing or a sudden gust. They bolted—ears back, tails up—cutting hard to the left through a patch of brush.

Hank didn't hesitate.

He stood slightly in the stirrups and spurred his gelding forward. The horse responded like lightning, surging ahead with speed and agility. Hank pulled the lasso from his saddle horn, letting it uncoil in the wind as he gained ground.

One calf veered wide. Hank cut the angle sharply, his body moving with the gelding like a single organism. Dust exploded beneath them as they spun—a blur of hooves, mane, and grit. He threw the loop, a perfect cast, and it landed clean around the first calf's neck. With a sharp tug and a practiced hand, he checked the animal's momentum, slowing it to a confused halt.

The second calf juked right.

Hank dropped the rope, spun his horse, and gave chase. The gelding pivoted on a dime—true cutting-horse style—lowering into a deep crouch before launching into a sprint. Hank didn't rope this one—he used pressure, angles, and speed, driving the calf back with shouted cues and fluid maneuvers.

The third calf bolted for open pasture, hooves pounding.

Behind him, Marshall whistled sharp and loud, the sound slicing across the field.

From the rear of the herd, Jesse groaned audibly, pulling his horse out of a lazy walk. "Every damn time," he muttered, but kicked into a lope all the same.

Together, Hank and Jesse cut off the last escapee—Jesse from the flank, Hank from the lead. The calf wheeled in confusion and turned back toward the herd. Hank whooped and rode tight circles around the trio, steering them all into a wide arc and funneling them back to the herd's edge with the ease of a seasoned hand.

Don Antonio watched, eyebrows raised, a slow smile spreading across his face. "Madre de Dios. That boy rides like he was born in the saddle."

Marshall's voice carried low and proud. "Yep. That boy's got a way with anything on four legs."

Don Antonio's eyes drifted to Jesse, who had returned to a loose rein, tossing Hank a lazy thumbs-up. "And the eldest?" Don Antonio asked gently.

Marshall tipped his hat low. "We do our best," he said, voice neutral but firm.

Before another word could pass between them, a sharp whistle rang from the rear of the herd.

Tegan.

Marshall turned, catching sight of his daughter astride her paint mare, waving him down with urgency. Without hesitation, he turned his horse and galloped toward her.

Don Antonio gathered the reins and clicked to Patrón, leading the now-contained herd toward the waiting whitewashed pens at the foot of the slope. He opened the gate himself, waving the cattle through as they funneled into the corral, hooves clacking against the packed dirt.

The Millers moved into action like gears in a machine. Marshall directed; Hank and Jesse sorted the calves from the cows, working the alley gates and squeeze chute with synchronized ease. Each calf came through one by one, ears flicking, eyes wide.

Tegan moved among them with sleeves rolled and jaw set, administering vaccinations with deft precision. Her syringe glinted in the light as she murmured calming words to each animal.

Meanwhile, under their father's supervision, Hank and Jesse performed the castrations—clean, efficient, and respectful. Marshall stayed close, his voice low but commanding, guiding their every move with the steady hand of experience.

Don Antonio sat astride Patrón at the edge of the pens, watching the family work—dust rising around them, sweat glistening on their brows, movements swift and sure. A disheveled crew, maybe. But capable. Fearless. And true.

Estancia Castilla had never seen a crew quite like the Millers. But perhaps, he thought, that was exactly what it needed.

As Don Antonio released the last calf from the chute and the dust settled around the pens, he dismounted, brushing a hand over Patrón's glossy neck before turning to the Millers with a warm, commanding presence.

"But you must stay," he said, lifting his hands as if to halt any protest. "We have refreshments waiting on the veranda. You must be hungry after such noble work. Please—I insist."

Marshall wiped the sweat from his brow with a bandana and glanced at his sons. Hank and Jesse both shrugged with tired shoulders, indifferent but clearly not opposed. Then he looked at Tegan, who was beaming up at him with wide, pleading eyes.

"Please, Daddy," she said, breathless with excitement. "I've never been on a veranda."

Before Marshall could respond, Don Antonio swept in beside her, presenting his arm like a proper gentleman. "It's settled," he said, smiling as Tegan giggled and grasped his arm. Together, they ascended the tiled steps to the grand veranda.

The space opened like a dream—arched columns cast striped shadows across a tiled floor in warm terracotta and cobalt patterns. A round table, elegantly draped in a white linen cloth, sat beneath the shade of an old olive tree. Six wooden chairs encircled it, and the table gleamed with polished silverware, cut-crystal glasses, and a spread of Argentinian delights—empanadas, media lunas, ceviche, picada platters stacked with meats and cheeses, and delicate alfajores dusted in powdered sugar.

Don Antonio motioned them to sit and gave a small, silver handbell a ceremonial ring.

Tegan instantly slid into the seat beside him, smiling from ear to ear. Marshall took the chair on Don Antonio's other side. Across from them, Hank and Jesse sank into their seats, their dust-covered shirts a sharp contrast to the elegant setting.

A moment later, an older woman in a crisp apron emerged from the house carrying a silver tray lined with pitchers of lemonade, iced tea, and beer bottles nestled in ice. She moved gracefully, placing each option in the center of the table.

"Lemonade, please," Tegan said brightly.

"I'll take one too," Hank added, parched and sun-flushed.

Marshall hesitated, then sighed. "Make that three."

The woman poured with gentle efficiency.

"I'll have a beer," Jesse said, reaching forward with a smirk.

Marshall's head turned slowly, his look sharp and unamused.

Jesse raised his hands. "Kidding. Tea's fine."

A momentary silence fell, the kind that comes after long work and unexpected civility.

Then Tegan broke it, pointing to the golden pastries arranged in delicate spirals. "What are those? They look like little moons."

Don Antonio's eyes lit up. "Media lunas—'half moons,' as you say. Try one."

Tegan didn't hesitate. She reached across the table and grabbed two, taking a generous bite. Her eyes widened with joy.

"They're almost as good as Mama's," she declared, mouth half-full. "But not quite. Mama's the best cook in the county. You have to come over for dinner."

"Tegan," Marshall said gently, giving her a warning look.

She shrugged. "Well, she is."

Marshall chuckled, conceding. "Can't argue with that. June can cook with the best of them."

Don Antonio placed a hand on his chest. "Then I shall look forward to it. I will come—with great appetite."

The Millers exchanged surprised glances, and Marshall nodded slowly. "Let me check with my wife. I'll get back to you."

Don Antonio grinned, then turned toward Hank. "But you, young man. I've not seen a rider with your instincts in a long time. The way you moved with your horse—magnífico. I could use someone like you on my ranch."

Hank blinked, stunned. "You mean—me?"

Marshall sat straighter. "We'll talk with your mother first," he said, his voice even but firm.

Don Antonio nodded, satisfied. "Of course. The wife rules the house, no? My wife, Elena—Dios la tenga en su gloria—guided me always. She still does."

He reached across and slapped Marshall's back in friendship. "Whether Hank joins the Castilla family or not, I look forward to doing more business with you."

Just as the conversation settled again, a soft melody floated in from the open parlor window. A piano, played with delicate precision—notes soft as feathers.

Everyone paused. Don Antonio leaned back in his chair, eyes closing in recognition.

Jesse's posture straightened as the music floated through the open window—soft, aching, precise. Clair de Lune. He knew it instantly. The notes carried something he hadn't felt in a long time: quiet. Space. Possibility.

He used to play it back in high school. In secret. He'd sneak into the family room on his mother's upright and let his fingers find their way across the keys, chasing a softness he couldn't name.

Then Marshall caught him once, alone at the piano before chores. Stood there in the doorway, arms crossed. Jesse had looked up, halfway through the piece, hopeful maybe—waiting for something. Praise, maybe. Or just... interest.

Instead, Marshall had said, "That piano ain't gonna milk the cows."

Now, he turned toward the sound, drawn in despite himself. The music still knew how to find him.

"That's Clair de Lune... Debussy, right?" he said, but too offhand, like he didn't care either way. Like it hadn't ever meant a damn thing.

Don Antonio's eyes opened, surprised and pleased. "Yes. My niece plays it when she wants something from me," he said with a rueful smile. "She's visiting for the summer. Studying... always studying."

He turned his attention to Jesse. "You are an artist too, no?"

Jesse shrugged, downplaying it. "I dabble."

Tegan snorted. "He's the best musician and singer in the—"

"In the county," Don Antonio finished, winking at her.

Marshall shifted uncomfortably. He stood, brushing dust from his jeans. "We should be going. Got to fix the irrigation line before sundown. And grandma needs help with the garden."

He extended his hand across the table. Don Antonio stood and clasped it warmly.

"Thank you again, my friend. I look forward to hearing from you about Hank—and to your wife's famous cooking."

Marshall tipped his hat. "We'll be in touch."

He looked at his sons, nodding.

Hank stood and took Tegan's hand. Jesse gave the veranda one last look, eyes lingering on the open window, then rose and nodded respectfully.

"Thank you for the meal, sir," he said.

"Gracias, Señor," Hank added.

Tegan slipped from her chair, let go of Hank's hand, and wrapped her arms around Don Antonio in a spontaneous hug. "You're my new best friend," she declared.

15

Don Antonio chuckled, then gently took her hand. "Until we meet again, Señorita Tegan."

They turned toward the steps; the sun casting long shadows behind them. Estancia Castilla shimmered in the afternoon light as the Millers made their way back to Bess, the red-and-white Chevy, waiting faithfully to take them home.

PORCH SONGS AND A GIG

T he kitchen smelled of cinnamon, warm butter, and a hint of black coffee as the Miller family lingered around the dinner table, finishing off the last bites of Grandma Ginny's homemade apple pie—her secret crust recipe revered like sacred scripture. Plates clinked and forks scraped as laughter filled the room, full-bellied and bright. Even Marshall and Jesse, usually the quietest at day's end, had cracked smiles and let out the occasional chuckle.

Tegan, perched at the edge of her chair, launched into another spirited retelling of the day's events at Estancia Castilla.

"And then," she said with wide eyes, hands gesturing like a conductor mid-symphony, "he looked down at me, all serious and noble-like, and he said"—she shifted her voice to a dramatically smooth Argentine accent—"'Señorita Tegan, you are most impressive. I am in your debt.'"

The table roared with laughter.

She threw her arms up. "I ate media lunas on the veranda! Like a real one! With linen napkins and a bell to summon lemonade!"

June, seated beside Marshall, raised a single eyebrow and turned her gaze to her husband.

"I can't wait until he comes to dinner!" Tegan blurted, mouth full of pie.

Marshall gently patted June's hand reassuringly. "We'll discuss it later."

Across the table, Jesse leaned back in his chair, fork dangling from his fingers. "Settle down, T-Rex," he said with a grin. "Before you burst a lung."

The nickname landed perfectly—T-Rex, a holdover from when she was a screeching toddler with the lungs of a banshee.

Tegan giggled and pointed a fork back at him. "You're just jealous. Hank's got a job."

"I do not!" Hank said, laughing, and nudged her shoulder with his own.

Tegan bared her teeth and growled, low and playful. "Rawrrr."

June raised both hands and waved them gently, like a conductor calling for a diminuendo. The noise subsided.

She turned her focus on Hank. "Well? What do you think about this job opportunity?"

Hank shrugged, serious now. "Don Antonio just likes the way I ride. I dunno if I'd fit in with all that finery. But it could help the family. We need a new tractor."

Marshall leaned back in his chair and gave Hank a long, proud look. The boy was growing into a man—thinking not just about himself, but about all of them.

"I'll talk to you about it later, Mama," Hank added softly.

He then turned toward Grandpa Joe at the end of the table. "His saddle, Grandpa... the leatherwork was unreal. Nothing I've seen except your stuff. The hand tooling, the detail... I think you'd like it."

Grandpa Joe gave a thoughtful nod. "Looking forward to meeting this Don Antonio. A man who appreciates fine craftsmanship is worth knowing."

June's gaze shifted across the table to Jesse. "And what about you, sweetheart? Did you enjoy the outing?"

Jesse hesitated, his fork circling the pie crust. He glanced at his father before answering. "It was fine. Money was good." He took another bite, burying the rest of his answer beneath layers of cinnamon and sugar.

But Tegan wasn't done.

"Tell her about the music, Jess!"

June's eyes softened, curious. "Music?"

Jesse blinked, then leaned back in his chair, the faintest flicker of light in his eyes. "Someone was playing Clair de Lune on the piano. Sounded like a grand—Steinway, I bet. Like the one we saw at the concert in L.A."

June's smile returned, gentle and warm. "Maybe Don Antonio will let you play it next time."

But the openness in Jesse's face flickered out. He looked down at his plate. "May I be excused?"

June's smile faltered. "Of course. But you and Hank are on dish duty tonight."

"Yes, ma'am," Jesse replied quietly.

He looked to Hank, who gave him a nod, and the two brothers stood and began gathering plates, pie tins, and crumpled napkins.

The rest of the family began making their way into the family room, voices low, bellies full, the warmth of the meal lingering like a hearth fire.

Jesse moved slowly toward the sink, casting one last glance over his shoulder, as if trying to remember the sound of the piano.

The clink of dishes and the soft swish of running water filled the kitchen, accompanied by the rhythmic scrape of plates being scrubbed and dried. Jesse stood at the sink, sleeves rolled, water sloshing around his elbows as he washed with surprising efficiency. Beside him, Hank dried each dish with a well-worn kitchen towel, spinning to stack plates in the overhead cabinet and slide silverware into their drawers with practiced precision.

They worked like two cogs in a machine—fast, fluid, familiar.

"Got a gig later at the pub," Jesse said suddenly, breaking the silence. "Wanna come?"

Hank didn't miss a beat. "I don't know, Jess. I'm tired—and unlike you, I've got an early morning tomorrow."

Jesse shrugged off the jab with a grin. "Come on, Hank, we're the Miller boys. We never get tired."

Hank gave him a flat look, shaking his head. "Hard pass."

Jesse dropped the sponge into the soapy water and leaned against the counter, his voice softening. "I need you, brother. This one's different. Could lead to something big—someone's coming to scout talent. And you..." he nudged Hank with his elbow, "you could use a little fun. Too much work makes you dull with the ladies."

"I'm not dull," Hank said, bristling.

Jesse raised his brows. "Of course not. I mean, tractors and irrigation lines are such enticing conversation topics."

That earned him a reluctant smile from Hank. "I see your point."

Jesse beamed. "Good. We'll leave once everyone turns in."

They turned back to their work, falling into rhythm again—rinse, dry, stack, rinse, dry, stack. A quiet hum settled over the kitchen.

Then, from the family room, the first notes of June's upright piano drifted through the house—soft, graceful chords that echoed through the walls with a lullaby's ease. Jesse paused, head tilted, a mischievous grin creeping across his face.

"You finish up," he said, wiping his hands on a dish towel. "I'm getting the strings to charm the fam."

Before Hank could protest, Jesse flicked a handful of suds in his direction and darted out of the kitchen.

"Jess!" Hank called after him, exasperated but smiling.

The family room glowed in the gentle lamplight of evening, each corner steeped in warmth and memory. Hand-built furniture crafted by Grandpa Joe anchored the space—rugged wooden tables with smooth, rounded edges, a sturdy sofa draped in handmade quilts, and two well-worn leather armchairs that bore the weight and stories of generations. The air carried the faint scent of cedar, old books, and pine smoke curling from the stone fireplace, which dominated the far wall.

Above the wooden mantel, a crucifix hung at the center. To one side, a folded American flag sat encased in glass. Flanking it were two distinct displays—WWII medals, proud and aged, labeled with Capt. Joseph Miller, U.S. Air Force, and another set marked Sgt. Marshall Miller, U.S. Marines—Vietnam. Beside them rested a framed photograph of a radiant young Ginny Miller in her Army nurse's uniform, eyes bright with hope and grit.

Framed photos covered the wall: a young Marshall in his Marine fatigues, posed beside a M48 Patton tank; Grandpa Joe, in crisp blues under an airbase hangar; Grandma Ginny, smiling in a field hospital tent. A photo of June, no older than eighteen, caught mid-performance at a concert grand piano, fingers floating over the keys. Tucked in the corner was her Yale diploma, the glass faintly cracked but proudly displayed. Below all of it was a family portrait—all five Millers smiling against a backdrop of golden pasture—and a newer photo of Jesse, Hank, and Tegan on horseback, grinning beneath wide-brimmed hats, eyes full of mischief and love.

June sat at the upright piano, finishing a gentle classical piece, her fingers tapering the notes into silence. The room sat still, all eyes on her.

Grandma Ginny rocked steadily in her chair, knitting a soft blue sweater, matching Tegan's eyes, needles clicking in time with the music. Tegan, nestled on the sofa between Marshall and Grandpa Joe, rested her head on her father's lap. His calloused hand stroked her hair in a slow, steady rhythm as her eyes fluttered, fighting sleep.

Hank entered from the kitchen, wiping his hands on a dish towel before sinking into the nearest leather chair, stretching out with a low groan of satisfaction.

A moment later, the front door opened, and Jesse stepped in from outside, guitar case in hand, hair tousled and cheeks pink from the breeze. He set the case down and pulled up a chair next to June just as she closed the lid over the keys. Applause rippled through the room. She gave a small bow of the head, eyes twinkling, and turned to her son.

Her expression softened into a playful grin.

Jesse returned it with a wink.

June counted them in. Her fingers hit the keys, brisk and syncopated. The notes of "Take the 'A' Train" burst into the room, jubilant and electric.

Grandpa Joe sat up straighter, his eyes alight. He stood, walked over to Grandma Ginny, and extended his hand with an old-world charm. "Let's show these youngsters how it's done."

Grandma Ginny chuckled, setting her knitting gently aside. "Try to keep up, flyboy."

She took his hand, and he led her to the center of the room. Together, they moved into a jitterbug, their steps still sharp despite the years, their bodies remembering everything their bones had forgotten. The room came alive.

Tegan's eyes snapped open.

She squealed and leapt to her feet, tugging Marshall's hand. "Come on, Daddy! Dance!"

Marshall chuckled, half-protesting, but she insisted. She dragged him up, and then spun around and grabbed Hank too.

Hank groaned. "Do I have a choice?"

Marshall and Hank exchanged a long-suffering look—then both gave in.

As Grandpa Joe and Grandma Ginny cut the rug, Marshall and Hank took turns spinning and swinging Tegan, her laughter piercing the air like wind chimes in a summer breeze. June and Jesse sang in harmony, Jesse's rich tenor winding through June's lilting alto. It was music from another time—joyful, timeless, deeply felt.

The song neared its finish. Grandpa Joe dipped Grandma Ginny with dramatic flair, both of them beaming.

Tegan leapt into Marshall's arms and kissed his cheek. "Best night ever, Daddy."

Across the room, June and Jesse shared a quiet, emotional moment. He leaned his forehead to hers.

"Love you, Ma," he whispered.

"I love you too, baby," she replied, eyes misting.

Grandpa Joe, still holding Grandma Ginny's hand, turned to the family. "That's enough excitement for one night. Goodnight, all."

Marshall clapped a hand on his back. "I'm with you, Pop. Early morning tomorrow."

June smoothed her dress, eyes twinkling. "Tegan, go wash up for bed."

Tegan crossed her arms. "Only if Jesse and Hank tell me a bedtime story and tuck me in."

June gave both sons a pleading look.

Jesse sighed, grinning. "Alright, T-Rex. Let's go."

He tickled her ribs, and she squealed. Hank rolled his eyes, but took her other hand.

They each grabbed a hand and swung her gently between them, legs kicking as she giggled uncontrollably.

"I'm gonna learn Spanish so good before I see Don Antonio again!" she declared.

She cleared her throat and, with theatrical flair, pronounced, "Señorita Tegan... por favor, más media lunas!" drawing out each syllable in a spirited imitation of Don Antonio's Argentine accent.

Jesse laughed. "That was awful."

"No, it wasn't!" Tegan insisted, puffing up. "Mucho gusto, Don Antoooooonio!" She rolled the R with all her might. "Gracias por los... mooostachoooos!"

"Right, Señorita, time for bed," Hank commanded, chuckling.

"Whatever," she said dramatically.

"She's ready for Buenos Aires," Jesse teased.

The three of them disappeared down the hallway—a cowboy, a musician, and a little girl turning language into song—her voice still echoing with exaggerated, affectionate Spanish as the farmhouse settled into the quiet of the night.

The light blue 1980 Chevy Caprice rolled into the gravel lot, headlights cutting through the dusk and brushing across the worn façade of the Long Branch Saloon. The chrome gleamed, the body spotless—June's car, clearly out of place in a parking lot full of rusted pickups and motorcycles.

Jesse parked with a satisfied grin. "She's asleep. Won't even notice it's gone."

Hank shot him a look. "You sure?"

"Left a note. Sort of. We'll have it back before sunrise."

Jesse grabbed his acoustic guitar and stepped out, energized. The saloon loomed ahead—a maroon-painted, weather-beaten building, the paint peeling from its planks. A plain white neon sign buzzed overhead, barely holding onto the word "SAL✱✱N."

Hank followed, pulling his cajón from the back seat, already second-guessing the decision. But Jesse was his brother—and sometimes that meant stepping into places you didn't belong.

Inside, the bar was alive. Music poured from the jukebox, mingling with laughter and clinking glasses. The floor, warped and sticky with spilled beer, bore the scuffs of years. Wooden tables surrounded a makeshift stage lit by a tired spotlight. Two microphones stood waiting.

To the left, a pool table saw a rowdy match underway. The crowd, already warmed by drink, barely glanced their way.

Behind the long oak bar, the owner—a thickset man with sharp eyes—glared at Jesse and pointed to his watch.

Jesse shrugged, knocked twice on the bar.

The man poured a pitcher of beer, slid it across. He raised his brows at Hank.

"Water," Hank said flatly.

"Set up the stage," Jesse told him. "I'll sweet-talk the man."

As Hank arranged the guitar, cajón, and a mason jar labeled "TIPS", Jesse chatted with the owner. Then he returned, pitcher and glass in hand, and passed Hank a cup of water.

Jesse tapped the mic. "Good evening. I'm Jesse Miller, and this here's my brother, Hank. We're gonna play some songs for y'all tonight—so dance, drink, or just enjoy. And don't forget to feed the tip jar."

With that, he strummed the opening chords to "Can't You See" by The Marshall Tucker Band. His voice cut through the noise—gritty, soulful, magnetic.

Heads turned. Conversations paused.

Couples drifted to the dance floor. In the corner, a group of young women leaned in, whispering and giggling.

Hank joined in at the chorus, voice tentative at first but finding its place. He tapped out rhythms on the cajón, letting himself relax into the groove. Jesse gave him a knowing nod—a moment of unspoken connection. For once, they were in sync.

The next few songs picked up the tempo. The crowd came alive, stomping, clapping, tipping generously. Jesse kept the energy high, even as he steadily worked through his second pitcher, unnoticed by Hank.

Then he leaned into the mic. "We're gonna slow it down. This one's for the ladies."

He turned to the corner table, locking eyes with a blonde in too much makeup, a denim corset, and tight jeans tucked into cowboy boots. He grinned and sang "Wonderful Tonight" straight to her, each note drawn out with effortless charm.

The women hollered. The crowd cheered.

"Thank you, thank you," Jesse said with a bow. "We'll be back in a few. Don't forget the tip jar."

He slung his guitar and sauntered toward the women's table.

Hank left on stage, shook his head, then climbed down. Needing a breather, he made his way to the bathroom.

When he returned, the mood had changed.

Near the wall, Jesse was pinned by the collar, shoved up against the wooden paneling by a thick-necked man with clenched fists—the blonde's boyfriend, clearly unimpressed with the performance.

Hank didn't hesitate. He charged.

He tackled the man, knocking him sideways into a table. Glass shattered. Chairs flew.

"Bam!"—a fist connected with Hank's jaw. He stumbled back and crashed onto another table, splinters flying as it gave beneath him.

Someone screamed. A beer bottle broke. And just like that—

The Long Branch erupted into a bar fight.

The metal door buzzed and groaned open as Hank Miller stepped out of the county jail, bloodied but steady, one boot scuffing the floor with every slow step. His black eye was swelling, his lip split, and his knuckles torn and caked with dried blood—a badge of honor earned not for himself, but for the brother still passed out inside.

Behind him, in the holding cell, Jesse lay slumped on a bench, snoring softly, a crooked grin still on his face. Not a scratch on him. Just mussed hair, a half-loosened belt, and the faintest trace of beer on his breath. He looked like he'd simply napped too hard on a couch.

Hank didn't glance back.

Deputy Wright gave him a sympathetic pat on the back. "Hell of a right hook, kid."

Hank offered a weak smile, eyes scanning the lobby where Marshall Miller stood like a carved figure from oak—stoic, arms crossed, his weathered face drawn taut with something between disappointment and reluctant admiration.

Hank lowered his gaze. "What about Jesse?"

Marshall's voice came low and flat. "He can sleep it off. Let's go."

No more was said as they stepped out into the cold blue light of dawn. The town still slept, but the weight of the night was alive in every echo of their footsteps.

They climbed into Bess, the red-and-white Chevy C20, and closed the doors with a heavy finality. The silence stretched thick and unmoving as Marshall started the engine and pulled away—not toward home, but in the opposite direction.

Hank glanced over, puzzled. "Where are we going?"

Marshall didn't answer.

The road wound upward through switchbacks and dusty gravel. Finally, Bess crested a hilltop, and Marshall eased her into park beside a weathered barbed wire fence overlooking the wide sprawl of the valley below.

Without a word, he stepped out, grabbing a thermos of coffee from behind the seat. He walked to the fence and stood tall, an unbreakable silhouette against the first blush of morning, watching the sun rise over the land that had raised him.

Hank joined him, shoulders stiff and tired face.

Marshall handed him the thermos.

Hank took it gratefully, unscrewed the lid, and drank deeply. The coffee was hot, bitter, and strong, and it hit his chest like a match to dry wood, burning the haze from his sleepless night.

They stood in silence, shoulder to shoulder, as the sky lit in oranges and golds, the first sunlight cresting the hills and spilling over the patchwork of fields and fences below.

Marshall spoke, voice rough like gravel under a tire.

"There are two types of people in life, son. The kind that floats through it, leaves wreckage behind, expects someone else to pick up the pieces. And then there's the kind who builds something—with pride, grit, and duty. A legacy."

He paused.

"I know you can be the man that builds something, Hank. But you have to decide if that's who you want to be."

Hank looked at his father—really looked—and for the first time saw not the invincible figure who held up their world, but a man shouldering the weight of love and disappointment at the same time.

"He's talented, Dad," Hank murmured, his voice raw.

Marshall flinched, blinked, turned his face slightly away.

"I know, son," he whispered. His voice cracked. "That's what makes it harder."

Hank saw it then—the flicker of pain, of love buried under years of restraint. It carved new understanding in him, solid and permanent.

No more words were necessary.

They stood together in the breaking light, two men bound not just by blood, but by the silent promise of something more: a legacy not yet written—but waiting.

HANK'S FIRST DAY

The midday sun shimmered off the hood of Bess as she rumbled down the long gravel driveway of Estancia Castilla, her engine humming low and steady like a heart at rest. Behind the wheel sat Grandpa Joe, his eyes squinting against the glare, posture upright, hands relaxed on the wheel like he'd been born there. In the passenger seat, Hank sat stiffly, fidgeting with his work gloves, his jaw tight with nerves—and lingering pain.

His ribs still ached from the night before. The bruises on his face had darkened overnight, and he winced every time the truck jostled over a pothole.

"You'll do just fine," Grandpa Joe said without taking his eyes off the road.

Hank exhaled through his nose. "I don't know, Grandpa. I've never worked for someone like Don Antonio before. Feels like I'm batting out of my league."

Grandpa Joe gave a small smile. "Boy, the Castillas are lucky to have you. They just don't know it yet."

Bess came to a halt at the edge of the Castilla courtyard, framed by arched porticos and flowering bougainvillea. As the engine quieted, Hank opened his door with a groan, carefully easing himself out of the cab. He rubbed at his side, jaw clenched. Grandpa Joe circled around the front, his boots crunching gravel, upright and composed in his worn work shirt and well-oiled belt.

Waiting for them beneath the veranda's shade were Don Antonio and his son, Agustín Castilla.

Don Antonio stood like a man born into the saddle and the boardroom—a trim figure in tailored riding pants, a white linen shirt, and polished boots that looked untouched by dust. His silver-streaked hair, bronze skin, and warm smile radiated hospitality.

Agustín, at his side, wore a fitted navy polo, clean khakis, and leather loafers that looked more Harvard Yard than cattle yard. He had perfectly combed hair, a crisp posture, and a reserved but kind expression—a young man accustomed to command but still learning when to wield it.

"Hank Miller!" Don Antonio beamed, stepping forward with open arms. "Bienvenido, my young friend."

Hank extended his hand, only for Don Antonio to clap it between both of his, shaking with firm affection.

"And this," he said, turning with pride, "must be the man who carved the very soul of this boy." He reached out a respectful hand to Grandpa Joe. "You honor me with your presence, Señor Miller."

"Joe's fine," Grandpa Joe replied, shaking his hand with a firm grip. "And thank you for having my grandson."

Don Antonio gestured to the young man beside him. "This is my son, Agustín. He runs the day-to-day operations of the estancia when he's home from his studies. Harvard, top of his class, valedictorian." His pride shone in every syllable.

Agustín offered his hand to both men. "Pleasure to meet you. We've heard good things about your family."

Then Don Antonio paused, his eyes lingering on the bruises along Hank's jawline, the way he moved a touch slower, favoring one side.

"You had quite the night, no?" Don Antonio asked, voice low but amused. "I heard there was... trouble at the saloon."

Hank looked down, embarrassed, but Don Antonio chuckled softly. "You defended your brother. We are our brother's keeper, no?"

Grandpa Joe stepped in with quiet pride. "Yes, sir. We Millers stand together. And my grandson—he's not only loyal, he's highly reliable."

Don Antonio nodded in approval, his gaze fond. "Then it is settled. Today, the Castilla family becomes stronger."

He turned to Hank and clapped a hand on his shoulder.

"We're excited you're joining us," he said warmly. "Agustín will show you around, explain your duties, and answer questions."

Agustín nodded briskly. "We start our employees at four dollars an hour. Does that sound acceptable?"

Hank's eyes widened. Four dollars an hour? That was more than he'd ever earned. He glanced at his grandfather.

Grandpa Joe didn't blink. "That seems fair."

Hank nodded quickly. "Yes, sir. Thank you."

"Excellent," Don Antonio said. "Agustín, take good care of him."

Then, with a twinkle in his eye, he turned to Grandpa Joe and looped an arm over his shoulders.

"Now, you, Señor Joe—I must show you something. My collection of antique rifles from Argentina. Family heirlooms. You will appreciate the craftsmanship."

Without waiting for a response, Don Antonio gently guided Grandpa Joe away across the courtyard, speaking animatedly.

Hank stood with Agustín, watching the two older men disappear into the shade of the house. He took a breath, tucked down his nerves, and squared his shoulders.

His first day had officially begun.

The early afternoon sun streamed through the windshield as June's light blue Chevy Caprice hummed along the quiet county road. Inside, the car was silent. Jesse, freshly released and still rumpled from a night in holding, sat slouched in the passenger seat, his gaze fixed out the window, avoiding his mother's eyes.

June said nothing at first, her hands steady on the wheel, her expression unreadable.

She reached for the radio and turned the chrome knob gently. The dial clicked softly as she tuned past bursts of static and chatter until the soft strains of J.S. Bach's Prelude in C Major filled the space—elegant and measured, each note familiar like an old lullaby through the worn speakers.

June smiled faintly and looked over at her son. "The first song I taught you," she said, her voice quiet. "I only had to play it once, and you already knew it."

Jesse glanced at her, his face shadowed with shame. "You got your car back," he murmured.

She nodded. "Your dad and Hank retrieved it before chores."

Jesse nodded too, his eyes falling to his lap. He whispered, "Sorry, Ma."

June reached over and gently tapped his thigh, her fingers warm and firm. "Never you mind," she whispered. "You're safe. That's all that matters."

They drove on in silence; the music wrapping around them like threadbare comfort.

As the Prelude ended and another classical piece began, June gave a small, purposeful tap on her handbag sitting between them on the bench seat. "There's something in there you should look at."

28

Jesse raised an eyebrow, then slowly reached over and opened the bag. Inside was a cream-colored envelope with his name written in his mother's careful script. He slid it out, opened it, and read the contents.

His eyes widened. "Wait... what? How?"

June kept her gaze on the road, but a knowing smile played on her lips. "Us Miller women have our ways. Tegan's been recording you every chance she got. And me..." she gave a soft shrug, "I sent in what mattered. You. Live auditions are in three months. Gives you time to prepare."

Jesse sat frozen for a second, stunned—and then a flicker of joy lit his face. But it was gone just as quickly, replaced by doubt. His fingers crumpled the letter slowly in his hand.

"Dad will never let me go," he said, voice flat.

Without hesitation, June pulled off to the side of the road and put the car in park. Gravel crackled beneath the tires.

She turned to him, her eyes fierce with something deeper than anger—conviction.

"You let me take care of your dad."

She held his gaze like a vice. "No more bars. No more drinking. And it would help if you showed some initiative at the barn. Help without being asked."

She leaned in just slightly. "Agreed?"

Jesse held her eyes for a long moment. Then, finally, he nodded.

June gave a satisfied nod, shifted the car into drive, and pulled back onto the road.

Neither of them spoke again. The classical music played on, the afternoon stretched ahead, and for the first time in a long while, the silence between them felt like hope.

The late afternoon sun angled low through the rafters of the barn, casting long golden streaks along the concrete floor. Hank, sweat-streaked and dust-covered, pushed a wheelbarrow heavy with manure, hay, and soiled bedding to the far corner of the compost area. With a grunt, he tipped it, the load spilling into the steaming pile. His arms ached, his ribs throbbed with every breath—but he was finished. Hours early.

He wiped his brow with the back of his arm, brushing away the salt and grime of the day, then glanced around, looking for Agustín to report in.

The barn was immaculate, its aisles swept, tack glinting from polished brass hooks. Hank moved toward the back, passing rows of neatly labeled stalls. That's when he saw the sign:

Do Not Approach
Dangerous Stallion

The words were carved into a dark wood plaque, bolted to a stall at the very end of the aisle.

Curiosity tugged at him.

He took a slow step forward, peering over the door's edge.

A blur of motion.

The stallion charged the door with terrifying speed, slamming his body against it, sending a loud crack echoing through the barn. Hank didn't flinch. Dust fell from the rafters. The horse's eyes rolled white, his nostrils flared, and his ears were pinned flat. He stomped the ground, snorting hard, trying to force a reaction.

But Hank didn't move. He just stood there, quiet, breathing slow.

The stallion's gaze locked with his, wild and full of rage—and something else: fear.

Seconds stretched.

Finally, the horse stepped forward into the light. His coat was a muted gold—a buckskin, dulled with sweat and neglect. Hank's eyes widened. Welts striped the stallion's sides, ribs visible, his body tense with hunger and pain.

Hank's chest tightened. "Son of a..."

He slowly reached into his back pocket and pulled out a horse cookie wrapped in a crumpled napkin. He extended it through the bars, careful not to make a sudden move.

"Hey there," he murmured. "You hungry?"

The stallion hesitated, nostrils quivering—then inched forward, muscles taut.

Snatch. The cookie vanished from Hank's hand.

Hank grinned. "You're a greedy fellow."

He pulled out another cookie and offered it. "You're okay," he said softly.

The stallion let out a low nicker, ears twitching, and glanced toward the back of the barn—the hay room.

Hank nodded. "Right. Food."

He hurried down the aisle, grabbed a flake of hay, and returned, gently placing it into the stall. The stallion lunged forward, devouring it.

Hank watched him, torn between calm and fury. Someone had done this. Someone had beaten and starved a good horse. He set his jaw.

"You won't go through this again," he whispered. "Not on my watch."

He turned, fists clenched, and marched toward the barn's front, anger fueling his stride. He didn't care who Don Antonio was—he wasn't going to work for horse beaters.

Then... he heard it.

Music.

Soft, classical—something elegant and foreign—floating in on the breeze. It drifted from the covered indoor arena nearby.

Curious, Hank followed.

The structure was stunning: arched steel beams, elegant Spanish-style motifs, and floral arrangements at each letter of the dressage arena. Sunlight streamed through high skylights, mixing with soft electric lighting to bathe the footing in gold. A small spectator gallery overlooked the space with tiled benches and wrought iron railings.

Inside, a young girl rode a magnificent grey PRE stallion, its mane braided, muscles rippling with every collected step.

Hank stopped cold.

The girl wore a crisp white button-down shirt, tucked neatly into white full-seat breeches, her black dressage boots polished to a mirror shine. Her dark hair was coiled into a perfect bun under a helmet and net, and she carried a jewel-encrusted dressage whip with effortless elegance. Everything about her was disciplined, understated—and striking.

But it was her emerald green eyes that held him.

She and the horse danced—truly danced—to the rhythm of the music. Pirouettes. Half-passes. Floating trot work that Hank had only ever seen in old Olympics broadcasts. It was the most beautiful thing he'd ever seen.

She looked like an angel.

And he... he looked down at himself. Sweat-stained shirt. Dust-caked jeans. Scuffed boots. Bruised face. His first time ever noticing his appearance—and feeling ashamed of it.

Just outside the ring, a man in European riding attire—neat breeches, gloves, a coach's stopwatch—watched intently. German, maybe, Hank guessed.

The girl finished her routine, the stallion halting with perfect stillness. She nodded at the coach as they exchanged words—he gave her a rare smile before leaving with a clipboard in hand.

She gave the grey a long rein and began walking him out.

As she turned the corner, she saw Hank.

Their eyes met.

Her expression flickered—curiosity, a question—but Hank's ears burned red. He looked down quickly, turned, and walked away fast, embarrassed by his intrusion.

He nearly collided with Agustín, who raised an eyebrow at him.

"You're finished?" he asked, surprised.

"Yes, sir," Hank said, still catching his breath. "Everything is done."

Agustín looked impressed. "Good. Then let's put that energy to use. We're bringing in another herd for branding. Think you're up for it?"

Hank's eyes lit up, the purpose returning to his bones. "Yes, sir. Lead the way."

The late afternoon sun bathed the Estancia Castilla veranda in a warm golden light, glinting off the lemonade glasses as Mirabella Castilla sat cross-legged on a white iron chair, sipping slowly beside her uncle Antonio. The stone table between them gleamed under the sun, its surface scattered with fresh citrus and half-finished pastries. Mirabella's cheeks were pink from her ride, her dark hair neatly tucked back in a bun, and her riding gloves rested in her lap.

They sat in companionable silence, watching the distant fields where Agustín, Hank, and several ranch hands drove a herd in for branding, the cattle kicking up dust beneath the long shadows of the approaching evening.

Mirabella tilted her head, eyes narrowing on a rider in a worn shirt and dust-streaked jeans. There was something different about him—how he moved with the horse instead of atop it, every shift of his weight precise and intuitive.

"Who is that?" she asked.

Don Antonio followed her gaze. "That's one of the Miller boys. Hank."

She continued to watch, captivated.

"He's riding El Diablo, isn't he?" she said suddenly, straightening in her seat. "None of the other hands will get on that horse."

Don Antonio's smile deepened. "Sí. And you're right. No one would—but him."

He took another sip of lemonade, then added thoughtfully, "It's like the boy can read the horse's thoughts. I haven't seen riding like that since your father." His voice softened. "He's a remarkable addition to the estancia."

Before Mirabella could respond, the faint rumble of a truck pulling into the driveway interrupted their conversation.

Don Antonio rose, brushing crumbs from his shirt. "That'll be the Millers."

Mirabella followed, curious.

The moment the truck came to a stop, Tegan burst from the passenger side before Marshall had even turned off the ignition. Her boots hit the gravel with a soft crunch, and she sprinted toward them—only to stop abruptly when she saw Mirabella.

She blinked, captivated, then walked straight up to her.

"Hi," she said confidently, sticking out her hand. "I'm Tegan. And you have the most beautiful eyes I've ever seen. What's your name?"

Mirabella turned to her uncle, momentarily startled.

Don Antonio chuckled, his eyes dancing. "Señorita Tegan, may I introduce my niece—Mirabella."

Tegan grasped her hand with both of hers and shook it firmly. "*Muy encantada a conocerlo,*" she said proudly, Spanish laced with effort but pure sincerity.

Don Antonio laughed aloud. "Well done!"

Tegan beamed. "We're going to be best friends."

Mirabella, charmed, smiled back. "I would love that."

Marshall walked up behind Tegan, placing his hands gently on her shoulders. "Where's Hank?"

As if on cue, Hank appeared from the barn, wiping his hands on his bandana, dust still clinging to his pants. His eyes lit up when he saw his family—but his expression shifted to solemnity as he approached Don Antonio.

"Thank you, sir, for the opportunity today," Hank began, "but I don't think I can work here."

Don Antonio's brow furrowed. "Why?"

Hank hesitated, looking from his father and sister to the Castillas. "I just... I can't be part of a place that would hurt a horse."

The words dropped like stones.

Don Antonio's expression darkened with concern. "Hurt a horse?"

Mirabella stepped forward before her uncle could speak, her voice firm. "We would never hurt a horse. We pride ourselves on providing the best care to every animal on this property. We Castillas take pride in our land—and in our horses."

Hank looked at her, confused. "Then why is there a buckskin quarter horse locked up in the back stall—ribs showing, welts all over him?"

Don Antonio turned sharply toward the house. "Agustín!"

Agustín emerged from the side entrance, eyebrows raised. "Yes?"

Don Antonio confronted him. "Do you know about the buckskin in the last stall?"

Agustín thought for a second and nodded. "That horse doesn't belong to us. I let one of the hands use the stall in exchange for work."

His father looks at him accusingly. "The horse is being abused by that hand."

Agustín's face paled. "I didn't know he was abusing him."

33

The silence tightened.

"I'll take care of it immediately," Agustín continued. "You know we don't tolerate that."

Don Antonio exhaled, shook his head in disbelief, and turned back to Hank. "Thank you, Hank—for your courage. I'm truly grateful."

He paused. "Will you reconsider?"

Hank looked to Mirabella, who met his gaze without blinking, a calm strength behind her emerald eyes.

"I'll stay," Hank said finally, "but only if I can take care of that horse."

Don Antonio rubbed his chin. "That animal may be too dangerous to keep here."

"Then let me feed him," Hank said. "Let me try."

Tegan, arms crossed and brow furrowed in exaggerated seriousness, piped up, "Well, then shake on it already."

Everyone burst into laughter.

Don Antonio stepped forward and extended his hand. Hank shook it, firm and resolved.

Then Mirabella turned to Tegan, eyes sparkling. "Would you like to come over? I have some books on Spanish... and a few ponies who love to be spoiled."

Tegan turned to Marshall, wide-eyed. "Can I, Daddy? Please? I'll do all my chores and help at the estancia!"

Marshall gave a weary smile. "Only if you keep your end of the bargain."

Tegan clapped her hands. "I get to work here too!"

Don Antonio, visibly relieved the tension had passed, gave a gracious nod. "I'll personally ensure the horse receives proper care. No more suffering on my land."

"Thank you," Hank said sincerely.

Marshall looked at the horizon. "Alright, kids—time to get going. Your mama's expecting us for dinner."

Tegan grabbed Hank's hand, already buzzing with excitement. "I can't *wait* to come back. Me, you, and Mirabella—we're gonna be like the *Three Musketeers!*" She skipped beside him. "We should name that horse Bob. Bob's a good name for our new horse."

Hank glanced sheepishly at Mirabella, clearly mortified by his sister's enthusiasm. But she just smiled, eyes twinkling.

He shook his head with a grin, and with Tegan still chattering about plans for Bob, he gently led her back to the truck—the dust settling behind them, and something new and hopeful just beginning to rise.

A Horse Named Bob

Sunlight streamed in golden shafts through the latticed rafters of the elegant tack room at Estancia Castilla, dust particles drifting like flecks of gold in the still air. The scent of oiled leather and saddle soap hung rich and clean, sharpened by a trace of sun-dried hay. Along the walls, bridles gleamed in neat rows, each one polished to a mirror sheen and hung beneath a brass plate engraved in precise lettering—Valeroso, Lucero, Esperanza, Patron. Saddles rested on custom wooden stands, their leather supple and spotless, silver fittings winking in the light. Below them, tack boxes carved with the Estancia Castilla crest lined the floor, corners burnished smooth from years of care. Framed photographs and faded ribbons adorned the walls—Don Antonio beside prize-winning stallions, gauchos mid-gallop, a young Mirabella in formal dressage whites. Between them hung traditional Argentinian gear: rawhide bosals, ornate silver spurs, woven ponchos folded with geometric precision. The room carried an air of reverence, as if each piece were part of a living legacy.

Tegan Miller sat cross-legged on an overturned feed bucket, cheeks flushed with contentment, as Mirabella Castilla gently parted her dusty blonde hair.

"You must always present yourself like a rider," Mirabella said with quiet assurance, her Spanish accent graceful and calm. She worked methodically, fingers nimble, weaving two neat French braids, tying them off with hunter green ribbons snipped from one of her old show shirts.

Something deeper, besides the braiding, mesmerized Tegan. A quiet understanding had blossomed between them.

"You're so graceful," Tegan said softly. "Like one of those ballerinas on horses."

Mirabella's smile warmed. "In Argentina, I rode Pas de deux with my cousins. Two horses dancing in harmony."

She stood, moved to one of the tall oak closets lining the tack room wall, and opened the door to reveal an array of pristine riding gear. She sorted through a few items, then pulled out a crisp white shirt with green trim and a pair of cream full-seat breeches.

Turning back, she held them out to Tegan. "These were mine. I think they'd look beautiful on you. If you want them, they're yours."

Tegan stared at the clothes in awe, blinking rapidly. "Really?" she whispered, taking them with trembling hands. "Thank you." She looked up at Mirabella, eyes shining. "It's always just been me, Jesse, and Hank. I never had an older sister before."

Mirabella knelt down and hugged her. "Now you do."

She stood and offered her hand. "Come, I want to show you someone."

Together they crossed the breezeway, stepping into the quiet grandeur of the main stable aisle, where sunlight filtered through tall windows and shone down on rows of gleaming stalls. A regal grey PRE stallion stood calmly in the last stall, ears flicking toward their approach.

"This is Valeroso," Mirabella said, her hand smoothing the stallion's shoulder. "He is half king, half poet."

Tegan grinned. "You talk about him like he's family."

"In a way, he is," Mirabella said. "He was born here. My father trained his sire. I've ridden him since I was smaller than you."

Tegan's hand hovered near the stall door. "Can I?"

Mirabella nodded. "Slowly. He likes calm hands."

Tegan reached out slowly, and Valeroso lowered his head to meet her fingers. "He's beautiful," she whispered.

Mirabella watched the quiet exchange, something easing in her posture. "You ride often?"

"Every chance I get," Tegan said. "Hank and I take the horses down by the creek. He says they move better when they're not told what to do."

Mirabella's brow lifted slightly. "He sounds...unconventional."

Tegan laughed. "That's a word for it."

Mirabella hesitated and then lowered her voice. "What's Hank like? Truly?"

Tegan tilted her head, thoughtful. "He feels things real deep, but doesn't talk about it. He acts like he doesn't care... but he always shows up. That's how you know he does."

Around the corner, Hank leaned silently against a post, a crooked smile tugging at his lips. His sister's words settled in his chest like a stone wrapped in velvet.

He stepped forward. "That's a fine horse. Never seen movement like that before."

Mirabella rested a hand on Valeroso's shoulder, her fingers tracing the soft curve of muscle. "The style I do with him—the dancing you saw—that's called dressage. It's about balance, discipline, and softness. The horse responds to the lightest cue, almost invisible. It looks like magic, but it takes years of training for both horse and rider."

Hank watched her for a beat, arms folded across his chest. "He moves real nice," he said. "But I don't know if I could ever get a horse to do that on purpose."

She smiled, but there was a flicker of challenge in it. "Were you ever formally trained?"

He shook his head. "No, ma'am. My dad showed me a few things, but he always said the real trainer is the horse. If you're paying attention, they'll tell you what they need."

Her brow lifted slightly. "But without structure, how do you know what they're capable of?"

"I let them show me," Hank said simply. "Not sure I believe in putting too many rules on something born to run."

Mirabella's mouth softened, but there was steel in her tone. "Dressage isn't about control. It's about partnership. Every movement is a conversation. Just—very fluent."

Hank gave a slow nod, but his gaze didn't waver. "Sometimes conversations don't need words—or choreography."

Valeroso flicked an ear toward Hank, then stepped forward with unexpected calm, as if weighing Hank's words himself.

Mirabella blinked. "He doesn't usually do that."

Hank offered a small smile. "Maybe he likes wild."

A quiet tension hung between them. Not hostile—just a spark of difference, like flint striking flint. Each of them, for the first time, unsure whether the other's way could still be right.

Tegan, sensing the atmosphere shifting into something too grown up for her taste, clapped her hands. "Let's go see Bob!"

They stepped quietly to the far end of the stable, where Bob, the battered buckskin stallion, stood hunched in his stall. The air was heavier here—dense with the sharp scent of sweat, fear, and old wounds.

His ears pinned flat as they approached. He snorted and backed into the corner, ribs visible beneath his coarse coat, welts crisscrossing his sides. His eyes flicked from one face to the next with wild distrust.

Tegan instinctively held her breath and then said. "I'm sorry, Bob."

Hank moved slowly, unwrapping a cloth bundle from his back pocket. Inside was a small mason jar filled with a pale, earthy salve.

"Hey, buddy," he murmured, crouching just outside the stall door. "Brought you something."

The stallion's nostrils flared.

Mirabella leaned closer. "What is that?"

"Salve," Hank said. "My Grandma Ginny made it. Chamomile, calendula, and some other stuff I don't know the names of. Smells strong, but it heals just about anything."

Mirabella's brow lifted. "Your grandma is a healer?"

"Yep," Hank replied, unscrewing the lid. The scent of herbs bloomed gently into the air. "Been healing our family since I can remember."

Mirabella's expression softened. "My abuela is a healer too. Back in Argentina, people come from all over just to see her. They say her teas and salves can cure what the doctors can't."

Hank looked at her, surprised and impressed. "If she's anything like Grandma Ginny... I'd love to meet her someday."

Mirabella smiled and held out her hand. "May I?"

Hank scooped a bit of the salve with two fingers and gently placed it in her open palm.

She knelt beside him, poised and respectful. Bob's gaze flicked between them, tense but curious.

"It's okay," she whispered. "No more pain."

Hank entered first, low and steady, showing his empty hands. He knelt and began gently applying the salve to one of the healing welts on Bob's hip. The horse shivered—but didn't move.

"See?" Hank whispered. "Told you it smells better than it tastes."

Bob shifted slightly, lowering his head toward him.

Tegan stepped forward, holding out a slender carrot. Bob sniffed it, nostrils flaring, then snatched it from her fingers with surprising gentleness.

Mirabella followed with another. Bob accepted it again—no flinch, no fear. His ears softened, flicking forward.

"It's working," Tegan whispered, eyes wide.

Hank continued applying the salve with practiced care, his hands moving like he was born to do it. "You're okay now," he murmured. "You're safe."

Mirabella leaned against the stall door, salve still on her fingers. "He trusts you."

"We're getting there," Hank said.

The three of them stood in companionable silence, the only sounds the occasional shuffle of hooves and slow breath of a horse learning what kindness felt like.

Back at the Miller farm, Jesse wiped a forearm across his dirt-smeared brow and hoisted a support beam into place beside his father. Marshall, steady and strong, guided it silently, the two of them moving in wordless rhythm under the afternoon sun.

They worked for a while without speaking, the sounds of hammering and birdsong filling the air between them.

Then Marshall said, "Ginny needs help with the garden. Netting's come loose again."

Jesse nodded, brushing sawdust from his shirt. "Want me to pick up Tegan and Hank while you fix it?"

Marshall gave him a sideways look. "You'll come straight back?"

Jesse smirked with affection. "Scout's honor, General."

As Marshall reached for the next board, Jesse ducked into Grandpa Joe's woodworking shed and returned with a small, hand-carved sign. He held it up with pride.

"Check this out," Jesse said. "Made it last night after chores. Thought we could hang it on the new coop."

The sign read in smooth lettering:

Casa de Cluck

Marshall squinted at it, then let out a rare chuckle. "Your mom and Tegan will love it."

Jesse beamed. "Got a few more ideas, too. Like what if we rig a rainwater catch system for the garden, or try a rotational pasture system for the livestock?"

Marshall's brows rose, surprised but pleased. "You were thinking of that?"

Jesse shrugged, but there was an earnest glint in his eye. "Just want to make the place run better. Maybe even expand someday. Less waste. More yield."

Marshall nodded slowly. "Draft up some plans. We can work on it together."

They stood there for a moment, the sun catching on the grain of the beam and the freshly carved sign. Marshall looked at his son—really looked at him—and for the first time in a long while, saw more than just the restless musician. He saw his son's care and commitment.

And Jesse, watching his father steady the post with care and resolve, saw the weight his old man carried every day to keep their world from falling apart. And he respected it.

Before heading to the truck, Jesse grabbed a hammer and two nails. Together, he and Marshall mounted the "Casa de Cluck" sign onto the new coop, stepping back to admire it for a moment.

"I'll head out now," Jesse said, grabbing the truck keys.

Marshall handed him a water jug and nodded. "Drive safe."

Jesse grinned, tossing the keys in the air. "Of course, carrying precious cargo."

Marshall watched him go, the corner of his mouth lifting ever so slightly—not a smile, but close. A glint of cautious hope flickered in his eyes, the look that said maybe, just maybe, he could start trusting his eldest son again.

Bess, Marshall's well-loved C20, rumbled into the courtyard, gravel crunching beneath her tires. The sun glinted off her red and white paint, proud and worn from a decade of devotion.

Don Antonio, immaculately dressed even in repose, greeted Jesse at the door with a glass of iced tea.

"They are with the horses," he said with a warm smile. "Come. Wait inside."

Jesse hesitated but followed him into the ornate Spanish-style mansion, jaw tightening with wonder as they passed vaulted ceilings, arched corridors, and mosaic floors that whispered stories of generations. Argentine paintings adorned the walls, bold with gauchos and stallions, and a faint scent of lemon and wood polish lingered in the air.

They entered a grand ballroom, its gleaming dance floor framed by tall windows and heavy velvet curtains. Argentine drums lined one wall beneath ornately carved sconces. In the center of the far wall, beneath an antique chandelier, hung a large oil portrait of a woman in a flowing dress—Don Antonio's late wife, captured mid-laughter, her beauty timeless.

A black Steinway grand piano gleamed beneath the chandelier.

Don Antonio took a sip of his tea, his tone casual but pointed. "You play?"

Jesse stepped forward, slowly circling the piano, fingers brushing its polished surface with reverence. "A little," he replied without looking up.

Don Antonio's smile turned mischievous, eyes narrowing in playful challenge. "Then play."

Jesse hesitated, his hand still resting on the lid. A flicker of memory rose.

He was five again. His mother had been playing Chopin—something soft and sorrowful—when he wandered over and asked if he could try. She'd smiled and lifted him onto her lap. He hadn't banged the keys like a child might. He'd listened. Note by note, clumsy but exact, he'd played it back to her.

She hadn't spoken at first. Just watched, stunned, as if a hidden door had opened and music was pouring through it.

From that day on, the piano had been more than an instrument. It had been a language. One he spoke before he understood anything else.

He blinked, returning to the present. With a quiet breath, he pulled out the bench and sat. His hands hovered above the keys, brushing across them once. Then he began.

Rachmaninoff.

The notes rang out, mournful and grand, flooding the ballroom. Jesse played with the poise and intensity of a concert pianist. His shoulders relaxed, expression distant, as if he were somewhere far away—lost in the music, unaware of everything else.

He didn't realize his audience had grown.

As the last note lingered in the air, he looked up to find Hank, Tegan, and Mirabella standing just inside the door.

Tegan clapped enthusiastically. Hank raised an eyebrow, a smirk tugging at his mouth.

Mirabella said nothing, her emerald eyes steady. She tilted her head, as if reading something no one else could see. Nobody had looked at him like that since his mother.

Don Antonio broke the silence, nodding with approval. "You are welcome to play anytime. Perhaps you will put on a concert for us someday."

Jesse glanced back at Mirabella, their eyes meeting like two quiet souls caught in a passing moment.

Jesse cleared his throat, suddenly too aware of the silence pressing in, of the way Mirabella's eyes hadn't looked away. "We should get back. Dad's expecting us."

As they walked toward Bess, Tegan teased, "Look at Jesse being all grown-up and fancy."

Later, with the evening sun slanting low across the barnyard, Bess stood in her usual spot, her hood popped open. Jesse, Hank, and Marshall huddled around her like surgeons mid-operation. Hank adjusted the alternator belt while Jesse passed his father a wrench, grease streaked across his knuckles.

Marshall leaned in, listening to the hum of the engine. "Sounds better already."

Jesse stepped back, squinting at the front bumper. "Chrome's got a couple of dings. I can fix that."

Marshall looked over, a trace of surprise on his face. "You know how?"

"Picked up a few tricks in Grandpa Joe's shop," Jesse said with a shrug.

Marshall nodded, impressed. "That'd save me a trip to town. Been meaning to get her touched up but didn't want to spend the money."

Hank wiped his hands on a rag. "Thanks for letting Jesse drive her over to pick us up."

Jesse grinned. "Don Antonio get a load of your cowboy charm?"

Hank rolled his eyes. "No. But I saw something I've never seen before. Mirabella, the way she rides—it's like the horse is part of her. Like music, but in motion."

Jesse smirked, nudging him. "Look out, Pa. I think Hank's gone all poetic on us."

Marshall raised an eyebrow. "Aren't you a little young to be thinking about girls?"

Jesse grinned wider. "He's almost driving age. Practically a man."

Marshall gave him a look that could sand wood. Jesse backed off, hands raised. "Alright, alright. I'll stay out of it."

Hank, quieter now, muttered, "She's Tegan's friend."

Marshall's expression softened. He closed Bess's hood with a firm clank and turned to his sons. "Doesn't matter who she is. What matters is how you treat her. Any woman. You respect her. Always. You lie, you play games—you're not just dishonoring her. You're dishonoring yourself."

The boys were quiet.

Jesse kicked at the gravel. Then, curious, asked, "You never told us how you met Mom."

Marshall looked surprised, then wary. "That's a long story."

Hank chimed in, earnest. "We want to know."

Marshall sighed, leaning back against Bess. "I was on leave. Some buddies dragged me to this recital at a fancy concert hall. I wasn't interested until she walked out to play the piano. Your mother lit up that stage. I'd never seen anything like it."

"She talk to you after?" Jesse asked.

Marshall chuckled. "She ignored me. I wasn't used to that. I brought roses. Chocolates. Nothing worked. Then one of her friends told me she liked poetry. So I started writing her poems."

Jesse nearly dropped his wrench. "You? Writing poetry?"

"They weren't any good," Marshall admitted. "But she didn't care. She said they were honest."

He smiled to himself. "Eventually got her number. Took her to see some foreign film she wanted to watch. Didn't understand a word of it. Didn't matter. She promised to write to me when I deployed. And she did. Every week. I knew after the second letter she was the woman I wanted to build a life with."

Hank glanced at Jesse, who looked genuinely stunned. Then Tegan's voice rang out from the house, the clanging of the old dinner bell echoing across the yard.

"Dinner!" she hollered.

Marshall pushed off the truck and tossed his rag aside. "Let's go. Before your mother thinks we've forgotten what a meal is."

Inside the kitchen, June stood at the sink, finishing the dishes with the radio humming softly in the background. The gentle melody of a classical waltz filled the space.

Marshall stepped in quietly, walked up behind her, and kissed her cheek. "Need a hand?"

June smiled, brushing her shoulder against his. "Always."

They worked in sync, wiping down the last plates and setting them aside to dry. When the last glass clinked into place, Marshall didn't let go of her hand. Instead, he turned the dial on the radio slightly louder and guided her into a slow dance, right there in the warm spill of kitchen light.

June laughed gently. "What's gotten into you?"

Marshall swayed with her. "The kids barely made it through dinner. Even Jesse was ready for bed by dessert."

June rested her head against his shoulder. "That's a first."

Marshall hesitated, then said, "He's been really showing up lately. Helping around the farm. Said he picked up some fabricating tricks in Joe's shop. I've been thinking... maybe I'll make a few calls. Look into a mechanics program. Could give him something real to work toward."

June went quiet in his arms.

He pulled back slightly to look at her. "What is it?"

She met his eyes. "Jesse got an invitation to audition for Yale. For music."

Marshall tensed. "What's he gonna do with a music degree? Teach?"

"You know we can't afford it," he added, the weight in his voice unmistakable.

June's gaze didn't falter. "Is that what you're really worried about?"

Marshall's jaw tightened. "I thought you were happy here. Thought this was the life you wanted."

She reached up and hugged him tightly, her voice fierce. "I love my life here. With the kids. With you. I wouldn't trade it for anything. It was my choice to leave that world behind—and I'd make the same choice again. But Marshall, you have to let Jesse make his choice."

He looked into her eyes, his expression softening. After a long pause, he said, "I'll think about it."

June smiled, that private, knowing smile he'd always loved.

He kissed her again, slower this time. And as the music played on, they continued to dance, held together by memory, love, and a future still being written.

THE THREE MUSKETEERS

It was Saturday, Hank's only day off—but you wouldn't know it. He was already out at Estancia Castilla, ponying Bob beside a steady ranch horse named Mateo, working the stallion through quiet exposure.

Bob's ears twitched nervously, his body tight with apprehension, but he followed. Reluctantly at first—like a kid dragging his feet to school—but he stayed beside Mateo, flicking glances up at Hank every so often, searching for reassurance.

"You're doing just fine, buddy," Hank said, his voice calm and warm.

The welts across Bob's flank—once angry, raw wounds—had faded under Hank's daily care and his grandmother Ginny's salve. The progress was slow, but it was honest. Bob began to trust him.

They reached a secluded field near the main barn, half-wild with scrub grasses and clover. Hank dismounted, tying Mateo to a fence post. Bob stood watching, muscles rippling with uncertainty.

Hank unhooked the pony line and stepped away, leading Bob by a rope.

They walked circles. Then zig-zags. Halt, go back again. Hank turned in different directions, shifted his weight, snapped his fingers. Each time Bob hesitated, Hank praised him. Each time Bob followed, he offered a treat and a soft word.

Eventually, the rope slackened. Bob moved with him, step for step, like thought alone tethered them.

Then Hank let go.

Bob trotted away at first, tossing his head, testing the boundary. Hank didn't follow. He stood still and waited.

After a beat, Bob turned and looked at him. Hank gave a low whistle.

Bob cantered straight toward him.

"You're a damn genius," Hank murmured, smiling as he fed him a carrot chunk. They worked another ten minutes with no lead rope—just body language, intent, trust.

Up the hill, Mirabella and Tegan watched from the shade of a sycamore.

"He's not even riding him," Mirabella whispered, her voice colored with awe. "But he's created a dance. A real one."

Tegan nodded. "He always does that."

Later, back at the barn, Hank led Bob into his stall, rubbing his neck with a curry comb. Mirabella and Tegan met him there.

"When are you gonna get on him?" Tegan asked, chin resting on the stall door.

Hank glanced at the stallion, who stood relaxed now, half-asleep. "Not sure," he said. "I guess Bob'll let me know when he's ready."

Bob let out a soft nicker, almost on cue, and nodded his head.

They all burst out laughing.

"I can't wait to see it," Mirabella said. "Have you ever broken a horse before?"

Tegan jumped in. "He does it all the time back home!"

Hank gave her a playful bump with his elbow. "I've started a few, sure. But every horse is different. I just try to give 'em the best chance at a relationship."

Mirabella tilted her head, curious. "My father started all our horses in Argentina. He had a method—structured, polished—but I've never seen anything like what you do. Who taught you?"

Hank shrugged. "I guess after being thrown enough times, I figured it's better to wait 'til the horse says yes. Beats eating dirt."

Mirabella and Tegan giggled.

Tegan suddenly stood tall and dramatic. "We're going swimming. There's a secret pond at the edge of the property. Hardly anyone knows about it. Want to come?"

Hank raised a brow. "Don't have trunks."

Mirabella grinned. "You can borrow Agustín's. He's at a friend's and won't mind."

Hank looked between the girls, then at Bob, who flicked his ears as if to say go on.

Hank smiled. "Alright. Lead the way."

The late morning sun blazed down as Hank, Tegan, and Mirabella galloped across the open pasture, hooves thundering like summer storm clouds on the dry earth. The trail to the pond wound through tall grasses and sloped gently toward a shimmering patch of blue tucked into the landscape like a secret.

Hank leaned forward in his saddle, urging Mateo into a faster lope. Behind him, Mirabella urged her sleek bay, and Tegan whooped from atop her pinto, laughing and kicking with wild glee.

"I saw that shortcut!" Tegan shouted as Hank cut between two shrubs and took the lead.

He twisted around, grinning wickedly. "Not my fault y'all don't know the terrain!"

He reached the pond's edge first, pulling Mateo to a stop with a flourish. Dust swirled around them as Hank dismounted with a satisfied smirk.

"You cheated!" Tegan cried as she rode up, flushed and windblown. "I demand a rematch."

Hank winked. "Catch me next time, lil' sis."

Mirabella arrived a beat later, dismounting with grace. "I believe he calls that strategic riding."

Tegan huffed, then kicked off her boots and ran into the water with Mirabella close behind. They shrieked as the cool pond enveloped them, the heat of the day peeling off their skin.

Hank stripped to his borrowed trunks and launched himself off the bank with a perfect cannonball, landing with a massive splash that drenched both girls.

"Hank!" they screamed in delighted outrage.

Laughter rang through the air as they splashed each other wildly. Water flew in arcs. Waves slapped the reeds. The pond erupted into a full-on war.

Tegan was the first to change tactics. "Shoulders! Shoulders!" she yelled and scrambled onto Hank's back. He bent his knees dramatically, submerging until only the crown of his head remained visible.

"Ready?" he growled.

"Launch me!"

Hank straightened in one powerful move, catapulting Tegan into the air with a splash. She howled as she soared, arms flailing, and crashed back into the pond with a wild whoop.

As she surfaced, she turned to Mirabella. "Your turn, Mia!"

Mirabella blinked in surprise, cheeks coloring at the nickname. "Mia?" she repeated, voice small.

Tegan shrugged with mischief. "It's yours now. I made it."

Mirabella hesitated.

Tegan swam closer, bumping her shoulder. "Don't worry. He's one of us."

With a nervous grin, Mirabella swam over to Hank and climbed onto his shoulders. He braced himself. "You ready?"

47

She nodded, barely containing her giggles.

He launched her skyward.

Mirabella shrieked, not with control but with pure, unrestrained joy. She hit the water with a laugh so real, so loud, it startled even herself.

When she came up, she gasped, covering her mouth in mock horror. "Oh no," she said between breaths, "I've become... uncivilized."

Hank and Tegan cackled.

They played until their limbs turned to jelly and the sun hung directly overhead. Soaked and smiling, they dragged themselves to the edge of the pond, where a checkered blanket waited beneath a tree's wide canopy.

Tegan and Mirabella had prepared a feast: Argentine media lunas, flaky and sweet; warm empanadas filled with spiced beef; juicy fruits and a tall canteen of lemonade sweating in the heat.

They collapsed onto the blanket, wordless with hunger. For several minutes, the only sound was chewing, sighs, and the occasional crunch.

Tegan finally broke the silence. "Mia... what's Argentina like?"

Mirabella wiped her mouth and leaned back on her elbows, gaze drifting to the clouds. "Big. Wild. Our ranch—Estancia Castilla—is 3,000 acres. My father inherited it from his father, and so on. Horses. Cattle. Mango trees. The whole family lives nearby and works the land. We ride in the morning, work all day, and by night, there's singing and dancing and grilled meat under the stars."

"Sounds like heaven," Hank murmured, eyes fixed on her.

She looked at him, steady and bold. "My uncle is trying to build something like it here. This estancia. This life. I wouldn't be here without him. He brought me to train with the best coaches. To learn English. To chase my dream."

"What dream?" Tegan asked, licking lemon juice from her fingers.

"To become a world-class Grand Prix dressage rider."

Hank leaned forward, captivated.

Mirabella tilted her head. "What about you, Hank? What's your dream?"

Hank blinked. No one had ever asked him that before. Not seriously.

He thought.

"I want to be the best cowboy in the country. Own land with a pond like this. Raise a family. Breed and train the best horses around. I guess... I want to carry on the Miller name, but build it even bigger."

Tegan snorted. "Boring. Hank'll live and die a Miller."

She flicked a pebble into the water.

Hank winced a little, hurt flickering across his face. "Alright then, Miss Tegan—what's your epic dream?"

Tegan sat up proudly. "I'm going to Argentina. Then I'll travel the whole world. I'll learn ten languages. I'll sing, dance, and become the best cowgirl the world's ever seen!"

Mirabella and Hank clapped in unison.

Tegan stood and held out her hands. "Let's make a pact. Best friends forever."

They joined hands, a triangle under the tree.

Mirabella and Hank looked at each other solemnly.

"Forever," they said in unison.

They sat back down, picking at fruit and laughing about Bob, about horses, about the possibility of growing up wild and free together.

For a moment, everything felt untouched by the cares of the outside world. Just three hearts, sun-warmed and full of hope.

The sun dipped low as the trio began their ride back from the hidden pond, golden light cascading over the fields like honey. Tegan rode ahead, her arms stretched wide like wings, belting out cowgirl songs at full volume.

"I'm a wild mustang, ain't got no reins! Kickin' up dust across the plains!"

Her voice echoed joyfully across the landscape, setting the rhythm for the ride home.

Hank and Mirabella followed at a slower pace, side by side, their horses relaxed and trailing in her wake. A breeze rustled through the cottonwoods lining the path.

Mirabella glanced over at him. "What are you going to do with Bob?"

Hank's brow furrowed slightly. "Well... first I gotta get on him."

Mirabella smiled. "Can I help?"

That caught Hank off guard. He turned to look at her, surprised and more than a little intrigued. "You want to?"

She nodded. "If Bob's open to it, I'd love to teach him some dressage. Nothing fancy. Just the basics. It might give him confidence. But only if you—and Bob—are okay with it."

Hank thought about it for a second, then smiled. "Sounds like a great idea. We could combine what we both know. Might be good for him."

"Thank you," she whispered. "For including me."

He tilted his head. "You act like people don't."

"They usually don't." She shrugged, her voice softening. "You and Tegan are the first real friends I've made here."

Hank blinked, surprised. "You don't have many friends?"

She shook her head. "I don't go to school like most kids here. I have tutors. English, math, French, biology. They're wonderful, but... it's not the same."

He nodded slowly. "Yeah, I guess that makes sense. I always figured you had your own circle, y'know? You seem... polished."

She laughed, brushing a strand of hair behind her ear. "Polished is lonely."

"What about back in Argentina?"

"I have cousins. And horses. But never anyone like Tegan."

He smiled at that. "She's one of a kind."

Mirabella glanced at him. "What about you? You probably have a bunch of friends."

Hank shook his head. "Not really. Between chores at home and working for your uncle, I don't have much time. I talk to some of the rodeo cowboys sometimes. Jesse and Tegan are my friends... and now you."

She looked at him, her expression warm. "That's enough."

They rode in silence for a moment, the horses' hooves thudding softly against the packed earth.

Then Mirabella asked, "What's school like in America?"

Hank shrugged. "It's fine. Depends on the teacher. But honestly? The best education I get is from my parents and grandparents. Real-world stuff. How to fix things, how to raise animals, how to listen more than talk."

Mirabella nodded thoughtfully. "I feel the same. My tutors are good, but I learn the most from my uncle and my family back home. Especially my father. They teach me how to live, not just recite facts."

Their eyes met, sharing the quiet truth between them.

"I guess we both love our families," she whispered.

"I guess we do," Hank replied with a grin. Then he looked ahead. "Speaking of which... we'd better catch up to Tegan before she takes over the entire Castilla estate."

Mirabella laughed, her face lighting up.

They nudged their horses into a light canter and caught up to Tegan, who had now switched to yodeling.

"About time!" she called out over her shoulder, hands on her hips. "I was about to annex the stables!"

All three burst into laughter, their silhouettes stretched long in the evening light as they rode on—three riders bound by something rare and real, heading home as the first stars winked into the sky.

As the sun dipped behind the hills, Hank and Tegan led their horses back up toward the gravel lot where their dad waited beside Bess, the family truck, sipping from an old thermos and squinting into the fading light. The horses' hooves crunched softly, and for once, Tegan wasn't singing. She walked beside him in thoughtful silence, her hair still damp from the pond, her cheeks flushed with the last of the day's joy.

It had been one of those rare days that felt whole. Nothing broken. Nothing rushed.

But as they neared the truck, Hank spotted Jesse sitting in the bed, legs crossed, sketchpad on his knees, headphones to his Sony walkman looped around his neck. He wasn't looking at them—just lost in whatever world he was drawing.

Their dad barely glanced up.

Hank adjusted Mateo's lead rope, eyes lingering on his brother for a beat too long.

Jesse had a way of being there without being there. He's always lost in thought. He perpetually pursued an elusive image and sound perceptible only to himself. Hank never knew what to say to him when he was like that. Their worlds didn't quite overlap.

He gave Mateo a gentle pat on the neck and looked toward the truck. *Maybe that's just how it is*, he thought. *Some of us dream out loud. Some of us just keep moving forward.*

He didn't resent Jesse—not exactly. But sometimes, like tonight, he wished their dreams pointed in the same direction.

He helped Tegan up into the cab, gave the horses one last look, and climbed in after her. The truck door shut with its familiar thud.

The sky outside had shifted to a velvet blue, the last of the sun's colors fading behind the distant hills. Mirabella Castilla sat at her small writing desk, tucked into the corner of her bedroom at Estancia Castilla, bathed in the golden glow of a brass lamp. The window was open just enough to let in the sweet scent of lavender and hay drifting in from the surrounding pastures.

Her room was a sanctuary of contrasts—elegant but lived-in. Stacks of books lined the built-in shelves, mostly in Spanish and English, with titles ranging from Martín Fierro to The Complete Training of Horse and Rider. A photo of her entire extended family gathered under the shade of an ancient ombú tree smiled at her from a carved wooden frame. Another picture, smaller and more faded, sat near her ink set: her and her father beside her first pony.

The furniture in her room—handmade in Argentina—was dark algarrobo wood, smooth from years of care. Her bed, topped with a pale embroidered quilt from her grandmother, had a rosary looped around the post of the night-stand, its beads catching the lamplight as they swayed with the evening breeze.

She dipped her pen into the inkwell and wrote in flowing Spanish:

Dearest Mamá, Papá, y familia—

I'm sitting at my desk tonight, looking at the moon over the fields of California, and I can't help but think about you.

Life here at Estancia Castilla has finally felt like home. Tío Antonio and Agustín have transformed this place into a reflection of our life in Argentina. The horses are thriving: the stables are clean: the staff works with heart—and there's music in the air again. We even had asado last weekend. Almost like we were all together again.

I continue to train every day with Valeroso. He has grown more expressive, more collected. We are working on our canter pirouettes and flying changes. There's a local show next month, and I feel more prepared than ever. Not just technically, but... spiritually. My connection to him has deepened. We are speaking without words. My instructor has taken my riding to the next level.

But what I really wanted to tell you is this:

I am no longer lonely.

I've made friends. Real friends.

There's a girl here—Tegan. She's ten, and she is the most outgoing, confident, fun little sister I never knew I needed. She's always laughing, singing, riding full-speed with her hair flying behind her. She's completely without fear.

And then there's Hank.

Hank is... different. He doesn't talk much, but when he does, you listen. He works hard, doesn't complain, and has a natural way with horses that I've never seen before—not in Argentina, not in Europe, not in any show barn. He doesn't train horses. He builds relationships with them. Someone badly mistreated a horse here, Bob. Everyone gave up on him. But Hank didn't.

He's been working with Bob patiently—day by day. And now, somehow, I'm a part of it. We're going to train him together. Hank will start him, and if Bob is willing, I'll teach him some dressage. I've never done anything like this before, and I've never worked with someone like Hank before, either.

He's kind. And brave. And he sees things in people—and animals—that others overlook.

I feel like... I belong here.

I miss you all more than words can say. I miss Papa's coffee in the mornings, Mama's singing in the kitchen, and the horses calling at sunrise. But for now, I am safe. I am growing. And I am loved.

Con todo mi amor,

Mirabella

She sealed the letter with wax and placed it gently atop her journal.

Rising, she crossed to the nightstand, her hand brushing the rosary before she extinguished the lamp. The room dimmed to silver, moonlight spilling across the floorboards.

Outside, a distant horse nickered. She smiled, knowing exactly which one it was.

DINNER WITH THE CASTILLAS

Morning haze lifted from the rolling pastures of Estancia Castilla as Hank, Tegan, Mirabella, Agustín, and a crew of seasoned ranch hands drove a large herd of cattle across the open land. Dust curled behind hooves and horse-shoes, sunlight catching on horn tips and tossing manes.

Mirabella, astride one of the ranch's seasoned Quarter Horses, wore tailored gaucho trousers, a crisp white blouse, and a flowing poncho pinned at one shoulder. Her hair was pulled back in a single braid beneath a flat-brimmed hat, and her boots—though polished—were dusted from the ride. She looked as though she'd stepped from a painting, but the way she rode said otherwise. She guided her horse with the precision of a reining champion, her posture refined, her leg cues sharp, and her eyes constantly scanning the movement of the herd.

Tegan rode beside her, wide-eyed. "You're like a cowgirl ballerina," she whispered.

Mirabella smiled. "I ride dressage, but cattle don't care about elegance. You have to read them like poetry."

Hank rode a few strides ahead, keeping the herd tight. When a group of yearlings broke off, Mirabella didn't wait. She pressed her heels in and cut them off in a graceful arc. Her horse responded instantly—quick, tight turns, steady pressure, fluid control.

Tegan's jaw dropped. "She's almost as good as you, Hank!"

Hank gave a short laugh, shaking his head. "She's not what I expected."

"What did you expect?"

"I don't know... pearls and side-saddle maybe."

"She's got style and grit," Tegan said. "Kinda like you, but cleaner."

Another calf darted from the flank. Hank caught Mirabella's eye, then turned his horse.

"I'll get it with her," he said.

They flanked the calf like instinct, one high, one low, wordlessly syncing their movements. Mirabella's poncho streamed behind her like a banner, catching the light in flashes of color. They circled and returned the calf with calm precision, the kind that didn't need words—just timing, trust, and the feel of the other's presence.

"You've done this before," Hank said, trying not to sound too impressed, though his heart still raced from the run—and not just from the chase.

"Plenty," she replied, her smile elusive. Hank noticed the way her hand lingered just a moment longer on the reins, like she was still riding the moment.

They reached the lower pasture, the herd calm and still. Agustín waved his hat. "That's it! Let them settle."

Hank slowed beside Mirabella. "You ride like someone who's done this their whole life."

"I work cattle on my father's estancia back in Argentina," she said evenly. "Smaller herds, same dance."

"Most folks don't expect someone dressed like you to know how to cut cattle."

"Clothes don't make the rider, Hank."

Tegan trotted up. "You two were like a real team! Hank, I think she might actually be better than you."

He raised a brow, smirking. "She's got style, I'll give her that."

They shared a laugh. Hank glanced at Mirabella—relaxed, poised, unreadable. His eyes lingered longer than he intended. There was something about her that didn't line up, something that made him want to know more. He couldn't decide if she belonged in a saddle or a storybook—or maybe both. He caught himself wondering what she'd look like under the same stars he watched back home.

Hank's horse shifted beneath him as they turned. He didn't say anything more, but her calm in the saddle still echoed through him like the last note of a song.

"Back to the barn," Agustín called, and they turned their horses for home.

As they dismounted, brushing dust from their sleeves and leading their horses back to the stables, Agustín wiped his brow and looked over at the Miller siblings with a gracious smile.

"What should we bring to the dinner?" he asked, ever polite.

Tegan squinted up at him, head tilted like she was solving a riddle. "Well, I would *hope* you'd bring yourself," she said, matter-of-fact, like it was the most obvious answer in the world.

Agustín blinked, then let out a laugh, charmed. "Of course. I'll be sure not to forget."

Hank groaned softly, rubbing the back of his neck. "She's still working on her social graces."

"But I'm not wrong," Tegan insisted, beaming. "You are coming, right?"

"I wouldn't miss spending time with Señorita Tegan." He replied looking at Tegan and then at Hank.

Hank chuckled. "Mom and Grandma have been cooking all day. Nothing else is needed."

"And I have something prepared just for you." Tegan pointed at Agustín with dramatic flare.

Agustín smiled. "Then we'll come hungry."

Grandpa Joe pulled up in Bess, and the Millers climbed in, the setting sun casting long shadows behind them.

Meanwhile, back at the Miller ranch, Marshall and Jesse worked side by side repairing the outer fence.

Wire clinked, wood creaked, and the rhythmic clack of hammers filled the air. The sun had started its slow descent, bathing the field in warm amber light.

Marshall leaned on a fencepost, watching Jesse. "You really want to audition for Yale?"

Jesse froze mid-swing, the hammer pausing just above the nail. "You know about that?"

Marshall nodded slowly. "Your mom mentioned it."

Jesse let the hammer drop into the tool belt and turned away slightly. His voice was quiet, almost wary. "Didn't think you'd bring it up. Let alone ask me."

Marshall rubbed his palm against the grain of the post. "Didn't think I knew how. I'm not great at... this kind of talk."

Jesse picked up a nail and rolled it between his fingers, buying a moment. "We don't usually talk about stuff like this. Not really."

"No, we don't," Marshall said. "Doesn't mean we shouldn't."

Jesse looked up, face unreadable. "I didn't plan on you understanding it. I just wanted you to know it matters to me."

"You love it?" Marshall asked.

Jesse nodded. "Yeah. I love the farm, it's home, but music's different. It's... who I am."

Marshall looked down, kicked gravel with his boot. "It's not the kind of future I imagined for you. I was hoping you'd take over the farm. But maybe that's not mine to decide."

"I know it's expensive," Jesse added quickly. "I'll work more. Contribute."

Marshall met his eyes. "I respect that. Means something, you wanting to earn your way."

Jesse's expression softened. "Thanks, Dad."

Marshall placed a hand on his son's shoulder. "We're Millers. We stick together. We'll figure it out."

The two men worked in silence, side by side, their rhythm natural and unspoken.

That evening, the Miller dining room glowed with the warmth of flickering candles and polished wood. The long table, dressed in June's best linen—ironed crisp—waited like a promise beneath Grandpa Joe's handmade chandelier. At its center, Grandma Ginny's china gleamed softly, ivory with faded blue trim, each plate a fragment of family history passed from mother to daughter. It came out only for weddings, Christmases, and nights like this, when guests of true importance were seated at the table. The silverware, polished to a mirror shine, caught the candle light beside mason jars filled with wildflowers Tegan had gathered from Grandma Ginny's garden.

The Castillas arrived just as the sun dipped low. Don Antonio, dressed in a tailored linen shirt and dark slacks, carried a bottle of Malbec from the original Estancia Castilla in Argentina. Agustín wore a smart, casual blazer over a crisp shirt, while Mirabella, in a flowing pale-blue blouse and riding pants, held a bouquet of wildflowers—lavender, daisies, and rosemary.

She handed them to June with a shy smile. "From our garden."

June accepted them graciously. "They're beautiful. As are you, dear."

Tegan darted over and clasped Mirabella's hand. "Come on! You're sitting with me."

Everyone gathered at the table, where platters of brisket sat beside Argentine empanadas and grilled vegetables. Bowls of chimichurri and roasted potatoes circled the main dishes.

Don Antonio poured wine, raising his glass. "This comes from our vineyards back home. The last vintage before my father passed. May it bring you joy tonight."

As the meal unfolded, Marshall turned to Agustín. "So what's your story? You've clearly got a good head on your shoulders."

Agustín, modest but confident, smiled. "I studied economics and agricultural science at Harvard. My goal is to bring our family's estancia into the 20th century—automation, sustainable practices, and strategic expansion into Europe and other territories. We're exploring distribution partnerships now."

Don Antonio nodded proudly. "His ideas are brilliant. But I remind him always—never forget where we come from. Honor the land, the horses, and the people."

Marshall raised his glass. "That I can get behind. Millers have worked this land for generations. Nothing fancy, but built with grit."

Grandpa Joe chimed in with a chuckle. "And good hands. Always been good with our hands."

Don Antonio turned his attention. "I've heard about your woodworking. I'd love to see it sometime."

Grandpa Joe nodded, smiling. "It started with my father. After the war, I used my GI Bill to go to trade school. I've been building ever since. I built the table you're sitting at."

Don Antonio caressed the table admiring the work, "Yes. I can tell this table was built by a true craftsman." He raised his glass to Grandpa Joe with respect and drank.

Don Antonio took another bite and sighed. "This food... exquisite."

June beamed. "I was excited to try some Argentine dishes tonight. I hope I did your culture justice."

Don Antonio grinned. "Almost as good as my madre's. Don't tell her I said that."

Everyone laughed.

As dessert was served, Agustín took a bite of the apple pie and leaned back, savoring. "This pie... this is the best I've ever tasted."

Grandma Ginny winked. "Highly guarded family recipe—passed from mother to daughter, each generation adding their own twist. All written down in the Miller family cookbook."

June nodded proudly. "Tegan created the most recent innovation."

Tegan sat up with pride and said, "I don't think we need any more tweaks, Grandma."

Grandma Ginny looked lovingly at her star pupil and responded, "This one has mastered most of the Miller recipes and she's becoming an adept healer too."

Agustín looked at Tegan with newfound admiration. "My stomach is in your debt, Señorita Tegan."

Tegan leaned toward him and spoke directly to his midsection. "You're very welcome, Agustín's stomach."

Laughter erupted around the table.

June smiled. "Shall we retire to the living room for some entertainment?"

She glanced at Jesse, who nodded and stood to fetch his guitar.

Tegan and Hank rose to help clear the dishes, and Mirabella moved to join them.

June stopped her gently. "Don't even think about it, dear. You're our guest. Come with me."

Mirabella smiled and followed June and the others into the family room.

The family room glowed with lamplight, its hand-built furniture polished and worn from years of use. Quilts folded over stuffed leather chairs, and a fire crackled in the hearth beneath the mantel, where family photos and military medals stood in silent testimony.

June sat at the upright piano, her fingers lightly touching the keys, waiting. Jesse sat beside her, guitar in hand. He tuned a string with quiet focus. Hank lingered at the threshold, hesitant. Jesse looked up and motioned with a nod toward the wooden cajón beside him. "C'mon, brother."

Hank glanced at their guests—Don Antonio, Agustín, Mirabella—seated with Grandpa Joe and Grandma Ginny in the cozy room. His father stood at the liquor cabinet, pouring a whisky for Grandpa Joe and Don Antonio.

Still uncertain, Hank stepped forward and took his seat beside Jesse. He rested his hands on the cajón, posture stiff until Tegan appeared with a tray of lemonade and tea, handing refreshments to her grandmother and Agustín. She then plopped down beside Agustín, laying her head on his shoulder.

Agustín smiled down at her, amused. When he looked at his father, Don Antonio returned a wink and a knowing grin.

June looked at her sons and gave a small nod. She counted them in.

Jesse strummed the first aching chords of "Fire and Rain" by James Taylor. The room stilled. June followed on the piano, her hands gliding in support of her son's voice. Jesse's singing carried heartbreak and longing—like he was spilling secrets into the quiet.

Marshall, glass in hand, froze. He turned slowly, caught by the voice he had never truly heard before. This was not the Jesse he thought he knew—this was something deeper. Raw. Real. A gift passed down from June, blossomed in quiet corners.

Then Hank joined in. His hands tapped the cajón in rhythm, steady and sure. At the chorus, he lifted his voice—not loud, but strong, warm, and grounding. It was the sound of two brothers weaving something sacred together.

Marshall's eyes shifted to June. She met his gaze with a quiet smile that said, *I told you.* Her music had lived on—in both their sons.

Tegan leapt up and dragged Agustín to the center of the room. They danced, hand in hand, laughing as they twirled.

Mirabella, watching, caught Jesse's gaze as he sang. There was something in his eyes—shadowed and aching—that she recognized. His voice held that ache too, like something cracked open and spilling. She understood it. She felt it. Being so far from home, from her father and the familiar weight of the land she'd grown up on—it left a space inside her that didn't always have a name.

Then her gaze shifted to Hank. He was nothing like Jesse. While Jesse seemed full of storms, Hank was the quiet before them—solid, still, with something steady in the way he sat and listened. She had wondered how two people so different could be brothers, but in their voices, the connection became clear. Jesse pulled things open. Hank held them together.

Her eyes lingered on Hank longer than she expected. There was something in his presence that made her feel steadier too, but also... restless, in a way she didn't quite understand. A warmth had settled in her chest, unfamiliar but not unpleasant. Whatever it was, it felt important—like noticing the horizon for the first time and realizing how far the world might go.

She stood and joined the dancing, Agustín spinning her and Tegan in turn, laughter rising like birdsong.

The last chord hung in the air like a blessing. Jesse glanced toward Marshall.

Marshall nodded slowly, his voice lost, but something in his expression had softened—warmed. He had never heard them like this. Never let himself listen. And now he saw it—the legacy his wife had passed on, the beauty she had nurtured. What she had given up for him.

Don Antonio stood and applauded, his eyes glassy with emotion. "That was... transcendent. Thank you for sharing such beauty."

Agustín took a sip of tea. "You have a strong voice," he said across the room. "Have you trained?"

Jesse looked up, caught slightly off guard. "No formal training. Just my mom. But I'm auditioning for Yale's music program."

Agustín nodded. "Ah. That explains the control. They'll want technical excellence, of course."

Jesse raised a brow, then smiled faintly. "Technique's important. But if it doesn't say anything real, what's the point?"

Agustín tilted his head, not unkind, but analytical. "Still, sometimes what's real needs refinement to be understood."

Don Antonio set his glass down with a gentle click. "Agustín," he said in Spanish, lightly but with meaning, *"recuerda dónde estamos."*

Agustín softened. "Of course. I meant no offense. It was a beautiful performance."

Don Antonio turned toward Jesse, his voice warm. "You reminded me of a singer we knew in Mendoza—he had no training at all, but his songs made you feel like the mountains were singing back."

June chuckled, her hand over her heart. "That's Jesse, all right."

The laughter returned gently to the room, like a ripple smoothing the surface of a pond.

Don Antonio raised his glass. "I would like to invite all of you to be honored guests at our upcoming festival—Olive Oil and Lavender. Agustín will announce plans for our new vineyard of Malbec grapes, imported from Estancia Castilla in Argentina. In time, we hope it becomes the Olive Oil, Lavender, and Wine Festival."

He smiled. "There will be food, music—a little Argentina in California. We hope you can all come."

Tegan leapt up. "Of course we'll come! The Millers never miss a party." Her eyes widened with sudden inspiration. "Will I be a VIP?"

Marshall groaned. "Tegan—"

Don Antonio chuckled. "I would be honored if Señorita Tegan were my personal guest."

Tegan squealed and jumped in place.

June clapped her hands gently. "Time for bed."

Jesse and Hank stood and guided a jabbering Tegan down the hall, her chatter filled with outfit ideas and imagined VIP duties.

Tegan returned briefly to give Don Antonio, Agustín, and Mirabella big hugs. "Thank you for being such great friends. I have the best friends in the whole county."

The Castillas laughed warmly, touched by her sincerity.

Agustín took the small basket from Grandma Ginny and beamed. "Thank you, Señora Ginny. The pie was incredible."

Grandma Ginny hugged him tightly—an older version of Tegan in every way. "You're always welcome here, Agustín. Especially if you're craving apple pie and some company."

"I'd be delighted to partake of your and Señrorita Tegan's inventions and learn of your healing methods. Until then." Agustín kissed Grandma Ginny on the cheek; she blushed and smiled smitten at the young man's attention.

Don Antonio turned to June and took her hand gently. "Thank you, June, for the unforgettable meal and music. This evening... it's one I'll never forget."

Grandpa Joe clasped Don Antonio's hand. "We'll be seeing each other soon. I'll show you the shop."

As the Castillas stepped into the night air and their car pulled away, the Miller homestead felt both smaller and bigger than ever before—humble, rooted, but now linked to something grander, a friendship newly forged between two families bound by land, tradition, and heart.

Later, on the porch, Marshall stood alone, cradling his whisky, listening to the night.

Crickets sang. The firelight flickered faintly behind him through the windows. He took a sip, slow and deliberate, the echo of Jesse's voice still humming in his ears.

He looked up at the stars, then down at his hands. Strong hands. Callused. Hands that had worked the land, built fences, carried children.

But tonight, they'd done nothing. Tonight, it was his sons' hands that had built something—a sound, a harmony, a truth he hadn't been ready to hear until now.

June stepped into the doorway behind him but didn't say a word. She didn't have to.

Marshall's jaw clenched softly. He didn't turn around. Just nodded once, almost to himself.

"I hear it now," he murmured.

OLIVE OIL AND LAVENDER

The morning sun climbed steadily as the Miller family made their final preparations for the day ahead. Weeks had passed since the Castillas had dined at the Miller homestead, and anticipation buzzed like electricity in the air. Today was the Olive Oil and Lavender Festival, and the Millers were determined to arrive in style.

Marshall and Jesse stood in the driveway, polishing every inch of Bess, their beloved C20 pickup. Jesse crouched low, buffing the chrome to a mirror-like shine. The front bumper, which he had promised to fix weeks ago, now gleamed with a finish so flawless it caught Marshall off guard.

Marshall stepped back and gave an approving nod. "Looks better than the factory."

Jesse smirked, wiping his hands on a rag. "She deserved it."

Nearby, Grandpa Joe put the finishing touches on a small wooden box on his workbench beneath the old oak tree. He gently slid out a pair of handcrafted salt and pepper shakers, each etched with the Argentine flag on one side and the Castilla Estancia emblem on the other. The craftsmanship was impeccable; the wood stained and polished until it glowed with pride and history.

June's voice rang out from the kitchen window. "Boys! If you want to make a good impression, you better come in and get dressed. We're leaving in twenty!"

Inside, Grandma Ginny was hemming the last stitch on Tegan's handmade dress—a cornflower blue cotton with delicate white embroidery along the hem and sleeves. June helped press Hank's shirt and iron the creases into Jesse's slacks. The entire house hummed with anticipation.

Time passed quickly as the family bustled with final touches—buttons fastened, hair slicked back, cowboy hats dusted, boots polished. By late morning, they stood assembled on the front porch, dressed in their Sunday best. Tegan twirled once for Grandma Ginny, who gave a satisfied nod. Hank adjusted his collar, and Jesse tucked in his shirt under June's watchful eye.

Hank grinned at his sister. "You clean up pretty nice, T-Rex."

Tegan growled playfully. "A dress won't stop me from being wild."

Everyone laughed.

Jesse shoved Hank with a grin. "You're not bad looking yourself, lil' brother. Hearts are going to break tonight."

Marshall gave him a pointed look.

Jesse smiled uncharacteristically and pulled Hank into a headlock. Hank wriggled out with ease, swatting at him.

June shook her head. "Boys, that's enough. We're not showing up looking like a wrestling match."

"Alright, everyone," Grandpa Joe said, lifting his old camera. "Let's get one for the scrapbook."

"Marshall, scoot to the left. Jesse, chin up. Hank, stand taller. Tegan, sweetheart, stop spinning."

The family stood together in front of Bess—clean, proud, and ready for the festival.

"Smile!" Grandpa Joe called.

The shutter clicked, capturing a moment just before the day turned unforgettable.

The gravel road crunched under Bess's tires as the Millers pulled into the grand circular drive of Estancia Castilla. Marshall, June, and Tegan rode in Bess while Grandpa Joe, Grandma Ginny, Hank, and Jesse followed close behind in June's light blue Chevy Caprice. Gone was the quiet ranch they had visited weeks ago—today, it had transformed into a celebration of culture and tradition.

Banners in vibrant blues and whites—the colors of the Argentine flag—fluttered overhead, streaming between trees and across the arched gates of the estate. The music of a traditional folk ensemble swelled from the central stage: the reedy hum of a bandoneón, the rhythmic beat of a bombo legüero, the sweeping harmony of violins, and the lively trills of a piano intermingled with the warm strum of guitars. The air was rich with the scents of grilled meats, pastries dusted with sugar, and blooming lavender.

Booths lined the walkways, offering everything from yerba mate and handmade leather goods to jars of olive oil and handwoven shawls. Performers in folkloric costumes spun and stomped to the music, ribbons twirling through the air.

Grandma Ginny stepped out of the Caprice and approached Don Antonio with a wide smile, holding a carefully arranged gift basket. "For you and your family," she said warmly.

Don Antonio accepted it with grace. "Señora Ginny, you honor us."

Inside the basket were bundles of dried herbs from her garden, jars of homemade salves, a fresh-baked apple pie labeled "For Agustín," and the finely crafted salt and pepper shakers carved by Grandpa Joe. Don Antonio inspected them with reverence. "Exquisite," he said, and then looked at Grandpa Joe. "God has blessed your hands."

Grandpa Joe tipped his hat modestly.

Don Antonio motioned them toward a beautifully set table beneath a shaded canopy. At the center of the table sat a vivid placard inscribed with "La Familia Miller" , and a small white placard rested at the head seat, elegantly scripted: *"Señorita Tegan—VIP."*

Tegan squealed with delight. "I'm a VIP!" She ran up and hugged Don Antonio tightly. "Gracias, Don Antonio!"

He chuckled and patted her back. "The honor is mine."

As they took their seats, the Millers couldn't help but notice the curious eyes watching them. Most of the festival attendees were Latino families, dressed in vibrant traditional attire, their faces open with friendly curiosity. The Millers were among the few white families there—and it felt, for a moment, like stepping into another world.

But there was no hostility, only warmth and welcome in the smiles of strangers.

Grandpa Joe lifted his camera and snapped photos of the stunning decor—hand-stitched flags, lavender garlands wrapped around posts, children in folkloric dress twirling with laughter.

Once seated, the Millers watched as Don Antonio gave a brief nod, excused himself, and proceeded to the center stage. It was time for the festival to begin—and for the Castilla family to shine.

The sun dipped low, casting a warm amber glow across the arena as a hush fell over the crowd. From the far gate, Mirabella Castilla entered astride her grey PRE stallion, Valeroso. The stallion's mane shimmered silver in the light, his every step deliberate and precise.

Mirabella wore a traditional Argentine riding ensemble: a crisp, high-collared blouse tucked into a sweeping navy skort that fell in flowing folds to the ankles of her boots. The fabric caught the breeze as she turned, flaring behind her like a flag of motion. A wide leather belt cinched her waist, and a slate-blue hat shaded her focused emerald eyes. She rode without embellishment—no showmanship, only grace, control, and quiet command.

The guitar music rose, and they moved.

Valeroso stepped onto the narrow wooden bridge, ears forward. Each hoof struck the planks with assurance. They turned sharply and approached a gate. Without hesitation, Mirabella opened it one-handed, pivoted through, and closed it behind her, never once dropping the rhythm. She guided her stallion through a serpentine of lifted poles, around barrels, and into a precise square halt. Then came a burst of lateral work—haunches-in, shoulder-in—followed by a pirouette that spun like silk.

She cued a flying change pattern across the diagonal, each step like music pressed into earth.

When she halted at the center, she dropped her reins, bowed low from the saddle, and Valeroso dipped his head in kind.

A beat of stunned silence—and then the arena erupted. "¡Eso! ¡Eso!" the crowd shouted, leaping to their feet.

At the banquet table, Tegan Miller's fork clattered to her plate. "That was like... ballet and bravery had a baby," she whispered.

Neither of her brothers spoke. Jesse leaned forward slightly, eyes fixed on the arena. Hank just stared, slack-jawed, barely blinking. The performance had silenced them both.

"She's unreal," Tegan added, more to herself than anyone else.

Mirabella rode out slowly, lifting her hand in quiet thanks. Valeroso arched his neck as if proud of the attention.

Music continued in the background as stagehands reset the space. Guests returned to their food, though many still glanced toward the gate where Mirabella had disappeared.

Don Antonio strode to center stage, lifting the mic with theatrical flair. "Amigos, we now present a dance passed through generations like stories by firelight—la chacarera!"

Bright guitars struck up. Dancers in vibrant traditional dress flooded the platform. Mirabella returned, now in a flaring white skirt embroidered at the hem and high boots laced to the knee. A sky-colored sash wrapped her waist, and ribbons flowed from her braid. At her side stood Agustín Castilla—hat tipped, vest buttoned, smile ready.

They moved—light, quick, defiant. Boots stomped, skirts twirled, and glances passed like sparks. The audience clapped along, swept into the beat. The dance was flirtation and pride, heritage and joy, all channeled through polished foot-work and knowing smiles.

Tegan cheered as Mirabella stomped and spun. "She's a cowgirl princess and a storm."

Jesse and Hank still said nothing.

The dance ended in thunderous applause. As the lights dimmed again, a steady, deep drumbeat filled the air.

Agustín stepped forward with a set of boleadoras—weighted cords tipped with leather-bound stones that caught the light like dull bronze. He swung them low first, the cords whispering through the air before the rhythm built, a blur of motion and sound that coiled around him like a living thing. He leapt, snapping the cords against the ground, in sharp, percussive beats, the rhythm carrying the echo of gauchos who came long before him.

Then, without warning, he called out, "Jesse Miller—join me!"

Jesse blinked. "Wait, what?"

"Go!" June urged, laughing.

He stood, straightened his shirt, and jogged to the stage, picking up one of the bombo legüeros set by the platform. A few warm-up taps—and then he found the rhythm.

Agustín's boleadoras sang in the air while Jesse's hands pounded out a com-plex, driving beat. The two rhythms—air and earth—met in perfect tension, climbing toward a shared crescendo. Agustín looked at Jesse and nodded.

The last crack of the cords and slap of the drum landed in unison.

For a heartbeat, everything held.

Then the crowd exploded. Cheers echoed into the hills.

Jesse, still breathless, looked across at Agustín. What he saw was no longer the clean-cut Harvard graduate from across the valley—but a man who lived between tradition and brilliance, between precision and fire.

And Jesse—musician, rebel, wanderer—recognized him.

As twilight deepened over the California hills, the festival at Estancia Castilla settled into a slower, more soulful rhythm. Lanterns hung between oak trees swayed gently in the breeze, casting flickering light across the courtyard. The scent of asado still lingered, drifting between bursts of laughter and the soft melodies of guitar and bombo.

In the courtyard, Tegan Miller spun barefoot across the flagstone, trying once again to master the chacarera. Her cheeks glowed with excitement and effort, her braid whipping as she turned.

Mirabella, calm and precise, clapped out the rhythm beside her. "You're starting too early on the turn," she said, stepping close, demonstrating the footwork with ease. Her long white skirt flared as she moved, floating over her tall boots. "Listen to the rhythm. It will carry you."

Tegan tried again—clap, stomp, sweep, spin—and this time, she landed the last step with a flourish.

From a quiet corner, Grandpa Joe raised his old Leica and snapped a candid shot of Tegan mid-spin. He smiled behind the lens, winding the film with care.

Nearby, June Miller and Grandma Ginny sat at a table draped with embroidered linen, sipping wine and watching the girls dance. The lantern light caught the silver in their hair.

"She's in heaven," June said, eyes on Tegan.

Ginny nodded. "That girl needed a big sister."

Tegan threw her arms around Mirabella. "Okay. That was it. I did it!"

Mirabella laughed. "You did, hermanita."

Tegan beamed. "You're officially stuck with me."

"Good," Mirabella said. "I was hoping."

Across the courtyard, Marshall Miller leaned against a low stone wall, arms crossed, watching the scene with quiet thoughtfulness. June stepped up beside him, nudging his shoulder gently.

"They fit in here," she said.

"They really do," Marshall agreed, nodding toward Hank, who stood by the grill with Agustín, talking cattle and saddle fit like they'd grown up together.

"You know," June said, glancing toward Mirabella and Tegan, "when we first met the Castillas, I never imagined they would become such good friends. But aren't you glad they did?"

Marshall took a slow sip of wine, his gaze resting on the dance floor. "I'll admit it. I wasn't sure at first. Fancy ranch, Argentine traditions, imported horses—felt like a world apart from ours."

"But?" June pressed.

"But I was wrong." He looked around the courtyard, at the mingling families, the uninhibited laughter, the music that made even old boots want to move. "They're good people. And they've opened their world to ours."

June smiled. "And Hank's job with them has been the best thing for him."

"Better than any classroom," Marshall agreed.

Just then, a cheer rose from the far end of the courtyard. A wiry old gaucho with quick feet and a mischievous grin had swept into a dance, Grandma Ginny.

She laughed and matched his steps, her shawl trailing like a flag, her boots striking the stones in perfect rhythm.

"Look at her go!" June laughed.

"She'll be sore tomorrow," Marshall muttered.

"She'll say it was worth every ache," June said.

Grandpa Joe snapped another photo, lowering the camera only to smile. "That one's going in the album," he said.

As the stars blinked overhead and music wrapped around the ranch like an old story retold, the Millers remained grounded in the moment—neighbors, yes, but something more now. Not just living beside the Castillas, but living with them—tied together by the land, by laughter, and by a shared rhythm that felt more and more like family.

The music from the courtyard had faded to a mellow murmur, the last notes of guitar drifting lazily in the night air. Laughter rose occasionally, but softer now—like the dying embers of a fire. Hank Miller walked away from it all, drawn not by frustration, but by something quieter. Something truer.

He made his way across the moonlit gravel toward the barns, the crunch of his boots muffled by the hum of crickets. Inside, the air was warm and familiar—hay, dust, saddle soap, and the earthy scent of horses. Lantern light glowed low along the aisle.

From the far stall came a low nicker.

"There you are," Hank murmured.

Bob, the buckskin stallion, stepped forward from the shadows. The golden sheen of his coat caught the light, his black mane and points giving him the look of something half-wild, half-royal. He wasn't the most trusting horse, not yet—but he recognized Hank.

The stallion's ears flicked forward.

Hank unlatched the door and stepped inside, grabbing a soft brush from the hook. He worked along Bob's shoulder in long, methodical strokes.

"Hey, Bob. You and me," he whispered, "we do better in the quiet. No dancing. No crowds. Just this."

Bob exhaled, leaning into the brush, guiding Hank to his favorite spot. Hank smiled and willingly obliged his friend. He continued down Bob's back, his own body relaxing to the comfort of just being–not on display, just the quiet sounds of the horse and him.

The barn door creaked open behind him.

Hank didn't turn. He knew that step—the hush of skirts over straw, the pause at the threshold.

"I thought I might find you here," Mirabella said gently.

She wore a shawl over her blouse now, her long skirt trailing just above her boots. Her hair was half-down, loose waves catching in the lantern glow.

She leaned on the stall gate, hands folded over the wood.

"Hank," she asked softly, "will you come back to the party?"

He kept brushing.

For a moment, only the sound of bristles against hide and the quiet breath of the stallion filled the space.

"I just feel more comfortable out here," Hank said at last. "With the horses. With the quiet. It's where I make sense."

Mirabella didn't push. She nodded, eyes on the buckskin stallion as Hank moved down his side, pausing at the haunch to check a healing scrape. The stallion stood calmly, trusting the hands that touched him.

"I understand," she said. "Most of the guests have left. It's just family now. Your sister's already curled up in my room, fast asleep. Jesse and Agustín are still at the fire, trading music. Don Antonio asked all of you to spend the night. Your parents have left the truck for you to return in the morning."

She paused. "Agustín would love for you to stay. So would I."

Hank ran his hand along Bob's ribs and down to the stallion's dark legs, noting the ease in the horse's stance, the subtle signs of healing. He set the brush back on the hook.

"If I stay," he said, "I can work with him first thing in the morning."

Mirabella stepped forward and extended her hand.

Hank looked at it for a long second, then at her—her steady gaze, the softness in her expression that never made him feel small.

He reached out.

Her hand fit perfectly in his—like he'd always imagined it would. He'd never held a girl's hand before. Not like this. Not with the quiet meaning tucked inside the touch. But somehow, he knew it was right.

She didn't squeeze. She didn't pull.

She simply led.

And he followed, through the dim barn aisle and out into the cool night air, where the music waited like an open door.

Twilight bathed Estancia Castilla in shades of violet and gold as the last of the guests filtered out. The once-bustling festival grounds now glowed softly with lantern light. The music had quieted to a gentle background murmur, a final note of farewell to a day filled with joy.

Marshall, June, Grandma Ginny, and Grandpa Joe had already left for the Miller ranch, leaving the younger generation behind. Near the stables, Mirabella stood beside Don Antonio, her face still warm from the evening's accolades.

"Buenas noches," Don Antonio said, placing a hand on Jesse's shoulder. "Thank you all for being a part of today. It meant more than you know."

"It was incredible," Jesse replied.

Mirabella offered each of them a kiss on the cheek. As her eyes met Hank's, they lingered for a heartbeat longer than the others—an unspoken something passed between them.

Jesse and Agustín, both perceptive and amused, exchanged a knowing glance.

"Sleep well, boys," Mirabella said softly, before she and Don Antonio disappeared into the house.

The trio went to the grass just outside the stables, where wool blankets lay spread beneath the stars. The firelight danced across their faces as they settled in.

Jesse lazily strummed his guitar, his eyes half-closed in contentment. "So, Agustín," he said, "what'd you think about college? Worth it?"

Agustín leaned back on his elbows, watching the sky. "College opened my mind. It gave me tools—not just knowledge, but perspective. I see this place differently now. The estancia, our traditions—they aren't something to escape. They're something to evolve."

Jesse strummed slowly. "Four years is a long time."

Hank lay quietly nearby, listening.

Agustín turned his gaze to Jesse. "And think of what you could do with a degree from Yale. You could open doors, Jesse. Leave your mark."

Then he looked toward Hank. "What about you? What do you want to do?"

Hank shrugged, plucking a blade of grass. "I haven't thought about it much. I like the farm. Riding, training horses. Feels right."

Jesse chuckled. "You can't take the cowboy out of Hank."

Agustín smiled thoughtfully. "Maybe not. But if you want a family someday, a future with stability—degrees help. Quality women don't fall for cowboys."

The comment landed with a thud. Hank's jaw tightened.

"I'm gonna check on the horses," he snapped, rising to his feet.

He strode off into the quiet barnyard; the shadows swallowing him whole.

Jesse shot Agustín a look. "Smooth."

Agustín raised a brow. "Just being honest."

Jesse strummed a melancholy chord and let it fade into the stillness.

The stars blinked overhead, as if waiting for what tomorrow might bring.

The moon hung low over Estancia Castilla, casting silver light across the olive groves and stables. Crickets chirped softly, and the breeze rustled through lavender and olive branches, whispering secrets only the land could understand.

Hank's boots crunched against the gravel as he made his way from the barn, still feeling the sting of Agustín's words. He paused near the grove, instinct pricking at the edges of his awareness. A flicker of movement caught his eye—something dark slipping between the rows of olive trees.

He narrowed his gaze. Not an animal.

Someone.

He turned and jogged back toward the stables, where Jesse and Agustín sat beside the dying fire.

"Something's out in the grove," Hank said, low but urgent. "Could be someone trying to steal or cause trouble."

Jesse stood at once, already grabbing the flashlight from his pack. "You sure?"

"I'm sure."

Agustín's expression darkened. "Not again."

The three young men mounted their horses and rode quietly toward the grove, flashlights in hand. The soft clop of hooves blended with the wind until they came to a halt beneath the gnarled boughs of the olive trees.

Then they heard it—metal clinking. Low voices. The unmistakable sound of something being forced open.

Hank dismounted first, creeping toward the source of the sound. Behind a low stone wall, two men were working to pry open an olive oil barrel while another poured what looked like bleach onto an irrigation valve.

Jesse swore under his breath. "They're trying to ruin the crop."

Agustín's face hardened. "Those are ex-workers. One of them is Esteban—the groom who used to handle Bob."

The mention of the name lit a fire in Hank. His jaw clenched. "That's the one who beat him."

Without another word, Hank surged forward, a flashlight beam cutting through the dark. "Hey!"

The intruders froze for a second—then bolted.

Chaos erupted.

Jesse lunged and tackled the one with the barrel lid, only to get clocked hard in the eye and fall back, swearing.

Agustín swung off his horse and went after another, pinning him against a tree.

Hank, with speed born of adrenaline and rage, leapt onto Esteban and wrestled him to the ground. Esteban fought back hard, but Hank was stronger—and furious.

"You're not taking him," Hank growled through clenched teeth. "Never again."

The struggle churned dirt and olive branches until Hank finally subdued him. Just then, floodlights snapped on.

Don Antonio and Mirabella, flanked by two uniformed security guards, appeared at the edge of the grove.

"What's going on here?" Don Antonio demanded, striding forward as the security detail grabbed the intruders.

"We caught them sabotaging the trees," Jesse said, wiping blood from his lip and pointing at the broken barrels and chemicals.

"And this one," Hank added, yanking Esteban to his feet, "was trying to steal Bob."

Recognition flared in Don Antonio's eyes. "Esteban," he spat. "You have shamed this land for the last time."

Mirabella placed a hand over her heart, visibly shaken. She looked at Hank, eyes wide with gratitude and worry.

Don Antonio turned to the Miller brothers, his voice grave but filled with sincerity. "You've protected not only our land—but our legacy. I will never forget this."

Jesse winced, touching his blackened eye. "Next time, maybe let security go first."

Hank gave a tired chuckle. "Next time, don't tackle someone twice your size."

Agustín clapped them both on the back. "You were brilliant. Thank you."

Don Antonio motioned to the guards. "Get these men off my property. Call the authorities."

Guards led the intruders away in handcuffs, and Mirabella stepped closer to Hank. Her voice was soft but firm. "Thank you for protecting him. For protecting all of us."

Hank, still catching his breath, simply nodded. "He wasn't taking Bob. Not again."

She smiled, and for a moment, the tension lifted.

They stood together beneath the moonlight, the grove safe once more.

The looming morning cleansed last night's battle. The horizon bloomed in soft strokes of lavender and gold as dawn unfurled across Estancia Castilla. Mist clung to the fields, curling along the fence lines and around the barns like breath on glass.

In the paddock behind the stables, Hank stood alone with Bob.

He hadn't slept. Not after the fight, not after seeing Esteban's face in the moonlight. So he turned to the one thing that always calmed the storm inside him—working a horse.

Bob moved freely at liberty—no halter, no lead—just trust. The buckskin stallion's coat had grown sleeker, his ribs no longer visible. His amber eyes were brighter now. When Hank stepped, Bob mirrored. When Hank paused, Bob settled.

"I got you," Hank murmured, holding Bob's gaze. "You're safe now."

He reached into his pocket and pulled out a homemade treat. Bob accepted it with a low nicker, brushing his velvet muzzle against Hank's hand.

At the gate, Don Antonio watched in silence before stepping forward. His stride was deliberate, his expression weary but resolute.

"You didn't have to stay out all night," he whispered.

Hank wiped the sweat from his brow. "Didn't want to leave him alone."

Don Antonio extended his hand—firm, warm. "The Castillas are lucky to have the Millers as allies. You've earned a place here. Both of you."

Footsteps sounded behind them. Jesse approached, shirt wrinkled, eye bruised, still in the clothes from the night before. Despite the shiner, he wore the faintest grin.

"Could've done without the black eye," Jesse muttered. "But I've had worse from Hank in a wrestling match."

"You got cocky," Hank replied.

Don Antonio chuckled. "Come by tomorrow. We'll open something stronger than last night's wine."

He left them with a proud smile and a clap on the shoulder.

The house stirred behind them. Tegan burst into the courtyard in her party dress and bare feet, arms folded tight across her chest.

"You fought intruders and didn't wake me up?"

Jesse smirked. "You would've screamed louder than the horses."

"I would've helped," she shot back, eyeing his bruise. "That looks nasty. I'll put some salve on that when we get home. Hank, you better tell me everything in the truck."

Then, her energy shifted as she spotted Mirabella emerging from the house, wrapped in a wool shawl. Tegan ran to her and hugged her tight.

"Best night ever," she whispered.

Mirabella returned the embrace, emotion flickering across her face. "I'm glad you came."

They didn't bring extra clothes, so the three Miller kids piled into Bess in their party outfits, wrinkled and stained from sleep and dust. As the truck rolled down the gravel drive, Mirabella caught Hank's eye one last time. He tipped his hat. She nodded, a soft smile on her lips.

In the truck, Jesse drove while Hank sat next to the window, the wind tousling their hair. Tegan jabbered between them, reliving every detail of the night she missed—the music, the dancing, the imaginary fireworks.

Hank leaned back, eyes on the sky warming into full daylight.

Jesse looked at him. "Not a bad party."

Hank cracked a smile. "Not bad at all."

Bess rolled on, dust trailing behind them—one family heading home, stitched a little tighter than before.

TRAINING WOES

The morning sun stretched across Estancia Castilla, warming the round pen just enough to lift the mist off the railings. Hank moved with quiet purpose, the saddle pad slung over his arm, lead rope slack in his hand. Bob stood at the center—tail swishing, ears twitching, muscles coiled beneath his buckskin hide.

Hank stepped in, soft and slow.

He held out the pad. Bob sniffed it, wrinkled his nose, then flung his head and snorted like Hank had handed him a wet rag.

"Yup, definitely got opinions today," Hank murmured.

He rubbed the stallion's withers, laid the pad gently over his back. Bob stood for a heartbeat, then launched into a short, snorting buck. The pad flew, hitting the dirt like a gauntlet tossed at Hank's boots.

He sighed and bent to retrieve it. "Alright. Message received."

It took time. Hank didn't rush it. One pass at a time, the pad stayed longer. Finally, Bob let it rest without flinching. Hank led him in a few circles—loose, steady, letting the stallion move. The tension drained from Bob's stride, each lap loosening something deeper.

"You two look different today," Mirabella called from the fence rail. Her voice held its usual polish, but her tone was warmer now. Approving.

Hank turned his head.

"You mean calmer?" he said.

She nodded. "Progress is a better word. He's beginning to trust you."

Hank considered that a second, then nodded toward the tack stand. "Think you can bring the saddle to the center?"

She raised a brow. "Already?"

"He's ready. Least he says he is."

Mirabella entered with the saddle balanced on her hip, the movement graceful and effortless. She set it down gently, dusting her gloves. Hank gave her a quick 'thanks' then led Bob toward it.

At first, Bob followed willingly.

Then his eyes locked on the saddle.

He balked.

Ears pinned, neck arched—then came the explosion. He squealed and twisted, yanking the lead rope and flinging himself backward. The saddle wasn't even on him, but he acted like it bit him.

Hank let the rope slide, giving him room. Bob bucked twice, kicking up a storm, and galloped a half-circle before skidding to a halt at the far end of the pen.

Hank stood where he was, hand on his hip, scratching his head.

Mirabella watched from the center. "So... not quite ready."

Hank didn't look at her. "No. He's ready. Just not the way I expected."

Hank's eyes drifted toward the barn. "Valeroso still in his stall?"

"Yes," she said cautiously. "Why?"

"I've got a theory. Saddle him. Bring him in."

Her brows drew tight. "Ride him in the round pen? That's not part of his program."

"I need him here."

Mirabella hesitated. "It's a small space. He's never—"

"Trust me." Hank's voice didn't rise, didn't press. But when he looked at her, calm and steady, something in her posture shifted.

She held his gaze for a beat longer, then nodded once. "Five minutes."

As she disappeared toward the barn, Hank started again with the saddle pad. This time, Bob tolerated it without a fuss. Hank didn't touch the saddle. Not yet.

When Mirabella returned, Valeroso was beneath her—regal, polished, every step a statement. His grey coat glimmered in the light, his black mane slicked and braided. Mirabella rode him in with silent authority, guiding the Andalusian to the perimeter.

Bob turned to face them.

His ears snapped forward. His body shifted with interest. The buckskin puffed his chest slightly, tail lifting, like he'd suddenly remembered there was an audience.

"Now we're listening," Hank muttered.

He brought Bob to the center again, carefully, watching the stallion's eye. Bob stayed soft. No fire. No fuss.

Hank lifted the saddle—slowly and measured. Bob tensed, but didn't bolt. Hank eased it down onto his back. No buck. No squeal.

"Look at that," Mirabella called softly, circling the edge. "He's showing off."

"He's competing," Hank said. "Let's lean into it."

He handed her the lead rope. "Pony him. Let him follow Valeroso."

She took it without question.

Valeroso stepped off—elegant, collected. Bob moved with him like a rival, stride for stride. When the grey walked, Bob walked. When Valeroso trotted, Bob surged forward, knees high, movement exaggerated. When Valeroso halted, Bob braced and stopped clean, ears pricked, eyes burning with purpose.

"He's copying everything," Mirabella said, astonished.

"He wants to outdo him."

They continued for three more laps. Bob stayed steady in the saddle, not a flicker of resistance. His head dropped, jaw soft, legs moving like he'd worn that saddle all his life.

Hank approached, taking the rope. Bob stood square, still puffed up and proud.

"I'm gonna get on."

Mirabella blinked. "Now?"

"He's telling me it's time."

"Do you want Valeroso to stay?"

"In the center. He's the reason we're this far."

Mirabella nodded and halted Valeroso inside the circle. The grey cocked a hind leg and lowered his head, calm and sure.

Hank rubbed Bob's shoulder. He checked the cinch again, ran a hand along the saddle's edge, then slipped his foot into the stirrup. No fast movements. He breathed with the horse.

Then, slowly, he draped his upper body across the saddle.

Bob shifted under him.

Hank kept his weight balanced, hand sliding down Bob's withers, his voice low and even.

"I'm here. Nothing bad's gonna happen."

He waited until Bob sighed. Then he pressed upright and swung his leg over, sitting deep in the saddle, quiet as snowfall.

Bob held his breath, shifting with uncertainty. Hank hovered, patient. A deep sigh from the stallion told him it was time. Hank again sat deep in the saddle.

"Easy," Hank murmured.

He gave the faintest nudge.

Bob walked—then hopped once. A quick, irritated buck. But Hank stayed loose in the saddle, riding it like he'd known it was coming.

"I'm still here," he whispered.

In the center, Mirabella released the reins. Valeroso lowered his head as if to signal calmness.

Bob glanced, then mirrored the gesture.

He relaxed.

Hank guided him into a walk around the ring. They circled, changed direction, stopped. Bob listened to every cue, subtle and clean.

At last, Hank brought him to a halt facing the center.

He dismounted slowly, boots settling in the dirt.

"Good boy," he said, rubbing the stallion's face.

Bob exhaled, leaned into his palm.

Hank pulled a peppermint from his vest and handed it over. Bob crunched it, triumphant.

Valeroso nickered low. Bob pawed the ground once, satisfied.

Mirabella watched, quiet for a beat. "I've never seen him like that."

Hank gave a half-smile. "Guess he just needed someone to listen to him."

She hesitated. "Would you mind if I joined you for a walk? After I put Valeroso away."

He looked at her, surprised. "Course. You're more than welcome."

She turned to lead Valeroso out. Bob watched her go, then bumped Hank in the ribs with a thud.

Hank laughed, rubbing his side. "Yeah... she's something special."

He clicked his tongue, and together they walked out of the round pen—one steady step at a time, side by side, no lead rope needed.

The barn was quiet. Dust particles drifted in shafts of golden light, and the leather of Valeroso's saddle creaked as Mirabella slid it from his back. She moved on instinct, hands going through the motions: unbuckle the girth, loosen the noseband, fold the saddle pad. But her mind wasn't on the tack.

The dirt from the round pen still clung to her sleeves. She brushed at it absently, then stopped, fingers resting over the crease in the saddle pad. Still watching that boy from the Miller ranch sit astride a half-wild stallion with no more than a whispered word and a quiet seat.

She rested her hand on the stall door, fingers still tingling from the halter's leather. The image of Hank's quiet seat and Bob's breath settling under him replayed like a secret she wasn't meant to see.

Hank's voice echoed in her memory—not raised, not commanding. Just steady. Listening.

She hadn't known a horse could respond to silence like that.

She brushed Valeroso's flank slowly, her fingers trailing the fine muscles beneath his dappled coat. He turned his head and blinked at her, calm and curious.

"You liked him, didn't you?" she whispered.

The stallion gave a slow blink, then lowered his head until it hovered near her shoulder.

Her throat tightened.

All her life, she'd relied on rhythm and rule. Diagonal aids. Shoulder-in. Pressure and release. She could name every principle drilled into her from childhood—but not what she'd just seen in that ring.

That hadn't been theory. That had been... trust.

She looked into Valeroso's eyes—seen a thousand times, and never like this. There was still more inside him. Layers untouched. Emotions unread. And suddenly, she was hungry to know them. To know *him*.

To go deeper than she ever had before.

A quiet smile touched her lips. "There's more to you, isn't there?"

Valeroso nudged her arm gently, a subtle answer, and she laughed softly under her breath.

She set his halter gently on the peg and leaned against the stall door for a moment, arms folded, gaze unfocused.

Hank hadn't done anything grand. He hadn't shown off. He hadn't raised his voice or driven the horse into submission. But he'd *moved* something—first in Bob, and now, unexpectedly, in her.

There was a side of horsemanship she'd never considered.

A side she was suddenly desperate to explore.

She looked once more at Valeroso, standing relaxed in his stall, the light catching the grey of his coat like mist over stone.

"I think I owe you an apology," she whispered.

She opened the stall door and stepped inside, but not to halter him.

Not even to touch him.

She just stood there, near the wall, hands at her sides. Still.

Valeroso turned his head to look at her. His ears flicked once, then settled.

He stayed at the far end of the stall, chewing softly, the slow rhythm of his jaw the only sound in the barn.

Mirabella watched him for a long moment. No commands. No cues. No agenda.

This is what Hank did, she realized. *He waited.*

And so did she.

After a minute or two, Valeroso shifted. He walked to her. Stopped a breath away.

She didn't move.

He lowered his head, and only then did she lift her hand—slowly, letting him decide.

He pressed his forehead to her palm.

Not a trick. Not a task.

Just contact.

Her eyes burned suddenly. She swallowed hard.

So this is what it feels like.

True connection.

She stroked his face once, then quietly left the stall and closed the door behind her.

She didn't say a word. But when she stepped outside, her chest felt lighter. Her hands were empty. And for once, that felt like enough.

The sun had risen above the tree line, casting long streaks of gold through the olive groves. Sunbaked clay clung to Hank's boots and the cuffs of his jeans, but he didn't mind. Bob walked beside him, untethered now, the lead rope looped in Hank's hand more out of habit than necessity.

They followed a worn path that wound past the back paddocks, a path nobody planned—worn into the earth by hooves and time.

Bob drifted toward a patch of wild grass and lowered his head to graze. Hank stopped with him, watching the stallion chew in lazy, rhythmic bites.

"I think this is what I want," Hank whispered. Bob flicked an ear. "Just this. Horses. Land. Something that doesn't lie to you."

He paused, letting the breeze carry his next words: "I don't know if I need anything more than that."

He looked out over the fenceline, where the pasture rolled into distant groves. The wind stirred through the olive branches, carrying the scent of lavender and sunlight.

"Agustín says college's the only shot at something real. Without a degree, nobody takes you seriously."

He paused, rubbing his thumb along the braided rope in his hand.

"But when I'm with you," he said, glancing down at Bob, "when we're working through something, or just walking like this... that's when I feel the most like myself."

Bob tugged another clump of grass, chewed slowly, unbothered by the weight of Hank's confession.

"I want my own place one day," Hank continued. "Not something big or fancy. Just a few good horses, a strong barn, and enough pasture to let them stretch out when they need to. I want to train horses the right way. Build something of my own."

Bob dropped his head lower, grazing deeper into the thick patch.

Hank gave a soft laugh. "You're not much for giving advice, are you?"

The stallion gave no sign he'd heard, though his ear turned briefly in Hank's direction.

Hank stepped closer and ran a hand along Bob's withers. "I'll make sure there's good pasture for you. Lots of it. That way you can eat all day and never have to hear me ramble again."

Bob lifted his head for a moment, gave a short exhale, then resumed grazing.

Hank smiled.

"I'll take that as approval."

He stood there a while longer, the silence comfortable between them. In the quiet, he felt something settle inside him—something steady and sure, like a nail driven deep into oak.

The old upright piano filled the front room with its warm, worn presence. Afternoon light spilled through the gauzy curtains, casting soft streaks across the scratched wood and yellowing keys. June sat beside Jesse on the narrow bench, her back straight, hands folded neatly in her lap.

Jesse hunched forward, his brow furrowed in concentration, fingers poised above the keyboard.

The opening of Liszt's *Sonata in B Minor* unfolded under his hands—halting, uneven. The emotion was there, but the execution fought him. Notes stumbled. Timing slipped.

His fingers stuttered again, the left hand dragging like an anchor. He could almost feel his family's savings pressed into each note—lessons, plane tickets, applications. All of it riding on the hope that he could turn talent into something that mattered.

But what if he couldn't?

He skipped a measure, rushing the tempo. June opened her mouth to speak—but stopped herself. He wouldn't hear it. Not yet.

He growled under his breath and slammed both palms against the keys. The piano barked in protest.

"This is impossible," he snapped. "Why can't we do the Rachmaninoff?"

June remained perfectly still, like the sudden outburst hadn't touched her.

She turned her head, calm and sure. "Because everyone will be doing Rachmaninoff."

Jesse blinked, frustrated; sweat beaded at his temple.

June's voice stayed soft. "You want to stand out, don't you?"

"You're asking the impossible," he snapped, voice cracking just slightly before he turned away.

He stood from the bench, hands tense at his sides, and began pacing toward the hallway.

June said nothing. She rubbed her palms together, adjusted her seat slightly, and without fanfare, placed her fingers on the keys.

She played.

The first sequence of the sonata spilled into the room—fluid, effortless, haunting. It filled the space with aching elegance, each note threaded with emotion, not for show but from memory. From love.

Jesse froze.

He turned halfway back, watching her. The music wound its way into the center of his chest, rattling the foundation of everything he thought he knew. She didn't just play. She listened—with her whole body—to the story in the keys. Jesse had never thought to do that.

He had no idea his mother could play like that.

When the final chord settled into silence, he stood motionless, shame pressing at his throat. His confidence cracked, his pride exposed.

Jesse stared at her hands. Her fingers had more truth in them than he could find in a whole page of sheet music.

He didn't know if he wanted Yale. But he knew he wanted *that*—whatever lived inside her hands when she played.

A knock at the doorframe broke the moment.

Marshall poked his head in, grease-smudged and holding a pair of worn gloves. "I'm heading into town. Need some parts for the tractor and a few gallons of diesel."

Jesse latched onto the excuse like a lifeline. "I'll come with you," he blurted. "I need a break."

He didn't even look back. As if quitting was easier than admitting he didn't know how to stay.

Marshall looked at June. Concern etched across his brow. "He alright?"

June kept her fingers on the keys, touching the silence that still lingered.

"He's fine," she breathed. "He's just feeling the weight of it."

Marshall gave a slow nod and disappeared down the hallway.

Alone again, June rested both hands in her lap, eyes closed. The notes still lingered inside her, bright and private. She'd given Jesse a glimpse—not to shame him, but to remind him: this path is hard, and it is worth it.

She smiled—faint and wistful—and reached forward to close the lid over the keys.

The bell above the gas station door jingled as Jesse stepped inside. The air smelled of burnt coffee, old jerky, and floor cleaner. Fluorescent lights buzzed overhead as he stepped up to the counter, pulling a crumpled bill from his back pocket.

"Diesel. Pump four."

Outside, Marshall was already working the nozzle into the first red gas can, the back of his shirt streaked with grease and sun.

Jesse turned to leave when a familiar voice stopped him cold.

"You've been missed. Place hasn't been the same without your guitar and voice."

Jesse turned.

It was the owner of the Long Branch Saloon, leaning against a rotating rack of lighters like he had all the time in the world. Denim vest. Scuffed boots. Laughter lines around his eyes that never really went away.

Jesse managed a polite nod. "Hey."

The man pushed off the rack and stepped closer. "You still pickin'? Or you traded all that in for... what was it—Yale?"

"Preparing for the audition," Jesse said, hearing how stiff it sounded even as he said it. "School of Music. Yale."

The owner chuckled. "Sounds good, Mozart."

He gave Jesse a little nudge with his elbow. "But this weekend, we've got music agents swinging through. L.A. types. Talent scouts, they say. Looking for something real. Gritty."

He raised an eyebrow. "You show up, your slot's still yours. Mic'll be hot."

Jesse kept his expression neutral, though something shifted behind his eyes. "I'll think about it."

He tapped Jesse on the shoulder with two fingers, the way he always did before a set. "I'll keep the lights on for you."

The bell jingled again as the door swung shut behind him.

Jesse stood still for a second longer, eyes fixed on the floor, the rhythm of old memories pulsing in his ears—crowded tables, the clink of bottles, the hum of his own voice tangled with six strings and cigarette smoke.

Outside, Marshall tightened the lid on the last can and loaded it into the truck bed. Jesse walked back across the lot and climbed into the passenger seat. The sun had climbed higher, washing the dash in pale gold.

Marshall glanced at him. "Who was that?"

Jesse buckled his seatbelt, eyes forward. "Just a guy asking for directions."

Marshall didn't push it. He started the engine, and they rolled back onto the main road, tires humming over the asphalt. Loose gravel kicked up behind them, and the horizon stretched wide.

Jesse leaned against the window, tapping faint rhythms on his thigh. The road unwound ahead of them, but his mind was caught somewhere else—in smoky light, the hum of a crowd, his hands on the strings again, this time for someone who could change everything.

He stared out the window, a flicker of conflict in his eyes.

At first it was random—fidgeting. But then a pattern emerged.

His fingers moved with ghostly purpose: the sonata.

He tried to remember it the way she'd played it—fluid, clean—but his left hand dragged behind again, muddling the lines, just like before.

Still, he kept going.

Not for practice. Not for Yale.

Just to remember what it felt like—before everything got so damn hard.

The sonata belonged to Yale. But the pull in his chest—that belonged to somewhere else. The melody clung to his skin like something unfinished.

Outside, the road stretched toward a future he didn't know how to name. The road ahead looked clean. Prestigious. Mapped. But it didn't sound like his voice. Not yet.

The late afternoon light painted the trees in amber as Hank and Mirabella walked side by side along the gravel path, Bob trailing slightly behind them, his lead rope draped casually in Hank's hand. A few birds called from the olive trees, and the distant hum of bees drifted in on the warm breeze.

They hadn't spoken for several minutes, and they didn't need to.

Bob's hooves crunched softly with each step. The stallion walked with his head low, his body loose—calm in a way Mirabella had never imagined he could be.

She glanced over at Hank. "What happens next?" she asked.

Hank looked out toward the pasture. "I'm not sure yet. I'll ask. He'll answer. Just not with words."

As if on cue, Bob let out a low nicker, almost amused.

They both laughed.

"Well," Mirabella said, smiling, "I can't wait to see what the two of you accomplish. You've got something rare."

Hank looked at her, sincere. "You're part of this too, you know."

Mirabella blinked, touched by the weight in his voice.

He meant it.

She nodded, letting a small smile rise. "Then I'll do my best to keep up."

They continued on, winding through the shade-dappled rows of trees until the barns came back into view. The stall doors stood open to the breeze, and Bob led himself the rest of the way, stopping at his own stall as if he belonged there now.

Hank gave the stallion a pat along the shoulder, unclipped the rope, and let him step inside.

"Thanks," he said, turning to Mirabella. "For helping. For today."

She met his gaze. "Anytime."

He hesitated a second, then adjusted his cap. "I've got a couple of things to finish for Agustín before I go. Nothing fancy—just some loose ends."

Mirabella nodded. "Of course. Go."

She watched as he walked off toward the equipment shed, sleeves rolled up, lead rope still in one hand.

Bob lowered his head to the hay, chewing in quiet contentment.

Mirabella stood at the stall door for a moment longer, a strange warmth blooming in her chest. A breeze stirred the leaves in slow spirals across the gravel path. She watched them scatter and settle, like a thought forming she wasn't quite ready to speak aloud. Then she took a step onto the path Hank had left behind.

Beside her, Bob gave a quiet snort, and Hank's footsteps crunched ahead without hurry.

SADDLE AND STAGE

S unlight slanted through the blinds, painting Jesse's bare chest in broken stripes. He stood in front of the mirror, holding up shirt after shirt. Nothing fit him right. Nothing looked like the guy he needed to be.

His black eye, now a bruise painted in murky golds and purples, stared back from the glass. It didn't hurt anymore, but it made everything look worse—like the fight had followed him home.

On the dresser, the sheet music for Liszt's *Sonata in B Minor* piece lay open, corners curled from use, red pen markings of a battle that had just started. A sticky note was stuck to the margin in his mom's handwriting:

Went over phrasing in the second movement—check my notes tomorrow?
Proud of you.
Love, Mom.

Jesse stared at it a second longer than he meant to, then looked away. Not tonight.

On the bed: a mess of denim and cotton. At the foot, his guitar rested against the post, its tuning pegs catching the light. Nearby sat a crumpled flyer from the Long Branch Saloon, a playlist, and a notebook full of second-guesses.

Jesse slipped into a maroon Western shirt, checked the mirror, then glanced down at the playlist in his hand. He scratched out "Simple Man" and scrawled "Copperhead Road" in its place. The pen hovered mid-air before he set it aside. His fingers brushed a chord on the guitar out of habit.

Boot steps thudded up the stairs. One knock.

The door creaked open before Jesse could answer.

"You coming?" Hank stood in the doorway, dirt and sweat streaking his clothes like he'd rolled through the day backward. "Dad's waiting for us to finish the sort. Told him you were fixing the chicken coop."

Jesse flinched. He lunged for the flyer, shoving it under his notebook. The playlist went under the guitar. Too late. Hank had already clocked it all—the boots, the shirt, the guitar. The mood.

"You've got to be kidding me," Hank said, stepping inside. The door swung shut behind him like a trap snapping closed.

"I'm playing tonight," Jesse said. "Long Branch."

Hank's face didn't change. Just hardened.

"Again?" His voice was quiet. Too quiet. "You seriously think that's smart after last time?"

"I'm not looking for trouble."

"You never are," Hank said. "But I still remember waiting three hours in a drunk tank while you slept it off. That brawl nearly got you blacklisted from half the county."

Jesse turned toward the mirror, buttoning the maroon Western shirt like armor. "It's different now. Scouts from L.A. are gonna be there."

"Oh, scouts." Hank's laugh had no humor. "That your big plan? Another night of half-baked dreams and a set list full of maybe?"

"It's not like that."

"No?" Hank stepped in closer. "Then what is it, Jesse? Because from where I'm standing, it looks like you're walking out on everything we've been holding up for you."

Jesse bristled. "I'm still practicing. I'm still showing up—"

"Not to do chores. Not to dad. Not to anything that doesn't have your name in lights."

Jesse's voice snapped. "I didn't ask for any of this! The audition, Yale—Mom set that up. Not me."

Hank blinked like he'd been waiting for that truth to land—and hated that it did.

"Yeah, well, she believes in you," he said, the words dragging gravel behind them. "We all do. That's the only reason no one's saying what we're all thinking."

"And what's that?"

"That you don't want it bad enough."

Jesse's jaw set. "No. I just don't want it their way."

Silence. Hot and mean.

"I've backed you every time," Hank said, voice low now, worn out more than angry. "I've lied for you. Covered for you. Pissed off dad, kept Tegan out of it, got you home when you couldn't walk straight. Every damn time."

Jesse looked away.

"I believed you when you said you were serious," Hank added. "That this time was different. But if you're going to keep choosing the bar that put you in cuffs over the school that might put you on a stage, then maybe I'm the idiot here."

Jesse ripped off the Western shirt and let it fall in a heap.

He grabbed the worn work shirt from the closet and shoved his arms through the sleeves.

"I'm not quitting Yale," he muttered. "I just need to know if this other part of me still fits."

Hank stared at him for a beat, the muscles in his jaw twitching.

"Yeah. Well. Try not to start a riot this time."

That look hit harder than the punch that gave him the black eye.

"I'll be down in five," Jesse muttered.

Hank didn't answer. He turned and walked out, boots thudding each step like punctuation.

Jesse sat on the edge of the bed, elbows on his knees, the guitar silent beside him.

The maroon shirt lay rumpled at his feet, like it never belonged. He glanced at the flyer, the edge still peeking out from under the notebook. A quiet resolve settled over him.

He was going to play that gig. But not alone.

If he was going to pull this off, he needed Hank and Tegan in his corner. Otherwise, the music wouldn't matter.

The sun poured honey over the hills, warm and slanted, lighting up the silt kicked up by the slow-moving herd. Tegan rode high on her shaggy pony, ponytail bouncing, while Jesse and Hank flanked her on either side—each on stocky ranch horses that moved with purpose, heads low, eyes locked on the cattle.

Tegan spotted Jesse first and lit up. "You made it!"

Jesse tipped his hat with a half-smile. "Wouldn't miss it."

Hank gave a curt nod but kept his eyes on the herd, his posture stiff, reins tight in callused hands. Jesse didn't expect a warm welcome, but the cold shoulder still stung.

They worked in practiced silence, shifting calves toward the sorting pen. Dust drifted lazily in the golden light, catching in the creases of their clothes, clinging to sweat-slick skin. Jesse took the left flank, Hank the right, and Tegan in the middle, playing quarterback.

Eventually, Tegan steered closer. Her reins were loose, and her eyes were full of something secret.

"T-Rex," Jesse said, squinting at her. "What are you scheming now?"

"I'm going to Argentina someday," she said.

Jesse blinked. "That right?"

"Yup. I'm gonna ride across Patagonia on a horse named Comet. Or maybe Eclipse. No fences, just sky and mountains and me and the wind."

He smiled. "You and Comet against the world, huh?"

"And after that," she went on, eyes gleaming, "Spain. I'll ride through olive groves and find castles. Take a train to France. I want to see fields of sunflowers taller than me."

"You ever even been on a train?"

"Not yet," she said proudly. "But when I do, I'll send you a postcard. With a hoofprint on the back."

He looked at her—so full of belief, like nothing could stop her. He looked over at Hank, shaking his head. Tegan looked at Hank as well and eventually asked, "So... why aren't you and Hank talking?"

"It's nothing," he said, eyes forward.

"It's never nothing," she replied, shifting in her saddle. "It's always something."

Jesse sighed. "I've got a gig. Tonight. Long Branch. Scouts from LA will be there."

Her brows shot up. "Really?"

He nodded.

She didn't speak immediately. The cows groaned and shuffled in front of them, the creak of leather and the steady clop of hooves filling the space between them.

Then she hit him with it—soft but direct. "What about Yale?"

That one landed harder than she knew.

Jesse's throat tightened. He gave a bitter smile and looked away. "Not you, too. I never picked Yale. Mom did."

Tegan's brow furrowed. "Doesn't mean it doesn't matter."

He sighed. "It's not that I don't care. It's just... this other thing? It's not noise. It's not rebellion. It's me."

Tegan was quiet for a moment. Then: "You know, when you play, your face changes."

Jesse looked at her, surprised.

"Not in a creepy, alien way," she added. "Like... like you remember who you are. It's the only time you're not trying to be what everyone else wants."

Jesse swallowed. "Yeah. That's the problem."

Tegan's brow furrowed. "Hey..." she reached out and nudged his arm. "If it's your dream, then I'll help. Dreams are important, Jess." She professed beyond her years and then quickly shifted back; "You have to show me what you're wearing."

His smile returned, cracked but real. "You get all fashion approval, T-Rex."

"Good," she said, satisfied. "And I'll smooth things over with Hank."

Before Jesse could say more, one cow veered sharply, bolting toward a gap in the fence line.

"There!" Hank barked. "Go!"

Jesse and Hank moved without thinking—boots to stirrups, reins snapping. The brothers cut through the dirt, splitting to box in the stray. The cow dodged and kicked, but they circled fast, pressing her in tight. Jesse veered wide, drawing her back toward the herd as Hank sealed the gap.

A cloud of particles hung over the pasture as the cow rejoined the group, huffing and defeated.

They slowed their horses, breath steadying. The unspoken rhythm between them still worked—even if the rest of it didn't.

The silence settled in again as they rode back; the herd moving slower now in the late light.

Tegan broke it. "Hank?"

He grunted. Didn't look up.

"I'm real tired of this tough-guy, silent-cowboy crap," she said, loud and clear. "We don't get that many brothers out here. So maybe stop acting like you can afford to lose one."

Hank's jaw flexed. Jesse held his breath.

"You think Jesse's selfish. Fine. But you're stubborn," Tegan said. "You think being mad means you don't care. But it's the opposite."

"I'm not mad," Hank muttered. "I'm just tired of watching him throw things away."

"And I'm tired of being the glue every time you two come unglued," she shot back.

Silence.

Then she softened and gave him that wide, pleading look—the one he could never ignore. "How would you feel if Jesse didn't support you?"

He exhaled. Looked from her to Jesse, then back again.

"If you're gonna go," Hank muttered, "go all in. Make 'em remember you."

Jesse blinked, surprised. "Thanks," he said, low.

Tegan lit up. "Alright, now we're *really* talking! Operation Jesse Takeover is on."

Jesse laughed and shook his head.

"You have to let me and Hank see your playlist."

"I don't stand a chance, do I?"

"Nope," she grinned.

As they rode toward the barn, Tegan jabbered nonstop.

"You better be doing 'Dream On.' And not the lame radio cut—the real one. Or 'Go Your Own Way.' Oh! What about 'Tumbling Dice'? That one makes Grandma dance. Or 'You Make My Dreams Come True'—but only if you smile when you sing it. No moody cowboy stuff, Jesse. And if you don't do something by James Taylor, I swear I'm walking off this ranch and never coming back."

Jesse and Hank both laughed. Jesse let the dust and her words wrap around him like armor.

The sun dipped behind the barn roof as they rode in together.

Jesse swung down from his saddle, but Hank didn't follow him into the barn right away. He stayed by the gate, hand resting on the horn of his saddle, staring out toward the far pasture like there was something unfinished out there. For a second, Jesse thought he might say something. He didn't. Just nodded once—more to himself than to Jesse—and turned his horse toward the house.

The loft hummed with late summer heat, thick with the scent of boot oil and wood dust. Jesse sat hunched at the foot of the bed, pulling tight the laces on his scuffed boots. A folded playlist sat beside him, corners worn soft. Across the room, Jesse cracked open the window, letting in the murmur of cicadas and the scent of hay.

Tegan sat cross-legged near the headboard, watching him like a hawk. She rested her chin on her hands, elbows on her knees.

"You nervous?" she asked.

Jesse didn't look up. "I've played the Long Branch before. I got it."

She raised a brow, clearly unconvinced. "Yeah, but you've never played with agents watching. From Los Angeles."

He paused mid-lace. "Still got it," he said, though the edge in his voice dulled. He tied the knot slower this time, like buying time would make it true.

Before she could press further, the stairs creaked.

Hank's boots appeared first, followed by his familiar shape—broad-shouldered, arms crossed, something unreadable in his expression.

"You're set," Hank said. "Told Mom you're coming with me to Estancia Castilla. She's letting you take the Caprice. Keys are in the ignition."

Jesse blinked. "You—wait, really?"

Hank gave a small nod. "Try not to scratch it."

Tegan grinned like she was in on it the whole time. Jesse stood, unsure what surprised him more—Hank covering for him or how easily he made it sound.

"Thanks," Jesse said, voice quiet.

Hank shrugged. "Don't make me regret it."

He turned and thudded back down the stairs.

Jesse stood there a beat longer, staring after him. Then he looked back at Tegan. She tilted her head. "He's got your back, you know."

Jesse gave a half-smile, the nerves slipping back in behind his eyes. "Yeah. I know."

He grabbed the guitar case leaning against the wall and took one last glance in the cracked mirror. His reflection didn't look ready. But he was going anyway.

The Caprice purred down the darkening county road, headlights carving twin tunnels through the dusk. Crickets sang in the ditches. Jesse's guitar case rode shotgun, seat belt slung lazily across it like a passenger.

His fingers tapped out the rhythm of his opening song on the steering wheel. A good beat. Familiar. He could do it in his sleep.

But the nerves still buzzed under his skin.

He thought of his mom—her hands hovering over piano keys, her voice soft but firm as she corrected his phrasing. The long afternoons she carved out to rehearse with him, even when her joints ached, even when he was half-listening. The Liszt still wasn't polished. Not yet.

Guilt flared in his chest, hot and sharp.

He gripped the wheel tighter. "Not tonight," he muttered.

This was his chance. The one he'd dreamed about when he played in the hayloft for the horses, when the applause was only in his head. This was real. The Long Branch. Agents. His name on a flyer—even if it was crumpled now in his back pocket.

Jesse exhaled hard and rolled his shoulders.

Showtime.

He pushed the Caprice a little faster. The headlights caught the sign for the Long Branch up ahead—weathered wood, crooked letters, but lit like a beacon.

He didn't look back. He already knew what was behind him.

Paper Dreams

The Long Branch hadn't changed—same warped floorboards, same neon hum, same stink of spilled whiskey and pine cleaner trying too hard. But Jesse had. Or was supposed to.

He hadn't played there in weeks. Not since he started chasing the Liszt piece instead of beer money. Not since those long afternoons with June at the piano, parsing every measure like scripture. She never pushed. Didn't need to. She looked at him as if he already belonged at Yale. He didn't have the heart to tell her he wasn't sure he believed it.

Not because he didn't want it. Because maybe he didn't deserve it. It wasn't his dream to have.

Jesse adjusted the strap on his guitar, fingers already sweaty. The stage creaked as he stepped into the low amber light. No mic. He didn't need one here. He'd built a reputation in this room back when he still thought talent would carry him the entire way. Back before Liszt clawed him open.

He strummed once—low and open—and the room quieted. Maggie looked up from behind the bar, raising a brow like a challenge.

He answered with "Lodi". Played it slow. He leaned into the melancholy. His voice—warm, smooth, a little cracked at the edges—wound through the verses like a cigarette curling in cold air. People listened. Really listened.

He followed with "Fire and Rain." More delicate. Less anger, more ache. Every note landed softly and certainly, as if it knew where it belonged.

Then came one of his own. A new one. Raw. No title yet, but the chorus circled back to home and the sound of screen doors and the echo of boots that didn't come back.

By the end, the Long Branch had stilled.

Applause came in hard claps and hollers. One guy in a Levi's jacket slammed his palm on the bar. Someone near the back let out a low whistle. Jesse nodded once and stepped down, adrenaline humming through his spine.

Jesse was packing up his guitar when the owner, Walt Smithers, leaned a forearm on the bar beside him. "One of 'em's here," Walt said, low enough not to draw attention. "Back booth. Name's Ray Navarro."

Jesse followed his gaze. A man in pressed denim and polished boots sat alone, half in shadow, nursing a glass of bourbon. He looked like someone who belonged on a tour bus—or maybe ran the thing.

"That one?" Jesse asked. "He doesn't look like an agent."

Walt shrugged. "He's come through a few times. Bought a round for a kid named Grady North last year. Helped him cut a demo down at Red Rooster Studios. Nothing huge, but I heard it got some college radio play."

Jesse squinted. "That true?"

"Far as I know. Ray talks straight, pays his tab. Doesn't hang around unless someone's worth his time."

Maggie, wiping down glasses nearby, said nothing. But when Jesse caught her eye, she gave a small shake of her head—barely a twitch. Not a warning. Just... 'be careful'.

"You want the real thing?" Walt added. "Sometimes you just gotta take a shot."

Jesse exhaled. The idea had felt abstract last week when Walt first mentioned it. But now the man was real, and watching him.

"He asked for me by name?"

"Didn't need to," Walt said. "He heard the set."

Jesse nodded once, grabbed his bourbon, and made his way across the room. Ray stood as he approached. "Hell of a voice," he said, holding out a hand. "Ray Navarro. Sit with me."

Jesse shook his hand—firm, dry, practiced. They sat. Ray poured two glasses from a half-empty bottle of Wild Turkey sitting on the table.

"You local?" Jesse asked.

Ray smiled faintly. "Born in Barstow. Based in Burbank now. Been on the road more than not."

He slid a business card across the table. Gold letters. No phone number. Just a name and a P.O. box.

Jesse turned it over. "No number?"

"Makes it harder for folks to waste my time when they're unsure. I check my mail regularly. But I'll be coming back through here on Thursday, headed toward Fresno."

"You'll be back here?"

"That's right."

Jesse nodded slowly.

Ray tipped his glass. "I find talent. Help shape it. You've got the hard part already."

"You with a label?"

"Something like that," Ray said. "I float. Plug artists into places that make sense. You, for instance... you're not a conservatory kid."

Jesse frowned, surprised.

"You're a storyteller. There's road in your voice—weathered, not rehearsed. It's honest. That doesn't get taught."

Jesse didn't speak. He let the Wild Turkey burn a little.

"Have you been playing here long?" Ray asked.

"Since I was sixteen."

"Took a break, though. Walt said this was your first set in a while."

"Working on an audition," Jesse said. "Yale School of Music."

Ray let out a low whistle. "Heavy stuff. That your idea?"

"My mom's. But she's not pushing. She just... believes in me."

"And you don't."

Jesse looked up sharply. Ray's smile was soft, unreadable.

"Seen it before. Kid gets told he's got something, but no one tells him what to do with it when it stops being easy." He reached into his jacket and pulled out a folded sheet. Jesse scanned it—studio specs, engineer contact, a penciled number at the bottom.

Ray tapped it with one finger. "I can get you in at Red Rooster Studios, Bakersfield. Real setup. Warm sound. Vintage boards. You cut five tracks, clean and honest. I take care of the rest—distribution, press kit, shopping you around. You're the kid that labels remember."

Jesse didn't speak. The number sat like a snake on the page: $4,500.

"Studio fee," Ray said. "All upfront. I don't touch a cent. You cover the tracks. I cover the road."

Jesse stared at it. Four thousand five hundred. He didn't even have enough gas to get to Bakersfield.

Ray leaned back. "Think about it. Like I said. I'll be passing through again Thursday night. You want it, bring the check then. If not, no hard feelings. But momentum? It's a fragile thing."

He stood. Left the sheet, the card, and the rest of the bottle.

Jesse picked up the paper again, though he already knew what it said. Maggie's glance flickered back in his mind. Just a twitch. The number hadn't changed. But something in him had.

The light over the estancia had gone gold and low, bleeding across the paddocks like honey over cracked earth. In the arena, Hank sat astride Bob, with the reins loose in his fingers, breath slow and even. The stallion moved at a steady walk, weaving between cones with cautious precision, muscles alert but willing. Hank was now riding Bob daily, developing more trust with each ride.

"Good," Hank murmured. "That's it."

He shifted in the saddle, guiding Bob toward a low bridge built from plywood and railroad ties—flat, sturdy, nothing dramatic. They'd approached it before, but never crossed.

Bob stopped dead.

Ears forward. Hooves braced. Breathing loudly in the quiet.

Hank clicked his tongue, nudged with his heels. "C'mon."

Bob flicked an ear but didn't move.

Hank gave a firmer cue.

Bob spun—sharp and fast—his flank twisting, back legs kicking. Hank lost the rhythm and hit the ground hard, landing on his shoulder and hip. Dust bloomed up around him. Bob bolted across the arena, reins flying behind him like a wild ribbon.

Hank stayed down a moment, blinking up at the sky, dirt in his teeth.

Footsteps came slowly and surely.

Mirabella appeared at the fence line, braid swinging, a frown already on her face. She didn't call out. She watched. When Bob circled, she opened the gate and stepped into the arena, quiet as smoke.

By the time she reached him, she already had the reins in hand. Bob snorted and shook his head but didn't pull away. Her hand on his neck was steady. She turned to Hank, still sitting in the dirt.

"I thought we were working on Bob together."

He didn't answer.

He stood up, brushed off his jeans, and took the reins from her without meeting her eyes. Climbed back into the saddle like nothing had happened.

They circled again.

This time, when they reached the bridge, Bob threw his head and bucked—hard. Hank flew sideways, landed with a grunt, and rolled once in the sand. Bob charged off again, tail high, righteous.

Hank sat up, fists buried in the dirt.

Mirabella walked over, but slower now. She lowered herself to the ground beside him, tucking her legs to one side.

"You okay?" she asked.

He nodded. "Yeah."

"You don't look okay."

He looked across the arena at Bob—now standing by the far fence, sides heaving, reins twisted around one stirrup.

"It's not about him," Hank said.

"I know."

She waited quietly.

After a moment, Hank exhaled through his nose. "I lied to my mom today. Told her I needed to come here. I did it so Jesse could take the Caprice. For the Long Branch gig."

Mirabella didn't speak.

He picked at the dirt beside his boot. "I cover for him all the time."

"Why?"

Hank's shoulders sagged. "Tegan. She wanted him to go so badly. She thinks he's on the edge of something big. When she looks at him, it's like... she already sees who he's gonna be."

Mirabella nodded. "It's hard to say no to Tegan."

"Yeah," he breathed. "I'd do anything for her."

A long pause.

Mirabella brushed some dust off her knee. "I thought Jesse was auditioning for Yale."

Hank gave a half-laugh, no humor in it. "He is. Kinda. Says he wants options."

She heard it in his voice—that thread of dread twisted into the words.

"I'm guessing that means he doesn't know what he wants," she said.

Hank looked at her finally. "No. He knows. He wants it all. And he wants it to come easy."

Mirabella didn't judge. She just nodded, the way someone does when they've lived long enough to understand more than they say.

"I'm glad you get it," Hank said, voice quieter now. "Most people don't see how it works. With me and Jesse. And Tegan."

"I do," she said. "I see it."

She held out her hand.

"I've got an idea about Bob."

Hank didn't ask. He just took her hand.

They stood together and walked toward the far side of the arena, where Bob waited in the deepening light—head high, body tense, but watching.

Together, they went to meet him.

The following morning, the light in Jesse's loft was too bright for how he felt. Slanted morning sun sliced through the curtain gap, landing in broken bars of shadow across the crumpled shirt on the floor and the empty glass on the nightstand. His guitar lay face-down near the bed, one string slack, one tuning peg bent.

He sat up slowly, head pounding—not from drink, but from something heavier.

A knock at the door.

"Jesse?" June's voice was gentle, not unsure. She never asked permission to care.

He didn't answer.

The door creaked open. She stepped inside holding sheet music, the familiar pages of Liszt's Sonata fluttering in her fingers. Her eyes scanned the room without judgment—just quiet understanding, like she already knew the night had gone late.

"You said today," she whispered.

Jesse groaned and flopped back down, arm draped across his eyes. "Didn't sleep. Not feeling it."

June didn't sigh. Didn't scold. She set the music on the desk and walked to the edge of the bed.

"Come downstairs," she said. "Let's try once."

Jesse didn't move.

She waited.

Something in the stillness shifted. He sat up and rubbed his eyes. "Fine."

The piano sat in its usual corner of the family room, polished, waiting, bathed in a morning light that spilled through the lace curtains. The bench creaked as Jesse sat. June laid the music in front of him, her pencil already tucked in the binding, red ink fresh along the second movement.

He flexed his fingers. Stared at the keys like they might bite.

Then he began.

It fell apart fast. A missed note. Then another. Too fast. Then dragging. Then too fast again. His foot hovered near the pedal but never committed. The phrasing—they'd worked it over last week. He'd had it then. But now, nothing landed.

June said nothing until he stumbled onto the third page and dropped a chord entirely.

She lifted a hand. "Again. From the start."

He exhaled sharply through his nose, jaw tight. "I had it. I don't know what's—"

"Start again, Jesse."

He pressed the heel of his hand into his forehead. Then lowered it to the keys. This time was worse.

The rhythm splintered halfway through the first phrase. He reached for the shape of a run—like chasing a melody already fading—and missed. Then silence.

The silence pressed in.

"I don't get it," he muttered. "It was there last week."

June stood behind him, arms crossed loosely, eyes on the sheet.

"You're trying to muscle through it," she said.

"I'm playing it the same way."

"You're not."

He spun on the bench to face her. "Why do you care if I play this exactly the same? You always say music should breathe."

She didn't rise to it. "It should. But it can't breathe if you don't show up for it."

The words landed sharper than her tone. He looked away.

She softened. Sat beside him on the bench. Her voice low now, like they were conspiring again instead of clashing.

"You're scared it's slipping," she said. "That if it's hard, maybe you were never good at it to begin with."

Jesse swallowed. Didn't answer.

June stared at him. "You are. You always have been. But talent doesn't mean much if you won't meet it halfway."

He stared at the keys.

The bench between them had never felt so wide.

She stood. "Try again later. Or don't. But don't lie to yourself about which one you chose."

She left the sheet music on the stand, then tiptoed out of the room, her footsteps soft on the hardwood.

Jesse sat at the piano, hands in his lap, sunlight inching across the floor like a held note. The silence wasn't just absence—it was a rest too long, a measure left unfinished.

The silence was worse than a mistake. It was the sound of distance.

The light slanted through the upper window of the barn, thick and golden, catching in the swirls of dust that danced like smoke above the stalls. Below, the horses shifted—hooves clinking against wood, tails flicking lazily. The smell of sweat, hay, and sun-warmed tack hung in the air.

Jesse sat on a hay bale in the loft, guitar balanced on his knee. He plucked a few notes from one of his originals—half melody, half memory—letting the tune drift upward, unfinished.

His shoulders still held the tension from that morning's piano session. His fingers hadn't moved right, not like they were supposed to. But here—bare feet in the straw, strings under his hand—everything made sense again.

Boots hit the ladder rungs.

Hank climbed up slowly, arms crossed before he even cleared the edge.

"You're not working on the Yale piece?" he asked.

Jesse didn't stop strumming. "Already did with Mom. Didn't go great."

Hank stepped fully into the loft, eyes narrowing. "Did she say that, or you?"

Jesse shrugged and kept his head down. Hank didn't push it.

After a moment: "So? How was the gig?"

Jesse's face shifted—brighter. "Killed it. Place was packed. People were into it." He sat up straighter, a grin breaking through. "Got offered a shot to cut a demo."

Hank blinked. "A real studio?"

"Yeah," Jesse said casually, confident. "L.A. guy. Says he's worked with a bunch of up-and-comers."

He didn't look up. Didn't have to. He knew the name-drop and the shine of it would do the work.

"So what, you dropping Yale now?"

Jesse's grin faltered.

"No," he said too quickly. "I'm just... looking at options."

Hank raised an eyebrow. "Thought this was *the* option. The whole family's been pushing for it. You worked your ass off these past months preparing."

Jesse's fingers slowed on the strings. "Yeah. I know. It's just—"

He stopped. Tried again. "When I'm on stage, it feels like I already *am* something. Not trying to be. Not waiting for someone to approve it."

Hank didn't say anything. Jesse kept going.

"With mom, with the Liszt... it's like I'm studying how to *prove* I'm good. But when I played my stuff at the Long Branch, no one needed convincing. They just *felt* it."

A pause. Then:

Hank studied him. "Sounds expensive."

Jesse didn't flinch. "Nah. He's covering it. I just have to get down there."

There was a pause. Not long. But enough to hang between them.

Hank nodded once. "Well... guess that's something."

He stood there a second longer. The air shifted. Not quite trust. Not quite doubt. Just that edge Hank always carried when Jesse started talking too fast.

Then Hank turned and walked back toward the ladder.

The wood creaked as he climbed down, each step fading softer than the last.

Jesse kept playing until the sound of boots disappeared.

Then he stopped.

The guitar rested quietly on his lap. The song, whatever it was, faded unfinished into the barn's hush.

Particles hung in the beam of light like a held breath. And Jesse sat in it, still as a stone, while silence folded around him.

The door creaked open without a knock.

Jesse slipped inside, quiet as a stray dog. He didn't bother with the light—sunlight filtered through the narrow window behind the desk, casting long bars across the floorboards like cell bars. The air was still, edged with the scent of tobacco, old varnish, and the faint copper tang of machine grease.

Marshall's office looked like it belonged to someone who measured time by task, not clocks. Everything had a place. A straight-backed chair, pushed in flush. A line of invoices squared at the corner of the desk, paperweights placed like guard posts. Wrenches and bolt catalogs sat shelved by size and category. Even the framed photographs—rodeos, county fairs, the boys in boots with sunburned cheeks—were level to the nail.

A dog-eared farm equipment catalog sat open near the calculator, a baler circled in heavy blue ink. The only softness in the room was a faded photo of

Tegan tucked into the corner of the mirror above the filing cabinet. Someone had recently cleaned even that—leaving no fingerprints on the glass.

Jesse moved behind the desk, careful not to drag his boots. He opened the top drawer. Pens, aligned. Paperclips, rubber bands, a folded map of the irrigation lines.

Second drawer.

There it was.

He slid the checkbook out from under a stack of feed receipts. Turned it in his hands like it might whisper something he didn't want to hear. His thumb brushed over the thick white edge of a blank check. His father's name printed in bold ink, sharp and final above the empty line.

The boots came first—measured, unhurried—then the creak of the door hinges.

"What are you doing in here?"

Jesse turned fast, heart thudding once against his ribs.

Marshall stood in the doorway, hands on his hips. Not angry. Not surprised.

"Looking for the gas card," Jesse said. "Mom asked me to fill her tank."

Marshall didn't move. He just looked at the drawer, then at Jesse. His eyes then flicked to the mirror above the filing cabinet. To the photo tucked into the corner.

Tegan. Five years old, with dirt on her cheeks, missing a front tooth, grinning like the world had never said no to her. She was holding a bucket too big for her arms, one boot untied, eyes bright.

He looked at it for a beat too long. "Glove box," he said. "Same place it's been since February."

Jesse nodded. Too fast.

He slid the checkbook back and closed the drawer with practiced ease. The room felt smaller now. The sun through the window seemed colder than it had a moment ago.

Marshall's voice came low and level. "How's the Liszt piece coming?"

Jesse hesitated. "Almost have it down."

"That right?"

Jesse forced a breath. "Been hitting it every morning. Mom thinks it's close."

Marshall studied him for a moment. Not blinking. Not smiling.

"Well," he said at last, "if you're that far along, we could use the help around here. A lot of weight's fallen on your brother and sister."

Jesse's mouth opened, but no words came.

"You wanna chase that dream, I'm behind you," Marshall continued. "But don't forget whose hands are keeping this place running while you're figuring it out."

The words landed like a slow hammer—not loud, but heavy.

Jesse managed a nod. "I'll grab the keys."

He started past him.

Marshall didn't move, but his eyes followed Jesse like a cattle dog watching the gate.

"You don't bug me," he said, just loud enough, "when you tell the truth."

Jesse didn't look back.

The screen door clicked behind him, sharper than it needed to be.

Outside, the sun dipped low behind the barn roof, throwing long shadows across the gravel. The Caprice sat in the drive like a getaway car, passenger seat waiting.

Ray Navarro's card sat like a dare in his back pocket. He could feel it there, as steady and silent as his own pulse.

No Shortcuts

The sun was still low, slung between the sycamores, casting long ribbons of light across the dust. Shadows of railings stretched across the sand, and the smell of alfalfa hung on the breeze, sharp and sweet.

Tegan sat tall—taller than usual—atop the big bay mare Mirabella had paired her with. Her stirrups were a hair too long, reins too tight, heels too far forward. But she held her chin up as though she belonged there.

Mirabella paced in the center of the arena, one hand holding the lunge whip like a conductor's baton, her braid looped over one shoulder. "Again," she called, accent clipped but even. "Your twenty-meter circle is more like a potato."

Tegan huffed. The mare slowed, confused.

"I'm trying," she said, glancing down at the wobbling arc they'd carved into the sand.

"I know," Mirabella replied. "So try better. Inside leg. Think bend, not steer."

Tegan straightened her spine, squared her shoulders. She picked up the trot again, jaw set.

Along the far rail, the gate opened.

Hank led Bob into the arena, reins over his shoulder, his boots coated in dirt. The buckskin stallion moved loosely beside him, head high, ears alert. A line of ground poles stretched out in a staggered arc near the far end—Mirabella's idea. Build footwork. Build trust.

"Watch the rhythm," Hank said under his breath. "We're not sprinting barrels."

He mounted clean, settled deep in the saddle, and guided Bob toward the poles.

Mirabella spared them a glance, then turned back to Tegan. "Don't lean. Let her find the balance. You're not a passenger."

Tegan nodded, teeth clenched. Sweat beaded on her brow. She circled again, this time a little rounder, a little more honest.

Hank urged Bob into a steady trot. They approached the poles. The stallion's stride shortened, eyes narrowing. His front hooves hovered—but he stepped through clean. One pole. Then another. Then the rest.

Hank smiled faintly. "That's my boy."

From outside the arena, tires crunched on gravel.

Bess rolled to a stop at her usual crooked angle, dust settling behind her like a curtain. Jesse stepped out, boots scuffing the edge of the drive, eyes narrowed to slits.

He leaned against the fence and took in the scene.

Tegan circled again. This time smoother.

"That's better," Mirabella called. "You're feeling it."

Tegan sat taller. "I am feeling it."

"Don't say that," Mirabella muttered.

Tegan ignored her. "Hey Hank," she shouted. "That circle's looking more like a circle."

Hank glanced over. "Debatable."

"Oh yeah? You do it, cowboy."

Hank gave Bob a nudge. The stallion turned neatly, picked up a balanced trot, and carved the circle with precision—shoulders lifted, rhythm even.

Tegan let her mouth fall open. "How'd you do that?"

Hank shrugged. "Pretended he was on a lunge line. Also, I've been working with him for months. There are no shortcuts in riding."

Jesse, still leaning on the fence, felt Hank's words thud against his chest: nothing worth learning came cheap.

Inside the arena, Tegan sighed dramatically. "I'll make it a circle by next week."

Mirabella smiled. "That's what practice is for."

Tegan grinned, flushed from the heat and the win. "Are you always this bossy?"

Mirabella arched an eyebrow. "You're still alive, aren't you?"

From the fence, Jesse finally lifted a hand. "You all look like you're being tortured."

Tegan spun in the saddle. "Jesse! About time. You missed my almost-perfect potato."

"You mean your sweet potato," Hank called. "Still had lumps."

Tegan pointed at him. "I'm gonna write a song about you and Bob. It's called 'Lumpy Cowboy Blues.'"

Jesse laughed. "Sounds like a hit. You might be the songwriter in the family."

Mirabella smirked. "That is a terrifying thought."

Tegan leaned down and patted her mare's neck. "We've been working hard. You missed all the action."

Jesse didn't answer right away. He kept his hands in his pockets, watching his brother circle again, watching his sister beam with pride. Dust clung to Jesse's sleeves—same sweat, same grit he saw on Hank and Tegan.

He didn't say it out loud, but it crept across his mind.

They're doing the work.

Bob's hooves stirred the footing in slow, deliberate steps as Hank walked him toward the rail. Tegan followed on foot, bouncing lightly beside her bay mare, still flushed from the ride, with a few strands of hair stuck to her temple.

Mirabella coiled the lunge whip with practiced ease, eyes on the horse, but ears tuned to the approach of familiar boots crunching gravel.

Agustín appeared at the gate, clipboard in one hand, sleeves rolled high. Green soot from the olive grove streaked his forearm, and sweat darkened the back of his collar.

"Found my workforce," he said dryly.

"You need something?" Hank asked.

"Nets came loose in the south rows. We're behind. Could use an extra pair of hands—maybe two."

"I'm in," Hank said without hesitation, handing Mirabella the reins.

Tegan brightened. "I'll help too!"

Mirabella raised an eyebrow. "You don't want to come to the lesson?"

"I mean—" Tegan hesitated, torn. She looked from Mirabella to Hank, then back again. "I wanted to see you play."

"You've seen me play," Mirabella said. "You mocked me last time."

"I did not."

"You said Mozart needed a nap and that my wrists were too tense."

Tegan grinned sheepishly. "Well... they were."

She looked again toward Hank. "But I promised I'd help him today."

"You don't have to," Hank said.

"I want to." She turned back to Mirabella. "I mean, unless you really need—"

"I got it," Jesse said, stepping in. "I'll go."

All eyes turned to him. He gave a loose shrug, casual.

"I could use a few pointers. Might as well learn from the best."

Tegan blinked, surprised. "You sure?"

He smiled at her. "One of us should keep an eye on Mirabella. She's liking Mozart a bit too much."

Mirabella gave him a flat look. "I tolerate Mozart."

Tegan laughed, then stepped toward Hank, who had already unsaddled Bob and handed him off to a stable hand.

"You ready?" she asked.

Hank nodded. "Let's go shake some trees."

Agustín tipped his head toward the far paddock. "Meet me at the south gate."

As they walked off, Mirabella and Jesse veered toward the main house, the light slanting across the gravel in warm, stretched lines. Jesse walked half a step behind, hands in his pockets, the rhythm of hoofbeats and laughter fading behind him.

Two directions. Two sets of choices.

And Jesse, once again, chose the quieter path forward—where he wouldn't get dirt under his nails.

Estancia Castilla's ballroom opened before them like a breath held too long—wide, hushed, and golden with afternoon light. Tall windows lined one wall, casting slender columns of sun across the polished floor. Velvet curtains hung like stage wings, and Argentine drums rested beneath carved sconces, as if frozen mid-celebration.

Jesse slowed his steps as they entered. The Steinway grand waited beneath the chandelier, a black mirror of curves and brass that caught the room's silence in its lid.

He'd played this piano before—months ago, when Don Antonio had first asked him to play. That day, he hadn't known what to do with the sound that filled the room. Today, it felt heavier.

The portrait of Don Antonio's wife still hung on the far wall, her captured laugh softening the grandeur. She'd watched him play, too, in her way.

Mirabella walked ahead, braid brushing her shoulder. Jesse trailed a few steps behind, his fingers twitching already at the sight of the keys.

Sitting at the Steinway was Emerson.

Tall and elegant, with an easy poise that didn't try too hard. He wore dove-gray trousers and a crisp white shirt, sleeves rolled to the elbow. His skin held the rich brown tone of polished walnut, and his hands—refined, long-fingered, still—rested on a page of marked Mozart like dancers awaiting a cue.

He stood as they approached.

"Mirabella," he said warmly. Then, with a curious glance, "And you must be?"

"Jesse." He offered his hand. "We've met. Sort of. I've played this piano before."

Emerson's handshake was firm but light. "Ah. So you already know her temperament. She only misbehaves with people she likes."

"I'll keep that in mind," Jesse said.

Mirabella settled on the bench, flipping open her score. Emerson tilted his head as she positioned her fingers.

"Back to the sonata?" he asked.

She sighed. "Reluctantly."

She launched into the piece, hands precise but a touch too restrained. Jesse recognized the tension immediately—how her wrists didn't quite loosen, how the tempo clung too close to the page.

"Stop," Emerson said gently after a few bars. "You're playing like he's watching."

"He probably is," she muttered, glancing at the chandelier.

"Then you owe him a better party; loosen the tempo, flirt with the phrasing."

He sat beside her and replayed the same phrase—looser, lifted, with a subtle rubato that made the notes wink. Then he twisted the last run into a flirtatious jazz flourish, his fingers fluttering like silk.

Jesse raised an eyebrow. "That's not Mozart."

Emerson grinned. "That's an invitation to enjoy Mozart."

Jesse laughed softly. "I needed that. I've been stuck on Liszt."

Emerson perked up. "Which one?"

"Sonata in B minor. For Yale."

Emerson gave a low whistle. "No joke. Play what you've got."

Jesse slid onto the bench, took a breath, and began.

Technically sound, the opening lost its breath somewhere between the second page and the rest. The phrasing faltered. The dynamics stiffened. It came out like a letter written in a language he hadn't practiced enough.

When he finished, Emerson was quiet for a moment. Then: "You're muscling it."

Jesse nodded. "That's what my mom says."

Emerson tilted his head. "Your mom's a pianist?"

"She used to be. A concert pianist before she married my dad."

Emerson leaned forward slightly. "What's her name?"

"She went by June Sinclair back then."

Emerson sat up straight, eyes wide. "Wait—June Sinclair? Are you serious?"

Jesse blinked. "Yeah. That's her maiden name."

"Holy hell." Emerson stood and started pacing like caffeine had struck him. "I have one of her records. The Debussy recital from '62? My college professor used it as an example of perfect pedal phrasing. I wore the grooves out."

Jesse sat a little straighter, stunned. "You're kidding."

"Not at all." Emerson pointed at him. "That warmth in your voicing? That's her. Your left-hand control isn't there yet—but the raw tone? It's genetic, man."

Jesse flushed. "She still plays. With me. She's the one who got me started."

Emerson nodded, almost reverently. "Well, now it makes sense. You've got a legacy under your fingers—you just haven't learned how to let go of it."

Jesse looked down at the keys, silent.

Mirabella, who had been watching from a few feet back, finally spoke. "So you'll help him?"

Emerson looked at Jesse. "If he wants it."

Jesse hesitated, his eyes flicking to Mirabella. She stood still, unreadable, though something in her look said this hadn't been an accident. He almost smiled—surprised she'd gone this far for him.

No one besides his mother had ever believed in the music buried under his noise. Not like this. Not quietly.

Jesse hesitated... then nodded. "Yeah. I do."

Emerson smiled. "Good. Next time, bring the Liszt. And bring your mother's phrasing with you. I'll help you breathe again."

Outside, the wind stirred the olive trees, whispering across the Estancia. Inside, the chandelier flickered over ivory and lacquer, and Jesse—still seated at the bench—wondered if maybe, just maybe, he wasn't stuck after all.

Pot roast, mashed potatoes, roasted carrots, and June's skillet cornbread, golden on the edges, crowded the warm table. The scent of rosemary and browned butter hung in the air. Evening light slanted across the floorboards, painting soft shadows across the table and the hands resting around it.

Grandma Ginny folded her napkin neatly, looking over the gathered family. "Hank," she said. "Say grace for us?"

Hank nodded. Chairs shifted. Heads bowed.

"Lord," he began, his voice steady, "thank you for this food, and for the work that brought it here. I'm grateful for my new job at Estancia Castilla—and especially for Bob. He's the toughest, best horse I've ever been around."

He paused, hands laced in front of his plate. Grandpa Joe's fork dropped to the floor, creating a harsh sound, disrupting the solemnity of the blessing, to the delight of Tegan and sharp disapproving glare from Grandma Ginny. A quick 'sorry' from Grandpa Joe, and Hank resumed the blessing.

"He's teaching me more than I thought a horse could. Trust, patience. He makes me earn every step. But I think he's going to be something really special."

"Amen," Ginny said with a soft smile.

"Amen," the rest echoed.

Marshall leaned an elbow on the table. "Is that the same Bob who bucked you off several times when you tried to saddle him a couple of months ago?"

"The very one," Hank said, smiling faintly. "But he's a thinker. Smart. Not mean—just... guarded. You get through to him, and he gives you everything. Today we worked poles at a trot. It's the first time he didn't flinch or fight me. He listened to my seat and followed."

"He'll be yours before long," Marshall said, not unkindly. "You've got a way of sticking with the ones that don't give it easy."

Across the table, Tegan leaned forward, fork spearing a roast carrot. "Mirabella nearly killed me today."

"Dressage?" June asked.

"More like boot camp on horseback," Tegan muttered. "Twenty-meter circles over and over. I thought I had it, and she'd say, 'Again.' I thought horses wanted to do stuff. Turns out they need a lot of convincing."

She glanced at Hank. "Hank and Mirabella make it look easy. But it's not. It's hard. And sweaty. And kinda fun."

"Your circle was almost a circle," Hank offered.

"It was a sweet potato," she corrected, grinning. "But I'll get there."

"You looked strong in the seat," Hank added. "That mare's not a pushover."

Tegan sat a little taller.

Jesse, who'd been quiet till then, reached for the cornbread, broke it open, then spoke without looking up.

"Mirabella's piano instructor—Emerson—offered to help me with the Liszt."

June looked up sharply. "He did?"

Jesse nodded. "His approach is... different. He doesn't focus on control and exactness as I thought piano teachers would. He listens for rhythm under structure. For personality inside the phrasing. It felt like—" he paused, searching, "—like he saw what I was trying to do. Like he heard me. Not just the notes."

He looked across the table. "He had one of your records, Mom. The Debussy recital. Said he wore it out in college. Called your pedal phrasing perfect."

June's breath caught. A faint blush colored her cheeks.

"You're famous, Mom," Jesse said, a crooked smile breaking through. "His words."

June laughed—quiet, almost embarrassed. "Well, not anymore."

"He knew your playing," Jesse said. "Said he could hear it in me."

Silence lingered for a moment—soft and reverent. The only sound was the quiet clink of silverware, then the low hum of cicadas rising through the open window.

Jesse finished his cornbread, nodded, the gratitude plain on his face. "I'm really glad Mirabella introduced me to him." He paused, tapping the side of his glass.

"Watching him coach Mirabella... it helped. She was stuck on something in the Mozart piece—her phrasing wasn't landing right. He didn't correct her with finger positions or tempo drills. He asked her what story she thought the notes were trying to tell."

He looked up, catching June's gaze.

"It made the Liszt feel possible again. Not easier—but... reachable. And it was good seeing someone like Mirabella have to work at it. To see her struggle a little and keep at it. I needed that."

June leaned in. "I think you should keep working with him. Let him challenge you in new ways."

Jesse met her gaze, softer now. "I want to."

Across the table, Hank was watching—not the words, but the surrounding space. Jesse spoke with the right tone, said the right things. But something in his shoulders stayed too still. Something didn't click. Hank couldn't name it, but it pressed against the back of his ribs like a storm not yet formed.

Marshall noticed. His eyes shifted to Hank, and then to Jesse and back to Hank, quiet but sharp.

He didn't say a word. He just tucked that glance away.

The conversation carried on—Tegan teasing Hank about Bob's lumpy circles, Grandma Ginny offering second helpings, June asking who had left boots by the back door again.

But underneath it, the thread ran taut.

Jesse smiled, nodded, and laughed in the right places.

But Hank had known him for a long time.

And something wasn't breathing right.

The loft pulsed with heat.

A box fan spun overhead, slow and rhythmic, its blades groaning like tired gears. Crickets outside chirped in syncopated runs—faint, but insistent. Together, they built something that sounded almost like the Liszt piece—fractured notes hiding in the night hum. Arpeggios in the fan's whir. Broken cadences in the rasp of the crickets. A ghost of the sonata, out of reach.

Jesse twisted under sweat-damp sheets. One leg tangled. One arm flung across his face like it might stop the dream from finding him.

But it did.

He was back on the stage—grand and cold, the spotlight white and brutal. The black Steinway waited in front of him, stretched wide like a jaw about to snap. The keys shimmered, not with promise, but with pressure.

He sat. Lifted his hands.

They didn't move right. Fingers felt rubbery. Detached.

The opening phrase came out too heavy; the next wobbled like a drunk on ice. Chords splintered. The pedal slipped. The room packed with faces shifted. The silence of judgment weighed more than any noise.

June sat in the front row, her hands clutched together in her lap. Emerson beside her, frowning slightly, arms folded. She leaned toward him—whispered something—but Jesse couldn't hear it over the ringing in his ears.

Then, Tegan and Hank, standing at the back of the theater, started laughing.

Not loud, but surgical.

Someone clapped slowly.

He tried to fix it. Started again. The piano rejected him—hammering out a sound like broken glass dropped down a stairwell.

The lights flared white—blinding.

Then black.

And from black: the warm flicker of neon.

The Long Branch.

The bar glowed softly around the edges like a memory misfiled. Walt wiped down glasses. Maggie stared down at the register. And there stood Ray Navarro—at the back near the jukebox, boots polished, the tilt of his shoulders easy and certain.

Jesse called out to him.

Ray didn't turn.

Jesse shouted again—voice catching like static.

Ray turned toward the sound and shook someone else's hand.

A kid. Blonde, clean-cut, guitar case over one shoulder, bright eyes and a notebook in his back pocket.

Ray clapped the kid on the shoulder and said something Jesse couldn't hear. Laughed.

Jesse tried to move, but his feet wouldn't lift. His boots were glued to the floor. He reached for the demo sheet in his hand, but it was already burning—edges curling, letters bleeding together, the number—$4,500; still legible until the whole thing turned to ash.

Smoke curled between his fingers.

He jolted upright.

Chest heaving.

The loft was still. Fan blades spinning. Crickets keeping time. A rivulet of sweat traced his spine. He blinked into the dark, heart hammering like a timpani roll.

He dragged both hands down his face and sat at the edge of the bed, bare feet on warped wood.

The air smelled of old varnish and dust, thick with choices not yet made.

Somewhere in the back of his mind, the Liszt still played. Disjointed. Demanding.

But this time, it wasn't the hardest thing echoing through him.

It was the look on Ray's face—smiling at someone else.

The hallway stretched long and dark.

Moonlight spilled in through the windows, striping the worn wood floor in pale silver. The old boards groaned under Jesse's weightless steps, each creak a warning swallowed by silence.

He moved barefoot. Careful. Hands loose at his sides, but clenched just enough to show the tremble. The ranch house slept behind closed doors—his sister, his brother, his parents, all dreaming of horses or harvest or nothing at all.

Jesse's heart drummed like a distant hoofbeat, steady and far too loud.

He reached Marshall's office door. He waited, counting his own heartbeat to four until it settled. Behind him, the house breathed: Tegan murmured in a dream, a pipe ticked as it cooled, somewhere a horse nickered at shadows. He closed his fist until the pulse dulled, then turned the knob with two fingers, catching it just before the latch could complain.

The room inside held stillness like a held breath. Same precision. Same order. The desk, the file drawers, and the calculator left squarely centered on its pad. The dog-eared farm equipment catalog still open, the corner circled in blue ink. It felt colder here somehow. Like the walls had seen too much.

Jesse stepped inside.

He didn't turn on the light.

He moved straight to the second drawer. Opened it with the ease of someone who'd already done it once.

The checkbook lay beneath a stack of receipts. He lifted it, surprised by its ordinary weight, and set it on the desk where a stray bar of moonlight plated the leather cover in silver. Hank's voice drifted up from the arena; "Hard work, no shortcuts," he said.

He opened to the last leaf. The paper crackled like thin ice. Pay to the order of: he wrote slowly, pressing just enough to bite. **Red Rooster Studios**. Figures next: **$4,500.00**. Each zero felt louder than the last. In the memo, he stopped himself from writing 'dream' and left it blank.

The signature came last. He let the pen hover, wrist trembling, then dropped into the practiced shape: the bold M, the sprawled A, the slanted S that always flew a touch too high—perfect forgery birthed from too many signed permission slips. As the last stroke bled into the paper, his stomach turned light, as if the ink were siphoning marrow. His father's name in the bottom right, traced in Jesse's hand—an imitation so good it made his chest ache.

He recapped the pen. Time restarted: the tick of the hallway clock, the fan stuttering in the kitchen vent, his own breath suddenly ragged.

He let the pen fall beside the ledger. Folded the check once. Slipped it into his pocket.

He closed the drawer and turned, ready to leave—but paused.

On the mirror above the filing cabinet sat the photograph: Tegan, five years old, mud on her cheeks, gap-toothed smile wide, holding a bucket too big for her arms, one boot untied, eyes bright. Jesse stared at it for a long moment.

His mouth twitched as if he might say something to her.

He didn't.

He turned the knob again. Pulled the door closed behind him until it clicked. The sound was soft. Final.

The hallway remained dark. The moonlight kept its pattern on the floor.

And Jesse disappeared into the quiet, a lie folded sharp as sheet-metal, thudding with every heartbeat.

THE GOOD SON

T he note on the fridge was cheerful, almost buoyant:

Running into town to grab groceries.
Back before lunch — J

He even added a smiley face. June would see it after her ride with Tegan. He'd circled two items from the list—flour and coffee—to make the lie look real. Thoughtful. Helpful. The son people bragged about.

The Caprice rumbled to life in the driveway, the engine slow to catch in the warm morning. He tapped the wheel in rhythm, humming the chorus of his new song, the lyrics just out of reach.

By the time he pulled into town, the knot in his chest had twisted tight enough to burn.

He stopped for groceries. Two bags—coffee, flour, sugar, vanilla extract, and local honey. He walked past a kiosk of glass Coca-Cola bottles and stopped at the gum display. Bubble Yum. He smiled and snatched a pack for Tegan. He even asked the checker how her day was going. The receipt felt like a receipt should: proof of something simple. He placed the bags in the trunk, closed it softly, then turned the wheel toward the Long Branch like he wasn't doing anything wrong.

The bar was dim and hushed, even with the late morning sun trying to crawl through the blinds. Only two regulars hunched at the counter. The smell of lemon cleaner mixed with the dull trace of stale beer.

Ray waited in the same back booth. Elbow draped across the worn vinyl, a bourbon already sweating in front of him. He didn't look up as Jesse slid into the seat across from him.

Jesse's hand found the inside pocket of his jacket, fingers brushing the folded check like it might bite.

Ray still didn't speak. Just stared at the bottle, then finally flicked his eyes upward.

"You bring it?"

Jesse nodded and set the check on the table, its creases sharp, the handwriting steady but too neat—deliberate.

Ray took his time. Didn't even glance at it right away. He let it sit there like a bet already won.

"You said five tracks," Jesse said, trying to sound confident. "All originals."

Ray nodded once. "That's the idea." Ray finished his bourbon.

"When do I hear from you?"

Ray picked up the check slowly, turned it once in his hand. "I'll call when it's lined up. Could be a few days. Week, maybe."

"That's not really an answer."

Ray finally met his eyes, calm as ever. "It's the only one I've got. Give me your number and I'll call you."

Jesse rattled off the home line. Ray scribbled it on the back of the check with a pen pulled from his inner pocket, like he'd known this moment was coming.

"Do you want this or not?" Ray asked, not unkindly, but looking for full commitment and exoneration.

Jesse hesitated. "Yeah. I want it."

Ray gave the faintest smile. Like he'd been waiting for Jesse to say it out loud.

He slid the check into his coat pocket like it was nothing more than a receipt.

And then he stood.

No handshake. No toast. No thanks.

As he walked away, Jesse blinked—and for a split second, the room stuttered. The lights flared too hot. The bar faded, and the Long Branch stage flashed in his mind—the nightmare a couple of nights ago.

Ray's back turned away.

Jesse called after him.

Ray never looked back.

Only this time, in real life, Ray reached out and shook someone else's hand near the door. A stranger in a leather vest holding a guitar case.

Jesse's stomach turned. Cold and hollow.

He sat alone in the booth, heart punching against his ribs, the smell of bourbon and lemon cleaner thick in his throat.

They said the first lies tasted bitter. He thought as he exhaled slowly, closing his eyes. This one tasted like nothing at all—and that scared him worse.

The receipt from the grocery store was still in his pocket. Proof that he was still the good son. Still the helper. But he wasn't.

Not anymore.

What chilled him wasn't the lie. It was how easy it came out of his mouth.

And how Ray had known—before Jesse ever did—that he'd go through with it.

The ballroom of Estancia Castilla sat in a hush, the kind that made sound feel like an intrusion. Sunlight filtered through tall windows, painting the parquet floor in long gold stripes. The chandelier hung motionless above, its crystals catching light but giving nothing back.

Emerson sat at the Steinway with the patience of a man practiced in waiting. One leg crossed over the other, a hand resting on the lid like it might open itself. His grey trousers and crisp white shirt held no wrinkles. His posture was easy, almost elegant. The only thing that moved was his right hand—fingers sketching a slow arpeggio in the air, as if weighing the silence.

Mirabella stood near the far wall, arms folded. Her riding boots were still dusty from the arena. Her eyes skimmed the clock and fled.

"He's late," she said.

Emerson didn't look up. "Artists always are."

Mirabella didn't smile. "He said he was coming."

He touched one key—middle C—and let it ring. "He still might."

Out the window, a horse whinnied from the paddock. Mirabella turned to the window, dust from the paddock swirling beyond the glass. "It's not like him to say one thing and do another."

Emerson struck the opening bars... The ballroom answered, then fell silent, the sun shifting higher in the sky marking the day's progress.

"Maybe," he said, "he's afraid of not being who we think he is."

She turned to him. The words caught her off guard. "What do you mean?"

"I mean, he plays like someone who's used to being praised. Not corrected. He leads with instinct, not discipline. Which works—until it doesn't."

He kept his eye on the keys. "He has talent. And the audition is in less than a month. But he's running from the part that requires something deeper."

Mirabella said nothing.

Cicadas outside droned a counter-rhythm, stitching through the quiet like a second pulse.

"I've worked with musicians like him before," Emerson continued. "They shine fast. But the real question is what they do when it stops coming easy."

Heat rose in Mirabella's jaw; she forced it slack.

She walked toward the piano and ran her finger along the polished rim of the lid. Her expression had shifted—less irritation now, more unease. She didn't like not knowing where Jesse stood. She didn't like how the silence crept in where the music should've been.

"He'll come around," she said at last, though the certainty in her voice wavered.

Emerson nodded and closed the sheet music gently, folding the pages over like a lullaby no one asked for.

"We'll be here if he does."

Mirabella offered a small nod, but her gaze lingered on the empty bench.

The chandelier above them flickered as a shadow passed through the glass panes.

Outside, the sun kept rising.

Inside, the piano stayed quiet.

Late afternoon sun angled through the high barn windows, laying honey-colored stripes across the sawdust floor. The heat had softened into something gentler. Horses shifted in their stalls, tails swishing, the air thick with the scent of sweat and hay.

Hank stood beside Bob, brushing slowly down the stallion's ribcage. No halter. No rope. The horse stood quiet, at ease. Every so often, Bob would blink and shift his weight, but he didn't step away.

Trust had taken time. But now, it moved between them like a breath.

"You're coming along," Hank murmured. "There's no rush. We'll get there."

He set the brush aside and reached for a sugar cube from his back pocket. Bob took it gently, like a horse who finally believed the world might not bite first.

Boot steps padded down the barn aisle.

"Of course you're here," Mirabella said, leaning on the stall door.

Hank glanced over his shoulder but didn't stop what he was doing. "Figured I'd catch up on grooming before heading home."

Mirabella folded her arms, one boot crossed over the other. Her braid was coming loose again. A few wisps of hair clung to her cheek.

"I waited with Emerson," she said. "Sheet music out. Piano open."

Hank moved to Bob's opposite side. "Jesse had to help Grandma Ginny. Should've told you."

Mirabella didn't respond right away. She ran her finger along the stall rail, as if tracing a thought. "That's the reason?"

Hank hesitated for a moment, but kept his focus on Bob. "It's the one I've got."

She studied him—his silence, the way he moved slower now, like maybe the lie weighed more than the truth.

"You know," she said, voice lower, "I don't need the cleaned-up version. Not from you."

He let out a soft breath, not quite a sigh. "It's not about you."

"But I'm here," she said. "If you ever feel like talking."

He looked at her then. Not defiant. Not closed off. Just caught somewhere between wanting to let her in—and wanting to keep her out of the mess entirely.

"I know," he said. And he meant it.

She nodded once, stepped into the stall beside him. Bob flicked an ear but didn't move.

"He's different around you," she said as she stroked Bob's neck.

"So am I."

They stood there in the quiet, Bob's flank rising and falling between them. Dust floated in the light like ash that never burned. He clenched the currycomb as the internal debate continued.

Hank wanted to tell her. About his misgivings about Jesse's behavior. About the piano lesson Jesse skipped. About how deep the pattern ran—Jesse walking ahead while someone else cleaned up the tracks behind him.

But he didn't. He couldn't.

She didn't deserve to be dragged into that.

Not when she looked at all of them like they were still worth believing in.

Mirabella stroked Bob's neck in slow, even circles. Then, without looking at him, she said, "Do you ever wonder what happens if he doesn't stop?"

Hank froze.

He looked at her—really looked—and marveled that she understood more than she let on.

And still, she didn't judge.

"I'll see you tomorrow," she said, hand brushing the stall rail as she turned.

Hank watched her walk away. The residue from her boots hung in the air long after she disappeared down the aisle.

When it cleared, he slipped the lead rope around Bob's neck and led him out into the amber light of the pasture. The day was cooling now. Sun slipping behind the olive trees. Shadows long across the fenceline.

Bob walked beside him, ears forward, steps slow. They didn't need to rush. At the gate, Hank paused and rested an arm on the rail as Bob wandered out into the tall grass.

He watched the stallion for a long moment—steady, uncomplicated. No masks. No damage trailing behind him.

Hank's thoughts drifted to Jesse. Lately, it wasn't shame written across his face. It was distance. Like he was already somewhere else. Not lost—just... absent.

And Mirabella. She hadn't said much. But the look she gave him before she left—the flicker of disappointment behind her calm—stuck harder than he expected. Not because she was angry. But because she wasn't.

She had expected more. Not from Jesse.

From him.

He reached into his pocket, pulled out another sugar cube, and tossed it gently into the grass where Bob stood grazing.

"You don't lie," he whispered. "That's why this works."

And in the hush that followed, Hank couldn't help wondering how much longer he could keep pretending that the people he loved weren't slipping through his hands.

The feed room smelled of grain dust and fresh hay. Evening crept through the half-cracked barn doors, streaking the floor in orange light. Jesse dumped the last bucket of oats into the trough too fast—grain clattering like hail against the tin. He forced a whistle past his lips, but it faltered, tuneless.

He didn't look up when Hank appeared in the doorway, arms crossed, boots planted.

"You skipped the lesson," Hank said.

Jesse kept his back turned. "Yeah. Had stuff to do here."

"Mirabella waited."

"I didn't ask her to," Jesse muttered.

"You didn't even tell her."

Jesse wiped his hands on his jeans and finally turned. His smile was thin. "Why do you care so much?"

"Because I covered for you—again. Told her you were with Grandma."

Jesse scoffed, sharp and small. "What's the big deal? It's one lesson."

Hank stepped forward. "It's not about the lesson. You're slipping, and you keep dragging people into it."

"I'm not dragging anyone," Jesse said, voice rising. "You don't know what I'm dealing with."

"No," Hank said, quieter now. Steadier. "But I know what lying looks like. And I know you're doing it."

Jesse met his eyes—and for a second, the mask slipped. Guilt. Panic. Shame. It all flickered across his face, and then vanished behind a practiced smirk.

"You want to play sheriff now?" Jesse said, arms folding. "I don't need this crap."

A long pause. Hank's jaw tightened. He looked at Jesse like he wanted to reach something that had already gone out of reach.

"You think I'm jealous," Hank said. "That I don't get it. But I watched Tegan write a song about you after your set at the Long Branch. She thinks you walk on air. I lie to people I respect so she can keep believing that version of you."

Jesse didn't respond.

"You think this all falls on you?" Hank snapped. "Mom defends your choices like scripture. Dad breaks his back to give you the room to chase music. And me—I carry your mess like it's my job."

"You don't understand—"

"No," Hank said, stepping in close, poking Jesse in the chest. "You don't."

Jesse's hands balled into fists. "You think this is easy? That I don't feel it every second?"

Hank hesitated. One breath. One second. He looked down, jaw flexing like maybe—just maybe—he'd stop.

Then Jesse smirked again.

That broke it.

"Stop lying to me," Hank said. "I'm sick of it."

Boots pounded down the path.

Tegan skidded into the feed room, hair tangled, boots too big, breath coming too fast.

"Hey!" she shouted, throwing herself between them, arms out wide. "Stop it!"

They froze.

"You're scaring the horses," she said—quieter now, but not soft. Her voice held.

Hank backed up first. His fists dropped. Jesse turned away, running a hand over his face.

Tegan looked between them, eyes wide and wet.

"You're brothers," Tegan said. "You're not supposed to make other people feel scared.

A silence fell. Not ashamed. Just...hollow.

"And if Jesse leaves," she added, "who's gonna fix my saddle for me. Or tell stories at night?"

Jesse opened his mouth, but nothing came out.

"You both act like being mad, means you don't love each other anymore," she said, blinking hard. "But it doesn't."

From the house, the dinner bell rang once, twice—June's rhythm. Sharp. Calling them home.

No one moved.

Tegan backed away, brushing straw from her jeans. "You better get it together. We're having pot roast."

Then she turned and walked out. Her boots slapped the dirt like a drum fading away.

Jesse stared down at his hands. Open now. Empty.

Hank didn't say another word.

They followed her path out of the barn, slower than usual, each one carrying more weight than when they walked in.

Behind them, the trough still overflowed. Oats scattered in the dirt, uneaten, crushed under boots that didn't look back.

The fence line stretched in long, uneven ribs across the north pasture. Dry earth crumbled beneath their boots as Hank held the cedar plank flush to the post. Sunlight had yet to bake the soil hard, and the morning air still carried a trace of chill.

Marshall knelt beside the tool bucket, pulling out a coil of baling wire and a tensioner. "You were quiet at dinner last night," he said, not looking up. "Tegan too."

Hank adjusted the board, lined up the nail. "Long day."

"She barely touched her plate," Marshall said. "You notice that?"

Hank hesitated. "Yeah."

"Pot roast night," Marshall added. "She never skips seconds."

The hammer hit the wood—thunk, clean and measured.

Marshall stood slowly, wiping his hands on a rag. "Something happen that I should know about?"

Hank kept his eyes on the fence. "Jesse and I talked."

"Looked like more than talk."

This time, Hank didn't answer right away. He drove the next nail harder than needed, though not enough to crack the board. The sound echoed sharply across the open field.

Marshall waited.

"There's something going on with him," Hank finally said. "He's... slipping. Lying about stuff."

"Stuff like what?"

"I don't know," Hank admitted. "But it's more than missing a lesson or two."

Marshall's brow creased beneath the brim of his hat. "You think it's the audition? That it's getting to him?"

Hank shrugged. "Maybe. Maybe it's bigger than that."

"You think I should talk to him?"

Hank nodded, slow. "Might be time."

Marshall looked out across the pasture, eyes narrowing against the sun. "He's always walked his own line," he said. "But I never thought he'd drift too far."

They went quiet again. Just the wind in the grass and the slow creak of wire settling into tension.

Hank picked up the next board. His grip was steadier now, but the knot in his chest hadn't eased. Not yet.

And down the fence line, the bent nail from earlier still caught the light—crooked, splintered, and unmissed.

The morning light sifted through lace curtains, painting the floor in threads of gold and dust. The piano sat in its usual place in the family room corner, lid open, sheet music already in place. Liszt's Sonata in B minor. Pencil marks curved along the margins like whispers she'd once shared with Jesse, bar by bar, note by note.

June stood beside the bench, one hand resting on the lid, the other smoothing her skirt—something to do while she waited.

Footsteps creaked down the hallway. She turned slightly, expectant.

Jesse appeared in the doorway, hair tousled, shirt wrinkled like he hadn't changed from yesterday. He paused when he saw her there.

"You said this morning," June whispered.

Jesse scratched the back of his neck, eyes drifting to the floor. "Can't. Got chores. Dad wanted help with the pump."

Silence bloomed. June blinked once. That tiny pause, the smallest inhale. Her shoulders drew back almost imperceptibly.

"You sure?" she asked, her voice still soft, but it held a note that used to pull truth from him when he was ten.

"Yeah," Jesse said. He didn't quite meet her eyes.

They both knew.

She gave a small nod—more of an acknowledgment than agreement. Her hand dropped from the lid to the bench, fingers brushing the wood as if it might steady her.

"Later, maybe," he added, already backing toward the hallway.

She didn't stop him.

He left without another word.

The silence he left behind was louder than the click of his boots on the floorboards.

June sat down slowly, knees folding like they carried more weight than they had a minute ago. She stared at the open sheet music, its red pencil markings suddenly foreign.

She played.

The first phrase faltered—right hand outpacing the left, the run muddied. She paused, adjusted, tried again. This time she missed a chord entirely. Her hands froze above the keys. A tremble worked up her arms, quick and unseen, until her hands dropped gently into her lap.

"That's not how it's supposed to sound," she whispered.

She closed the lid with care, like sealing off a wound.

Across the room, a picture of the three kids on horseback smiled from the mantle—Jesse in the middle, reins in one hand, the other lifted in mid-laugh. Her eyes lingered there.

She didn't cry. She didn't call after him. She simply sat, listening to the stillness, as if waiting for something to return that had already walked away.

Jesse's loft breathed shallow in the dark. Nighttime had not come soon enough.

One window cracked for air, but the breeze had died hours ago. The fan turned overhead with a sluggish rhythm, cutting the silence into slow, uneven pieces. Jesse sat cross-legged on the floor, guitar limp in his lap, the wood warm and useless under his hands.

126

Five songs laid around him—his handwriting jagged in the low light. Some finished. Some half-birthed. A few still smelled like promise. He reached for one. The river song. Three chords. Easy flow. He used to hum it while walking the fence line.

He played. But his hand trembled on the second chord. The G came crooked. His thumb slipped. He hit a dead note. He tried again. This time the D slipped, his pinky locking wrong. His fingers dropped away from the strings as if they didn't belong to him.

He didn't belong to him.

He stared at the pages. His songs. His voice. But it all felt borrowed now—like it came from a better version of himself. The one who hadn't lied to Hank. Who hadn't flaked on Mirabella. Who hadn't looked his mother in the eyes and handed her silence instead of truth.

The version of him that might've had a shot at Yale, once.

That dream was gone now. A ghost with no shadow. And he'd chased it so hard that by the time he caught up, it had already turned to smoke.

He pulled himself up and crossed the room.

Ray Navarro's card sat where he left it—gold letters catching the lamplight like a trick coin. Jesse picked it up, turned it once. Again. Fingers twitching. He opened the drawer and took out the check stub. Folded. Thin. Heavy.

His father's name was still printed across the top in sharp, dark ink.

He held them both. One in each hand.

He told himself it would be worth it.

Ray would call. The studio would be real. The demo tape, sharp and clean. Someone would hear it. He'd get picked up, backed, managed. He would tour. Theaters would sell out when he performed. Maybe stadiums.

And when the money came, he'd pay it back. Every cent. With interest. Fix the barn roof. Buy Tegan a better saddle. Replace the well pump before it failed again. Take the weight off his father's shoulders.

Take care of everything.

He stared at the stub hoping it might nod back. But the lie wouldn't hold still. It wavered, slipped, slid under his grip like a wet stone. He exhaled, and something in him came unspooled.

His back hit the wall. His knees bent until he was on the floor again. The guitar still facedown where he left it, strings to the wood like it was ashamed of him too. His chest tightened. No tears. No sound. Just the stinging pressure of everything cracking inward.

He couldn't go to Hank. Couldn't face Mirabella. His mother... he'd lied to her too. The one person who'd always seen the best in him. Who'd handed him music like a key and trusted him not to drop it.

And he had.

He'd dropped it, stomped it, sold it.

He stared down at the check stub and Ray's card—one for the past, one for the future—and knew they were both fictions now.

He closed his hands around them, anyway.

Because the lie, at least, was warm.

WHEN THE PORCH LIGHT DIES

Weeks passed and the morning came golden and slow. Light spilled through the lace curtain above the sink, warming the tile and curling at the toes of June's boots as she stood at the stove. The smell of cinnamon and browned butter drifted through the house. A pan sizzled low.

Jesse sat at the table, hair still damp, sleeves pushed up, a mug resting in his hands. No circles under his eyes. No twitchy glances toward the phone. Just a quiet hum under his breath—the Liszt piece, distilled into its simplest rhythm.

He leaned back and bumped his foot against Tegan's. "Easy, T-Rex. Don't swing that fork like it's got a license."

Tegan narrowed her eyes. "You call me a dinosaur one more time and I'm writing a song called Lame Brother Lullaby."

"Great," Jesse said. "I'll produce it. Drop it next week."

Grandma Ginny chuckled behind her tea. "Make sure it's in a key that won't scare the chickens."

Next to her, Grandpa Joe set down his fork and reached for more jam. "Kid's got a hook. That one might go platinum."

Hank walked in, boots brushing the doorframe as he passed. He gave Jesse a nod, then snagged a piece of toast off Tegan's plate.

"Hey!" she shouted, lunging for it.

Hank chewed. "Too slow."

Jesse grinned. "See? Velociraptor. Told you."

Tegan growled, but the sound melted into a laugh, the kind that came from some place easy.

June flipped another pancake onto the stack and slid it onto the table. "Sit down, Hank. That toast was a bribe, not breakfast."

Marshall folded the paper and set it aside. "You two heading to the estancia today?"

"After chores," Hank answered. "Agustín is going to show me how to run the olive press, Mirabella's is adding more drills to Tegan's dressage lesson, and Emerson wants Jesse on the Steinway."

Jesse nodded. "Yeah, we're digging into phrasing. He says I'm finally not muscling the notes."

June smiled as she poured coffee. "He said you're finding the music inside the music."

Jesse tilted his head. "That's one way to put it."

Marshall gave a rare nod. "Long as you're still showing up."

"I am," Jesse said, eyes steady. "Feels good."

Grandma Ginny reached into her knitting basket and pulled out a small jar wrapped in cloth. "Before you go, Hank—Don Antonio asked if I'd send more of the arnica salve. Said it worked wonders on that stallion of yours."

Hank took the jar and tucked it into his coat pocket. "Thanks, Grandma. I'll drop it off in the tack room."

No one argued.

The clink of silverware filled the quiet. A quiet that stretched wide across the room—not awkward, not heavy. More like the silence before a bow draws across string. Still. Tense in its stillness, but not yet broken.

Jesse reached for the syrup. Tegan reached for her toast. Hank leaned back in his chair and watched his brother, watched their mother watching him with pride.

Everything held its place.

Outside, clouds gathered behind the hills. But no one saw them yet.

Later that morning, June worked the lattice across the top of the apple filling, fingers quick and sure, humming faintly to something only she could hear. Beside her, a second crust rested on a floured board. Sunlight filtered through the window above the sink, warming the counter in long golden strips.

The kitchen smelled of warm apple, sugar, and nutmeg—love made edible.

The phone rang. Sharp. Two tones in.

Marshall wiped his hands on a dishtowel and crossed the kitchen.

"Miller Farm," he said.

"Marshall? It's Dave over at Ranch Supply."

Marshall nodded, already picturing the ledger. "Hey, Dave. Is everything alright?"

"Well... we've got a slight issue on the last order. That squeeze of alfalfa and the grain pallet from last week."

"Yeah, I remember it."

"Check didn't clear," Dave said. "Came back NSF. Insufficient funds."

Marshall blinked once. "That can't be right."

"I figured it had to be a mix-up," Dave offered. "Didn't sound like you. Thought I'd call before putting a hold on the account."

"I appreciate it. I'll stop by the bank this afternoon and sort it out."

"Thanks, Marshall."

He hung up and stood still for a beat, the receiver resting in his palm longer than necessary.

June glanced up from the counter. "Who was that?"

"Feed store," he said, returning the phone to its cradle. "Nothing urgent."

She wiped her hands and slid the pie into the oven, tying off her apron with practiced ease. "That was nice of them to call."

He gave a slow nod. "Yeah."

He crossed the kitchen again, slower this time, eyes drifting to the mail stacked neatly beside the fruit bowl. Bills. A few catalogs. Nothing out of place.

Marshall walked down the hall and stepped into the small side office. He pulled open the desk drawer and retrieved the check register. Flipped through. Everything appeared in order. Every stub in his own handwriting. Nothing out of place there, either.

He leaned on the edge of the desk, one hand resting on the old wooden surface. Someone had already fed the cows. Chores almost done. The quiet settled deep within the walls.

Back in the kitchen, June set a timer and wiped a trace of flour from her cheek.

Marshall stared through the office window at the pasture beyond. The late morning light stretched across the fence rails, everything painted in familiar calm.

But a crease formed across his brow.

The Long Branch crouched low against the dusk, its windows smeared with dust and neon flicker. Jesse parked the Caprice half a block away. He'd dropped

Hank and Tegan at the farm ten minutes earlier, claiming he needed air. A drive. Something.

Inside, the bar reeked of lemon cleaner, spilled beer, and something sour underneath. A few regulars hunched over their glasses. Maggie wiped the counter with a rag that had given up long ago.

Jesse didn't sit. "Have you seen Ray?"

Maggie froze mid-wipe. Her gaze didn't lift.

From the far end of the bar, a man with a busted cap and a beard tangled like wire laughed once. "Aw, hell. You're his mark."

Jesse turned. "What are you talking about?"

"Ray Navarro," the man said, lifting his drink. "Been running that 'record deal' scam across three counties for a decade. Promises a demo, takes the cash, gone before the echo fades. He's good at it. Knows the notes to hit."

Jesse's heart thudded against his ribs. "No. He said—he said—"

"I tried to tell you," Maggie said reluctantly, her voice cracking like an old record. "But Walt's the one who gets a cut. I say too much, I lose my job. And I need this job, Jesse."

Jesse stepped back, as if the air had tilted.

He turned and bolted down the hallway, past the glowing jukebox, past the crumpled flyers. His fist hit Walt's office door hard enough to rattle the hinges. He shoved it open.

Walt looked up from his desk, mid-bite of a sandwich. "Kid. What the hell?"

"You knew," Jesse said. "You vouched for him. Ray. You said he was the real deal."

Walt blinked, still chewing. "Kid, you're barking up the wrong damn tree."

"I gave him everything I had," Jesse snapped. "That was my family's money."

Walt stood, slow. "You need to calm down."

"You sold me out."

Walt's face went hard. "You handed over the check. Don't cry foul now 'cause you woke up dumb."

Jesse lunged—hands curled into fists, breath ragged. Walt met him halfway, grabbing him by the collar and slamming him into the office wall. A plaque clattered to the floor.

"You don't get to barge in here and blame me for your mistakes."

"Let go—"

"You want someone to blame? Look in the damn mirror."

Walt dragged him out into the main bar like a dog on a chain.

"Hey!" Jesse barked, twisting, but Walt's grip clamped harder.

"Out."

Every eye in the bar snapped toward them. Maggie froze mid-pour. The seed cap man chuckled again.

Walt shoved Jesse through the front doors. He stumbled down the stairs, boots skidding in the gravel.

"And don't come back," Walt called after him. "You're done here. Permanently."

The door slammed behind him.

Jesse stood alone under the dying neon sign, light flickering across his face like a bad omen.

He took one step toward the Caprice—then doubled over beside it, hands on his knees. Bile surged up. He vomited into the dirt.

Shaking, he wiped his mouth with the back of his hand and pressed his forehead to the car's fender. Couldn't breathe. Couldn't think. The pressure in his chest wouldn't release. He slid down the side panel until he was crouched low to the ground, arms wrapped around his knees. Ray was gone. The money was gone. It welded the lie shut.

And now there was no stage, no tape, no voice strong enough to call it all back.

Minutes passed, or maybe more. Eventually, the shaking dulled. His hands steadied. He climbed into the driver's seat, started the engine with trembling fingers. Ray was gone, and the lie was real.

The Caprice ticked in the silence, headlights cutting through the dusk. The engine droned, headlights skimming fence posts.

And suddenly he wasn't a fool with bruised knuckles and bile on his breath—he was sitting at the family piano playing the Liszt sonata in B minor. He played with a confidence that revealed months of work with his mom and Emerson. For one impossible moment, Yale had felt less like a dream than a doorway.

When he lifted his hands, the sound lingered in the mahogany belly of the piano, shimmering. June pressed her fingers to her mouth. 'You found the music inside the music,' she whispered, eyes shining as if the notes had lit the room themselves. She touched his shoulder—light, proud, certain.

A pothole jarred the Caprice—and the memory—loose.
Dashboard warning: LOW FUEL. Of course.

Jesse didn't look back.

The bank's lobby smelled faintly of ink and old carpet, cooled by the hum of a swamp cooler in the back wall. Fluorescent lights buzzed overhead, flickering slightly above a row of orange plastic chairs lined up along the paneled wall. A poster for a savings promotion—featuring a cartoon piggy bank—curled at the corners.

Marshall pushed through the glass door, hat low against the late afternoon sun. He paused, wiped his boots on the mat, and made his way to the counter.

"Afternoon, Lisa," he said, voice even.

The young teller glanced up from her typewriter. "Hi, Mr. Miller. You're here kinda late."

He gave a small nod. "Need to check on something. Is Douglas in?"

"Yeah, I think so." She leaned toward the intercom, pressed the button. "Doug? Marshall Miller here to see you."

A crackle, then a voice: "Send him in."

Lisa smiled, unsure. "Everything okay?"

"Yep," Marshall said with a slight hesitation.

He adjusted his hat and walked past the rope divider, down the narrow hallway. The carpet changed to linoleum outside the manager's office—yellowed and curling at the seams. Inside, Douglas Haynes rose from behind his desk, hair parted with a ruler, and shirt collar a half-size too tight.

"Marshall," he said, offering a hand. "What can I do for you?"

Marshall didn't take the seat offered. "Got a call from the feed store this morning. Said the check bounced. That shouldn't have happened."

Douglas slid a ledger from the top drawer. "Let me take a look."

The pause wasn't long, but Marshall could hear the flipping of pages like a slow clock. Douglas stopped, tapped a page with the back of his pen.

"There it is. NSF."

"NSF?" Marshall repeated.

"Non-sufficient funds."

Marshall stiffened.

Douglas adjusted his glasses and continued. "The account had enough to cover your deposit from last week, but there was another check cleared just before it hit. That's what tipped the balance."

He reached into the folder and slid a slip across the desk.

Check #5924 Payable to:

Red Rooster Studios Amount: $4,500

Signed: Marshall J. Miller

The handwriting was clean. Too clean. Perfect where it shouldn't be.

Douglas studied him over the rim of his glasses. "We have your signature on file from the truck loan. This one's... close."

Marshall didn't speak. He folded the slip once, then again. Slipped it into his pocket like it belonged to someone else.

Douglas cleared his throat. "Do you want to file a fraud—"

"No."

"Marshall, I don't mean to pry, but if someone got hold of your checks—"

"I'll take care of it."

The manager nodded slowly. "Alright."

Marshall tipped his hat and left the office.

Lisa gave him a polite wave on the way out. He didn't see it.

Outside, the sun had dropped lower, bleeding orange across the hood of the truck. The air still held some of the day's warmth, but it was cooling quickly. He climbed into Bess, started the ignition, and gripped the wheel like it needed anchoring.

He'd told June he had a few errands before dinner. It was supposed to be simple. Grain store. Hardware. Home. He took the turn off Main too fast. The back tires caught the loose edge where the pavement met gravel. The truck slid wide, but he corrected it, boot firm on the brake, hand steady on the wheel. No music played. No dust lingered behind him. Only the rising blur of heat on the road ahead.

The Miller truck tore onto the gravel drive, engine growling like a threat. The tires barely stopped before the door flew open. Marshall didn't slam it—he left it gaping.

He moved fast. Past the porch. Past June in the kitchen, who called after him—but he didn't answer. The stairs to the loft groaned under each heavy step.

Inside, Jesse's world was still. The scent of guitar strings and old cologne. A music notebook sat on the bed, one page folded back, five songs in various stages of half-belief. A forgotten metronome clicked, ticking time that no one could regain.

The drawer caught at the halfway mark. Marshall yanked it open.

There it was. Check stub. **Red Rooster Studios. $4,500.** His name—signed, stolen. And the card.

Ray Navarro, Producer, P.O. Box as the address—an obvious scam.

The paper trembled in his grip. Or maybe it was his hand. The door creaked behind him.

Jesse's voice, easy, unaware: "I thought I shut the—"

He froze. Saw the papers. The stance. The silence.

"Dad..."

"How long," Marshall said without turning, "has this been going on?"

Jesse stepped forward, swallowed hard. "A couple of weeks. I didn't mean—"

"You forged my name," Marshall said, quiet but blistering. "You stole from me. From this family."

"I was gonna pay it back." Jesse replied–another lie.

"Was Yale a lie too?" Marshall turned now, eyes locked. He held up Ray's card. "Was all that practice a scam?"

"No—" Jesse shook his head, chest heaving. "I was gonna go. I still—still might."

"You think you can cheat your way into the future and not burn everything behind you?"

"I didn't want this life!" Jesse snapped. "You and your barns and chores and cattle. You wanted that. Not me!"

"I gave you room to dream; we all did," Marshall said. "I gave you space to leave. You spit on all of it."

Boots thundered up the stairs.

June's voice below. "Marshall?"

Hank burst in, followed close by Tegan.

"You lied to your mother. You lied to your brother. You lied to me." Marshall stepped forward. "And you let Tegan worship you like some kind of damn saint."

"I didn't ask her to!"

Marshall's fist flew, cracking against Jesse's cheek with a sound like snapped wood—and even as it landed, horror flooded Marshall's face. Jesse reeled onto the desk. A framed photo of the kids on horseback crashed to the floor, glass shattering.

Jesse didn't raise a hand to defend himself.

"Dad—!" Hank rushed in, grabbed his father's arm.

Marshall shoved him hard—Hank stumbled into the doorframe, ribs thudding off the wood, knocking the wind out of him.

Marshall turned back to Jesse, fists clenched, breath heaving—

But Tegan was already there. She threw herself between them, guarding her brother with her life.

"Daddy, please!"

Marshall stopped cold.

Her face—stricken. Her big blue eyes were wide with fear. Lower lip quivering.

That look hollowed him out. He looked back at her, trying to hide his pain to no avail. He took a half-step back; the rage draining slower than his breath.

No one moved.

No one spoke.

Then Tegan, tears streaming down her face, turned and ran—down the stairs, through the yard, out into the dusk.

The screen door slammed behind her like a final chord.

The stunned quiet stretched long.

And in it, Hank's voice came low. Hoarse. Pained. Cracked.

"What did you do?"

Hank flew down the stairs like the house was on fire, shoulders grazing the wall, boots pounding the wood.

"Tegan!" he yelled, voice splitting the silence.

June shouted his name from behind, panic rising. Jesse stumbled after him, dazed, still holding his jaw. Marshall hadn't moved. He stood in the middle of the loft like a man already buried.

The screen door banged open. Outside, the light had shifted—gray now, strained and strange, like the sky had sucked the color from the world. Grandma Ginny stood on the porch, white as a bedsheet. "She took the black filly—Midnight. Didn't saddle her. She's already through the gate!"

Hank didn't answer. He cut across the yard, legs stretching, lungs tearing open. Grandpa Joe met him at the barn with a gelding already in hand, the reins flapping, saddle half cinched.

"She's headed toward the north fence," Grandpa Joe said, voice cracking. "Go."

Hank vaulted into the saddle. No plan. Just fear ripped through his chest like barbed wire.

The gelding surged forward, wind slicing his face. Dust kicked high behind him. The slope dropped, and there—far ahead—he saw them.

Tegan held on to Midnight's mane, clinging to the filly's bare back. Midnight galloped flat-out, untethered and wild, tail flying like a black flag.

"Tegan!" Hank roared, standing in the stirrups. "Pull her in!"

But she didn't hear. Or couldn't. Her head pressed low to the filly's neck, her fists twisted in the mane, tears streaked her face, and the wind loosened her braid.

She wasn't guiding the horse, and the filly felt the fear. The fence loomed ahead—six feet of old pine and wire, braced for cattle, not children. Midnight barreled toward it, eyes rimmed white, ears pinned, breath hitching.

Hank's voice broke. "No!"

Tegan kicked hard, heels slamming into the filly's sides in a final, desperate cry for flight.

Midnight's legs jackknifed beneath her, a black knot of panic.

Tegan's body didn't. It flew.

She struck the top rail shoulder-first. There was a snap—quick, sharp, wrong—and her body twisted mid-air before crumpling like dropped cloth on the far side of the fence.

She didn't move.

Not a twitch. Not a gasp. Just stillness.

The filly whinnied—a high, wild sound—then wheeled and tore back across the pasture, reins snapping, eyes rolling, lost to fear.

Hank didn't feel the ground as he dismounted. His boots barely hit dirt before he was climbing the fence, heart slamming his ribs.

He reached her in two strides and dropped to his knees.

"Tegan..." he breathed.

Her arm bent backward beneath her. Her head lolled. Tegan's braid had come completely undone from the impact.

"Tegan," he choked again, touching her face. "No. No—come on."

Her lips were parted, as if about to speak. But the light behind her eyes had already gone out.

He pulled her into his arms. Her neck gave too easily.

A sound tore from his chest—hoarse, broken. He rocked her against him like she was still small enough to carry. Like he could undo it if he held her tight enough.

"Come on, T-Rex, please." His hand shook as moved her hair from her face.

Footsteps thundered behind him—June first, shrieking, hands outstretched. She dropped beside them; her scream a sound no mother should ever make, raw and animal. Her knees hit hard. She clawed at Tegan's shoulders, cupped her daughter's face, kissed her forehead with shaking lips.

"No, no, no, no—Tegan, wake up—baby, wake up—"

Grandma Ginny reached them, collapsing beside June, pulling her into her arms.

June wouldn't let go of her daughter.

Grandpa Joe stood back, trembling. One hand over his mouth.

Jesse arrived last, stumbling across the field. His chest rose and fell as if someone had punched him. He didn't speak. He couldn't.

He looked at Hank—at Tegan—and dropped to his knees.

"I didn't mean—" he started, but the words wouldn't come.

June turned to him with eyes that no longer saw him, no longer cared. He was a stranger to her. Her hand lashed out. The sound of her palm striking his cheek snapped across the field.

Jesse didn't flinch. He didn't lift his hand. He bowed his head as if he had earned it a thousand times over.

Marshall stood on the hill above them. Motionless.

The wind caught in the cottonwoods. The filly disappeared behind the barn, still running.

And in Hank's arms, his baby sister lay broken, the last warmth draining from her skin. The silence pressed down like dirt on a grave.

Evening folded around the ranch like a worn quilt—soft, heavy, unbearable.

A lone county coroner's vehicle idled in the driveway, engine low, a steady hum against the hush. Its lights weren't flashing. There was no need.

On the porch, June sat on the steps, her skirt bunched beneath her, her hands slack in her lap. Her eyes fixed forward, unblinking, still in the same clothes from that morning, before the world shifted on its axis. Dust covered her boots. Her lips parted slightly, as if she might ask where Tegan had gone.

She didn't move.

Grandma Ginny sat close, arms wrapped around June's narrow frame like bark over a storm-bent tree. She rocked them both with no rhythm. No comfort. Only presence.

At the far end of the porch, Grandpa Joe stood behind Marshall, one hand clamped on his son's shoulder. Marshall knotted his fists at his sides; his eyes were hollow, and his jaw locked. His face gave away nothing—but his chest barely moved, like even breathing was more than he could bear. Grandpa Joe's grip never wavered. If he let go, they'd both fall.

The gurney eased down the walkway on hushed wheels. Tegan's body was small under the white sheet. Too small. The man guiding the stretcher said nothing—he moved as if silence was part of the uniform.

Hank walked beside them, step for step, as far as the tailgate would let him. His boots dragged. He hadn't taken off his cowboy hat. Dirt caked his jeans from the pasture.

At the open door, he paused. The man gave him a small nod and stepped aside.

Hank peeled the sheet back—careful, reverent—and smoothed the edge down until her face was visible. Still. Peaceful. A single curl had fallen across her cheek.

He reached with shaking fingers and tucked it behind her ear. Then, as he had so many mornings before school, he swept her hair forward, gently placing it over her shoulder. His hand lingered there, not wanting to lift away.

The caretaker cleared his throat. "We'll take good care of her."

Hank didn't answer. His eyes were like glass. His mouth pressed into a hard line.

He nodded once, barely.

The door closed with a whisper. Metal on metal. Final. The stretcher lifted into the back. The latch clicked shut.

No one spoke as the engine rumbled into gear. Gravel crunched under the tires, and the county vehicle turned slowly down the drive, its taillights fading behind the cottonwoods.

Stillness followed. Heavy. Endless.

From the far edge of the pasture, Jesse stood hidden beneath the windmill's frame, knees half-bent, one hand braced on the fence post like it was the only thing holding him upright.

He didn't move. He didn't call out.

No tears came. They were somewhere too deep to reach. Above, the sky drained of color, dimming from gold to ash.

The porch light flickered, then died, leaving the ranch in the same darkness that had swallowed Tegan's last breath. And somewhere out past the cottonwoods, a horse still ran.

WHAT CAN NOT BE FIXED

The bell tolled slow and deep, each note rolling through the streets like the weight of the day itself. St. Robert's rose from the corner lot, its stone walls weathered but proud, the arched wooden doors polished by decades of parish hands. Inside, colored light spilled from tall stained-glass windows, pooling across the polished oak pews. The scent of incense hung in the air, mingling with wax from the flickering votive candles.

A pipe organ loomed in the rear loft, its brass pipes catching the dim light. Above it, the choir—women in black skirts and men in pressed white shirts—sang low and slow, voices carrying over the mourners like a tide pulling them toward the altar.

The Miller family sat in the front pew. Marshall's broad shoulders squared, hands clasped tight on his knees. Grandpa Joe sat beside him, his hat in his lap. On the other side, June stared forward, unblinking, her face pale and hollow. Grandma Ginny leaned close, her hand resting lightly over June's. Hank sat between his father and mother, jaw set, eyes fixed on the marble floor.

The seat at the far end remained empty. Jesse's absence was a shadow of its own.

Behind them, the Castilla family sat together. Mirabella wore a black dress with a lace veil draped over her dark hair, her rosary looped between steady fingers. Don Antonio and Agustín flanked her in tailored black suits, their expressions solemn. The church brimmed with neighbors, ranch hands, and townsfolk—faces familiar and foreign, all drawn here by loss.

At the pulpit, Father Facklar cleared his throat. "Would any member of the Miller family like to say a few words?" His voice carried through the vaulted space, soft but certain.

No one moved. Marshall's stare didn't waver. June remained still. Hank's throat tightened, but words wouldn't come.

After a moment, Mirabella rose. Her heels clicked softly against the stone floor as she stepped forward. She turned to the crowd, hands clasped over the rosary.

"Tegan was the sister I never knew I needed," she began, voice low but steady. "She was my very first friend in the United States. From the first moment we met, she made me feel like family. She had this gift—this rare way of including everyone, making you feel you belonged exactly where you were. Her light always shone bright, with an unwavering loyalty that could not be shaken."

Her breath caught, and for a heartbeat she closed her eyes, holding the moment still. "She left us too soon," she continued, the words trembling now, "but I know—" her voice broke, "I know she's riding ponies in heaven."

Silence followed, thick and unmoving.

Marshall lifted his gaze to her, something unspoken passing between them—gratitude, perhaps, or the recognition of courage in the face of pain.

Hank met Mirabella's eyes for a moment, a flicker of connection in the heavy air. He looked away before it could root too deep.

The choir began again, voices rising like a slow wave against the cold stone walls.

The wind came softly off the hills, carrying the dry scent of hay and dust. The family burial plot above the barn stood quiet, the grass pressed flat where they had opened the earth. A pine box rested above the grave, its wood pale against the dark soil.

Hank stared at the grain of the box, tracing the lines the way Tegan once traced her fingers along the wooden fence rails, naming the knots and swirls as if they were constellations. She'd laughed when she found one shaped like a heart and made him promise not to paint over it. Now he searched the coffin for another hidden heart, knowing he wouldn't find it, knowing it wouldn't have made a difference if he did.

Tegan's burial was private—only family had come. The Castillas stood with them as though they had always been part of the bloodline.

When the ropes lowered Tegan into the ground, June's knees buckled. A thin cry escaped her. She folded forward. Marshall caught her before she fell, gathering her against his chest. She pressed her face into him, her sobs muffled in the wool of his jacket. He held her tight. His jaw locked.

He would not break.

The thud of earth hitting wood came slow and steady until the grave was filled. No one spoke.

Before anyone turned away, Mirabella stepped forward. She knelt, placing a small bouquet of wildflowers on the mound, her fingers lingering in the loose soil as if the touch alone could bridge the distance. She whispered something in Spanish, rose, and walked back to Don Antonio's side.

Agustín and Marshall walked June down the slope toward the house, her steps small, as if her weight had doubled. Don Antonio rested a hand around Mirabella's shoulders, guiding her behind them. Hank moved to Grandpa Joe's side, steadying him as they helped Grandma Ginny navigate the uneven ground. The old woman clutched Hank's arm, lips moving in quiet prayer.

At the foot of the hill, Hank and Marshall both turned toward Jesse's loft above the garage. The curtains were drawn. No movement. They looked at each other, the silence between them carrying the weight of two losses—Tegan gone forever, and Jesse somewhere neither of them could reach. Hank's chest tightened, the truth cutting sharper than he expected: the family would never be whole again.

Inside, the Miller house felt heavy, the air still. Mirabella moved through the kitchen, setting plates in front of the men, her own hunger gone. Grandma Ginny led June upstairs without a word.

At the doorway, Don Antonio placed a hand on Marshall's shoulder. His voice dropped low. "If you need anything, just ask."

Marshall gave a single nod, his eyes fixed on the floor.

Agustín turned to Hank. "Take your time coming back to work."

"I'll be there tomorrow," Hank said, the answer quick, leaving no room for argument.

Later, Mirabella approached him, a plate in her hands. "Hank—eat something. Please."

He shook his head, eyes fixed somewhere past her. "Got chores to do."

"You don't have to do this alone," she whispered.

"I'm fine," he replied, the words short, clipped. He moved toward the door before his voice could betray him.

Marshall, standing in the kitchen doorway, let him go.

Outside, the barn doors stood open, the dim interior swallowing Hank as he walked inside. The clink of a latch and the shuffle of hooves were the only sounds left on the wind.

Dusk bled across the hills, the last orange light catching on the barn roof before slipping away. The grave on the family plot was still raw, the soil uneven and dark, the scent of it fresh in the cooling air. Mirabella's bouquet lay at its center, petals dim in the fading light.

Jesse had stayed away that morning. The family noticed, but no one said a word. The silence had been sharper than anything they could have spoken.

Now he came alone. Boots slow on the slope, a small cloth bundle cradled under one arm, guitar slung over his back. Each step seemed to press deeper into the ground, as if the earth wanted to claim him too.

From the far pasture, Hank spotted him, a dark shape against the pale dirt. He stood still, one hand on the fence rail. The last time they'd been this close, they'd both been leaning over Tegan's bed, trying to get her to sleep while she jabbered on about how she was going to be the VIP at Estancia Castilla's Olive Oil and Lavender Festival. She'd kicked the blanket off twice, grinning between every sentence, certain they'd allow her to stay up late describing every detail of her dress and the brother's outfits. There was no anger now—only something hollow and aching. He didn't move closer. He couldn't.

Jesse reached the mound and lowered himself to his knees. For a long time, he didn't move, just stared at the soil as if it might breathe. Finally, he loosened the knot in the cloth. Inside was a small wooden dinosaur, the grain worn smooth by his hands, *T-Rex* carved deep into the belly. It was supposed to be for Christmas—something she'd laugh at and hold on to forever. Now, forever was a word that didn't mean what it used to.

He set it on the grave with a care usually reserved for something breakable. Then he pulled the guitar forward, the strap creaking in the quiet. The first notes came soft, hesitant. The song was one of their kitchen tunes, the silly ones that made her dance barefoot on the tile while he sang louder than necessary. Tonight his voice cracked on the second verse, his throat closing tight until the words came out in pieces.

The last chord trembled and died. He bowed his head, shoulders shaking. "I'm sorry," he whispered, barely more than a breath. "I didn't deserve your love." His hand went into the soil, pressing down until the dirt crumbled between his fingers. For a moment, he kept it there, as if the warmth of the earth could pass through her. Then he let the grains fall, slow, like the last thing he could give her.

The wind pressed cold against his back, tugging at the loose strands of hair along his temple. Somewhere far off, a dog barked, and the sound carried over the hills like a reminder of a world still turning without her. The grass hissed in the breeze, each blade bending in the same direction, as if bowing toward the grave. Jesse closed his eyes and let the sounds fill the hollow space inside him, because he feared what they would leave if they stopped.

Hank turned away, walking back down toward the barn before Jesse could see him. The tune stayed with him like a splinter under the skin, a sound Hank would carry for a long time.

Jesse stayed a moment longer, looking toward the farmhouse. Light glowed in the windows, but it might as well have been a world away. He didn't climb the porch steps. Instead, he turned into the dark; the hill falling behind him, his own shadow stretching long in the last scrap of light.

The days after Tegan's burial blurred into a steady grind. Hank rose before sunrise, heading straight to Estancia Castilla. He worked until the light turned gold in the late afternoon, then rode home for supper and evening chores.

Most of his hours belonged to Bob. The buckskin stallion met him at the gate now, ears pricked, the old wariness softened into curiosity. In the arena, Hank put him through the paces of working equitation—guiding him over narrow wooden bridges, between gate panels, past a stuffed bull on wheels. They wove through barrels, sidestepped along a fence, and dragged a rope looped to an old tire across the sand.

Bob still startled at the slam of a gate or the rattle of chains, but he came back quicker each time. His muscles had filled out, his stride lengthened, his stops sharper. Trust had taken root, quiet but unshakable. Where Tegan's laughter once filled Hank's days, the stallion's steady breathing had taken its place.

The sound of boots on gravel broke the rhythm. Mirabella walked up to the rail, hair shifting in the breeze, eyes following every move.

"You've been here a lot," she said.

"Yeah."

"You're working him well. He looks... different. Stronger. His top line and haunches have really developed. "

"Thanks."

She hesitated, then rested her hands on the rail. "Do you want help?"

Hank slowed Bob to a walk, considering. "Don't need it," he said finally. "We're in a good place."

The words came out flat, final.

Mirabella stayed silent, her gaze steady on him. She waited for more, but he had nothing else to give. If he let her in—if he said what working with Bob had meant—he wouldn't be able to hold it together. Not for her. Not for the family.

"I should get him cooled out," he added, turning Bob toward the far end of the arena.

Mirabella watched him lead the stallion away, the sun catching the dust as it drifted in their wake, closing behind him like a door.

The Miller house felt dim, even in daylight. June kept to her bedroom, blinds half-closed so the sun only leaked in as a pale wash across the carpet. The air inside was still, a quiet that pressed into the walls.

Mirabella came by in the afternoons, slipping into the room with a book in hand. She'd sit in the chair beside the bed, reading aloud in a low, steady voice. June would listen for a while, her gaze fixed somewhere past the ceiling.

"How's Hank?" she asked one afternoon, her voice thin.

Mirabella closed the book over a finger. "He's thrown himself into work."

A crease formed between June's brows, concern flickering for a moment. But then her gaze drifted back toward the shadows. "That's good," she murmured, and the wall between reality and dream closed again.

Downstairs, Grandma Ginny had taken over the house—cooking meals, keeping the floors swept, feeding the animals before sunrise. Her steady presence kept things running, but it wasn't the same. The sound of June's piano no longer floated through the rooms. The Liszt sheet music sat on the stand in the family room, its margins marked with her neat, slanted handwriting, a relic from a different life.

Late one evening, after someone cleared the dinner table and the house grew quiet, Jesse slipped through the kitchen door. He always came after everyone else had eaten—avoiding his father's steady glare and Hank's colder silence.

Grandma Ginny was waiting for him. "I saved you a plate," she said, sliding it across the counter.

He took it but didn't eat, his eyes drifting toward the family room. The sheet music sat on the stand, catching the dim lamplight. He walked over and lowered himself onto the piano bench and touched the sheet music as if it would bring Tegan back, as if it would bring his mother back. But that dream was over. His hands hovered over the keys but never pressed down.

"You'll always be a part of this family," Grandma Ginny said gently from behind him.

Jesse gave a short, bitter laugh. "Mom hates me."

"She doesn't," Grandma Ginny replied firmly. "She just... needs time."

He shook his head, staring at the empty keys. "This is all my fault," he mumbled. "Everything would be better if I just left."

"That's not true," she told him, stepping closer. "You leaving would break her worse."

But Jesse was already on his feet, pulling on his jacket. He didn't meet her eyes. "She wouldn't even notice."

The screen door creaked open and shut. By the time Grandma Ginny reached the porch, Jesse had already gone up the stairs to his loft.

The morning light stretched long shadows over the gravel drive as June's Caprice rolled to a stop outside the main barn at Estancia Castilla. The engine idled for a moment before Jesse stepped out, guitar slung over his back, duffel bag gripped tight in one hand.

Agustín was crossing the yard, sleeves rolled, a clipboard in hand. "Hank is working the cattle this morning," he said, his eyes falling to the duffel. "Come to my office."

They walked in silence through the barn's wide aisle, the air cool and smelling faintly of hay and leather. The office was small, tidy—maps of the property pinned to the walls, a stack of invoices on the desk. Agustín shut the door behind them.

"What's going on?" he asked.

Jesse set the duffel down at his feet. "I'm leaving town."

Agustín leaned back against the desk, arms folded. "You can stay here. Guest room, bunkhouse—whatever you need."

Jesse shook his head. "Couldn't do that to Hank. This place... it's the only thing keeping him from falling apart. Me being here would just make it worse."

For a moment, Agustín studied him, then whispered, "You should mend things with him. Before you go."

Jesse hesitated, looking down at his boots. "It's too late for that." He reached into his jacket and pulled out two envelopes, one marked *Hank*, the other *Mom*. He handed them to Agustín. "Give these to them after I'm gone."

Agustín glanced at the names, then back at him. "Where?"

"San Francisco. Nine a.m. bus."

Agustín pushed off the desk. "I'll take you."

"You don't have to—"

"I'll take you," Agustín repeated, his tone leaving no room for argument. "We'll take the Caprice. I'll bring it back to your family's farm."

They left the office without another word. The Caprice rumbled down the empty road, the morning sun breaking over the hills. Neither man spoke on the short drive to the bus stop; the silence carried more weight than any conversation could.

When they pulled up to the curb, Agustín put the car in park.

"I'll make sure she gets home," he said, nodding toward the steering wheel. Agustín pulled out cash from his wallet and handed it to Jesse.

Jesse shook his head. "I can't take this." He handed it back to Agustín. Agustín pushed it back to Jesse.

"Take it. I insist."

Jesse opened the door, the guitar strap creaking over his shoulder. "Thanks," he said, his voice low.

Agustín gave him a nod, not trusting himself to say more.

Jesse stepped onto the sidewalk, duffel and envelope in hand, and didn't look back as he walked toward the waiting bus.

The light was thinning, stretching long across the yard, when June's Caprice rolled up the Miller's driveway. Dust trailed behind it, catching the last gold of the day. Behind it came Don Antonio's truck, the engine a steady, low hum.

Marshall straightened from the pigpen, one boot braced on the fence post he'd been setting. He watched Agustín ease the car to a stop, Don Antonio pulling in behind. For a moment, the only sound was the metallic clink of Marshall's hammer in his palm.

Their eyes met. Agustín's eyes carried the weight of what he wasn't saying. Marshall didn't ask—he didn't need to. Jesse was gone.

Marshall gave a curt nod, tipping his hat toward Don Antonio in quiet acknowledgment, then turned back to the gate, driving the hinge bolts home. Don Antonio stayed in the truck, hands on the wheel, gaze steady on the yard.

The scent of hay drifted in from the pasture. Agustín stepped out of the Caprice and glanced across the field. Hank was moving with a determined rhythm, the wheelbarrow piled high, the hay fork working in steady arcs. He was doing the chores that used to belong to Tegan and Jesse both—carrying the weight without complaint.

Agustín's hand brushed the inside pocket of his jacket, feeling the shape of the two envelopes. His gaze lingered on Hank for a long moment before he decided. Now wasn't the time. The letters would wait.

He shut the car door quietly and walked back toward Don Antonio's truck, the sound of Hank's work carrying on in the cooling air.

The house had gone still; the only sound was the slow tick of the mantle clock in the front room. In his office, the light from the desk lamp cut a narrow circle across the farm ledger. Columns of numbers sat untouched. Marshall's eyes weren't on them.

His eyes focused on the small photograph pinned to the mirror above the filing cabinet—five-year-old Tegan, pigtails jutting from under a floppy straw hat, front teeth missing, her grin wide enough to take up half her face.

He leaned back in his chair, elbows on the armrests. "I miss you, Peanut," he murmured. "Thought I'd have more time. I wanted to see you walk across that stage in a cap and gown. Wanted to give you away someday. All those things... they're gone now." His voice thinned, the words catching in his throat. "And I'd trade every acre, every horse in the barn, to have you sitting here in that chair, swinging your legs and telling me what a fool I am."

The door creaked. Grandpa Joe stepped in without a word, lingered behind him, and rested a hand on his son's shoulder.

Marshall didn't look up at first. "Jesse's gone," he said finally. He uttered the words flatly, as if he had worn them smooth by turning them over in his head all day. "Left this morning."

Grandpa Joe's hand tightened on his shoulder. "He'll be back."

Marshall gave a brief shake of his head. "Don't think so. And maybe... maybe that's for the best right now."

They sat in silence for a beat before Marshall spoke again, his tone lower. "It's not just that. We're in trouble here, Dad. Real trouble. The bank's given us a month, maybe two, to make the mortgage. If we can't, we lose the place."

Grandpa Joe's hand didn't move. "I've got savings. Take it."

Marshall turned toward him, his expression set. "No. That's for Normandy. You've been saving for that trip for half your life. You're not giving it up because I couldn't keep this place above water. And...it's not enough, dad."

"It's just money, son. This farm has been a part of this family and—"

Marshall shook his head. "It's more than money. I'll find another way."

In the hallway, Hank stood in the shadows, one shoulder against the wall. At the first mention of Jesse's name, his jaw had locked. Now, hearing his father speak of the farm's danger, a low heat rose in his chest. He wanted to storm in, demand answers, ask how Jesse could walk away and leave the rest of them carrying the load. But he stayed still. He had to be the strong one now, for his mother, for the land, for what was left of his family.

The words from inside the office kept turning over in his mind—Jesse's gone. We could lose the place. They sank deep, heavy as stone, and he knew they weren't going anywhere.

Without a sound, Hank pushed away from the wall and walked back down the hall, the weight of it all pressing into his shoulders like an extra yoke he'd chosen to carry.

Hank stepped out onto the porch, the night air cool against his face. Across the yard, the barn stood dark; the pastures stretching out beyond it under a moonless sky. Somewhere in the distance, a coyote called, its cry sharp and lonely. Jesse was gone. Tegan was gone. And now the farm—the only thing left that felt certain—was slipping toward the edge. Hank tightened his fists, the muscles in his forearms flexing. He didn't say it out loud, but the promise settled in his chest all the same: he would not let this place fall. Not while he was still here to fight for it.

THE FORGOTTEN BIRTHDAY

I t had been only a few weeks since Tegan's funeral and Jesse's quiet disappearance. Long enough for the shock to dull into a constant ache, but not nearly long enough for anything to feel steady again. The Miller farm moved forward because it had to—chores didn't wait for grief—but the rhythm was different now. Slower, off-beat. There were gaps in the day where voices used to fill the air.

Hank's sixteenth birthday had come and gone the week before without so much as a mention. No cake. No candle. Not even a nod from his parents. He wasn't expecting much, especially this year, yet the silence felt like a weight in his chest.

On the day itself, he'd been out by the shed with his mother's Caprice, the hood propped open, the sharp tang of oil and metal thick in the air. Midmorning blackened with grease, his fingers, each movement deliberate: drain the old oil into the pan, wipe the threads clean, spin on a new filter. The work gave him something to measure, something he could finish. Easier than thinking about what wasn't there.

That absence made the memory sharper. Back before the accident, in early spring, Tegan had turned eleven. June had spent the morning in the kitchen, flour dusting her apron, the scent of vanilla and cocoa so rich it hung in the hall. She'd baked what Hank still thought was the most perfect cake he'd ever seen—three layers, smooth buttercream swirled with pale pink rosettes, tiny fondant ponies prancing in a circle like they might leap from the icing.

June always made each child's cake a masterpiece—Jesse's topped with guitars or musical notes, Hank's with horses or cowboy hats. For Tegan, it had been a carousel, each pony hand-painted with eyes and manes, the poles shimmering with edible gold.

That afternoon, the entire family gathered on the porch, paper crowns sitting crooked on their heads. Marshall hoisted Tegan onto his shoulders, the crown sliding down over her eyes, and she'd laughed so hard she almost dropped the slice of cake in her hand. Hank remembered the sun warming his face, the frosting melting a little on the plate, and how the world had felt right in that moment.

Now, a week after his own forgotten birthday, dawn was just breaking when the scent of coffee drifted through the kitchen.

Grandma Ginny stood at the counter, her back straight but her movements quiet, deliberate. The cast-iron skillet was already warming on the stove, butter softening in its center. Marshall sat at the table with a parts catalog, flipping pages slowly, eyes glazed with thoughts he didn't put into words.

June moved between the mudroom and the yard, scattering feed for the barn cats before heading toward the pig pen. She was out of her bedroom these days, taking on chores again. Her pace was slower; still listening for footsteps that would never come.

"Let Hank sleep in," Grandma Ginny said as she passed behind Marshall, setting a fresh cup of coffee by his elbow. "That boy deserves a day off."

Marshall glanced up but didn't argue.

"I'm spending the day with him," Grandma Ginny added, her tone soft but immovable.

From the mudroom, June's voice drifted in. "What plans?"

"The kind that'll remind him he matters," Grandma Ginny replied, turning back to the skillet.

Marshall's gaze dropped back to the catalog. June came in a moment later, brushing a piece of hay from her sweater. Neither spoke, the kitchen settling into the quiet sizzle of butter meeting hot iron. Outside, dew clung to the fence rails. Upstairs, Hank slept on, unaware that—for the first time in weeks—the day ahead would be different.

The morning air carried a damp chill as June stepped into the chicken yard, a metal scoop of grain in her hand. The hens clustered at her boots, their clucks low and insistent, wings rustling against one another. She tipped the scoop, scattering feed in slow arcs. The kernels pattered against the dirt, the sound oddly hollow in her ears.

Her hands moved out of habit, but her mind drifted. She could see a smaller, barefoot Tegan slipping between the hens years ago, her laughter startling them into a flurry of feathers. She'd been fearless, scooping eggs straight from beneath the warm, complaining hens. June could still hear her voice—"You've got to be quick, Mama, before they change their mind!"

The present returned with the weight of the empty scoop. She moved on to the barn. The cows stood waiting, their breath rising in slow clouds that mingled with the faint scent of hay and manure. She settled onto the milking stool beside the first one, leaning in with the pail between her knees. Her fingers curled and pulled in a rhythm that had been second nature for years. The warm streams of milk hit the tin with soft, steady splashes.

She didn't think about the sound. She thought about the last time Jesse had come in to help—half-distracted, humming some tune under his breath. He'd been different even then, his eyes set on something far away. She'd noticed. She just hadn't asked.

When June finished with the cows, she lingered in the barn for a moment. The light filtering through the high windows caught the dust in a golden haze, and the soft shifting of hooves filled the space like a heartbeat. She let it steady her before heading back toward the house.

Inside, the faint smell of coffee lingered from earlier, mingling with the sharper scent of the cold air she carried in. Her gaze moved to the counter—bare now—but in her mind, she could still see the parade of birthday cakes she had baked there. Each one had been different, each one personal, each one a piece of her love turned into sugar and flour.

Her feet carried her into the front room, to the piano. Dust lay faintly on the closed lid. She lifted it; the hinges creaking in the quiet. The keys were smooth under her fingertips, but she didn't press them. Instead, her eyes shifted to the sheet music still resting on the stand. Liszt, with small notations in her own slanted handwriting—the reminders she'd written for Jesse's Yale audition.

She traced one note with the edge of her nail, remembering how he'd roll his eyes, then play the passage exactly as she'd asked.

The house was silent. She closed the lid again, careful not to let it slam, and stepped away. Sounds, colors, even the air seemed muted now. But she was moving again. That had to count for something.

The smell woke him before the light did—warm biscuits, pancakes, and sausage, a breakfast that used to mean a holiday or company coming over.

Hank blinked against the pale stripe of sunlight spilling through the narrow gap in his curtains. For a moment, still half-caught in sleep, he expected to hear Tegan in the hall, singing off-key to some song only she knew. The quiet pressed in instead.

153

Then it hit him. Morning chores. He sat up fast, heart jumping, and swung his legs over the edge of the bed. The floorboards were cold under his bare feet.

He pulled on jeans and a flannel, ran a hand through his hair to push it into place, then jammed his feet into his boots. The stairs creaked under his weight as he headed down, bracing for his father's voice or the sharp look that usually came with being late.

Instead, he found Grandma Ginny at the stove, an apron tied snug at her waist, a spatula in one hand. The air was thick with the smell of sausage sizzling in the cast-iron skillet, pancakes stacked high on a plate, and biscuits split open to let the butter melt right into their centers.

She turned toward him; her face breaking into a smile that reached her eyes. "Happy Birthday."

Hank paused in the doorway, surprised. "That was a week ago," he said, scratching the back of his neck. "And I missed morning chores."

"I told your mother and father to let you sleep in," Grandma Ginny replied, flipping a pancake with practiced ease. "I didn't tell them about your birthday. Just said I wanted to spend the day with you. Make sure you're okay."

He leaned against the counter, unsure what to do with the lump in his throat. "You didn't have to—"

"I did," she cut in gently. "You've been carrying more than your share. Today, you get a little breathing room." She set the spatula down, meeting his eyes. "Church first. Then your driver's test. Maybe a few surprises along the way."

Something eased in his chest, enough for the corner of his mouth to twitch upward. "Sounds like a plan."

"Good. Now sit. Eat. We've got a full day ahead of us."

He slid into a chair, the wood warm from the sun coming in through the window. Outside, dew still clung to the pasture fences. Inside, Grandma Ginny set the table; the kitchen smelled like it used to, and for the first time in weeks, he felt the weight on his shoulders lighten—just enough to notice.

It was the first time June had walked up the hill since the day they laid Tegan to rest. The climb felt steeper than it used to, her breath shallow, her boots pressing into the dry grass with a weight that had nothing to do with her body. Every step pulled her farther from the farmhouse and closer to the place she had been avoiding for weeks.

The late morning sun spilled across the pasture, casting long shadows from the twisted oaks at the hill's crest. The air was still except for the soft rustle of leaves and the far-off creak of the windmill turning in the breeze.

When she reached the top, her eyes fell on the tombstone. She hadn't pictured it—not really—but there it was, gray granite standing against the bright sweep of grass, simple and exact in a way that made her chest tighten.

Tegan Virginia Miller
1972 – 1983
Beloved daughter, sister, and friend.
May her light shine as bright in heaven as it did on earth.

June traced the letters with her fingertips. The quote was pure Ginny—hope wrapped in scripture's softness. June didn't even know someone had ordered the stone. The days since the funeral had blurred into one long stretch of sleepless nights and muted mornings.

At the base of the stone sat a bouquet of wildflowers, stems bound with twine, still fresh enough to carry the meadow's scent. Beside them, a small wooden dinosaur—its edges worn smooth—waited. She bent down, lifting it carefully. The carved letters on its belly read *T-Rex*. Jesse's work. She pressed the cool wood to her chest before slipping it into the pocket of her dress, her fingers curling over it like she could keep it safe there.

Footsteps sounded in the grass behind her.

"Mirabella leaves the flowers," Marshall's voice said, steady but quiet. "Almost every day."

June kept her eyes on the stone. "Where's Jesse?"

There was a pause. "He left. Weeks ago. I don't know where. Agustín took him to the bus stop."

Her head snapped up. "And you didn't tell me?"

"I didn't know how," he said, eyes shadowed under the brim of his hat. "Didn't want to make things worse."

Her voice cracked. "There is nothing worse than losing a child, Marshall. And now I've lost two."

"I was trying to protect you."

She shook her head slowly. "You can't protect me from what's already happened." Her gaze lingered on the grave a moment longer before she turned toward the slope. "I'm going to warm up the lunch Ginny prepared this morning."

She walked down the hill without looking back. The tall grass whispered against her skirt. Marshall stayed where he was, his shadow stretching across the granite. The bouquet swayed in the faint breeze, the empty patch beside it marking the dinosaur's absence. He stared at his daughter's name until the letters blurred, but he didn't move to follow June.

The heavy wooden doors of St. Robert's swung inward with a low groan, letting in a slice of pale winter light before closing again behind them. Inside, the church was warm in a way that seemed to come from more than the heating vents—it was the warmth that seeped into stone over decades, stored in the walls like memory.

The air carried a faint, sweet tang of incense that clung to the polished pews and high stone arches. Above, painted saints and angels looked down from the vaulted ceiling, their faces serene, untouched by the chill of the world outside.

Hank followed Grandma Ginny down the central aisle, their footsteps hushed on the runner. She moved with quiet purpose, her hand brushing the carved ends of each pew as if greeting old friends. The colored light from the stained glass windows spilled across her hair and coat—patches of crimson, sapphire, and gold shifting with every step.

They stopped at the side altar, where rows of candles stood in brass holders. Most were unlit, waiting. Grandma Ginny chose a tall white one from the box, struck a match, and held it until the flame steadied. She placed it in the front row, among the few already burning, their flicker bending shadows against the stone.

They both knelt. Grandma Ginny bowed her head, lips moving in silent prayer. Hank stared at the candle's flame.

It danced once, then grew still, its glow reflected in the glass before it. He thought of Tegan—not in the moment they'd lost her, but in the dozens of small ways she'd filled his life. The way she'd draped herself over the barn fence to watch him work Bob. How she'd pretended to hate his bad jokes but always laughed. How she could make a room brighter just by walking in.

The memory warmed him, the way the candle seemed to push back the dim. He let it warm him, even if only for the length of a prayer.

When Grandma Ginny rose, Hank followed. They stepped back into the wide, quiet space, leaving the candle behind to burn in Tegan's name, its light holding steady in the shadows.

The DMV squatted between a laundromat and a shuttered hardware store, its brick facade dulled by years of sun and rain. Inside, the fluorescent lights hummed overhead, casting a pale glow over a scuffed linoleum floor and a long row of metal-framed chairs. People sat hunched with forms in hand, eyes flicking to the red digital number board as if willing it to change faster.

Hank followed Grandma Ginny to the counter, the faint smell of coffee and paper mingling with the sharp tang of disinfectant. He felt the weight of the morning still in him—the church, the candle—but he pushed it aside, focusing on the task ahead.

"You've been driving farm trucks since you could see over the wheel," Grandma Ginny said, leaning in just enough for him to hear over the murmur of the room. "This'll be the easiest thing you do all week."

A corner of his mouth twitched upward. "Guess we'll see."

When his number was called, they stepped forward. The clerk, a woman with half-moon glasses perched low on her nose, glanced at his paperwork before directing him toward the testing area.

Outside, the air bit at his cheeks. The examiner, a tall man with a clipboard, greeted him with a nod. "You ready?"

Hank slid into the driver's seat, adjusting the mirrors with practiced efficiency. The engine turned over with a low rumble, and they pulled out of the lot. The route wound down Main Street—past the feed store, the post office, and the barbershop with its faded candy-cane pole—before cutting toward the edge of town where the road widened and the horizon opened up.

He kept both hands steady on the wheel, checked his mirrors, signaled early, and took each turn like he was hauling a full load of hay. Years of dawn feed runs and hauling water tanks had made this second nature.

By the time they rolled back into the lot, the examiner was already scribbling. "Congratulations," he said, tearing off the top sheet and handing it to Hank.

The words landed with more weight than he'd expected—not joy, exactly, but something close. A step forward.

Inside, the camera flashed, capturing a faint, almost shy smile—the first true one since Tegan's death.

Grandma Ginny's eyes crinkled at the corners when he showed her the temporary paper license. "Looks official to me. You did good, Hank."

He folded it carefully into his wallet. "Feels official."

Outside, the winter sun had climbed higher, and the air seemed a little warmer as Grandma Ginny handed him the keys. Hank took the keys, the metal cool in his palm. As they climbed into the Caprice, he glanced at the paper license again. It wasn't just a card—it was a piece of something new, a small claim on the future.

"Your turn to drive," she said. "And I know exactly where we're going next."

The Caprice's engine hummed as Hank eased it out of the DMV lot, the paper license tucked snug in his wallet. Grandma Ginny leaned back in the passenger seat, her eyes scanning the storefronts they passed like she was looking for something she hadn't seen in years.

"Take us to Pie and Burger," she said suddenly, her tone bright in a way that made Hank glance over.

"The diner?" he asked, turning onto Main.

"That's the one. Haven't been there in ages. Perfect way to mark the day."

The neon sign came into view first—a pink and turquoise glow against the pale winter sky. The building itself was a squat corner diner with a wraparound row of windows, each one rimmed in chrome trim. Inside, Hank could see the gleam of the long counter and the flash of the jukebox lights.

Stepping through the door felt like stepping into a memory that wasn't entirely his. The black-and-white checkered floor stretched out beneath their boots, the tiles worn smooth in the high-traffic paths. Red vinyl stools lined the counter in a perfect row, each one with a ring of scuff marks at its base from decades of customers swiveling in and out.

Framed black-and-white photos of smiling faces—high school football teams, families dressed in their Sunday best, couples sharing milkshakes—crowded the walls. Faded posters of 1950s movie stars, their colors washed to sepia, filled the spaces between.

A jukebox in the corner spun a Buddy Holly tune, the soft scratch of the record needle weaving under the sound of clinking dishes and low conversation.

They slid into a booth by the window, the vinyl seat squeaking under Hank as he settled in. He glanced out at Main Street—bare trees, a pair of kids pedaling past on bikes too big for them—then back to the menus Grandma Ginny was already studying like she didn't know exactly what she wanted.

When the waitress arrived, Hank ordered a cheeseburger with fries. Grandma Ginny grinned and ordered the same.

The food came quickly, wrapped in waxed paper that was already spotted with grease. Hank unwrapped his burger, the smell of grilled beef and melted cheese hitting him all at once. The first bite was almost overwhelming—savory and salty, the cheese stretching before melting completely into the meat. He chewed slowly, letting the flavor settle, realizing it was the first time in weeks that food had tasted like more than fuel.

Grandma Ginny watched him over the rim of her coffee mug. "Told you we needed to celebrate," she said.

They polished off their burgers, the pile of golden fries shrinking between them, before ordering a slice of warm apple pie with vanilla ice cream to share. The crust flaked under Hank's fork, steam curling from the spiced apples, the melting ice cream pooling in sweet rivulets across the plate.

Hank swallowed his bite, leaning back in the booth. "Almost as good as yours," he teased, his eyes glinting.

Grandma Ginny raised a brow in mock offense. "Almost? Boy, my pies are revered throughout the county. Agustín can't get enough of them."

He smiled at her in a way that softened both of their faces. "Would you teach me?"

The question landed heavier than the words themselves. Baking had been Tegan's territory with Grandma Ginny—something Hank had always left for them.

Grandma Ginny's eyes softened even more, and she reached across the table, her hand warm over his. "I'd be honored."

The jukebox clicked over to another track—Elvis this time—and for a moment, the hum of the diner wrapped around them like a blanket from a time when laughter came easier.

The Caprice purred along the two-lane road, its tires humming over the cracked asphalt. The late afternoon sun hung low, catching in the winter stubble of the fields on either side, turning the dull gold to fire.

Hank drove with both hands on the wheel, his paper license folded in his wallet but still fresh in his mind. He could feel Grandma Ginny studying him now and then from the passenger seat, though she said nothing. The road stretched quiet ahead.

Finally, he broke it. "Grandma... I overheard Dad and Grandpa in the office the other night."

Ginny turned her head slightly, her silver hair catching the light. "About what?"

"The bank," Hank said, eyes fixed on the faded center line. "About the farm being in trouble. It sounded bad—like we might not keep it." His grip on the wheel tightened. "I could take more hours at the estancia. Or... something else. I could help."

Grandma Ginny rested her hand on his, warm and steady against his knuckles. "Hank, you've been carrying more than your share since..." She stopped, the weight of the unspoken hanging between them. "Your father and grandpa know this farm better than anyone. They'll find a way."

"What if they can't?" His voice was quiet but edged with something harder.

She looked out at the stretch of road ahead, the bare branches reaching over it like fingers. "The Lord has carried this family through harder times than you can imagine. He'll do it again. You've got to trust Him—and trust your father and grandpa to steer this farm through." She squeezed his hand before pulling hers back. "That's where your strength is needed right now."

Hank gave a brief nod, but the question still burned in his chest. He didn't press it.

They drove in silence for a while, the farm's fence line finally appearing in the distance, posts casting long, thin shadows over the pasture.

Grandma Ginny tipped her head toward the driveway. "Pull in nice and easy. Don't go tossing gravel—your grandpa's been patching that drive for thirty years."

A faint smile tugged at Hank's mouth. He braked smoothly; the gravel crunching softly under the tires. But even as they rolled toward the house, the talk of the bank sat heavy in him, like a stone he couldn't set down.

The sun had dropped lower by the time they turned onto the long drive, painting the horizon in deep golds that bled into violet at the edges. Thin clouds caught the last light and burned like embers against the darkening sky.

Hank eased the Caprice forward, the tires crunching over the familiar stretch of gravel. The winter air slipped in through a crack in his window, carrying the scent of wood-smoke from the stove and faint hay from the barn.

The farmhouse came into view first, its porch light already glowing in the early dusk. Beyond it, the silhouette of the barn stood against the fading light, doors shut, the yard quiet except for the low rustle of wind in the bare trees.

Hank parked beside the porch, letting the engine idle for a few seconds before turning the key. The tick of the cooling engine was the only sound between him and Grandma Ginny for a long moment.

He glanced toward the barn, picturing Jesse leaning against the doorframe with his guitar, or Tegan darting out with her hair flying, laughing as she raced him to the house. The images hit fast and sharp, like photographs someone had shoved into his hands.

Today felt... almost normal. Burgers and pie, Grandma Ginny's uninhibited laughter, the quiet pride of holding his first driver's license. For a while, the weight in his chest had eased.

But as the last light drained from the sky, it settled again—changed, heavier in some ways, softer in others. It wasn't the same jagged ache. It had shifted, found a deeper place to rest inside him, where it would live alongside everything else he carried.

Grandma Ginny opened her door, the hinges creaking. She paused before stepping out, resting a hand briefly on his shoulder. "Good day, Hank." Her voice was gentle, but it held the firmness that left no room for doubt.

He nodded, not trusting himself to speak.

As she climbed the porch steps, framed in the warm light spilling from the kitchen, Hank glanced back toward the hill where the oak tree stood. He could almost hear Tegan's voice ringing out beneath it— *"Let's make a pact. Best friends forever."*

He could see it now: the three of them, hands joined in a triangle, Mirabella's eyes shining, Tegan's grin wild and sure, the sky above them wide and endless.

"Forever," he whispered.

Hank stepped inside, closing the door gently behind him. The sound was soft, but it felt like something settling into place—like finding his place again.

Later that night, once the porch light had gone off, and the windows glowed faintly with lamplight, Marshall stepped out into the dark alone. Marshall didn't take a flashlight—he knew the land by feel. He stood beneath the oak, boots sinking into the cold, brittle grass, the night pressing in on all sides. He didn't kneel. Didn't speak. Just stood there a while, hands in his coat pockets, the same way he used to stand behind the bleachers at Tegan's 4-H shows—close enough to be there, far enough to stay unnoticed. When the wind picked up, he tilted his head slightly, as if listening for Tegan's voice in the rustle of the leaves. Then he turned and made his way back down the hill without a word, the dark swallowing his shape.

GHOSTS OF THE SKY

The kitchen smelled like bacon and coffee, the scent that clung to wood and fabric seemed to say home. Warm light filtered through the curtains, bouncing off the polished table that Grandma Ginny had scrubbed clean at dawn. The radio on the counter hummed with country music, low and steady, a voice crooning about highways and heartbreak.

June stood at the stove beside Grandma Ginny, sleeves rolled past her elbows, apron tied neatly around her waist. A skillet of eggs sizzled as she crooned to the tune, the same way she used to when Tegan helped her measure flour or stir cake batter. The sound was quiet but steady, as if her voice was learning to live again.

Grandma Ginny plated bacon while June pulled biscuits from the oven, their golden tops glistening. The rhythm of their movements overlapped, familiar and practiced, like life before grief had broken it. The house still carried silence where voices used to be, but now there were hints—soft and fragile—that it could be whole again.

June wiped her hands on her apron and stepped onto the porch. She reached for the iron triangle that hung from its hook and struck it with the steel rod. The sound carried clearly over the yard, a high, ringing summons that had called the Miller men to the table for generations.

Boots sounded against the porch steps. Marshall came in first, smelling of hay and dust, his hat pushed back on his head. Grandpa Joe followed, leaning on his walking stick, his movements slow but steady. Hank trailed last, dust clinging to his jeans, his shoulders squarer than they had been weeks ago. They settled into their chairs, filling the table once more, though not completely. Two places remained empty, and the quiet there spoke louder than any prayer.

Grandma Ginny bowed her head. "Heavenly Father, we thank You for this meal, for the hands that prepared it, and for the family gathered here today. Bless those who are absent from this table and guide us through the days ahead. Amen."

A murmur of amen followed, and the dishes were passed—biscuits split open with butter melting into their centers, bacon disappearing piece by piece, eggs spooned onto plates. Conversation stayed light at first, drifting to weather, fences, and cows. Yet, in the pauses, the weight of absence returned.

For a month now, the kitchen had lacked Tegan's giggle, bright and untamable, and Jesse's music floating in from the loft above the garage—scales and the haunting lines of Liszt played over and over for his Yale audition. The ghosts of their sounds still clung to the walls, like echoes the house wasn't ready to let go.

Between bites, Grandpa Joe cleared his throat. "Marshall, I've got an order to deliver into town. A table and a pair of chairs. Could use an extra hand loading."

Marshall nodded. "Soon as I take Hank over to work, I'll give you a hand."

"I can take him," June said quickly, glancing at her son. "It'd give me a chance to get out of the house."

Hank set down his fork. "Actually, I was going to drive myself. I've got my license now. I was planning on taking the Caprice."

The words seemed to stall in the air. Marshall froze halfway in lifting his coffee. June's lips parted, but nothing came. Their eyes shifted toward Grandma Ginny. She didn't look up, only buttered her biscuit, her mouth twitching at the corners like she'd been waiting for this moment.

The realization landed on Marshall and June at once. Shame flickered between them, hot and heavy. Their son had turned sixteen a week ago, crossed a threshold, and they had let it pass without a word.

June reached for Hank's hand under the table. He met her eyes, steady.

"It's okay, Mom." His fingers squeezed hers once, firm, before letting go.

Her throat tightened. "I still want to go with you."

Hank gave a small nod and went back to his eggs.

Marshall drew a breath, habit pushing him to argue, but stopped. He caught Grandma Ginny's glance and let the words die in his throat.

The meal carried on, but the weight pressed in around them. The scrape of a chair, the clink of a fork—they all seemed louder because of what was missing. Tegan would have teased Hank about being old enough to drive. Jesse would have argued about taking the Caprice next.

Now the voices were gone, and though the table was full, it still felt hollow.

Hank sat taller, the morning sun catching him across the face. Manhood was coming for him faster than anyone wanted to admit. It was in his license, in the quiet resolve in his tone, in the way his parents' guilt only deepened his calm. He was stepping into a sky wide and endless, haunted by ghosts, but opening to him all the same.

The Caprice turned up the winding drive to Estancia Castilla; the estate sprawling across the hillside with its whitewashed stucco walls glowing in the late-morning sun. Terracotta roof tiles shimmered red and orange, bougainvillea climbing in cascades of fuchsia and magenta along the arched corridors. The scent of lavender and rosemary drifted on the breeze, mingling with the faint sound of cattle lowing from the pens below.

Don Antonio was already waiting at the portico, dressed immaculately in a black suit with a silk kerchief tucked into his breast pocket. He opened his arms warmly as June and Hank stepped from the car.

"Señora June, Hank," he greeted with his usual flourish, his smile easing the formality of the grand setting.

Hank shifted his weight, then touched the brim of his hat. "Morning, Don Antonio. I should get to the barns."

Don Antonio's eyes glimmered with pride. "Sí, of course. They are waiting for you."

Hank strode off, shoulders squared, his long frame moving with quiet confidence toward the stucco barns, where a group of vaqueros was already gathering. June's gaze lingered on him before Antonio gestured gently for her to follow him into the house.

As they entered the cool, shaded corridors, June lowered her voice. "Is Agustín here?"

Don Antonio gave her a knowing look, the corners of his eyes softening. "He is in the office, speaking on the phone with one of our distributors. It will not be long. Come, I will take you to the veranda."

He led her through the arched hallway to a wide veranda overlooking the pastures. The view stretched endlessly: cattle dotted the rolling hills, the sun flashing off the tiled roofs of the barns. And there, astride a dark bay, was Hank.

She stopped in her tracks, her hand tightening around the wrought iron rail. Hank sat tall in the saddle, issuing calm but firm instructions to the other cowboys. They obeyed without hesitation, moving cattle across the pens under his direction. His voice carried across the wind—measured, confident. He was no longer just a ranch hand. He was leading them.

Don Antonio's chest swelled. "He has taken charge of the cattle operations. Agustín trusts him completely. Hank's leadership allows my son to handle the business without distraction."

June pressed her lips together. The sight filled her with both pride and ache. Her boy—her quiet, steady boy—was becoming a man, and she had missed it.

Words gathered before she could stop them. "I missed it." Her voice scraped. "I missed his birthday."

Don Antonio turned slightly, waiting.

She swallowed. "I forgot my son's birthday." The sentence landed between them like dropped iron. "Ginny had to take him for his license. It should've been me. I should have baked the cake, driven him to town, made a fuss... anything. And here he is..." She gestured toward the pen, hand shaking. "He's turning into a man while I stand on a porch and watch. What kind of mother forgets the day her son came into the world?"

Don Antonio did not answer at once. He placed a steady hand on her arm, his voice low, kind. "Come with me," he said. "There is something I want to show you."

He guided her back inside toward the grand ballroom, his steps unhurried, giving her time to steady herself.

Don Antonio guided June through the hushed corridors until their footsteps echoed into a vast, gilded space. The ballroom opened before her—high ceilings painted with cherubs and clouds, crystal chandeliers catching the midday light. At the far end stood a grand piano, its surface gleaming like a black anchor in a sea of gold and marble.

But Don Antonio stopped at the fireplace, where a single portrait hung.

"She was my wife," he breathed. "Isabela."

Her painted face was serene; her eyes, kind.

"She died bringing our child into the world. And I—" He drew a breath, jaw tightening. "I wasn't there. Out with friends. Cards. Drink. Foolishness." He pressed a hand briefly to his temple. "When I returned, it was too late. She was gone. I buried myself in my shame."

June stood silent, her eyes on the portrait.

"It was my brother who pushed me to come here," Don Antonio said, gesturing toward the window where the California sun poured over the land. "He said, 'Begin again.' This place saved me. This work. My son... and now Mirabella."

He turned to her, voice raw. "You are not alone, Señora June. You will find joy again."

Her gaze drifted to the piano. Jesse had played here once—the Liszt piece, full of hope. She crossed the room slowly.

Don Antonio stepped back.

"Will you play for me? For them?"

June lowered herself onto the bench. Her fingers hovered over the keys. Then, she began.

The notes rang out—haunting, sharp, aching. Jesse's music, but reshaped by grief. Every crescendo a cry, every quiet passage a prayer. She played for Jesse, her prodigal son. For Tegan, her little light. The music filled the grand room, echoing off marble and up to the painted sky.

When the last notes faded, silence held its breath.

From the doorway, a soft sob broke the stillness. June turned, startled, to see Mirabella and Agustín standing there. The girl stepped forward first, not hesitating. Her green eyes were wet but steady, her dark braid trailing over one shoulder like a tether.

She didn't speak at first. Just crossed the room and wrapped her arms around June with the certainty of someone far older than thirteen. June froze, then folded into the embrace. Mirabella pressed her cheek to June's shoulder.

"She loved it when you played," Mirabella whispered. "She said it made the house sound alive."

June's throat closed. "Tegan told you that?"

Mirabella nodded against her. "She said your music could chase ghosts."

The words broke something loose. June's tears came freely now.

"Thank you," she managed, her voice cracking. "For visiting me. Reading to me when I couldn't get out of bed. For the flowers on her grave."

Mirabella's arms tightened. "Tegan was my best friend, my sister. I'll never stop bringing flowers."

Behind them, Agustín waited silently, giving them the moment.

The chandelier light glimmered above, soft and golden. June closed her eyes, and in that instant, she felt it—not the absence, but the lift. As if the ghosts weren't gone, but rising—carried by music, memory, and a girl brave enough to love through loss.

The loft above the garage smelled faintly of sawdust and turpentine, the air still holding Jesse's presence though he hadn't slept there in weeks. Dust motes floated in the slanted shafts of light that slipped through the small window, settling over a space frozen in time.

Marshall stepped inside, the boards creaking beneath his boots. The silence pressed heavily, broken only by the faint hum of the wind against the eaves. It was as if Jesse had only stepped out for an afternoon and might return at any moment—though Marshall knew better.

The guitars lined the wall, most of them propped carelessly on stands or leaning against old amps. Sheet music lay scattered across the small table by the bed, notations scribbled in Jesse's slanted handwriting. Sketchbooks, open to half-finished drawings, sprawled across the desk. Posters curled at the corners on the walls—bands Jesse admired, places he'd wanted to see. But the one thing missing was the old Martin guitar June had saved for months to buy him. His favorite. The one Jesse had carried out with him when he left.

Marshall's gaze fell on the desk. At first, he thought the stack of papers was just more doodles, but as he leaned closer, he realized these weren't idle sketches. They were plans—detailed, practical, drawn with care.

A new sign for the chicken coop, "Casa de Cluck," rendered in bold letters with exacting measurements for wood and paint. Marshall paused, remembering the day he and Jesse had hammered the original sign into place. Jesse leaned on the post, grinning, and said he had 'a hundred more ideas for making this farm run smoother'. Marshall had been hopeful, if only for a moment, that his boy was serious about contributing to the Miller Farm. But he had dismissed the words then as youthful talk, empty promises thrown out to please a father he didn't truly understand.

Now, seeing the sketches spread before him—plans for a rainwater catch system to irrigate Grandma Ginny's garden, a carefully laid-out pasture rotation chart for the cattle—Marshall realized Jesse hadn't been spinning idle words. He had been thinking, planning, shaping a vision for the farm in his own way.

Marshall's jaw tightened. Pride and anger pulled at him in equal measure. Here were the ghosts of what could have been: a son who might have stood beside him, working shoulder to shoulder to keep the place alive. But Jesse's theft, his betrayal, and his quiet departure on a bus north had shattered that future. Marshall could have had both—the talent of the musician and the grit of the farmhand—but Jesse left sketches and silence.

He gathered the papers into a neat stack and tucked them under his arm. "Alright, son," he murmured, his voice low, almost a whisper. "If you can't be here to build it, I will."

He cast one last look around the loft—at the guitars, the drawings, the space where Jesse should have been—and then turned for the stairs.

The ghost of Jesse lingered in every corner, but in Marshall's hands were the blueprints of a boy's hope, sketches that might yet shape the farm's future.

The office smelled faintly of cedar and ink, a clean order that came from Agustín's meticulous habits. Sunlight slanted through the tall windows, striping the polished floorboards in gold. Behind the desk, Agustín arranged ledgers and binders in precise rows, as if he could maintain Estancia Castilla's business in perfect balance while the rest of the world spun out of control.

June sat in a leather chair across from him, her hands clenched together in her lap. She stared at the gleam of brass on the desk lamp, afraid of what he might say next.

Agustín leaned against the edge of the desk, arms folded loosely. He studied her with quiet patience, weighing his words. "It was the nine o'clock bus," he said at last. His voice was steady, but gentle. "North to San Francisco."

The air seemed to leave her chest. She forced herself to swallow. "So it's true. He's gone."

"I drove him there," Agustín admitted, nodding once. "He asked me not to tell anyone right away. He thought it would be easier that way."

June closed her eyes, her throat tightening. Easier. Easier for him to slip away like a shadow in the night, easier for Marshall not to face it, easier for her... not to see her son walk out the door.

Agustín crossed to the desk, opened a drawer, and withdrew two envelopes. His fingers slightly wore the paper edges as he turned them over again and again. He set them carefully on the polished surface between them. One bore her name in Jesse's uneven scrawl. The other: Hank.

June reached forward, her hand trembling as she touched the envelope. She traced the word MOM with her fingertips, the same way she way she soothed Jesse's hair when he was a boy, as if tenderness could summon him home. She didn't open it. Couldn't. Not yet. She slid both into the pocket of her dress; the fabric sagged with their weight.

"He wanted me to give them to you after he was gone," Agustín said quietly. "I've been holding onto them until I thought the moment was right. But perhaps... there is never a right moment for such things."

168

June looked up at him, her vision blurring with tears. "Do you know how to reach him?"

Agustín's expression softened with regret. "No. No address or number. Only his word." He paused, then spoke with a firmness that cut through the heaviness in the room. "But he promised me he would call once he was settled. And Jesse—" he gave a small, almost reluctant smile—"he keeps his promises when it matters."

A watery laugh broke from June's throat. She pressed her fingers to her lips. "That sounds like him." Reckless. Restless. He was always sure he'd land on his feet, even if he never thought about those he left behind.

For a long moment, neither spoke. The tick of the mantle clock filled the silence, steady and unrelenting. June lowered her gaze to the desk, trying to gather herself. Agustín leaned forward slightly, his voice quiet but certain. "Señora June, I know it feels as though he is gone for good. But the sky is wide. Messages find their way home. You will hear from him."

She nodded, though her chest ached with doubt. She wanted to believe him. Needed to.

Agustín straightened, glancing through the window where the Caprice gleamed in the courtyard, its chrome catching the afternoon light. "Let me drive you home," he offered. "Leave the car for Hank. He should have it now."

June hesitated, then nodded. Hank had earned that freedom—his license, his work, his steady presence. He was still here. He needed her more than Jesse's ghost did.

She rose slowly, pressing her hand against the envelopes in her pocket, as if to steady their weight. "Alright," she whispered.

Agustín opened the office door for her. As June stepped into the hall, she thought of her son carried north under the California sky, like a ghost already beyond reach—despite that, perhaps, tethered by paper and ink and the promise of a phone call.

The light had turned honey-gold by the time Hank made his way across the yard. The air smelled faintly of hay and wood smoke, the last warmth of the sun clinging to the barn roofs. He paused outside the workshop, the weathered door half open, and breathed in the familiar scents of sawdust and linseed oil. Inside, the glow of two oil lamps flickered across the walls, casting shadows over neatly hung tools—chisels, hand planes, hammers all in their places like soldiers in a line.

Grandpa Joe stood bent over a workbench, his strong, knotted hands guiding a plane along the edge of an oak board. His cane leaned against the bench within arm's reach. He looked up as Hank entered, his lined face breaking into a quiet smile.

"Grandma sent me," Hank said, shifting awkwardly in the doorway. "Thought you needed some help."

Grandpa Joe chuckled low in his throat, his eyes narrowing knowingly.

"Help, is it? Sounds more like she thinks I ought to talk some sense into you." He tapped the board with his knuckles. "Well, grab that sander then. Let's see if we can smooth this out."

Hank obeyed, setting the tool in his grandfather's palm. They worked in silence for a time, Grandpa Joe with the plane, Hank with the sander, the rhythmic scrape and hum blending into something steadying. The air filled with the scent of raw wood, sharp and clean.

It was Hank who broke the quiet, his voice rougher than he meant it to be.

"I should've saved her."

Grandpa Joe paused, his hands stilling on the board. He turned slowly, resting both palms on the bench. "Saved whom, son?"

Hank's jaw tightened. "Tegan. I wasn't fast enough. If I'd just gotten to her sooner..." His throat closed around the words. He set the sander down hard, dust scattering across the bench. "I should've saved her, Grandpa."

For a moment, the only sound was the faint hiss of the lamp wick. Grandpa Joe reached for his cane, pushing himself upright with a soft grunt. "Come with me."

They stepped outside, the cool evening air wrapping around them. Gravel crunched under Hank's boots, Grandpa Joe's cane tapping a slow rhythm against the dirt road. They walked in silence toward the edge of the fields, the sky above them painted in streaks of pink and purple, fading to indigo at the horizon.

Finally, Grandpa Joe spoke. "When I was about your age, I thought life was simple. Do right, work hard, and things fall into place. Then the war came. I ended up flying C-47s over Europe, hauling paratroopers behind enemy lines. I did it dozens of times—Normandy, Market Garden, places you'll only ever read about in history books." He tapped his cane once, his gaze fixed far ahead. "Got medals for it, too. Folks back home thought I was a hero."

Hank glanced at him. "Weren't you?"

Grandpa Joe gave a weary shake of his head. "No. The actual heroes were the boys jumping out the back of that plane. Eighteen, nineteen years old, parachuting into flak and tracer fire, knowing they might not live through the night.

They were the brave ones. But me?" He swallowed hard, the weight of memory dragging down his words. "I just flew the plane."

They walked a few more paces before Grandpa Joe stopped, leaning heavier on his cane. "But here's the thing—I carried guilt for years. Every time I came home safe, I thought about the ones who didn't. Thought maybe I should've done more, flown lower, turned back, something. Anything." His voice thinned, almost breaking. "But the truth is, they made their choice. Just like I made mine."

He turned to face Hank fully, his eyes sharp even in the dim light. "We all make choices, son. Tegan chose to ride that horse. You chose to go after her. That's all anyone could've done. You hear me? That's all."

Hank's chest ached, but something in his grandfather's words slipped beneath the weight he carried, easing it just enough to breathe. He nodded slowly.

"Come on," Grandpa Joe said, starting down a narrower path that led toward an old shed tucked behind the orchard.

He stopped at the door and pulled a ring of keys from his pocket. With a twist and a groan, the lock gave way. Grandpa Joe swung the door wide, and the fading light spilled over a shape draped in a dusty tarp. With a small flourish, he pulled it back, revealing a 1956 Chevrolet Apache pickup, its body painted a deep, gleaming green, chrome grill catching the light like a grin.

Hank's eyes widened. "Is that...?"

Grandpa Joe's smile deepened. "Apache Green. Spent the last year tinkering with it. We all had a hand in getting her running. We meant it for your birthday, for you and Jesse to share." His voice caught for a moment. "But now it's yours."

He held out a set of keys; the metal worn smooth from years of turning. "Your dad's not giving up Bess anytime soon. Time you had your own wheels."

Hank took the keys, his hand trembling. He climbed into the driver's seat, the cracked vinyl familiar under him. Grandpa Joe slid into the passenger side, tapping the dash affectionately.

"Go on," he said.

Hank turned the key. The engine sputtered, coughed. Then it caught with a low rumble. He gave it a little gas, and the sound steadied, strong. A grin broke across his face, the first in what felt like months.

Grandpa Joe chuckled. "That's more like it. Now ease her out—don't tear up my shed."

Hank guided the truck carefully onto the dirt road. As the headlights flickered on, throwing pale beams across the fields, they rolled past the main barn where Marshall was hauling tools back inside. Marshall glanced up at the sound, surprise etched on his face. Hank lifted a hand from the wheel in a wave. After a beat,

Marshall raised his own hand in return, a small, almost reluctant smile tugging at his mouth.

Grandpa Joe leaned back in his seat, pride softening his features. "Think you can take me to the hardware store?" he asked.

Hank's grin widened, the engine humming beneath him, the wheel steady in his hands. "Yes, sir."

They drove on into the deepening dusk, the old truck carrying them forward—two generations, each with ghosts behind them, but both choosing to keep moving under the wide, endless sky.

The 1956 Apache rumbled into the gravel lot of Greer's Hardware, headlights cutting across the storefront windows. The sky above had dimmed to a deep violet, the last streaks of daylight fading behind the hills. Inside, the glow of old fluorescent tubes spilled through the windows, steady and familiar.

Hank eased the truck into a spot near the front, cutting the engine with a satisfied twist of the key. The smell of oil and aged vinyl still clung to his hands. Grandpa Joe swung his cane down with a practiced thump, the sound echoing in the quiet evening.

The bell above the door jingled as they stepped inside. The place was exactly as Hank remembered—wooden floors worn soft by decades of boots, the air carrying the mingled scent of feed, lumber, and oiled tools. Rows of shelves stretched back in narrow aisles, stacked with everything from nails in old pickle jars to rolls of barbed wire.

"Joe Miller!" Trevor called from behind the counter, his face splitting into a wide grin. "You're just the man I was hoping to see."

Grandpa Joe tipped his cap. "What's that?"

"My wife's been after me for months. Our anniversary's coming up, and I'd like a proper dining table. Something sturdy. None of that factory junk."

Grandpa Joe's eyes twinkled. "Think I can make that happen."

The two fell easily into conversation, discussing dimensions, lumber quality, and finishes, their words drifting toward the back aisles as they examined planks. Hank hung back, only half-listening.

Something on the counter caught his eye—a bright flyer, corners curled from other curious hands. He stepped closer. Bold letters announced:

Local Rodeo – This Month Only Events: Saddle Bronc, Calf Roping, Steer Wrestling, Barrel Racing... And at the bottom, underlined in heavy ink:
Open Jackpot Race – Cash Purse $3,500

Hank's heart gave a small, quick kick. He traced the words with his eyes, lips moving silently. Jackpot Race. Open entry. No draws, no stock assignments. Just rider and horse fighting the competition for the prize.

Bob's face rose in his mind—the buckskin stallion's dark, alert eyes, the raw power coiled in his muscles when he stretched out at a gallop. The horse wasn't polished yet, not by a long shot, but he was fast. Faster than anything Hank had ever swung a leg over.

For a moment, Hank imagined it: the crowd pressing against the rails, the whistle cutting the air, and Bob surging forward beneath him, hooves tearing into the dirt, mane whipping his face. He could see the stallion's ears pinned tight, muscles driving with every stride, eating up ground like it belonged to them. No bronc ride, no borrowed mount—just the two of them, the way it had always meant to be.

And in the ranch rodeo section, there it was: team sorting, penning—work Bob was already learning, the sharp, cattle-minded moves they practiced daily. Bob, green but game, threading cattle with the quickness of thought, responding to Hank's cues like an extension of himself.

The purse amount burned into Hank's thoughts. Enough to matter. Enough to ease the weight of the mortgage, removing the ghost of the bank's deadline hanging over the farm.

He folded the flyer in half and tucked it into his back pocket.

When Grandpa Joe and Trevor returned, still debating finishes, Hank was standing straighter, his jaw set. He didn't say a word, but his mind was already far ahead—out on the arena dirt, chasing both the purse and the proof that he and Bob could do it.

For the first time in weeks, the ache of loss loosened its grip. A new pull took its place, strong and unyielding.

Bob wasn't just a horse anymore. He was the way forward.

THE THREAD THAT HOLDS

T he morning sun rose pale and cold over Estancia Castilla, stretching thin
beams across the silver-green rows of olives and down into the open
pastures. Hank swung into Bob's saddle before most of the hands had finished
their coffee. The buckskin stallion shifted under him, eager, ears pricked, steam
puffing from his nostrils in the crisp air.

Normally, Hank would have walked Bob out slowly, giving him time to settle.
Today he pressed his spurs and drove him forward at a lope, jaw tight, eyes fixed
on the far fence line. He hadn't slept. The flyer he'd found at the hardware
store still burned in his pocket like a secret he couldn't put down—local rodeo,
jackpot race, prize money big enough to make a difference. Big enough to mean
something.

He'd replayed it all night: Tegan's face the moment before she fell. Grandpa
Joe's words—*You couldn't have saved her.* His own answer to himself—*then I'll
save something.* If he and Bob could win, it would prove he wasn't the failure he
felt in his bones.

But Bob was still green. Too green.

They cut across the lower pasture, dew scattering under hooves. A few of the
hands glanced up from the pens, surprised to see Hank riding hard so early.
One called after him, but Hank didn't slow. Bob stretched into a gallop, mane
whipping, the rhythm pounding in Hank's splintered chest like a war drum.

The narrow wooden bridge came into view—a small span over the creek bed,
slick with moss where the water still pooled from winter rains. Bob had crossed it
before, always hesitant but manageable. Hank leaned low, pushing Bob forward.

"C'mon, boy. You've done this," he muttered through clenched teeth.

But Bob planted hard at the edge, nostrils flared, muscles bunched. The jolt pitched Hank forward. He jerked the reins short, jaw locked.

"Quit it! We don't have time for this."

He circled him once and came back to the bridge. Bob balked again, pawing at the boards, ears pinned.

Hank's patience snapped—so unlike him even he registered the turmoil rolling inside. Normally he'd back off, let Bob settle, and find another way. Not today. He swung out of the saddle, boots hitting the dirt. *Why did Tegan have to ride that mare? Why couldn't she just have listened to me?*

"Fine. You follow me, then."

He took the reins close to the bit and stepped onto the boards, tugging firmly. Bob snorted, eyes rolling white. His hooves clattered against the first plank.

"Easy. Easy, boy," Hank said, though his voice was sharp, not the calm drawl Bob trusted. "It's just a bridge. You've done this—"

The stallion lunged sideways, jerking the reins from Hank's hand. In a flash of buckskin and raw muscle, Bob surged forward, half rearing, half bolting. Hank had no time to move.

The impact knocked him flat. Hooves crashed into his side, a crushing weight driving the breath from him. Something cracked—once, twice—sharp as gunfire inside his ribs. His head hit the planks hard, stars exploding behind his eyes.

He dimly heard shouting. Boots thudded on wood. The world tilted sideways in a blur of sky, mane, and pain so deep he couldn't breathe.

Bob, wild-eyed, leapt clear of the bridge and tore into the pasture, reins flying.

"Hank!" Mirabella's voice sliced through the ringing in his ears. She was running, skirts gathered in her fists, hair streaming.

Hank tried to sit up, but fire ripped through his chest. His vision doubled. He collapsed back against the boards, groaning.

"Please don't... don't be worse than it looks," she whispered, eyes darting toward the distant riders galloping closer. Her hand trembled as it hovered above his temple, afraid to touch, afraid to hurt him.

She looked back down at him; her face pale, eyes wide. "You're going to be alright," she said, more to herself than to him. "You have to be."

When one cowboy shouted, closing in, she lurched to her feet, waving both arms high. "Here! Over here!" Her voice carried sharply across the pasture.

Then she dropped back beside Hank, dust streaking her knees, her braid hanging wild across her shoulder. Her voice softened to a steady rhythm, as if he might hear her through the haze. "Hold on. They're coming. Just hold on."

Two cowboys dropped to their knees beside him. One checked his pulse; the other shouted for a stretcher.

"He's busted up bad—get him to the house!"

"I'm fine," Hank rasped, though his voice sounded like broken glass. His right arm wouldn't lift. His chest felt like it was caving in.

Mirabella knelt beside him, tears streaking her cheeks. "No, you're not fine—you can't move! Don't you dare move."

Cowboys lifted him carefully, rolling him onto a rough canvas stretcher. Pain lanced white-hot through his ribs, stealing his breath until he almost blacked out.

"Concussion," one muttered. "Ribs too. Lord help him if a lung's punctured."

Mirabella grabbed Hank's hand, her grip fierce. "Stay with me, Hank. Please."

He tried to squeeze back but couldn't. His eyelids sagged. The sky above him spun—blue and endless, the same sky Tegan had disappeared under.

"Don't sell him," he whispered hoarsely. "Don't sell Bob."

Then, the blackness closed in.

The cowboys rushed the stretcher up the slope toward the estancia, Mirabella running beside them, calling for help, her voice breaking against the morning air.

The guest room smelled faintly of lavender and polished wood, but beneath it lay the sharper scent of dust and sweat carried in from the pasture. Hank lay motionless on the wide bed, his face pale, a bruise already spreading dark across his temple. His breaths came shallow, uneven, each one pulling June tighter into her grief.

She sat beside him, clutching his hand as if sheer force could anchor him. Her tears fell onto his knuckles, staining them. "We can't lose another child," she whispered, her voice raw, almost broken.

Marshall stood at the foot of the bed, arms folded across his chest, his jaw locked hard. The silence pressed on him like stone.

"What happened?" His voice was low, measured, but there was an angry wound inside it.

Mirabella shifted near the door, her braid loose, dust streaking her riding clothes. She shook her head, blinking hard. "He was working with Bob. That's all I know. It happened so fast. He was alone out there."

Don Antonio's boots clicked against the tile as he stepped forward. His expression was grave, the weight of his authority in every word. "I'm selling that horse. A dangerous stallion has no place here."

June lifted her head, her eyes red and fierce. "He's right. That horse should have been gone long ago. He's dangerous, Marshall—dangerous like the one that took our little girl. Midnight. You sold her the next day. I won't sit here and watch it happen again." Her hand trembled as she brushed the hair from Hank's damp forehead. Hank groaned as he took a shallow breath.

Marshall's gaze flicked between his wife and the boy on the bed. He opened his mouth, then closed it again, his jaw working silently. Marshall knew what Bob meant to Hank. He knew how much that horse had already mended in his boy's heart. But June's grief was its own storm, and he had no strength to stand against it—not today.

Then, a sound cut through the room.

Hank stirred, his lips parting. The words came out rough, little more than a breath, but sharp enough to stop every heart in the room: "Don't... sell him."

June froze, staring down at him in disbelief. Marshall felt his chest tighten. Mirabella clutched the doorframe, her eyes filling with tears.

Hank's eyes cracked open for the briefest second, then slipped shut again. His chest rose and fell in a shallow rhythm, but his plea hung in the air heavier than the silence that followed.

June's face crumpled. "Hank doesn't understand. He's a boy. He doesn't see how dangerous that horse is." Her voice faltered, but she didn't take it back.

Marshall stood perfectly still, shoulders taut. He wanted to speak, to say that Hank understood—that Bob was his anchor in the storm of losing Tegan, his bond to something steady. But the look on June's face stopped him. She had already lost too much, and he wouldn't pile more weight onto her grief.

The silence deepened, thick and suffocating. Tegan's ghost hovered in that room—her laugh, her empty chair, her absence at every meal. Jesse's ghost lingered too, in the loft's emptiness, in the piano gone silent.

June pressed her lips to Hank's temple. "Please, Lord, don't take him from me," she whispered.

Marshall turned his face toward the shuttered window, the lines in his brow etched deeper than ever. He didn't say a word.

The bell over the diner door jingled as another customer left, letting in a rush of bay air that carried the faint scent of salt and diesel. Agustín Castilla sat in a corner booth, posture straight as ever, a small leather portfolio resting beside him. His meetings with a wine distributor had finished that morning, and the paperwork he carried could have filled his day—but that wasn't why he was here.

The real reason was weaving between tables with a tray balanced high, sleeves rolled back, hair grown a little too long. Jesse Miller.

Agustín almost didn't recognize him at first. The boy who once spent afternoons bent over sheet music, hands finding elegance on piano keys, now carried plates stacked with cheeseburgers and fries. He wore a worn shirt, and his apron had stains. Yet there was no mistaking the swagger, the way Jesse leaned in just enough to make people feel seen, special.

At the counter sat two older women in pressed blouses, their lipstick bright even under the harsh fluorescent lights. Jesse topped off their coffees, flashing a grin.

"Now tell me," he said, voice low and playful, "do you two come here for the pie, or just for me?"

The women laughed, one swatting his arm. "Oh, Jesse Miller, you are trouble."

"Trouble keeps life interesting," he quipped, sliding their cups back with a wink.

They giggled like schoolgirls, charmed by the attention. Jesse basked in it, soaking up their warmth like stage lights. But then, turning, he caught sight of Agustín in the corner booth. His smile froze. For a beat, color drained from his face. Then, just as quickly, the charm snapped back into place.

"Well," Jesse said, striding over with the tray tucked under one arm, "if it isn't Señor Harvard in the flesh."

Agustín's mouth curved faintly. "It has been some time."

Jesse set the tray down at the edge of the table and slid into the opposite seat without asking. He leaned back, arms crossed, as if daring Agustín to comment on the apron, the grease stains, the fall from the bright promise of Yale to this chrome-and-vinyl world.

"You came all the way to San Francisco just to watch me sling hash?" Jesse asked, voice sharp with practiced levity.

"I came on business," Agustín said evenly. "But yes—I wanted to see you."

Jesse gave a humorless chuckle. "Well. Here I am. Not exactly Yale, is it?"

Agustín didn't rise to the bait. "Why did you leave without a word to your family?"

Jesse's grin slipped. His hand went to the hem of his apron, worrying the fabric between his fingers. "Because it was easier that way," he said finally. "Easier for them. Easier for me. No fights, no dragging it out. Just...quiet."

He dropped his gaze, shoulders tightening as if bracing against something only he could see. "You don't know what it's like, waking up every day with the same

178

picture in your head—knowing you should've done something different, said something different. They don't need that shadow hanging over the house."

A humorless laugh escaped him, brittle and low. "I figured if I left, maybe they could breathe again."

The sugar dispenser between them caught Jesse's eye. He spun it once, twice, avoiding the weight of those words. Finally, he said, "I'm saving. There's a conservatory here. Local. Small. But it's a shot. A couple of years, maybe. Tips, shifts... whatever it takes."

The bravado slipped then, revealing a flicker of the old Jesse—the boy with dreams bigger than the valley sky.

Silence stretched before Jesse, softer now, asked, "How's Hank?"

Agustín leaned back, watching him closely. "He's head of cattle operations now. Your brother has become the backbone of the ranch. The men look to him."

Something flickered across Jesse's face, so fast it might have been missed. Pride—fierce and raw, quickly strangled by something darker. Jealousy. Regret. He masked it with a crooked grin. "Figures. Hank always was the golden boy."

"He has earned it," Agustín said simply.

Jesse's grin faltered. He tapped the table, a restless rhythm, then pushed up as if ready to leave. "Well, good for him."

Before he could stand, Agustín reached into his portfolio and slid a plain envelope across the Formica.

"What's this?" Jesse asked, suspicion sharp in his tone.

"Tuition. For the conservatory."

Jesse's hands hovered over it, hesitant. "I don't take handouts."

"It is not a handout," Agustín said. "It is belief. From me, from your family. We all wanted to see you reach Yale. That did not happen. But the dream does not end just because it changed its shape."

Jesse's throat worked. Slowly, as if it cost him, he pulled the envelope closer, sliding it beneath the apron. "Thanks," he muttered.

Agustín rose. "I will not tell your mother I saw you, if that is what you want."

"Please don't," Jesse said quickly.

Agustín inclined his head. "Very well. But promise me you will write. Or call. One day, they deserve to hear from you."

Jesse didn't answer. He just leaned back in the booth, arms folded tight, mask slipping into place again.

Agustín studied him for a last moment, then left, the bell above the door jangling as he stepped back into the city's bustle.

Jesse sat there, staring at the place where the envelope had been, fingers brushing over the lump in his apron pocket. Pride, guilt, and shame churned inside him like storm clouds. When the two old ladies called his name, he pasted the grin back on and went to refill their coffee, his voice bright, his laughter easy.

But behind his eyes lingered the ghosts of a brother he couldn't face, a home he'd abandoned, and a dream that still might burn him alive.

The guest room carried a faint, sharp scent of Grandma Ginny's remedies—dried herbs, liniment, and the earthy tang of poultices steeped in cloth. Hank lay propped against pillows, ribs bound tight under his shirt, each breath shallow and aching. Afternoon light filtered through lace curtains, striping the floorboards in gold.

Mirabella sat beside him, a small jar of salve balanced in her hands. She dipped her fingers, pressing the cool mixture gently to the bruise along his temple. Her touch was careful, steady, but her eyes were restless, searching for a spark in his eyes.

"You should say something," she said, the words breaking the quiet. "Anything. I thought we were friends—you, me, Tegan. The three musketeers, remember?"

Hank kept his eyes fixed on the ceiling beams, his jaw set.

Mirabella's shoulders stiffened. She set the jar down harder than she meant to. "You can't just lie there and shut me out. Not after everything." Her emerald gaze burned, and her voice rose despite her effort to steady it. "Tegan wouldn't want this—your silence. She wouldn't want you shutting me out."

Hank's hand tightened in the blanket, knuckles pale. His voice came out rough, almost a growl. "You wouldn't understand." He stopped, the words choking in his throat. "You have no idea—"

Mirabella cut him off, her voice trembling with anger. "Don't you dare say that. You're not the only one who lost Tegan, Hank. I visit her grave almost every day. I bring flowers because I can't stand the thought of her being forgotten." Her voice cracked. "Do you think it doesn't tear me apart to stand there alone?"

Hank turned his head, finally meeting her eyes. The force of her grief hit him like a fist. He wanted to tell her—everything—how every step he took carried the memory of that day, how he'd never forgive himself. But the words locked in his chest. If he opened his mouth, he feared the dam would break, and he'd never be able to close it again.

Mirabella stared at him, waiting for something—anything—but his silence was its own answer. Her hands curled at her sides, shaking.

"Fine," she whispered, her breath catching. "I guess we were never friends."

She turned, her dark hair swinging, and stormed toward the door. It slammed shut behind her, rattling the frame.

The silence that followed was suffocating. Hank stared at the ceiling, the echo of her words cutting deeper than the ache in his ribs. He shut his eyes tight, but that didn't stop the image of her face—the hurt in her eyes, the tears she fought back.

And in that hollow space inside him, he realized something he hadn't dared put words to before: what he felt for Mirabella was more than friendship. It had always been more.

His chest burned—not just from broken ribs but from the weight of everything he couldn't say. Tegan. The Rodeo/Jackpot Race. Mirabella. All of it pressed against him, demanding release.

But not yet. Not now.

He rolled onto his side, every movement a jolt of pain, and buried his face in the pillow, willing the pressure in his chest to stay locked inside—for one more night.

The barn was dim, dust drifting through slats of late light. Mirabella stepped into Bob's stall without a word. The buckskin turned toward her, quiet and alert. She grabbed a brush from the rail and started working down his side—short, firm strokes. Dust rose in soft clouds. Her jaw stayed tight, her motions sharp. Then slower. Then uneven.

The brush faltered. Her breath hitched. Tears slipped down her cheeks before she could stop them. She turned her face away, wiped at her eyes with the sleeve of her shirt, then kept brushing—faster now, like movement might outrun the feeling. Bob shifted. Stepped forward. Gently, he curved his neck around her and drew her in, his chin pressing into her side, wrapping her in the weight of his head.

She froze—just for a moment—then let the brush fall. Her hands slid into his mane. She pressed her forehead against his warm neck, shoulders shaking.

Bob stood still, breathing slowly. His flank rose and fell against her ribs, grounding her.

She didn't speak. She didn't need to.

And in that silence, everything she couldn't say found its place.

181

The woodworking shed glowed amber under two oil lamps. Sawdust hung in the air like smoke. Marshall measured a cedar board, marked it, and fed it into the table saw. The blade sang. Grandpa Joe stood at the vise, planing a bracket, shavings curling to the floor in butter coils.

On the bench lay Jesse's drawings—gutters, barrels, measurements. Clean lines and neat notes. A small irrigation system, clever and complete.

"Hold that end," Grandpa Joe said, sliding a bracket across.

Marshall steadied it as Grandpa Joe bored the pilot holes. Screws rasped into wood. They worked mostly in silence—mallet taps, file strokes, the quiet talk of men with grief between them.

They carried the gutter to the door. Evening pooled violet across the yard. Out on the porch, two wine barrels waited on blocks.

"Needs a touch more pitch," Grandpa Joe said, eyeing the level.

Marshall slid in a shim. The bubble centered. "Good," Grandpa Joe said. "Let's hang her."

They fastened the gutter to the shed's eave, fitted the downspout, and wrapped thread tape on the spigot fitting. Water would feed Grandma Ginny's tomatoes in the dry season. Jesse had thought of everything.

Marshall's hand hovered over the drawings. "Tegan always defended him. Said I couldn't see what she saw." His voice dropped. "Maybe if I'd handled him better, she'd still be here."

Grandpa Joe didn't look up. He wiped his hands on his pants and leaned on his cane. "Everyone made choices. Jesse. Tegan. You. Guilt doesn't change what happened."

Marshall stared at the gutter run. "I thought he spat on everything we built. Maybe he did. Still... he had a head for this."

"Same as his old man," Grandpa Joe said. "Stubborn too."

"Stubborn didn't stop a horse."

The words dropped hard. Grandpa Joe set the drill down, then picked up the screen box. "Let's finish. The garden won't water itself."

They mounted the screen and set the first-flush pipe. Marshall clamped the overflow hose and stepped back, knees stiff. He crossed the yard and opened the pump spigot. Water banged in the hose, spilled over the roof. The gutter caught clean. A silver rope ran into the barrel, rattled, and vanished.

They stood watching. The barrel thunked as the first inches hit. A faint burble rose, soft as breath.

"He wanted to make it right," Marshall whispered. "Built signs. Sketched plans. As if work could fix it."

"Work keeps a man from drowning," Grandpa Joe said. "Doesn't heal him. But it keeps his head above."

Marshall looked toward the dark porch. "She tried to stop me that day. I pushed past her. If I'd listened…"

"Don't rewrite the day," Grandpa Joe reminded. "Memory'll twist it if you let it."

Marshall lifted Jesse's drawings and folded them carefully. "We could've had both—the farm and his music."

Grandpa Joe sank onto the step. "You can break a man trying to make him choose. Or he'll break it for you by leaving."

Marshall rubbed a palm over the barrel. Actual work finished. Jesse's lines turned into something useful.

"Jesse's ghost lives here," he murmured.

Grandpa Joe grunted. "Ghosts don't hammer brackets."

Marshall's mouth twitched. "Maybe not. But they stand near a man who does."

A drip ticked through the screen, soft and steady—a sound like a promise.

The veranda lanterns burned low, their golden glow spilling across the wide stone floor. Beyond the balustrade, the night hummed with cicadas and the faint rustle of olive leaves in the breeze. Hank shifted stiffly in his chair, ribs still aching beneath their bindings, though he wouldn't admit it out loud.

Don Antonio approached with a long, cloth-wrapped bundle in his arms, Agustín just behind him. Mirabella lingered in the doorway, her face pale and set, eyes darting once toward Hank before turning away.

"These were meant for your birthday," Don Antonio said in a solemn yet warm voice. "But good things, sometimes, arrive late."

He set the bundle across Hank's lap. Hank glanced at June, who gave him a faint nod, then peeled back the cloth. The breath caught in his throat.

The chaps gleamed in the lantern light–rich brown leather tooled with intricate designs. Along one leg, in proud lettering, was etched: *Henry Joseph Miller*. On the other side, next to each other, lay an American flag and an Argentine flag. Across the back, in bold script, read: *Estancia Castilla*.

For a moment, Hank couldn't speak. His fingers traced the stitching as though he were afraid it might vanish under his touch.

Agustín crouched beside him. "Custom work from Córdoba. Every stitch by hand. They were made for you." His tone softened. "How are you feeling?"

"Like I lost a fight with a bull," Hank said wryly, though his hand lingered on the leather.

Mirabella's lips parted, as though she might say something, but then she closed them again. She turned sharply and slipped back inside, her skirts brushing the doorway.

June's eyes followed her, then returned to her son. Pride and ache knotted together inside her chest. The boy she had once coaxed into boots two sizes too big now sat holding a gift that declared him a man. The chaps didn't just belong to a ranch hand; they belonged to someone trusted, someone recognized.

Her breath caught as she realized the distance between them. Hank was no longer the child who needed her to stand guard at his side. He had become something steadier, broader, a presence that carried weight in the world. She felt pride blooming, but threaded through with the bittersweet sting of watching him grow into a place where she could only watch, not guide.

Hank finally looked up, eyes shining in the dim light. "Thank you," he said, his voice thick. He ran his hand down the leather one last time before hugging the bundle against his chest.

Don Antonio's smile was small but knowing. "You honor us by wearing them, Hank. They carry not just leather, but our legacy."

The cicadas droned on, steady and endless, while June stood quietly by. In the gift laid across Hank's lap, she saw both the weight of his future and the shadow of all they had lost. The night air pressed heavy, thick with memory, but for once she let herself rest in the stillness—no words, just watching her son step, however painfully, into the man he was becoming.

The following morning's air at Estancia Castilla smelled of hay, leather, and the faint tang of lavender drifting up from the orchards. Sunlight slanted through the stable windows, catching dust flecks as they floated in lazy spirals. Hank winced as he eased himself into a pair of jeans, every breath tugging at his bound ribs. The bruises down his side ached, but he forced the denim up anyway, jaw set against the pain.

The chaps Don Antonio had given him the night before hung from a wooden peg. He reached for them, tracing the stitched crest of *Estancia Castilla*, his own name beneath, flanked by the flags of Argentina and the United States. They felt like a declaration — that he belonged, that he was no longer a boy trailing after Jesse but a man carving his own path.

Behind him, June's voice broke the quiet. "Hank, please don't."

184

She stood in the doorway, hands wringing the apron she hadn't realized she still wore. Her eyes were red from too many sleepless nights; her face drawn. "Don't ride that horse again. Not after what he's done to you. I can't..." Her voice faltered.

Hank straightened, ribs protesting, and met her gaze. "It wasn't Bob's fault. I pushed him too hard. He just... reacted."

Marshall appeared beside June, his arms crossed, silent but watching. He looked older in the filtered light, worry etched deep into his brow. He didn't speak, but his presence said enough: he was listening, weighing, and not ready to choose sides.

From farther down the stable, Don Antonio stepped into view, his polished boots striking the stone floor with authority. His dark eyes took in Hank's struggle, then shifted to the family. "Señora June is right. A dangerous horse has no place here. I'm selling the horse by the end of the week."

The words hung heavy in the air, thicker than the dust. Mirabella stood just behind her uncle, lips pressed tight, eyes still swollen from last night's tears. She didn't speak, only looked at Hank as though begging him to say something that would change the course already set.

Hank drew in a ragged breath, his chest burning. He squared his shoulders anyway. "No. Bob stays." His voice cracked with pain, but he pushed through. "You take him, you take the last part of me that still makes sense."

The stable fell into silence. June's lips trembled, torn between anger and fear. Marshall's jaw clenched tighter, but he still didn't speak, torn between his wife's dread and his son's resolve. Grandma Ginny reached out, laying a gentle hand on June's arm, as if to steady her before grief could swallow her whole again.

Hank pulled the chaps from their peg and slung them over his arm. He grimaced as the movement sent fire through his ribs, but he didn't let it show on his face. He took one step toward Bob's stall.

Don Antonio's voice cut sharp through the stillness. "No, Hank."

Hank froze.

The Argentine's expression softened only slightly, but his words carried the weight of finality. "The stallion is finished here. This is not open for debate."

The words landed like iron. June exhaled in relief, her shoulders slumping, while Hank's heart clenched tight in his chest. He turned slightly, meeting Don Antonio's gaze with steady eyes, but said nothing.

He tightened his grip on the chaps instead, the leather biting into his fingers, and stepped into the shadows of the stalls.

Later that morning, they would gather at June's Caprice and drive back to the Miller farm. His body battered, his family fractured, but one thing had settled deep in Hank's chest:

If they took Bob, they took the last thread holding him together.

And Hank Miller wasn't letting go.

THE EDGE OF IT ALL

The morning lay pale and cool across Estancia Castilla. Mist curled low along the olive groves, clinging to the earth as if reluctant to leave. The barns were quiet, the hands not yet stirring, and the arena stood empty, its sand dark with dew.

Mirabella slipped through the stable door with her braid pulled tight, her boots muffled in the straw. She wore tan breeches tucked into polished black boots, a fitted jacket buttoned neat despite the early hour. In her hand, a coiled lead rope swung loose, brushing against her leg as she walked.

Bob lifted his head from the hay, ears flicking, nostrils flaring. That wild gleam—half distrust, half defiance—lived in his eyes. Mirabella pressed her palm to the door and murmured soft Spanish: words of reassurance, of patience.

She slid the halter on with practiced ease and led him out into the dim light of the yard. His hooves struck hollow against the cobblestones, echoing in the quiet. At the arena gate, she paused, let him sniff the wood, then guided him inside.

The work began slowly. She stood at the center, sending him out on the circle, the rope slack between them. Bob's head bobbed nervously, but he moved, ears flicking toward her, eyes sharp. She shifted her weight, changing direction, letting him find the rhythm on his own. No pressure. No force.

When she brought him back in, she rubbed his neck, whispering close to his ear. "You're not dangerous, Bob. You're brave. I believe in you."

Her hand lingered on his withers as she guided him toward the far end of the arena where the grooms laid a wooden bridge for working equitation. Its planks were rough, hewn, and weathered, built to resemble the same narrow bridge

Hank had tried to cross on the trail. The sight alone made Bob's muscles tense beneath her hand.

Mirabella didn't even try to mount. She walked beside him, rope loose, stopping when he stopped.

Bob stretched his neck, sniffed the boards. His ears flicked back, then forward. Mirabella didn't pull. She let him breathe, let him look, let him decide. After a long minute, he lowered his head and touched the wood with his muzzle. Mirabella smiled faintly, rubbing his shoulder. "See? You can face it. You're stronger than they think."

What she didn't know was that Hank had arrived.

He stood just outside the arena gate, leaning against the fence, ribs still bound beneath his shirt. He'd come earlier than usual, restless, and now he was watching in silence. His breath caught when he saw her hand resting steadily on Bob's neck, her voice low and calm.

Despite their fight, despite his silence, Mirabella hadn't turned her back on him—or the stallion. She was here at dawn, alone, believing when even he had doubted.

For a moment, Hank felt something twist inside him—pride, gratitude, and a shame he couldn't name. He had pushed her away, shut her out, but she was still here. Always here.

Mirabella turned Bob in another circle, then let him halt, stroking his muzzle as though sealing some quiet pact. She exhaled, brushing a stray strand of hair from her cheek. That was when she spotted him. Hank straightened, trying to school his face, but the look was already there. She froze, color rising in her cheeks.

"You're here early," she said, fumbling with the lead rope.

"Could say the same for you," Hank answered, voice guarded.

She lifted her chin. "He needed someone to believe in him."

The words landed between them heavier than she intended. Hank's jaw tightened. He wanted to tell her he knew, that he saw, that it meant something he couldn't put into words. But pride, guilt, and the wall he'd built around himself held him silent.

Mirabella looked at him for another heartbeat, then shook her head, tugging Bob gently toward the gate. "I should go."

She brushed past him without another word, the scent of lavender clinging faintly as she disappeared into the barn shadows.

Hank watched her go. For the first time, he noticed the heaviness in her steps, the shadows under her eyes. Not just angry—exhausted, worn thin by loss. Their fight had cut deep, but beneath it was something deeper still—the hollow ache of Tegan's absence.

A pang struck him as sharp as the ache in his ribs. Mirabella carried Tegan's ghost just as he did—maybe even more. Every flower she laid at the grave, every hour she spent here with Bob, was her way of holding on.

He opened his mouth, almost called her name. The words lodged in his throat. He closed it again, fists tightening at his sides.

Bob shifted beside him, ears flicking. Hank reached out, running a hand along the stallion's neck where Mirabella's hand had been moments earlier.

The sand was damp, the air cool, but the warmth of what he'd seen lingered. She hadn't given up—on Bob, or on him.

Even when he tried to push her away, Mirabella was still there.

The barn was hushed after Mirabella's footsteps faded, the morning light cutting thin through the slats. Hank eased the stall door open, ribs aching, and slipped inside. Bob stood tense in the corner, head high, ears flicking, the whites of his eyes showing.

When Hank raised the brush, Bob flinched, shifting his weight like he might bolt. Hank lowered his hand.

"I know," he whispered, voice ragged in the stillness. "I don't blame you."

He tried again, slower this time. The brush touched Bob's shoulder, light as a feather. The stallion's skin quivered, but he didn't shy away. Hank kept his strokes steady, long and even.

"I pushed you too hard," he whispered. "Tried to make you carry what wasn't yours. That bridge...I should've listened when you said no. I didn't. And you panicked. Can't blame you for that. I'm sorry, boy."

The stallion blew out a breath, loud but not sharp, and turned his head slightly toward him. Hank stayed with the rhythm of the brush, shoulders loosening as the tension bled away.

"You were scared. So was I," Hank admitted. "Guess we both lost our footing."

Bob stepped closer, muzzle brushing against Hank's chest with tentative weight. The contact knocked the air from his ribs, but Hank stood still, one hand sliding up into the thick black mane.

"Alright," he murmured. "You forgive me, I forgive you. Fresh start."

The stallion exhaled again, softer this time, leaning into him. It was enough—an answer in its own way.

As Hank rested there, forehead against the warm hide, a memory flickered unbidden. Tegan skipping at his side, her small hand tugging at his, blue eyes dancing with mischief. *I can't wait to come back. Me, you, and Mirabella—we're gonna be like the Three Musketeers!*" she'd laughed. "*We should name that horse Bob. Bob's a good name.*"

Hank had rolled his eyes, cheeks burning, especially with Mirabella standing right there. But she'd only smiled, her emerald eyes bright, and the silly name had stuck.

Now, standing in the stall, Hank felt the weight of it. That plain name, born of his sister's laughter, tied them together in a way nothing else could. Bob wasn't just a horse—he was a thread to Tegan, something alive that carried her memory forward.

Hank tightened his grip on the mane, a lump rising in his throat. For a moment he couldn't breathe.

Bob shifted again, steady against him. Hank let the silence hold, the air thick with dust, hay, and forgiveness. He didn't need to say more. The stallion had given his answer.

The sun stood high over the courtyard, bright and hot against the whitewashed walls of Estancia Castilla. Cowboys leaned on the fence rails, drinking from tin cups, their shirts dark with sweat. Somewhere, a windmill creaked lazily in the breeze. Hank wiped his brow with the back of his sleeve, ribs aching from the morning's work.

Agustín's voice carried from across the yard. "Hank. A word."

Hank handed off the lead rope to another hand and walked over, boots crunching on gravel. Agustín stood inside the verandah's shade, a ledger tucked under his arm. His dark hair was damp at the temples, his face serious.

"I wanted you to hear this from me," Agustín began. His tone was calm, but the weight behind it was clear. "We've found a buyer for the stallion."

Hank froze. "What?"

"A breeder from Texas. He's made an offer. He'll be here at the end of the week to see Bob."

The words struck like a fist to the gut. Hank's chest tightened, his ribs screaming with the sharp breath he dragged in. "You can't—"

Agustín raised a hand, steady but firm. "Listen, Hank. My father respects you. You've proven yourself here. The men follow your lead with the cattle, and he trusts your judgment. But the horse..." He let the words settle, his gaze steady. "Bob is different. My father won't risk him hurting one man—or Mirabella. He's firm on this."

Hank's fists curled at his sides. "Bob isn't dangerous. He just needs time. He needs trust. If anyone gave him half a chance—"

190

"We have given him chances," Agustín said, not unkindly. "But you saw what happened. You carry the scars of it now." His eyes flicked to Hank's bound ribs. "This is not about you alone. My father must think of everyone here. He won't change his mind."

Hank shook his head, heat rising in his chest. "You don't understand. He's all I've got left—" He bit the rest back.

Agustín's expression softened, but only slightly. "I understand more than you think. But sometimes, Hank, understanding doesn't change the outcome."

Bob—Tegan's Bob—sold off to a stranger. Unthinkable.

Agustín laid a hand briefly on Hank's shoulder. "Take the rest of the afternoon. Cool your head. This isn't your fight to win."

But Hank was already pulling away, jaw clenched, anger burning hotter than the sun overhead. He stormed across the courtyard, ignoring the stares of the hands.

As he passed the verandah, he glimpsed Mirabella standing in the archway. Her eyes followed him, curious, uncertain—she hadn't heard the words, but she read the anger and pain carved across his face. He didn't slow, didn't look back.

The crunch of gravel under his boots rang loudly in his ears. He wasn't sure if it was fury, grief, or both clawing at his chest, but he knew one thing: if Don Antonio sold Bob, a piece of him went with the stallion.

At the far gate, his hand brushed against the folded flyer tucked into his back pocket—the one for the local rodeo, the jackpot race advertised in bold letters. The prize money had caught his eye before. Now it glowed in his mind like salvation.

If he and Bob could win, the money might be enough to change things. Enough to prove Bob's worth. Enough to keep him.

Hank's ribs ached with each breath, but resolve settled in his bones heavier than pain.

He didn't just need to win for himself, or for the farm.

He had to win to save Bob.

The olive grove shimmered in the late afternoon heat, silver leaves flashing under the sun, shadows stretched long between the rows. Hank sat with his back to the trunk, hat tipped low, a hand pressed against his ribs. His chest ached worse than the break itself, worse than the bruises. It was the ache of something slipping from him, something he couldn't stop.

He didn't hear her until she was standing a few paces away.

Mirabella's braid swung down her back, the hem of her breeches stained with dust from the yard. Her cheeks were flushed, though not from running. From anger. From hurt.

"I heard," she said, voice taut. "About the buyer. Bob."

Hank's jaw clenched. He stared at the ground; the ants threading through the dry grass.

"They said a breeder from Texas. End of the week." She took a breath. "I know we're not friends anymore. You made that clear. But I came anyway."

He looked up, blue eyes blazing with something she couldn't name. Then he looked away again, hand gripping his knee until the knuckles whitened.

"You shouldn't have," he muttered.

Her voice softened. "Maybe not. But you shouldn't be alone either."

Something inside him cracked at that. A sound left his throat that was closer to a laugh, closer to a sob, and his head dropped into his hands.

"It's my fault," he said, voice muffled.

Mirabella froze. "What is?"

His hands fell; his face twisted with pain that had nothing to do with ribs. "Tegan." The name came out broken. "I wasn't fast enough. She took off, and I—I was right behind her. One more stride. If I'd been quicker, if I'd cut across the field—" His voice collapsed into silence, shoulders shaking.

"You chased her," Mirabella whispered. "You went after her."

"Too slow!" His voice rang sharply through the grove. Birds startled from the branches above, wings clapping against the leaves. He dragged a hand through his hair, eyes wild. "Every night I see it. Her braid flying, her scream—God, she screamed right before—" His voice cracked, and he pressed his fist against his mouth. "And then nothing. Just...nothing."

Tears stung her eyes, but she forced them back. He'd never spoken this way to anyone. Never let it out. She wouldn't stop him now.

"She always defended Jesse," Hank went on, voice hoarse. "Even when he stole. Even when Dad came down on him, she stood between them. Said he just needed time. Said we had to believe in him." He let out a bitter laugh. "And he left anyway. Skipped the funeral. Left Mom in her room, Dad breaking himself over the fields. Left me carrying it all. He didn't even say goodbye."

He bent forward, elbows on his knees, shaking his head. "House feels like a grave. Mom barely talks. Dad tries, but he's...hollow. And I can't—I can't let them see me break. Someone has to hold it together."

Her throat tightened. "So you carry it alone."

"I try to." His voice faltered. "But I heard them. Dad and Grandpa. In the office. The bank is ready to take the farm. A month, maybe two. Grandpa offered his Normandy money. Dad wouldn't take it. And all I could think was—it's on me now. Sixteen years old, and it's on me." He lifted his face finally, eyes raw and wet. "What kind of son, what kind of brother, just lets it fall apart?"

Mirabella stepped closer, her boots crunching on the dry soil. She crouched, her emerald eyes level with his. "Not your fault," she whispered.

He let out a choked sound. "I found a flyer in town. Rodeo. Jackpot race. Purse big enough to matter." He patted his pocket, though the paper wasn't there. "If Bob and I win, I can prove he's worth keeping. Buy time for the farm. Maybe—maybe fix something."

"Hank..."

"I know it's crazy." His voice cracked again. "But Bob—he's all I've got left of her. She named him, you remember? Called him Bob like it was the funniest thing in the world. She tied him to us. To me." His hand curled into a fist. "If I lose him, I lose her all over again."

The grove was silent except for his breath, the rattle of cicadas.

"And you," he whispered, words tumbling before he could stop them. "You're the only one who makes me feel like I'm not drowning. When you're around, I can breathe. When you're gone, it's gray. You matter to me, Mia. More than I can say without sounding stupid."

Her eyes widened. A tear slid free. "I didn't know. I thought you hated me. Thought I annoyed you."

He gave a broken laugh. "I told myself I did. But I could never hate you, Mia." His voice dropped, rough with honesty. "It's always been the opposite."

Her breath hitched. "Then why push me away?"

"Because when you're near, it's easy to breathe. Too easy. And that scared me." His shoulders slumped. "But I don't want to pretend anymore."

She reached for his hand. He didn't hesitate this time. Their fingers laced, strong and trembling all at once. For a long moment they just knelt in the grove, hands locked, grief and silence binding them. Then, as if drawn by the same pull, they leaned forward.

The kiss was clumsy, unsteady, raw with everything they couldn't say. Her lips were warm and wet with tears, his breath sharp with salt. It lasted only a few heartbeats, then they pulled apart, eyes wide, startled by their own courage.

Neither spoke. Neither apologized.

Mirabella pressed her fingers to her mouth, then let them fall, a small smile breaking through tears. "I'm here," she whispered. "Even if you push me away. I'll still be here."

Hank squeezed her hand, his chest aching but lighter. "I don't want to push anymore."

They sat in the grove, her head on his shoulder, until the shadows stretched longer, cicadas screaming in the heat. And for the first time since Tegan's death, Hank felt the weight shift—not gone, never gone, but shared.

The barn smelled of old hay and machine grease–the scent that lingered in wood and cloth long after the day's work was done. Evening shadows stretched across the floorboards, turning tools into silhouettes. Hank crouched beside the '56 Apache truck, sleeves rolled to his elbows, a wrench in his hand. His ribs still throbbed when he bent too far, but he worked anyway, jaw tight with concentration.

The sound of boots on wood made him glance up. Marshall stepped inside, hat low, a sliver of light catching the lines etched deep into his face. He said nothing at first, just leaned against the stall door, watching his son's hands move over the engine.

"Don Antonio called," Marshall said finally, his voice even but heavy. "I talked to him about Bob, but the buyer's still coming. End of the week."

The wrench slipped from Hank's fingers and clattered onto the floor. He stared at the engine block, jaw set hard, then pushed himself to his feet.

"I can't let them take him, Dad." His voice cracked sharply in the still barn. "I get why Mom's afraid. But Bob isn't just a horse to me. He's the work I started, and I have to see it through. You've always said a man finishes what he begins. I can't walk away from him now."

Marshall's eyes flickered, the weight of those words pulling at something buried deep. He shifted his hat in his hands, thumb worrying the brim.

"Your mother's been through more than most folks could carry," he breathed. "Give her time, Hank. She can't see straight right now. Fear's got a hold on her, and it doesn't let go easily."

Hank shook his head. "Time's exactly what I don't have. If I quit on Bob, if I let him be sold, then everything I've poured into him means nothing. That's not how you raised me."

Marshall stepped forward, boots crunching on stray gravel that had worked its way into the barn. He stopped beside the truck, looking at his son not as a boy but as something in between—half-grown, carrying burdens too heavy.

"I don't pretend to understand all of what Bob means to you," Marshall admitted. "But I can see it. You're standing taller because of him. Stubborn, sure. But he's kept you moving when the rest of us are stuck."

Hank swallowed hard, blinking back the burn in his eyes.

Marshall let out a long breath, gaze falling to the concrete floor. "I've already buried one child. I can't—" His voice faltered, and he started again. "I won't make promises I can't keep. Not about your mother, not about Don Antonio, not about that horse."

The words landed heavily, but they weren't a dismissal. They were an admission—of fear, of love, of a man trying to hold too much.

"But," Marshall said, his tone softer now, "I'm not telling you to give him up either."

Hank looked up, surprise flickering.

Marshall placed a steady hand on the truck's fender, the gesture grounding. "Sometimes a man needs something to anchor him. Maybe Bob's that for you. Maybe that's what your mom hasn't seen yet. Just...don't lose yourself trying to hold on to him."

The silence stretched, filled only by the creak of the rafters and the ticking of the cooling engine.

Hank nodded slowly, his throat too tight to speak.

Marshall reached for his hat again, settling it back on his head. "Finish up here. Supper'll be ready soon."

He turned and walked out, the barn door groaning shut behind him.

Hank stood alone in the fading light, grease on his hands, heart pounding with the weight of his father's words. Marshall hadn't promised. But he hadn't shut him down either.

For now, that was enough.

The farmhouse was hushed, the quiet that came only when every lamp was out and every door latched. Crickets hummed beyond the fence line, and the stars hung heavy above, a thousand cold lights stitched across the sky.

Marshall sat on the porch steps, hat tipped back, elbows resting on his knees. The screen door creaked, and June stepped out, robe drawn close around her shoulders. She paused, as if deciding whether to turn back inside, then sat on the step above him.

"He was quiet at supper tonight," Marshall said after a stretch of silence.

June glanced down. "Hank?"

Marshall nodded. "Didn't say more than two words. I think it's because of the sale. Don Antonio found a buyer for the stallion."

June's shoulders eased, and she let out a slow breath. "Good. I won't have to worry about that horse anymore."

Marshall turned his head, studying her face in the dim porch light. "You think it's good?"

She looked at him sharply. "That horse trampled him, Marshall. Nearly broke him in half. And after Tegan—" Her voice faltered, the name catching in her throat. She pressed her hands together in her lap, knuckles white. "I can't watch another child laid in the ground."

Marshall lowered his gaze to the porch boards. "He's not a child anymore. He's sixteen. Stubborn, hard-headed, sure, but he's standing taller than most men I know." He hesitated, then added, "Maybe that stallion's the only thing keeping him upright."

June shook her head quickly, her hair falling loose around her face. "No. Don't say that. That horse is dangerous. It's too close. Too much like—" Her voice broke, and she turned away. "I can't do it again."

She rose abruptly, robe brushing the steps as she moved to the door.

"June," Marshall whispered.

But she didn't turn. The screen banged shut behind her, leaving him alone with the stars and the creak of the windmill.

Marshall pulled the brim of his hat low over his eyes. He understood her fear, but what she saw as danger, he saw as Hank's anchor. And that difference stretched between them like the night sky — wide, dark, and unbridgeable.

The dream came fast, jagged, wrong.

Midnight's hooves didn't pound so much as *boom*, each strike like a drumbeat inside Hank's skull. Dust rolled in waves, choking the air, turning the pasture into a storm of brown and gray.

Tegan clung to the filly's mane, her braid flying apart, her face wet with tears—but in the dream her eyes glowed too blue, too bright, like shards of glass. She didn't look at him. She never looked at him.

"T-Rex!" Hank screamed, but his voice echoed back at him, empty, like shouting into a canyon.

The fence loomed ahead, but it warped in his vision, stretching higher, impossibly high, until it blotted out the sky. The boards twisted like ribs, pinning him on one side and her on the other.

Midnight screamed, a sound like tearing metal. Tegan kicked, heels slamming against the filly's sides—and then she lifted, not just over the rail, but into the air. Her body bent in the wind, arms outstretched, reaching for him at last.

Hank reached back, but his fingers passed through hers like smoke.

Her braid unraveled completely, strands whipping loose, carried away until nothing was left.

Then the crack came—bone against wood, louder than thunder, louder than anything—and she was gone. Only stillness. Only the weight of silence pressing on his chest.

Hank ran, legs pumping, but the ground stretched under him like taffy, pulling him farther away with every stride. He shouted her name until his throat burned, but no sound came out at all.

She didn't move.

He jolted awake, chest heaving, sweat dampening his shirt. His ribs screamed when he sat up, each breath jagged. The room was thick with shadow, moonlight slanting through the window. For a moment, he couldn't move. Couldn't breathe.

Finally, he shoved back the covers and swung his legs over the edge of the bed, shoving his feet into boots. He moved down the hall in silence, careful not to wake anyone, and pushed open the screen door.

The night air was cool against his fevered skin. Stars burned sharp above, and the windmill creaked in the distance, steady and hollow.

Hank sat on the porch steps, elbows braced on his knees, face in his hands. His breath slowed, but the images didn't fade. Tegan's scream, the crack of wood, her stillness—they lingered like ghosts, bright as the stars.

After a long while, he lifted his head and looked out toward the dark fields. His voice came low, raw, the kind meant for no one's ears but the night.

"You named him, T-Rex. Bob. Thought it was funny—this wild, stubborn stallion with a plain name. You laughed like it made perfect sense." His throat tightened, and he pressed his palms together. "Now he's all I've got left of you."

He dragged in a breath, ribs aching, and forced the words out. "They want to sell him. Don Antonio, Agustín, even Mom. They think he's too dangerous." His jaw clenched. "But you saw more. And Mirabella sees it too. She believes in him. She believes in me."

He stared into the dark, searching for something beyond the horizon. "I won't let them take him. Not Bob. Not the last piece of you I can still touch. I'll find a way."

The vow rang low but steady, settling into his bones.

The first gray of dawn bled across the fields, the windmill groaning once more as the breeze picked up. Hank pressed a hand against his ribs and whispered into the waking sky:

"Me, you, Mirabella—Three Musketeers. That's what you said. We'll carry it on, Tegan. I promise."

The sun crept higher, silvering the pasture, and Hank kept his eyes fixed on the horizon. Bob wasn't just a horse. He was Tegan's legacy—and Hank's last chance to make things right.

A Second Chance

The morning lay quiet over Estancia Castilla, dew silvering the rosemary hedges and fog still clinging to the olive trees. Most of the hands were still at breakfast, their laughter drifting faintly from the cookhouse. The main arena, bordered by whitewashed rails, stood empty in the stillness.

Mirabella slipped through the gate with Bob at her side, her small hand steady on the lead rope. The buckskin's ears flicked nervously, breath puffing white in the chill, but he followed her willingly, head lowered just enough to show his trust.

She wore breeches and tall boots polished from yesterday's ride. Her braid hung loose against her back as she clipped the reins to the bridle and swung lightly into the saddle. She breathed once, deep and measured, then nudged him forward.

"Easy, Bob," she murmured. "Just you and me now."

The first minutes were stiff. His strides rushed, his head flung high, muscles bunched beneath the saddle. Mirabella sat steady, quiet hands, seat soft but insistent. She guided him through wide serpentines, slowing her posting, coaxing his rhythm to match hers. Half-halts checked his speed, reminding him she was there. A few steps of leg yield, then back straight, patient repetition.

Bob snorted, tossed his head, and tried to brace. Mirabella didn't pull. She waited. She asked again, gentle but firm.

Gradually, the fight bled out of him. His back lifted, his stride lengthened, and his head lowered into the contact, the reins humming with softness instead of strain. His jaw worked, licking his lips, the tightness in his body melting.

Mirabella smiled, a flicker of triumph in her green eyes. "There you are," she whispered. "I knew you could."

From the shadows of the veranda, unseen until then, Don Antonio watched. He crossed his arms, his face carved with disapproval. This was the stallion he had already deemed too dangerous, too costly. And yet... the picture before him unsettled his judgment. The horse looked different. Calmer. His niece sat proudly in the saddle, seat balanced, hands steady like her mother's had once been.

Still, rules were rules.

He stepped out of the shade, boots striking the gravel. His voice carried sharply across the arena. "Bob is off limits. Did you not hear me the first time?"

Mirabella's cheeks flushed, but her back straightened. She did not argue. Instead, she brought Bob to a halt with quiet precision, swung out of the saddle, and led him toward the wash rack. Her silence was its own defiance.

Don Antonio followed, his shadow long behind her. At the wash rack, she looped the reins over the post, grabbed the sponge, and began cooling Bob's neck. Steam rose where the water touched his coat; the stallion sighed in relief.

Finally, Mirabella spoke, her voice trembling but strong. "If you're set on selling him," she blurted, "then I'll buy him." She scrubbed Bob's withers, jaw tight. "I'll use my birthday money. Every peso. I don't care. Hank deserves a second chance. So does Bob."

The words rang sharper than she intended, but she didn't look at him. She focused on the sponge in her hand; the horse leaned into her touch as if to shield her.

Don Antonio's jaw worked. He shook his head slowly. Anger simmered in him—not only at her disobedience, but at the sharp reflection of himself he saw in her. That same defiance, that refusal to bow even when outmatched. Her mother had carried it, too.

It frightened him, that fire. He had buried men who carried too much of it, men who rushed headlong where patience might have saved them. He had tried to stamp it out of himself once, bury it beneath business ledgers and responsibility. And yet, seeing it now in Mirabella—his blood, his family—filled him with something dangerously close to pride.

She had worked the stallion well. Better than many seasoned hands he had paid over the years. Fearless, steady, with a quiet determination he recognized and respected even as he tried to deny it.

"I will think about it," he muttered at last, his voice low.

He pivoted and walked away, his boots grinding against the gravel. His shoulders were stiff; his stride clipped with irritation. But pride gnawed at the edges of his anger. He would not praise her—he could not encourage such reckless defiance—but inside, he marveled at her steel.

Mirabella exhaled, pressing her cheek against Bob's damp neck. "They don't see you like I do," she whispered. "But they will."

Bob blew out a breath, warm and steady, as if agreeing.

After they penned and counted the cattle, the sun hung low and hot, smearing the pastures in gold. Hank's shirt clung damp with sweat, his ribs ached with every breath, and dirt streaked his forearms like war paint. He pulled off his gloves and wiped his brow, but instead of following the other hands toward the cookhouse, he turned his boots toward the house.

The halls of Estancia Castilla were cool and dim, the thick adobe walls keeping the heat at bay. He passed through the tiled corridor, boots echoing against the floor, until he reached Don Antonio's office. The heavy wooden door was ajar.

Hank paused, rubbed his palms against his jeans, then knocked once and stepped inside.

Don Antonio sat at his broad mahogany desk, a ledger open in front of him, spectacles perched low on his nose. He looked up, expression unreadable.

"Yes, Hank?"

Hank cleared his throat, nerves coiled tight, but his voice came steady. "I want to buy Bob."

Don Antonio blinked once, then leaned back in his chair, folding his hands over his middle. "Do you now?"

"Yes, sir." Hank stood straight, though his muscles burned with fatigue. "I'll take him to the Miller farm. Train him myself. He'll be mine to answer for."

The older man studied him, dark eyes sharp. "You're a bold one. Do you know what a horse like that is worth?"

Hank swallowed. "Enough that I have to earn it. And I will."

Amusement flickered across Don Antonio's face, though he masked it quickly. Two offers in a single day—one from his fiery niece, now this from the boy who had been through fire himself. He tapped a finger lightly on the ledger.

"And how," he asked slowly, "will you pay for such an animal?"

Hank's answer came without hesitation. "Dock my wages. Every week, every month. I'll work it off. And the rest—" He drew in a breath, steadying himself. "The rest will come from the rodeo. There's a jackpot race coming. Bob and I can win it."

Don Antonio tilted his head, studying him as if measuring weight on a scale. The boy's shoulders were squared; his voice carried no bravado, only resolve. Dust clung to his hair, sweat traced his temple, but his eyes were steady—blue and unflinching.

"You would gamble on the future of your farm with a green stallion and your own sore ribs," Don Antonio said.

"Yes, sir," Hank replied. "Because I believe in him. And I won't quit."

The room was quiet except for the faint tick of a clock on the shelf. Don Antonio let the silence stretch, testing the boy's resolve. Hank didn't look away.

At last, Don Antonio sat forward, closing the ledger with a soft thump. "I will consider your proposal. You shall have my decision by day's end."

Relief didn't show on Hank's face, but he nodded once, sharply. "Thank you, Don Antonio."

"Go on, then," the older man said, dismissing him with a wave of his hand. "Wash the dust from your throat. You've earned your supper."

Hank turned and left the office, the weight of his words still heavy in the air. He didn't know that only hours earlier, Mirabella had stood in the same defiance, offering her own future for the same horse.

Behind him, Don Antonio leaned back once more, eyes narrowing with thought. Two young hearts had laid claim to the stallion in a single day. He had expected obedience. Instead, he faced conviction.

And conviction, he knew, was harder to break than any horse.

The kitchen smelled faintly of biscuits and coffee from breakfast, though the table now sat empty and quiet. Afternoon light streamed through the curtains, painting long stripes across the worn wood. June stood at the sink, her hands in warm water, scrubbing slowly at the same plate she'd already rinsed twice.

The shrill ring of the telephone startled her. For a second her heart leapt, as if some part of her had been waiting for this very sound. She dried her hands quickly and snatched up the receiver.

"Hello?"

A pause, then a familiar voice, rough but trying for cheer. "Hey, Mom."

June's knees nearly buckled. "Jesse?" Her voice trembled, but joy bloomed in her chest, almost giddy. "Oh, Jesse—it's you."

He laughed lightly, though the sound was thin, forced. "Yeah. It's me. I'm doing alright. Got a job waiting tables at a diner downtown. Been saving up."

June pressed the phone tighter against her ear, eyes stinging. "You sound tired."

"Long hours," he admitted, but his tone shifted quickly, a mask slipping back in place. "It's fine. I'm getting by, thinking about enrolling at a conservatory here in the city. Not Yale, but—still music. You know?"

June closed her eyes. She knew that tone. She had heard it every time he had tried to convince his father of some scheme, every time he swore he'd practiced his audition pieces when he hadn't. It was a lie, or at least only half the truth. But she didn't challenge him. Not now.

"That sounds wonderful," she breathed, willing herself to believe it. "A school in San Francisco, that would be...that would be something, Jesse."

She hesitated, then asked, "Where are you staying?"

There was a beat of silence on the other end, just the faint hiss of the line. Finally he said, "With some friends. It's fine, Mom. Don't worry about it."

June's fingers tightened around the receiver. She wanted to believe him, but the hollowness in his voice told her enough.

"Jesse..." Her voice cracked. "Come home. Please. We need you here. Hank—he was in an accident with that stallion. He's alright now, but the family needs you."

The line went quiet again. She could almost picture him, head bowed in some dim diner kitchen, shame pressing heavy on his shoulders.

When he finally spoke, his voice was low, steady but heavy. "I can't come back. Not yet."

"Why not?" The plea broke out of her, raw. "You're my son. You belong here with us."

"I'll only make it worse." His breath hitched, almost too quiet to catch. "Hank can take care of himself. He always could."

The light in the kitchen seemed to dim, her second chance at happiness slipping away like water through her fingers. June pressed her free hand to her mouth, biting back the sob building in her chest.

"I love you, Jesse," she whispered into the receiver. "You'll always have a place here. Always."

He didn't answer, only gave a quiet sigh before the line clicked dead.

June lowered the phone slowly, the dial tone buzzing in her ear. She set the receiver back in its cradle and sank into the nearest chair. Her hand covered her mouth, but it couldn't hold back the hot tears spilling down her cheeks.

For one moment, when she'd heard his voice, she thought her family had been given back to her. She thought they might be whole again.

But the house was quiet, the chair beneath her cold, and she knew the truth: Jesse was gone. Maybe not forever, but for now—and that hurt more than anything.

The evening lanterns glowed warmly along the barn aisle, their light flickering across the whitewashed walls. Hank eased open Bob's stall, sore from the day's work but restless, needing to see him.

He stopped short.

Mirabella was already there, her braid slipping over her shoulder, brushing long strokes down Bob's golden side. The stallion leaned into her touch, eyelids heavy, utterly at peace.

She looked up, startled, then smiled—small, tentative. "I thought you might come."

Hank shifted his weight, suddenly aware of the dust on his shirt. He tried to clean up his appearance but relented. "Couldn't stay away," he admitted, his voice low.

For a moment, they just looked at each other, the air thick with something unspoken. After what he had told her in the grove, everything felt different now—new, fragile. Hank had never liked a girl before. He wasn't sure what to say, or what to do with the way his chest tightened just seeing her there.

"You're good with him," he finally managed.

Mirabella ducked her head, brushing another line down Bob's flank. "He trusts me. Maybe more than I deserve."

Hank moved closer, resting a hand on Bob's neck opposite hers. Their fingers nearly brushed, and both pulled back at once, cheeks warming. They laughed softly, nervous and awkward, like children caught sharing a secret.

Don Antonio stepped into the doorway, arms crossed, his shadow stretching long across the straw. His gaze swept from Hank to Mirabella, eyes dark but glinting with something more than anger.

"Well," he said, voice rich and steady, "this explains much. Two offers in one day—for the same horse."

Both of them froze, heads snapping toward him.

Don Antonio strode in, hands clasped behind his back. He let the silence draw out, his expression grave—though the faint curl of his lips betrayed him.

"Two children trying to outwit me," he continued, his accent lacing the words with music. "Both of you are certain you know best. What am I to do with such a rebellion under my roof?"

Mirabella bit her lip, eyes wide. Hank straightened, jaw set, but said nothing.

Don Antonio stopped before them, placing a hand on Bob's shoulder. The stallion flicked an ear but didn't shy away. Don Antonio gave a small nod, almost to himself, then looked between them with a sudden spark of mischief.

"I suppose the only answer," he said, drawing it out, "is that you will both own him. Half and half." His brow arched. "You will share the trouble, share the work, and share the glory—or share the blame."

Mirabella gasped, then laughed through it, covering her mouth with her hand. Hank blinked, stunned.

Don Antonio's tone softened, warm now. "He deserves a second chance. And so do the two of you."

Mirabella dropped the brush and flung her arms around his neck. "Gracias, Tío!" she whispered, muffled against his coat.

He chuckled, patting her back. "You see, Hank? I am too soft with her. She twists me like a rope."

Hank's mouth tugged into the faintest smile. He stepped forward and offered his hand. "Thank you, sir."

Don Antonio shook it firmly, his grip strong. "Agustín will draw up the papers tomorrow. We'll make it official. And..." he paused, his eyes glinting with pride, "Estancia Castilla will sponsor you in the rodeo, Hank. A Miller with Castillas at his back—think of the headlines."

Hank's eyes widened. "Sponsor me?"

"Sí," Don Antonio said with a wink toward Mirabella. "He has earned it. And it will be good for business. Now don't make me regret it."

Mirabella laughed, her eyes shining as she glanced at Hank. He looked back, still stunned, but something unspoken passed between them: the surprise, the relief, and the quiet knowledge that they had both fought for the same thing.

Bob shifted again, lowering his head between them, and Don Antonio clapped his hands once. "Bueno. Tomorrow we begin. For now, let the horse rest. You have both worked him enough."

With that, he turned, stride confident, humming to himself as he left the stall.

Mirabella bent to pick up the brush, cheeks flushed. Hank ran a hand down Bob's neck, their fingers brushing briefly as they worked side by side in silence.

For the first time in weeks, the future felt less like a weight—and more like a promise.

Mirabella was still laughing when she clipped Bob's lead and led him out of the stall, her excitement carrying her down the aisle. Don Antonio watched her go, fondness softening the edges of his stern face.

Then he turned to Hank, still lingering by the gate. "Hank," he said, gesturing with a tilt of his head. "Walk with me."

They crossed the courtyard, lanterns glowing against whitewashed walls. The olive trees whispered in the breeze; the fountain trickled steadily. Don Antonio slowed, studying Hank in the dim light. The boy's shoulders were dust-streaked, posture stiff with nerves—but there was steel in his eyes.

"You spoke well today," Don Antonio said. "And more important—you listened well. That is rarer."

Hank ducked his head, voice quiet. "Thank you, sir. For Bob, for trusting me."

Don Antonio inclined his head, seeing the sincerity plain as day. "I do not give trust lightly. But you remind me of my brother—strong, honest, loyal, pure of heart. Qualities that last longer than charm." His lips twitched faintly. "That is why you have earned a measure of my respect."

Hank shifted, boots scraping against the cobblestones. His jaw worked as though chewing words too big for his mouth. At last he blurted, "Would it be alright if I took Mirabella out for ice cream? To celebrate."

Don Antonio stopped, eyebrows lifting. "Ice cream," he repeated, savoring the word. "She is nearly fourteen. Too young for courtship."

Hank's ears went red. He rushed, "It's not a date. Just celebrating. We're partners now, with Bob. That's all."

A chuckle rolled from Don Antonio, low and warm. "Ah, to be young. You stumble over your words like a colt finding its legs."

Hank shut his mouth, realizing he couldn't win this one.

Don Antonio clapped him once on the shoulder, firm but kind. "Fine. Take her. But back before dinner. I will not have your grandmother sending a search party through town."

Relief washed across Hank's face. "Yes, sir. Thank you."

Don Antonio's gaze lingered on him, thoughtful, almost paternal. He knew Mirabella was far too young yet, and he would guard her fiercely. But this boy—this Miller—saw something good in him. A steadiness. The man who might one day be worthy of her.

"Enjoy it, Hank," Don Antonio said at last. His eyes softened, knowing. "There are moments in life that do not come twice. Do not waste this one."

The '56 Apache rattled down the two-lane road, its headlights cutting narrow tunnels through the dusk. Hank had scrubbed his hands and face at the pump before leaving, but dust still clung stubbornly to his shirt and jeans. He caught himself glancing sideways at Mirabella, worried she might notice, but she only sat with her braid over one shoulder, gazing out the window, a quiet smile tugging at her lips.

The diner came into view—a squat building with neon buzzing faintly in the twilight. Hank pulled into the gravel lot, the tires crunching loudly, and shut off the engine. For a moment, neither of them moved. Finally, Mirabella looked at him and grinned. "Are you going to open the door, caballero, or do I have to?"

Hank flushed, jumped out, and hurried around to pull the handle for her. She laughed, the sound light, and together they stepped inside.

The place smelled of coffee, fried onions, and sugar. Vinyl booths lined the windows; a jukebox hummed softly in the corner. They slid into a booth across from each other, and when the waitress asked what they wanted, Hank cleared his throat and said, "One chocolate sundae. Two spoons."

Mirabella's brows lifted, but she didn't tease.

When the sundae arrived, a mountain of vanilla ice cream smothered in chocolate sauce — they dug in eagerly. Between bites, the talk turned practical.

"We'll need to work on groundwork first," Hank said. "Get him steady with ropes and flags. Make sure he's listening before we even think of speed."

Mirabella nodded, licking a drip of chocolate from her spoon. "And balance. Lots of trot work, transitions, lateral exercises. He needs his back strong if he's going to carry you in the race."

He smirked. "You mean if *we're* going to carry each other."

She smiled, and for a long moment their spoons rested idle.

The conversation drifted. Mirabella traced circles in the condensation on her glass. "I didn't think you cared for me, Hank. Not really. Not until the grove, when you..." She trailed off, eyes soft. "You let me see you."

Hank caught himself watching her for too long. Not because she was beautiful—though she was—but because she saw him like no one else did. And maybe that was enough. For now.

Hank set his spoon down, heart thudding. He looked at her—really looked. The lamplight caught her dark lashes, the way her green eyes searched his face like she was afraid of what he might say.

"I've liked you since the first time I saw you," he said finally, voice low but steady. "That first day at the estancia when you were riding Valeroso. I couldn't believe anyone could ride like that." He paused, his throat tight. "You're my best friend, Mia. My only friend."

Her hand slid across the table, small and warm, covering his. "Musketeers forever."

Hank's chest tightened. He turned her hand palm-up, bent, and pressed his lips gently against her knuckles. "Forever," he whispered.

She smiled through tears she didn't bother to hide. Their laughter bubbled up again, softly at first, then fuller, carrying across the diner like sunlight breaking after a storm. For the first time in a long while, the world felt wide open.

The Miller farmhouse smelled of roast chicken and warm biscuits, the supper that once made Hank's mouth water after a long day. Tonight, though, he sat at the far end of the table with a faint smile tugging at his lips. His fork moved absentmindedly through the potatoes, but his thoughts were still at the diner—the jukebox humming, Mirabella's laughter spilling over a sundae, the way her hand had felt in his.

For the first time in months, he'd glimpsed a future worth wanting: Bob beneath him at the rodeo, Mirabella at his side, the farm saved if he could just hold it all together.

Grandpa Joe passed him the biscuits, and Hank took one without looking up, the smile still ghosting his face.

Then June cleared her throat. "I had a phone call today."

Her voice carried just enough weight to pull every eye toward her. She folded her hands in her lap, trying to be calm. "It was Jesse."

Hank's fork froze mid-air.

Marshall's knife paused against the chicken breast. "Jesse?"

"Yes." June's gaze flicked to each of them, lingering a moment too long on Hank. "He's doing well. He's saving for school in San Francisco. A conservatory. Not Yale, but still—music."

The words struck like a fist to Hank's ribs. The fragile warmth he'd carried into the room drained in an instant, leaving only the ache of old wounds.

His fork clattered against the plate. He shoved his chair back; the legs screeching against the floorboards. "That's enough." His voice was sharp, raw.

Napkin tossed onto his half-finished plate, he turned toward the doorway, jaw tight.

"Hank—" June called after him, her voice breaking.

Marshall reached across the table, laying a steady hand on her arm. "Let him go."

The screen door slammed, rattling against its frame.

Silence thickened in the kitchen. Grandma Ginny's lips pressed tight as she lowered her eyes. Grandpa Joe watched the empty chair at the table's end, his brow furrowed, concern etched deep.

June's hands trembled in her lap. "He hates his brother," she whispered.

Outside, the evening air hit cool against Hank's skin, but it didn't cool the fire in his chest. He paced down the steps and into the yard, fists clenched, ribs aching with each breath. The crickets hummed; the sky blushed faintly purple with the last of daylight.

But all he could hear was Jesse's name. Jesse, who had left them to pick up the pieces. Jesse, who had their mother's love no matter how deep the betrayal ran.

For a flicker, Mirabella's laugh came back to him—the warmth of her hand in his, the promise of forever whispered across a diner table. He clung to it like a lifeline, then let it slip as anger surged.

He drew a sharp breath, staring out at the dark fields. Bob, the rodeo, Mirabella—they were his now. Jesse was his past.

And Hank wasn't going back.

Night etched through the sky as Hank sat hunched over his desk, pencil smudges dark across his knuckles, his ribs aching when he leaned too close to the paper. The lamp at his elbow cast a pale yellow circle over the rough sketch—lines crossed and redrawn, eraser marks ghosting the margins.

It wasn't pretty. But it was his.

A bit for Bob.

He traced the mouthpiece one more time, the pencil's tip wobbling where his hand trembled. Not sharp, not punishing—just enough curve to sit gently on the bars of Bob's mouth, to guide instead of force. Functional. Honest. The tool a horse could trust.

A knock rattled the doorframe.

"Hank?"

His pencil paused. He didn't answer. The door creaked open anyway, and June stepped inside. Her hands twisted in her apron, her face drawn in the lamplight. For a long moment she only stood there, watching him.

Finally, she crossed the room, her eyes landing on the sketch. "You did this?"

Hank shifted in his chair, uncomfortable under her gaze. "Yeah."

She leaned closer, studying the lines. Surprise softened her features. "It's good."

Hank shrugged, defensive. "Not like Jesse's drawings. But it'll work." He lifted his chin, meeting her eyes. "Mirabella and I are buying Bob. We will train him. He's my responsibility now."

The words hung between them, heavy and certain.

June's breath caught. She searched his face; the boy she'd feared was lost replaced with someone sharper, steadier. A young man she hadn't expected to rise so soon. Hank replaced her with Mirabella. She nodded slowly, her voice low. "Forgive me. I feared too much."

Hank's jaw clenched. He slammed the pencil down harder than he meant to. "We're going to lose the farm because of him, Mom. And you forgive him like it's nothing?" His voice cracked, anger flooding through the cracks in his composure. "All of us are working ourselves to the bone, and Jesse—he steals, he runs, and now he's off in San Francisco like nothing happened."

June flinched, but she didn't look away. Her voice was soft, almost pleading. "He's trying, Hank. He's broken, but he's trying. And like Bob, we all deserve a second chance."

From her apron pocket, she pulled a folded envelope. She placed it carefully on the edge of his desk. "He left this for you. With Agustín. Read it if you can."

Hank's throat burned. He snatched the letter and tossed it straight into the wastebasket at his feet. "He's not my brother."

The words struck sharper than he intended, but he didn't take them back.

June's eyes glistened, but she only drew in a shaky breath. She stood, smoothing her apron as if it might hide the tremor in her hands. At the door, she turned, her voice steadier now.

"I love you, Hank. And I hope someday you'll forgive him. Forgive me, too."

She closed the door behind her, the latch clicking softly.

Hank sat rigid in the chair, staring at the crooked lines of the bit sketch. His chest tightened beneath the press of everything unspoken—his father's silence, his mother's grief, Jesse's shadow stretched long and familiar. Then he stood abruptly, the legs of the chair scraping against the floor, and crossed the room in heavy strides.

He stopped at the window, pressing a palm to the cool glass. Outside, the fields were dark, rimmed in moonlight. Barn lanterns swayed gently in the breeze, their glow soft against the walls. Somewhere, a horse nickered.

He watched the shadows shift for a long while, letting the quiet push back against the weight inside him. When he turned, the room felt smaller. Still thick with what hadn't been said.

He dropped back into the chair, elbows on the desk. The pencil waited beside the bit sketch, its lines rough and smudged—but solid. His eye drifted to the wastebasket.

The corner of the envelope stuck out, pale in the lamplight. Slowly, he reached down and pulled it free. He didn't open it. Just set it beside the sketch—two futures, side by side.

One he was building with his own hands.

And the other—unopened, uncertain—but not gone.

His gaze flicked to the lead rope hanging by the door, still dusty from the arena.

He thought of the diner. The jukebox. Mirabella's laughter over a shared sundae. Her hand in his, small and sure.

A second chance didn't always come loud. Sometimes it came quiet, with chocolate sauce and two spoons.

Hank picked up the pencil. For now, the bit came first.

FIRE IN THE BLOOD

The workshop breathed like an old beast in the morning stillness. Sawdust lay thick on the benches, its faint resin scent curling up into the air, catching in the beams of slanted dawn that spilled through the single window. Tools hung in an orderly grid along the back wall—chisels, planes, and saws polished with use but not neglect. An oil lamp hummed on the far bench, casting a warm circle of gold over the unfinished dining table.

Hank worked a rasp across the edge of a chair leg, the shavings curling onto his boots. His ribs still ached if he bent too long, but he set his jaw and kept the rhythm steady. Beside him, Grandpa Joe sanded the tabletop with the same even patience that had carried him through a lifetime of labor.

"Trevor's going to be pleased," Grandpa Joe said after a while, checking the grain. "Table and chairs like this—solid oak, strong joints. Should last his wife a hundred years. Fine anniversary gift."

Hank grunted, brushing sawdust from his wrist. "Glad for it. Lord knows we need the cash."

Grandpa Joe's eyes flicked up, sharp despite his age. "What do you mean by that?"

Hank hesitated, rasp stilling. The words sat like a stone on his tongue. Finally, he muttered, "I overheard you and Dad. Couple weeks back. Out by the house. Talking about the foreclosure." He swallowed, pressing the rasp hard against the wood. "I told Grandma Ginny when she took me to Pie 'n Burger. Couldn't keep it in."

The old man set down his sandpaper, dusting his palms on his apron. "You ought to speak with your father about it."

Hank shook his head quickly. "No. He's got enough weight on him. I'm not piling on more. I just..." He drew a breath, steadying himself. "I want to help. Earn his respect. Not his pity."

He shoved his hand into his pocket and pulled out a folded paper. Carefully, he spread it flat across the workbench—the sketch of a bit, its lines rough but clear.

"I've been thinking," Hank said, tapping the page. "Rodeo prize might be two grand. The jackpot race is thirty-five hundred. Together, I could clear five thousand. Enough to help with the payment."

Grandpa Joe leaned closer, squinting at the drawing. His weathered fingers traced the arcs of the cheekpieces, the curve of the mouthpiece. He studied in silence, then gave a single, firm nod.

"You've got your head on straight, boy."

Relief flickered through Hank's chest, quick as breath.

Grandpa Joe slid the sketch aside and walked to the forge. With practiced ease, he stoked the coals until the fire roared bright, heat pushing back the chill of morning. He set a length of steel in the flames until it blushed red, then handed the tongs to Hank.

"Hold it steady."

Together they worked—the hammer falling in steady rhythm, the metal bending under their will. Sparks spat into the dim air, the sound of each strike ringing like a church bell. Hank's arms shook with the weight, but he gritted his teeth and swung true. Grandpa Joe corrected with a nod here, a sharp word there, until the shape emerged.

They cooled it, filling the edges smooth. The rasp sang a clean arc across steel, a music of patience and labor.

As Hank worked, Grandpa Joe spoke, voice quiet under the hiss of metal. "Tools are only as good as the hands holding them. Same with second chances."

Hank's file slowed. He didn't look up, but he felt the words bite deep. The old man didn't have to name Jesse. The silence that followed spoke enough.

For a while, only the scrape of steel filled the shop.

For a moment, Marshall simply watched, struck by the steadiness in Hank's movements. That same steadiness he'd never seen in Jesse—Jesse with his restless hands, his eyes always turned toward some horizon far from home. The sound of steel on steel carried more than craft; it carried something Marshall hadn't let himself name: pride.

But guilt rode alongside it. Marshall remembered the night Jesse disappeared, remembered his own silence when June had begged him to bring their boy back. He remembered Tegan's fall—the raw ache of it—and how he'd told himself he had to hold everything together while his family splintered around him. He wondered, not for the first time, if he'd broken Jesse by pushing too hard, or by not holding hard enough.

Now, seeing Hank bent over the work, he felt the weight shift. One son gone. One daughter buried. But this boy—this boy kept showing up. Quiet, determined, carrying more than his share without complaint.

Marshall's jaw tightened. He let out a slow breath; the sound lost under the rasp of steel. Pride swelled in him, sharp as pain.

He turned away before they noticed him, carrying the sound of hammer and file into the morning air, a sound he knew he would remember when the time came to choose where he stood.

The noon sun poured hot over Estancia Castilla, bleaching the white rails of the arena and setting rosemary hedges shimmering with scent. Dust hung in faint veils, stirred by hoofbeats.

Hank sat astride Bob, seat steady, hands low. Mirabella leaned against the rail, braid dark against her pale blouse, her sharp eyes never missing a stride.

"Half-halt. Let him find the balance."

Hank closed his fingers, exhaled. Bob's stride shortened; his jaw softened.

"Good. Now trot—walk—trot."

Hank eased his weight. Bob slipped to walk, then into trot again with a smoothness Hank hadn't thought possible a month ago.

"Serpentine," Mirabella called. "Three loops. Don't let him rush the centerline."

Hank shifted his hands, legs brushing in rhythm. Bob curved across the arena, his topline stretching with each pass. Dust puffed up behind him, the air alive with motion.

Mirabella's voice held no doubt, only calm authority. "Inside shoulder. Free the ribs—ask for a touch of leg-yield."

Hank nudged, subtle. Bob's body softened, stepping sideways with a grace that surprised even Hank. The stallion's head lowered, chewing the bit, breath settling into Hank's seat.

"Good," Mirabella said, nodding once. "That's enough."

Hank slowed Bob to a halt and swung down, dirt sticking to his jeans. His hands moved quickly, practiced—saddle off, bridle off, halter left hanging on the fence.

Mirabella frowned slightly. "What are you doing?"

Hank patted Bob's shoulder, breath still quick from the ride. "My turn. Watch."

He stepped away, empty hands loose at his sides. Bob lifted his head, ears pricked. Hank drew in a breath, turned his shoulder just enough. The buckskin followed. One step. Two. Matching stride for stride.

Hank stopped. Bob stopped. Hank exhaled slowly, and Bob reversed softly, hooves whispering back through sand.

Mirabella's lips parted. She didn't speak.

"Draw," Hank murmured, lifting his chest a fraction. Bob came in close, shoulder to Hank's chest, eyes soft, no lines on his face. A hand signal sent him out to circle. No rope. No spur. Only space and breath. Hank shifted his gaze, and Bob changed direction, sand spraying in the light.

Mirabella leaned on the rail, fingers tight around the wood. She had read of such things, seen circus horses in Europe, but never like this—not a half-wild working stallion moving on whispers, a boy's body the only cue.

Bob trotted loose, then slowed as Hank angled his shoulder. The stallion stopped square, head low. Hank didn't chase, didn't demand. Only invited.

Mirabella stepped quietly into the pen, unrolling a flag she'd fetched. The white cloth snapped once in the air. Bob's muscles tensed, flank twitching.

"Easy, boy," Hank said, voice firm and low. The stallion's ears flicked toward him, then settled. He breathed out, and Bob's ribs softened. The cloth brushed his hip, slid down to hock. Bob blinked, sighed. The fear drained like water leaving a trough.

Two cowboys dragged a wooden bridge into the arena, narrow slats creaking, echoing the one that had once sent Hank to the dirt. Hank didn't touch Bob this time. He walked to the far side and stood, hands at his sides, waiting.

The stallion stretched his neck forward, nostrils flaring. One hoof touched the first plank. Pause. Mirabella whispered from the rail, "Good boy."

The second hoof followed. Weight shifted. The board groaned. Bob's eyes stayed soft, his steps careful but steady. He crossed without rush, each hoof placed like a promise.

Hank didn't praise with touch or sugar, only space. When Bob's hind feet found sand again, Hank breathed out, and the stallion mirrored him, lowering his head.

Silence filled the arena. Even the sparrows in the olive trees seemed to still.

On the edge, Don Antonio and Agustín had come, quiet as ghosts. They stood with arms folded, their faces unreadable. For a long beat, neither spoke.

At last, Agustín let out a breath and grinned crookedly. "You two should open a training yard someday. I'd invest."

Hank glanced up, startled, cheeks flushed with sweat. Mirabella's eyes shone, pride and relief woven together.

Don Antonio hid his mouth behind his hand, but the warmth in his gaze betrayed him. "Under my roof, perhaps."

Hank reached for Bob's forehead, rubbed the swirl at the center. The stallion pressed in, eyes half-closed. Mirabella nodded, a smile breaking through—soft, relieved, proud.

The three of them stood in the ring, shadows braided together: the cowboy boy with dust on his shirt, the girl with her dressage discipline, and the horse who carried both their hearts. A new language had been born between them, wordless but strong, and for the first time, even Don Antonio saw it—something he had never witnessed before on his estancia.

The office at Estancia Castilla was cooler than the afternoon sun, its wood-paneled walls lined with ledgers and neat stacks of correspondence. A faint tang of olive oil hung in the air from the crates stacked along the desk. Hank tugged the tape across one of them, sealing the carton with a sharp rip and press of his palm.

Agustín leaned against the counter, sorting shipping slips. He had rolled up his sleeves, and his dark hair fell across his brow. He watched Hank work, expression unreadable for a long moment.

"You pack as if the world depends on it," Agustín said with a half-smile.

Hank shrugged, keeping the tape taut. "Work's work."

Another box filled, bottles wrapped in brown paper and nested snug. Hank tucked the last one down, folded the flaps, pulled tape. The room filled with the scrape and snap of the dispenser.

Agustín broke the quiet. "You know, I saw your brother the last time I went north. San Francisco."

Hank's hands froze for half a beat before he set the carton aside. "So?"

But the memory rose like smoke—bitter and stubborn.

It had only been a few months ago, but it felt like another lifetime.

That night at the Long Branch. Jesse's voice, smooth as Tennessee whiskey, soaked up the spotlight, strumming chords into the bones of the bar. Hank had been there too, cajón steady beneath him, following like he always did—until Jesse spotted the blonde in the denim corset and decided "Wonderful Tonight" was his newest weapon.

The boyfriend hadn't appreciated the serenade. By the time Hank came back from the bathroom, Jesse was pinned to the wall, laughing, provoking. And Hank... well, Hank did what he always did. He jumped in. Fists flew. Tables broke. Someone threw a bottle. It all blurred until the cuffs clicked, and the police towed the Caprice from the lot like an afterthought.

Hours later, the jail door groaned open, and Hank stepped out—black eye swelling shut, lip split, knuckles raw. Jesse was still inside, sprawled on a bench, snoring like a baby. Not a scratch on him. Just a crooked grin and beer on his breath, as if he'd slept through the wreckage.

Marshall had been waiting in the lobby, carved from silence. Arms crossed. Jaw tight. When Hank asked, *"What about Jesse?"*, his father just said, *"He can sleep it off."*

They left in silence. Climbed into Bess and drove—not home, but nowhere Hank recognized. The taste of blood and shame filled the truck cab. And in that thick, unmoving quiet, Hank finally understood: Jesse might be the wildfire, but Hank was always the one left to smother the flames.

He didn't want to play cleanup anymore.

"I'll be heading up again tomorrow. Distributors near the wharf. I'll probably look in on him if I can." Agustín's voice was casual, as if it cost nothing to say. "Want me to bring him a message?"

Hank's hands froze for half a beat before he set the carton aside. "No," he said flatly. "Have a good trip."

He pushed the tape gun onto the table harder than necessary. The crack of plastic against wood made both of them flinch.

Silence pressed on. Dust specks drifted through the shaft of light from the single top window.

Agustín studied him. He set down the slip in his hand, the calm mask sliding away. "Anger eats time, Hank. I wasted years on mine when my mother died. Blamed my father, blamed the world. By the time I stopped, I couldn't get those years back."

Hank's eyes hardened, his jaw working. "I can forgive him," he said, voice rough. "Someday. But that doesn't mean I want him in my life."

The words hung there, heavier than the crates.

Agustín nodded slowly, a flicker of respect in his eyes. "That's a start."

They went back to work, the scrape of tape and shuffle of papers filling the space where Jesse's name lingered, a shadow that wouldn't quite leave.

Marshall adjusted his hat as he stepped through the doors of the Whitaker Falls Bank. The air inside smelled of polish and paper, too clean, too exact. A rope divider split the lobby, leading customers in a neat line toward the tellers. Marshall ignored the pens chained to the counters, the ledgers spread wide like schoolbooks. He walked past the divider, boots sinking into carpet worn thin in the middle but still stiff at the edges.

The carpet gave way to linoleum outside the manager's hallway—yellowed and curling at the seams. It clicked faintly under his heels, the sound too loud in the quiet.

He reached the office. Inside, Douglas Haynes rose from behind his desk, hair parted as if with a ruler, collar pressing tight around his neck. He smoothed his tie and extended a hand.

"Marshall," Douglas said, with a warm note that didn't quite hide the strain beneath it. "Always good to see you."

Marshall shook his hand, the grip firm, unhurried. "Douglas."

They sat. Marshall reached into his coat and pulled out a plain envelope, edges soft from handling. He set it on the polished wood and nudged it forward with two fingers. "It's not the full amount. But it's what I've got now."

Douglas opened the flap, counted the bills with care, then tucked them back inside. His expression stayed composed, but the lines around his mouth deepened.

"I respect the Millers," Douglas said finally. "Your family's been here longer than mine. Your father, your grandfather—everyone knows the work you've put into that land. Believe me when I say, I don't want to foreclose on you."

Marshall nodded once, jaw working.

Douglas folded his hands over the envelope. "But I've got superiors who don't care about history. Policy's policy. I can hold them off for a month. After that... if the balance isn't paid in full, foreclosure moves forward." He spread his fingers as if to show the helplessness in them.

Silence filled the office, thick and stale. Marshall studied the scuffs on the linoleum near the door, the places where countless boots had stood waiting for news—some leaving relieved, some hollow. He drew a slow breath and lifted his gaze back to Douglas.

"Thank you for the month," Marshall said. His voice was even, but iron lay underneath.

Douglas hesitated. He leaned forward slightly, lowering his tone. "Everything alright, Marshall? With you and yours?"

Marshall adjusted his hat brim, fingers brushing the sweat-stained edge. "I'll bring the money," he said flatly.

Douglas studied him for a long beat, then nodded once. "Alright."

They stood. Their handshake showed respect but also conveyed the weight of unfinished business, which they couldn't settle in that place.

Marshall stepped back into the hallway, his boots clicking again on the curling linoleum, then muffled as he crossed to the carpet. Outside, the noon light hit hard, bouncing off storefront glass and whitewashed walls. Dust lifted along the street, tugged by a restless wind.

Marshall squared his shoulders and set his jaw. All he'd bought was time—and time ran fast.

Late afternoon light bent low across the trail as Hank and Mirabella rode toward the pond. Bob carried Hank with ears pricked, his hide shining golden under the sun. Beside them, Mirabella sat tall on Valeroso; the stallion's grey coat rippled with each step, his gait collected and proud even at a walk.

They reached the water's edge without a word. Both dismounted, tying reins loosely so the horses could drink. Valeroso lowered his head first, his reflection warping in the ripples. Bob followed, blowing out a long snort that sent ducks scattering from the reeds.

The pond mirrored the oaks that ringed it, branches stretched wide, sky cupped between leaves. Hank bent, scooped up a flat rock, and flicked it across the surface. One, two, three, four, five, six, seven skips before it disappeared with a soft plunk. The ripples stretched and tangled until the pond stilled again.

"Days like this," he murmured like a prayer, "I wish Tegan were here. Singing nonsense, heckling me, calling him Bob." He rubbed the stallion's damp neck. "She thought she was so clever, giving a buckskin a plain name."

The ache in his chest pressed harder. Before silence could settle too deep, Mirabella stepped closer. She threaded her fingers through his, her grip delicate but certain. "She is here."

Hank gave her hand a small squeeze. "You're right."

They stood for a moment, horses shifting behind them, the air filled with the sound of water lapping the bank. Mirabella's gaze drifted across the pond, her voice thin as smoke. "I'm leaving at the end of the month. I should've gone last month, before my birthday, but..." She trailed off, shoulders stiff.

Hank slid his arm over hers, steadying her. "But you stayed."

She nodded, blinking quickly. "I miss my family back home. I miss Argentina—the language, the food, the air. But this..." Her breath hitched, and she pressed a hand to her face. "I love this family too. You. Bob. All of it. I don't want to forget. I'm scared I'll forget what she looks like."

Hank turned so she couldn't look away. "Will you come back?"

Her green eyes glistened. She nodded once.

"Then you'll take her with you," Hank said. "Tegan always said she was going to Argentina. Now she can—through you."

Mirabella's tears slipped free, but so did her smile. She leaned on his shoulder. "Thank you for saying that."

"Thanks for staying," Hank answered softly. "I couldn't do this without you."

She sniffed, swiped at her eyes, then managed a crooked grin. "I would never miss you becoming a world-famous cowboy."

He chuckled. "World-famous? Let's get through the jackpot race first."

They laughed together, the sound fragile but alive, carried across the water like a promise. Behind them, Bob and Valeroso raised their heads, ears swiveling, breath drifting in twin plumes.

Hank looked out across the pond. It had been only months ago that he, Mirabella, and Tegan stood on this bank, declaring themselves the Three Musketeers. They had been kids, shouting vows into the air as if forever were easy to hold. Now that Tegan was gone, her laughter was only an echo. Yet the pact hadn't broken—it had only changed shape.

Here, in the hush of evening, Hank felt it still alive. The Three Musketeers remained: Hank, Mirabella, and Bob.

And together, they would carry it forward.

The barns of Estancia Castilla lay hushed beneath the weight of midnight. Crickets pulsed steadily from the olive groves, their rhythm rising above the low creak of lanterns swaying in the rafters. Dust and hay carried their sharp smell even in the cool air.

Bob paced his stall, hooves pressing restless patterns into the bedding, muscles bunching along his shoulders. His breath came quickly, ears twitching at shadows.

Hank's boots clicked on the concrete aisle, the sound cutting clean through the night. Bob's head shot up. Recognition softened him at once—ears pricked forward, eyes wide but no longer wild.

"Easy, boy," Hank murmured, unclipping the latch. He slipped the lead rope onto Bob's halter. The stallion pressed forward, not anxious now, but eager.

They walked together down the quiet aisle. The barn doors yawned open to a sky salted thick with stars. The air outside was sharp and clean, the kind that stung the lungs after the heat of the day. Hank tilted his head back, letting the heavens fill his sight, then glanced at Bob, whose own gaze tracked the horizon as if he felt the same pull.

At the pasture gate, Hank slid the chain loose. Bob stepped into the dew-bright grass, head high, tail flicking once. He stood for a long moment, inhaling, then lowered his nose to graze, calm rippling through the restless muscle.

Hank leaned on the gate, watching him. "Pasture tonight," he whispered. "We work again at dawn."

Bob flicked an ear back toward his voice, chewing slowly. The stallion's frame looked less like fire threatening to break free, more like heat banked under coals, waiting.

Hank breathed deep, the night air cool as water over stone. He latched the gate and stood for a beat longer, boy and horse both dreaming beneath the same stars, trust stretched quietly between them.

The Miller farmhouse was quiet but not at peace. The old clock downstairs ticked in the stillness, each stroke marking time like a weight. In the master bedroom, a single lamp burned, its light pooling over June's hands as she folded and refolded a nightgown already put away. Marshall sat on the bed, bent over his boots, unlacing them with steady fingers.

He broke the silence first. "Hank's entered Bob in the rodeo. And the jackpot race."

June's head snapped up. She turned from the dresser, eyes shining with disbelief. "He did what?"

Marshall straightened, voice even. "Rodeo. Race. He's serious about it."

She pressed her hands against the dresser edge as though it might hold her upright. "It's bad enough he's training that stallion—after what happened. Now a rodeo? A race? Don't you see what this means? Stop him, Marshall." Her voice cracked. "That horse nearly killed him. I can't bury another child."

Marshall leaned forward, forearms resting on his knees. His gaze held hers steady, but sharp with conviction. "He isn't a child anymore. He's stepping into manhood, and he's doing it with more grit than most men I've known. You want me to stop him? Forbid him?" He shook his head. "That's not living, June. Living in fear isn't living at all. I won't live that way—and I won't make Hank live that way either."

June's breath came ragged, tears slipping down her cheeks. "You talk about living, but what about dying? That's what happens at rodeos. Wrecks, broken necks, bodies crushed. We've already lost Tegan. Jesse's gone. What happens when Hank falls too?"

Marshall stood, his shadow falling long across the room. "Then we'll face it. But I won't tie him down with fear. Hank's earned more than that. He's one of the best horsemen I've ever seen. I've worked with plenty, but that boy—" Marshall paused, his throat tightening before he went on. "The Castillas see it. Don Antonio. Agustín. Even Mirabella. They believe in him. We should too."

June shook her head, clutching at her sleeves as if to keep herself from breaking apart. "Believing won't stop the ground from taking him."

"No," Marshall said, softer now. "But believing will keep him standing tall while he's here. And right now, he needs us at his back. Not dragging him down."

She turned away, grief radiating from her in waves. "If he dies, Marshall—if he dies, I'll never forgive you."

He reached for the lamp switch, his voice steady as hammered iron. "Hank deserves our support. He's earned it. If you can't give it, don't. But I'll be there. Mom and Dad will too. You'll lose him just the same if you don't stand beside him."

The lamp clicked off, plunging the room into shadow. Moonlight slipped through the window, laying silver across June's rigid frame as she sat frozen at the dresser.

Marshall lay back against the pillows, staring at the ceiling, jaw set. He could feel the gulf between them as sharp as a blade. Yet beneath it, one truth steadied him: he had chosen his side.

For the first time since Tegan's death, he knew exactly where he stood—beside his son.

In the hallway, Hank stood barefoot, his shoulder against the wall outside his parents' room. Their voices had carried through the wood—June's sharp with fear, Marshall's deep and steady with resolve. He didn't mean to linger, but the words rooted him where he was.

When the lamp clicked off, silence fell. He let out a breath he hadn't known he was holding.

A hollow ache opened in his chest. His mother's voice still rang in his ears—her fear, her plea to stop him. Jesse had always had her faith, her music, her trust. Hank had never begrudged it before, but tonight it cut. He wanted her support, wanted her to see him for who he was, not just what she could lose.

Yet beneath the sting came something new. His father's words—plain, unpolished, but firm—settled deep. *He's one of the best horsemen I've ever seen.* Marshall Miller, a man who measured speech like a coin, had said it out loud.

Hank blinked hard, his throat tight. He hadn't realized how much it mattered to hear it.

Quiet as he could, he slipped back to his room. The house pressed around him, heavy with sleep, but his chest burned with a fire that fear couldn't smother.

If his father believed in him, then he would not fail. Not with Bob. Not with the rodeo. Not with the race.

He set his jaw in the dark, determination settling into bone. Whatever it took, he would win.

The fire in him was no longer dangerous—it was forged, shaped, and ready.

BRUISES AND BELIEF

Morning light slanted through the tall windows of Grandpa Joe's workshop, catching on sawdust that hung in the air like flecks of gold. The smell of oak and linseed oil pressed warm and familiar. Hank stood with his shoulder under one end of the dining table, ribs tightening against the weight.

"Easy now," Marshall grunted from the other side. His hands were firm on the polished edges, his jaw tight with focus.

Hank forced a steady breath through his teeth, hiding the stab in his side. The table wasn't heavy compared to hay bales or tack trunks, but his ribs screamed all the same. He straightened as soon as they set it on the truck bed, stretching his back as if the ache were only stiffness.

"You alright?" Marshall asked, eyes narrowing.

"I'm fine," Hank said quickly, brushing sawdust off his jeans. "Just sore from riding."

From the doorway, Grandpa Joe leaned on his cane, watching. His sharp eyes caught more than Hank wanted them to. "Fine or not, let your grandma have a look at you when we get home. Those ribs aren't mending on pride alone."

Hank nodded, though he didn't mean to. He wasn't about to be fussed over like a little kid.

The three of them worked in rhythm, chairs loaded after the table, each piece shining from hours of sanding and polish. Grandpa Joe's handiwork showed in every joint and curve, and Hank couldn't help feeling proud to have been part of it.

By midmorning they rattled into Greer's Hardware. Trevor Greer stepped out to meet them, wiping his hands on his apron. His round face split into a grin when he saw the dining set.

"Well now," Trevor said, running a palm over the smooth tabletop. "Joe Miller, you've outdone yourself again. My wife's going to think I robbed a city showroom."

Grandpa Joe chuckled, leaning heavier on his cane. "Solid oak'll outlast both of us. Treat it right, and it will be in your family for a hundred years."

Trevor whistled low and shook his head, impressed. "Worth every penny." He handed Marshall an envelope thick with bills. "And if you've got another set ready before summer, I'll take it. Folks are always asking after Miller work."

Marshall tucked the envelope inside his jacket with a quiet "Thank you."

Small victory. Everyone knew it. It was money, but not enough to keep the bank from circling. Hank's eyes drifted past the counter toward the bulletin board. The same flyer he'd seen before—bright ink against weathered cork.

Whitaker Falls Rodeo & Jackpot Race. Cash Prizes.

He stepped closer, scanning the prize list again. $3,500 for the open race. Close to $2,000 for the all-around cowboy. His ribs ached, but his pulse quickened. That kind of purse could save the farm.

"Are you thinking of entering?" a voice asked.

Hank turned. Clayton Briggs stood a few feet away, hat in hand. He wasn't young—lines carved his face deep, and his hair had gone more silver than black—but his shoulders were still square, and his eyes sharp as fence wire. He'd been winning the jackpot race for nearly a decade, Hank knew.

"Been running that race ten years," Clayton said, slipping the hat back on. His voice carried no boast, only fact. "Takes more than speed. Takes a horse that'll stand with you when the ground shakes, when the crowd's hollering, when every steer in the pen wants to scatter."

Hank held his gaze, saying nothing.

Clayton's eyes softened, just a fraction. "Most boys don't understand that part. They come for the money. They leave with dirt in their teeth." He gave a small nod. "Good luck to you."

And then he was gone, the bell over the hardware door jingling behind him.

Hank stood rooted, jaw tight, pulse thudding in his ears. He didn't need luck. He needed Bob.

On the ride home, the truck creaked beneath them, the envelope of bills resting in Marshall's jacket. None of them spoke for a long time.

Finally, Grandpa Joe broke the silence. "That money'll keep the bank quiet for a spell. But it won't keep us standing." He tapped his cane once against the truck floorboards. "Work will. That's what puts food on the table. Respect too. Both are earned the same way."

Marshall gave a curt nod, eyes fixed on the road ahead.

Hank shifted in his seat, ribs burning from the morning's strain, but he didn't wince. He sat straighter instead, the flyer still fresh in his mind. Work, respect, salvation—he'd find them all in the ring.

Bess rattled over the gravel on the road home, dust rising in lazy curls behind them. Marshall kept his hands on the steering wheel, eyes on the horizon. Grandpa Joe leaned back against the seat, cane next to his leg, quiet in that way of men who'd said their piece.

Hank sat between them, shoulders stiff, the flyer's bold letters burned into his mind. *$3,500 Open Jackpot.* More than numbers—hope, a chance, a way forward.

His thoughts slipped to Bob. The buckskin had come far—farther than most thought possible. From a skittish stallion that flinched at every shadow to a horse that mirrored his breath, turned on a glance, trusted his hand. They were more than rider and mount now; something unspoken stitched them together.

But Bob was still green. Still young. Hank knew it. Every cowboy at Whitaker Falls would bring horses hardened by years of work—steady under pressure, unshaken by crowds, bold at speed. Bob wasn't that yet.

A pang twisted in Hank's ribs—not from the break, but from doubt. He was asking too much of the horse. Piling all his family's salvation on four legs that had only just stopped trembling at a rope's flicker.

Yet he couldn't shake the truth that sat heavier than oak on his chest: if he didn't try, they'd lose the farm. And if they lost the farm, then Tegan's death—her laughter in the wind, her cowboy hat crooked on her hair at the pond, her wild cry when Midnight bolted—would feel like it had swallowed everything.

Redemption. That was the word Clayton Briggs hadn't said but had hung in the air after his warning. Hank wanted more than a purse. He wanted proof. Proof that when it mattered, he could save something. Proof that failing Tegan didn't mean he'd fail everyone else.

He pressed a palm against his aching ribs, staring at the road unwinding beneath the wheels.

Bob's not ready, he thought. *But neither was I, and I can't wait anymore.*

Bess rattled to a stop in the Miller yard, gravel spitting under the tires. Marshall cut the engine and climbed out, the thick envelope of bills still tucked in his jacket.

Grandpa Joe eased down next, cane steady, while Hank slid from the passenger side, ribs flaring from the jolt.

They headed up the porch steps, Marshall already striding ahead, when Grandpa Joe spoke over his shoulder. "Ginny ought to look at you when we get inside. You're walking stiff as a board."

Hank opened his mouth to argue but closed it just as quickly. There was no point—Grandpa Joe saw everything.

Inside, the air smelled of coffee and last night's biscuits. Grandma Ginny stood at the sink, sleeves rolled high, humming an old hymn as she scrubbed a pan. She turned at the sound of the screen door.

"You got it delivered?" she asked.

"Paid in full," Marshall said, laying the envelope on the counter before disappearing into the front room.

Grandpa Joe tipped his head toward Hank. "The boy is in pain."

Grandma Ginny wiped her hands on her apron and planted them on her hips. Her sharp eyes found Hank and didn't let go. "Sit. Shirt off."

"Grandma, I'm fine—"

"Sit. Now."

Hank sighed and dropped into the nearest chair. His fingers fumbled at the buttons, each tug dragging fire through his ribs. He peeled the shirt off slowly, trying not to wince, but when he glanced up, he saw the truth in her face.

His ribs displayed a mottled pattern of purple and black, with yellow spreading at the edges and swelling present. Every breath lifted shallow.

Grandma Ginny shook her head, muttering, "Lord help us." She pulled her willow basket from the shelf, the jars clinking softly as she set them down. The sharp scents of comfrey and arnica filled the kitchen.

She dipped her fingers into the salve, cool and green, and pressed it to his side with practiced care. Hank flinched once, then let his eyes close.

"You think you can work through anything by sheer will," she said, voice firm but not unkind. "That's not strength, Henry Joseph. That's pride."

Her fingers moved steadily as she wound a fresh bandage. Her voice softened into a murmur, almost like a prayer. "But those who wait on the Lord shall renew their strength; they shall mount up with wings like eagles; they shall run, and not be weary; and they shall walk, and not faint."

The words wrapped around him, stronger than the salve, steadier than the bandage.

And yet Clayton Briggs' voice rose unbidden in Hank's memory: *Most boys don't understand. They come for the money. They leave with dirt in their teeth.*

Clayton had spoken with the weight of years in the saddle, not malice. His warning had lodged deep, needling Hank with doubt. Was Bob too green? Was Hank too green?

But Grandma Ginny's verse answered that doubt, not with simple comfort but with a demand: endure, trust, keep moving forward.

"You believe that?" Ginny asked gently.

He swallowed, throat tight. "I want to."

"You don't have to want," she said. "You just have to trust. Strength comes from faith. Healing too."

Hank let the verse settle into him, deep as marrow. He thought of Bob, still young, still learning, yet meeting him stride for stride. He thought of the farm, the debt, the flyer tacked on Greer's board. And he thought of Tegan—her laughter, her crown, her last wild ride.

Grandma Ginny tied off the bandage snug, her hand resting briefly on his shoulder. "These bruises will fade. But don't forget—the worst wounds don't show."

Hank opened his eyes and managed a crooked smile. "Thanks, Grandma."

She smoothed his hair back the way she had when he was little. "Don't thank me. Just don't be foolish."

She gathered her basket and moved toward the door. The kitchen fell quiet again, save for the tick of the clock on the wall.

Hank leaned back, ribs aching but spirit steadier, the verse and Clayton's warning both echoing in his chest. One spoke of patience; the other of peril. Between them, he set his jaw.

They shall run and not be weary.

And Hank promised himself he would.

The kitchen sat heavy in the afternoon's stillness. The sun angled through the curtains, lighting dust particles that spun above the counter where Grandma Ginny's jars still lay open from tending Hank's ribs. Arnica, comfrey, and a bundle of dried yarrow waited to be packed back into her basket.

June entered, her steps dragging but her hands brisk. She stopped at the sight of the jars, her expression tightening. Her fingers closed around one of the brown glass bottles, holding it up to the light as though it were something suspect.

"Herbs," she muttered, almost spitting the word. "He needs a doctor, not weeds."

Hank had been leaning in the hallway, drawn by the sound of her voice. At first, he thought to slip away unnoticed, but her words pinned him where he stood. He stepped through the doorway.

"I don't need a doctor," he said flatly.

June startled, the jar nearly slipping in her hand. "Hank, you shouldn't be up—"

"I'm fine," he cut her off. "Grandma knows what she's doing. It helps."

June set the jar down harder than she meant to, the glass clinking against wood. Her voice sharpened. "It's not enough. You're getting worse every day. Do you think I don't see it? You're hurting yourself, and for what? Some fool's dream?"

Hank's jaw tightened. He stepped farther into the kitchen, the air between them heating. "It's not a dream. I'm going to fix what Jesse broke."

The words landed heavily. June froze, blinking as though she hadn't heard right. "What Jesse broke?"

Hank's eyes burned. "The money he stole, the trust he shattered—everything. He left us in a hole so deep we may not crawl out. I can't bring Tegan back, but I can save this farm. Someone has to."

June's mouth opened, then shut again. Her hand pressed to the counter as if she needed to steady herself. "Don't you talk about your brother like that."

"I'm telling the truth," Hank snapped. "You and Jesse never cared about this place. You had your music. He had his songs. But I care. I've worked on this ground every day. I've bled for it. And I'll do whatever it takes to keep it."

June reeled as though struck. She stared at him—the set of his shoulders, the fire in his eyes—and for the first time she saw not a boy but someone older, harder. Someone she didn't know.

"You're sixteen," she whispered, voice trembling. "Too young for rodeo bronc riding. Too young to carry this. Do you even understand what happens when those horses buck? When you hit the dirt wrong?"

"I understand enough." His voice was steel. "I've broken ribs, I've been trampled, and I'm still standing. This is my way. My chance to put food on the table, to make the payment the bank wants, to prove this farm matters. You don't have to believe in me. I'll do it anyway."

Her eyes filled, tears catching in the lines of her face. "Hank—please. You'll end up like—"

She stopped herself, choking on the name.

"Like Tegan?" he said flatly.

Silence snapped tight between them.

"I know what I'm risking," he went on. "But I can't live hiding from it. Not like you."

Her breath caught—like he'd slapped her.

"You don't believe I can do this," Hank said. "That's fine. But I do."

He turned on his heel and strode toward the back door, his boots thudding against the worn boards. The screen door banged behind him, the sound echoing in the silence he left.

June stood in the kitchen, one hand still pressed to the counter, the herbs spread before her like useless trinkets. The boy she had held in her arms, sung lullabies to, pushed on a swing—he was gone. In his place stood someone leaner, sharper, driven by a fire she didn't understand.

She pressed her fingers to her lips, her breath coming shallow. For all her fears, for all her grief, one truth rang through her like a bell: she no longer recognized the young man her son had become.

The estancia's barns glowed gold in the waning light as Mirabella ran a currycomb in steady circles across Bob's hide. Dust rose, catching in the shafts of the sun. The buckskin stood quiet under her hand, eyes soft, lower lip drooping. Every sweep of the brush drew out more shine until his coat gleamed, burnished like copper.

Hank leaned on the rail, ribs still sore, watching. He'd untacked Bob earlier, grateful that Mirabella had all but ordered him to save his strength. She worked with a kind of reverence, as if every stroke carried a promise.

"You'd think he was a prince the way you fuss," Hank teased, though his voice carried warmth.

Mirabella smiled without glancing up. "He is. Almost as beautiful as Valeroso." She tilted her chin toward Hank, eyes flashing playfully. "Don't tell him I said that."

Hank chuckled, the sound easing the ache in his chest. "Don't worry. Bob's already got a big enough head. Don't need him thinking he's prettier than your stallion too."

She set the brush aside and reached for a soft cloth, running it carefully along Bob's face. The stallion nosed at her braid, tugging gently. She laughed and pushed him back. "See? He knows he's handsome."

Hank shook his head, smiling. "He knows because you treat him like he is." His voice softened. "Most folks only ever saw a mean horse when they looked at him."

Her hands stilled on Bob's cheek. She looked over at Hank, serious now. "Not you. You saw more than that. That's why he follows you, Hank. You believed in him before anyone else did."

Hank swallowed, surprised by the weight of her words. "Sometimes I wonder if I believed enough," he whispered. "I pushed him too hard. That bridge...he could've killed me."

"He didn't," Mirabella answered quickly, almost fiercely. "And he won't. Not if you listen to him. Not if you work together." She gave Bob a fond pat, then added, more softly, "That's what I'm here for too. To remind you. To remind both of you."

Silence stretched, filled by the sound of Bob's steady breaths. Hank rubbed the back of his neck, searching for words.

"You know," he began slowly, "when I think about the rodeo and the jackpot, it's not just about the money. I mean, yeah—we need it. But it's more than that. It's about proving that Bob isn't broken. That I'm not, either."

Mirabella's expression softened. She stepped closer, the cloth still in her hand, and leaned against the rail near him. "You don't have to prove that to me. I already know."

Her words landed heavier than he expected. He looked at her—really looked at her—her braid loose from work, a smudge of dust across her cheek, eyes bright with belief he hadn't known he needed. The belief he wanted to come from his mother, came from her.

"Then maybe I need to prove it to myself," he admitted, voice rough.

Mirabella studied him for a moment, then reached for his hand. Her fingers were small, firm, calloused from reins and brushes, but steady. "Then we'll do it together. You, me, Bob. The Three Musketeers." Her smile flickered, wistful. "Tegan would like that."

Hank's throat tightened. He squeezed her hand once, hard. "Yeah. She would."

Bob blew out a long sigh, resting his chin against the rail between them as if to seal the pact.

Mirabella laughed softly, her other hand stroking his mane. "See? Even he agrees. You're not alone in this, Hank. You never were."

Hank nodded, his chest aching in a way that had nothing to do with his ribs. For the first time in a long while, the weight felt shared.

Dinner at the estancia was a warm affair, the long oak table laden with roast chicken, olives, and fresh bread still fragrant from the oven. Candles flickered in wrought-iron holders, shadows dancing across the arched beams above.

Partway through the meal, Don Antonio rose, napkin folded in his hand. "This evening, we make it official what has already been decided," he said, his voice carrying down the table.

Agustín stood as well, holding a neatly folded shirt. He set it before Hank. The white cotton was crisp, stitched with the insignia of Estancia Castilla on the chest pocket. On the sleeve, side by side, the American and Argentine flags fluttered in fine embroidery.

Hank touched the fabric as though it might vanish. "It's beautiful," he whispered.

Don Antonio inclined his head. "It is yours. Wear it at the rodeo and race. You ride not just for yourself, but for all of us."

Mirabella lifted her glass, eyes shining. "And for Bob. For both of us."

Don Antonio's eyes twinkled. "Ah, yes. To the strangest partnership I've ever permitted—two owners for one horse, and a horse as stubborn as both of them. May it bring victory."

Agustín chuckled. "And may it bring some peace to this household."

Glasses clinked, laughter softened the formality, and Hank raised his own glass, cheeks flushed with pride.

Later, in the grand room, the piano gleamed in the lamplight. Mirabella sat at the bench, fingers poised above the keys. She struck the first notes of a Chopin nocturne, filling the room with its aching beauty.

Hank lingered at the doorway, awkward in his new shirt, the embroidery still stiff against his chest. Mirabella looked up and beckoned him closer with a small tilt of her head.

"I can't play," he said, stepping reluctantly toward her.

"Then sit," she replied simply, sliding over enough for him to join her on the bench.

He sank down, shoulders stiff, hands folded in his lap. She shifted into a slower melody, simpler, inviting. Hank's voice joined hesitantly at first, low, almost swallowed by the notes.

But as she played on, he steadied. His voice grew stronger, weaving with her playing until the song belonged to them both. Not Jesse's polished talent, not June's teaching—it was something rougher, truer.

When the last chord faded, silence lingered, warm and whole.

Agustín, standing in the doorway, exchanged a glance with Don Antonio. The older man's expression was unreadable for a moment, then softened with a flicker of pride.

Mirabella turned toward Hank, her eyes bright. "See?" she whispered. "We can make our own music."

Hank met her gaze, a faint smile pulling at his mouth. "Yeah. We can."

The moment hung between them, fragile but real, as steady as the trust that had taken root between them, Bob, and the dream they now shared.

The Miller house lay quiet beneath a blanket of crickets and windmill creaks. The clock in the hall ticked with slow, steady patience.

In his room, Hank slept restlessly. The bandages around his ribs pulled with every shallow breath, and his brow furrowed as though he wrestled ghosts even in dreams. Sweat dampened the sheet on his chest. His lips moved, faint words slipping out in fragments.

"Tegan..." The name shivered into the dark, half-gasp, half-plea.

From the doorway, June froze. She'd meant only to check, to make sure the swelling had gone down, that he hadn't hidden a worse injury from them all. But the sound of her daughter's name on her son's lips rooted her in place, her fingers clenching the doorframe until her knuckles whitened.

The sight before her carved at her heart. She had thought of Hank as steady, quiet, her strong one—the boy who never asked for much. But now she saw what she had refused to see: the weight he carried pressed deeper than any bruise. He bore Tegan in his body, in his dreams, in the hitch of his breath and the grit of his jaw when he woke each day.

Her eyes blurred. She stepped into the room slowly, carefully, as though crossing holy ground.

Hank stirred, turning slightly onto his side. His face pinched, and he murmured again, the sound broken. June's chest ached at the truth of it—her boy hadn't let himself weep, hadn't laid down his sorrow where she could see. He carried it alone, and she had been blind.

She lowered herself onto the edge of his bed. For a long moment she simply sat, hands trembling in her lap, listening to the uneven rhythm of his breathing. Then, with a hesitant motion, she reached out and smoothed back the hair dampened on his forehead.

His body flinched at the touch, but he didn't wake. His brow eased slightly under her hand.

June bent close, her whisper catching in her throat. "I'm sorry, Hank. I see you now."

The words hung fragile in the night air, a confession and a prayer at once.

She stayed there, stroking his hair, until her own shoulders eased. Her thumb brushed across the bandage edge, tracing its edge like a border between old wounds and new strength. The boy before her was bruised—flesh marked purple, heart lined with fractures she had helped carve by seeing too little, too late. But she also saw something else. Beneath the bruises lived a will as fierce as Marshall's, a tenderness that echoed her own, a belief that still burned bright despite all it had cost him.

She thought of Jesse then—her other son, the one she had poured her music and dreams into. He was gone, chasing a life she couldn't follow, leaving behind broken promises and silence. Yet Hank had stayed. He carried the weight Jesse had dropped, shouldered the grief, the chores, the burden of keeping them together. She loved them both, but tonight the truth pressed in on her: Jesse had left, and Hank remained.

Maybe, just maybe, Hank had been the stronger one all along.

She rose carefully, tucking the blanket higher at his chest, her movements automatic but tender. In the faint glow of the lamp, she studied him a last time. The boy who had once been her quiet son now looked different—older, harder, and yet more fragile than she had imagined.

At the doorway she paused, hand on the frame again. "Hold on, Hank," she whispered into the stillness. "Hold on to that fire. I'll try to believe it too."

She closed the door halfway, letting the quiet settle back over him.

In the room, Hank shifted once more. His lips moved, but this time no sound came. His ribs ached beneath the bandage, and even in dreams he curled around the pain. Yet somewhere inside, the whispered promise of his mother lingered, brushing the edge of his sleep like balm over bruises.

Bruises, yes—but belief too. Enough perhaps for both of them.

DUST AND BLOOD

The Apache rattled across the gravel lot as dawn cracked pale over Whitaker Falls. The rodeo grounds were already awake—trucks and trailers packed in long rows, banners fluttering from poles, the air alive with the mixed scent of frying dough, manure, leather, and dust kicked up by boots and hooves.

Beyond the main arena, the parking rows looked like a patchwork village of cowboy life. Horses tied to trailer posts, cropped hay from hanging nets, tails flicking lazily at flies. Others stood in temporary pipe stalls, glossy backs already damp with sweat. Saddles gleamed from racks bolted to truck trailer sides, silver conchos catching the early light. Cowboys moved in and out of the lanes with feed buckets, spurs jangling, their laughter and calls rising above the bawl of calves penned nearby.

Hank gripped the wheel tighter, ribs aching whenever the Apache jolted over ruts. Beside him, Mirabella sat stiffly, her braid falling over her shoulder, hands folded in her lap. She tried for small talk—something about how Valeroso would have strutted here, tossing his head as if the whole rodeo were his stage—but her voice thinned with worry. Her eyes flicked toward Hank's side, knowing how much every movement cost him.

Hank didn't answer in words. He reached across, squeezed her hand once. His palm was rough; hers cool. He didn't need to tell her he was hurting—she already knew. What mattered was that he meant to carry it.

He eased the Apache between two long rigs, gears grinding as he parked. Dust swirled past the windshield. For a moment, the rumble of engines and shouts outside seemed louder than anything in Hank's head. Then he cut the ignition. Silence settled inside the cab.

Mirabella exhaled, pushed the door open, and hopped down onto the gravel. She shaded her eyes, scanning the rows of sleek horses being led in tight circles, tack polished bright. Hank followed, stepping carefully from the driver's seat, ribs tightening as his boots hit the ground. Mirabella was already circling the trailer by the time he caught up.

Around them, cowboys unloaded one horse after another, muscled bodies with coats burnished like glass. Some men had three, four horses tied side by side—one for roping, one for steer wrestling, another for speed. Each wore custom saddles trimmed in silver, reins braided with rawhide. Against that parade of polish, Bob was the only green one in the lot, a raw-boned buckskin whose best credential was the stubborn fire in his eyes.

"Don't let them get to you," Mirabella said, catching Hank watching the others. Her voice steadied. "They don't know what the both of you can do."

Hank nodded faintly. He had to believe that, too.

From near the chutes came a burst of laughter and backslaps. Clayton Briggs stood at the center, tall and broad, signing programs for kids with one hand while shaking with the other. His affable grin never wavered. The reigning all-around cowboy, his presence radiated command. When his eyes found Hank across the lot, he tipped his hat—a flicker of recognition, neither friendly nor dismissive. Just acknowledgement.

Hank's jaw tightened, but he didn't return it. He turned to the trailer door, unlatched the bar. Dust and straw drifted out as Bob stamped, ears flicking at the noise. The buckskin's hide glowed even in shadow.

"Easy, boy," Hank murmured as he stepped inside. He ran a brush down Bob's neck, steady strokes, whispering low. "It's just you and me. Don't mind the noise." Bob blew through his nostrils, then lowered his head to nudge Hank's chest. A soft nicker vibrated in his throat, tension melting under Hank's touch.

Mirabella leaned against the rail nearby, arms folded, relief softening her face as she watched.

Up in the bleachers, Marshall, Grandma Ginny, and Grandpa Joe were finding their seats. Marshall stood still a moment, brim low against the sun, eyes locked on his son. He gave the smallest nod—approval, cautious but real. Hank felt it like a spark in his chest. Grandma Ginny wasn't so restrained. She hurried down before Hank could lead Bob away, wrapped him tight in her arms. The squeeze made his ribs flare hot, but he didn't let it show. "Remember, strength and resolve comes with faith," she whispered. Grandpa Joe clapped him once on the shoulder, saying nothing, but his eyes told Hank all he needed.

June wasn't there. Hank felt the gap as if the bleachers had marked it. She had been there for Jesse's recitals, for Tegan's shows. But not for this. He stuffed the ache deep down, welding it into resolve.

The announcer's mic crackled overhead, testing sound. Vendors shouted about hot dogs and lemonade. By the chutes, murmurs rose louder—side bets passing from hand to hand. Clayton was the favorite, of course. But Hank caught his name, too. *The Miller boy. That buckskin's his. Long shot, but tough. He might surprise them.*

He straightened, brushing the dust from Bob's withers. Underdog or not, he had stepped into the fight. The dust underfoot hung thick with expectation.

And in it, Hank carried more than himself—he carried Bob, the farm, and the weight of every ghost that had brought him here.

By midday, the arena shimmered like a skillet left too long on the stove. Dust hung thick in the heat, stirred by hooves and the shuffle of boots in the bleachers. The announcer's voice boomed over the crackle of the loudspeaker, calling names for the calf roping. Hank pulled his hat tighter, ribs banded in fire beneath his shirt, and swung into the saddle. Bob's ears flicked forward, the buckskin shifting on his feet, tense but ready.

Mirabella leaned over the rail, braid loose against her shoulder, knuckles white on the wood. She whispered as if Bob could catch the words across the din. *You're brave. You're fast. Show them.*

The chute gate banged. A calf burst out, legs scrambling, tail whipping. Hank snapped his rope loose, the burn of the coils familiar against his palm. "Go!" he hissed.

Bob launched forward as if Hank had shot him from a gun. The sudden acceleration punched Hank back into the saddle, ribs screaming. He swallowed the pain, eyes locked on the calf zig-zagging across the dirt. The rope swung high, loop widening, shadow stretching. Hank leaned into it, the movement tearing fire across his side.

The loop dropped clean over the calf's neck. Bob checked himself on instinct, slowing just enough for Hank to dismount. Boots hit the ground, knees jarred, lungs clawing for air. He sprinted three steps, flanked the calf, hands working quick as lightning. A flip, a tie—dust coated his tongue. He threw his hand up.

The flag dropped.

The clock froze, **first place**.

For a beat, the arena was silent, as if everyone had to check the board twice. Then the cheer swelled—cowboys on the rail trading looks, nodding. They'd seen fast horses before, but not like this. Bob hadn't just run—he'd read the calf, adjusted, given Hank the split second he needed. Smart. Under pressure.

Hank patted Bob's neck, breathing ragged. "Atta boy." He wiped grit from his mouth, climbed back into the saddle slowly, ribs shrieking with every pull. He tipped his hat once toward Mirabella. She beamed, clapping until her palms stung.

The next event rolled fast—team roping.

Hank tightened the cinch, jaw set. His partner, an older cowboy with a scar carved across his chin and reins worn smooth, rode up beside him.

"Name's Wade," the man said, spitting tobacco in the dust. "You hold your end, kid, and we'll give 'em something to talk about."

Hank only nodded.

The steer burst loose, horns low, shoulders driving. Wade's loop sailed wide—miss. A groan rolled through the crowd. For a heartbeat, Hank felt the pressure clamp down, ribs pulsing like a drum.

"Easy," he muttered, more to himself than Bob. "Steady."

Bob responded to the low voice, muscles coiling, stride lengthening to cut the steer's line. Hank lifted, swung, the rope sliding through his palm. Pain knifed through his side, but he drove the loop down anyway. It snapped over horns with a jolt.

The crowd erupted, stomping on the bleachers. Dirt boiled under the steer's hooves as Wade swung in again, catching the legs clean. The animal toppled, rope tight.

Third place.

It wasn't perfect, but it was on the board. Hank leaned forward, pressing his forehead to Bob's mane for a breath. The buckskin's hide was hot, damp with sweat, but steady.

Across the arena, Clayton Briggs rode his sorrel gelding through the same event, every movement polished, practiced, the picture of control. His loop landed on the first throw, the steer turned neat, his partner cleaning it up. First place, easy. Clayton tipped his hat to the crowd.

Hank slid off Bob's back, legs wobbling. He grabbed a paper cup of water, the lukewarm liquid sloshing as he downed it. Sweat dripped from his jaw, ribs gnawing with every breath.

"Don't let it win," he muttered, crushing the cup.

By the fence, a pair of younger cowboys leaned on the rail, grinning. "That green colt won't last a season at that speed. Kid'll run the legs off him before the month's out."

Hank ignored them. He dismounted, crouched again, and ran his hands down Bob's legs, brushing the hooves free of stones, murmuring thanks. Bob lowered his nose into Hank's shoulder, blowing warm breath there, steadying both of them.

Then Clayton Briggs rode past, reins loose in his hand, his bay gelding gleaming with years of polish. Clayton tipped his hat toward Hank; his weathered face marked with lines of sun and wisdom..

"Good work, Miller. Keep your loops honest, trust your horse, and don't let the crowd set your pace. You're riding for yourself, not them."

Hank met his eyes and nodded, the respect unspoken but received.

On the rail Mirabella kept her eyes on Bob, murmuring in Spanish now, soft as a lullaby. The horse nosed toward her hand, ears flicking. She smoothed his face, whispering like she always did: *Good boy. Always a good boy.*

Hank tightened his cinch again, swung back into the saddle. His shirt clung dark with sweat, dust caked on his jeans, but his gaze never left the arena. Each bruise, each stab of pain became another stone in the wall of resolve building inside him.

The scoreboard tallied: Clayton Briggs on top, Hank not far behind. Whispers stirred in the crowd—*that Miller boy's tougher than he looks. That buckskin's no fluke.*

Hank spat grit, adjusted the brim of his hat, and set his jaw. They hadn't seen anything yet.

The announcer's voice boomed over the loudspeakers as Hank led Bob out of the arena after team roping. The crowd still buzzed, murmurs chasing him like a trailing dust cloud.

"Next up—steer wrestling. Hank Miller, riding the buckskin stallion, Bob!"

Hank's name cracked through the heat. He felt it settle into his ribs like another weight. He tightened the reins, ignoring the jeers of the younger cowboys along the rail. Bob's ears pricked forward, hooves drumming steadily on the packed dirt as if he, too, had heard the challenge.

The gate clanged shut behind them.

Hank took a breath, ribs tight, vision narrowed to the chute. He gave Bob a squeeze. The buckskin coiled and then exploded forward when the steer burst free, a blur of hooves and horns tearing down the arena.

Dust flew up in choking waves. Hank leaned low, hat brim cutting the wind, every jolt a dagger in his ribs. Bob surged alongside the steer, matching stride for stride, the crowd rising to its feet as the boy and the stallion closed the gap.

Hank launched himself out of the saddle. His boots hit hard; the world shuddered with the impact. Pain tore through his side, white-hot and merciless, but there was no stopping now. He wrapped an arm around the steer's horn, dug his heels into the dirt, and twisted with everything he had left.

The steer fought, eyes wild, muscles bunching against his grip. Hank's vision blurred, ribs screaming, but he drove his weight down, legs braced like stone pillars. The animal bucked once, twice—then collapsed with a crashing thud.

The dust cleared. The horn raked Hank's arm, smearing it red, but his grip didn't falter.

The flag dropped. The clock stopped.

The announcer's voice cracked, almost disbelieving: "New leader—Hank Miller!"

For a heartbeat, the arena fell silent, stunned. Then the roar hit—cheers exploding like thunder across the stands.

On the rail, Marshall gripped the post so tight his knuckles whitened. Pride flared in his chest, but fear pulled at him harder. Beside him, Grandma Ginny whispered a prayer, lips moving fast, eyes bright with tears.

In the shaded stands, Don Antonio shook his head slowly, arms folded across his chest. "Too much weight for one boy," he muttered.

Agustín, watching Hank drag himself upright in the dirt, answered softly, "But he carries it, anyway."

Hank staggered to his feet, chest heaving, blood streaking down his arm. Hands rushed forward to steady him, but he brushed them aside, jaw set. He walked out of the arena under his own power, Bob pacing the rail as though waiting for him.

Mirabella was there before anyone else, her braid flying as she pushed through the dust and noise. She caught his arm, her eyes blazing. "Are you okay?"

Hank forced a grin, though every breath stabbed deep. "Strength comes from faith." He tipped his hat toward the stands where Grandma Ginny sat, her hand pressed over her heart.

Mirabella scowled at his bravado but didn't let go, slipping her arm under his to take some of his weight. For once, Hank didn't fight it.

Together, they walked back toward Bob's trailer, the roar of the crowd chanting 'Hank' then 'Bob' still chasing them—dust, blood, and belief binding every step.

The shade tent buzzed with cowboy talk, the clank of tack, and the steady chomping of horses working through hay nets tied to trailer rails. Dust drifted through the canvas roof beams, cutting golden streaks in the dim.

Bob stood tethered, ice boots strapped snug on his legs, head lowered as Mirabella rubbed liniment across his topline. Her strokes were even, steady, the sharp scent of herbs filling the warm air. Bob sighed, stretching onto her hands, lower lip trembling loose.

"I'll take him for a walk before dark," she said, wiping sweat from her brow with the back of her wrist. "Keep him loose so he won't stiffen up. That's what I always do for Valeroso after a show. Bob will be ready for tomorrow's race."

Hank sat nearby on a folding chair, hat tipped back, ribs bound beneath his shirt. He studied Bob's ears flicking lazily, Mirabella's braid swinging as she leaned into her work. "He's already done more than I thought he could," Hank said, voice low. "Roped clean. Held steady. Didn't lose heart once."

Mirabella looked over her shoulder, green eyes catching his. "Because you didn't lose heart first. He trusts you. That's why he'll keep giving."

Hank didn't answer, but the words burrowed deep.

When she finished with Bob's back, Mirabella knelt beside Hank with Grandma Ginny's old jar of salve and a roll of bandage. Without waiting for his protest, she dipped her fingers into the cool paste and slid them under his shirt to smear it across the bruises striping his ribs. He stiffened, biting back a grunt.

"Stop fighting me," she said, her voice sharp but not unkind. "If you can throw steers, you can sit still long enough for this."

The ointment burned, then cooled, seeping relief into the ache. She wound the bandage tighter around his ribs, her hands sure and practiced. "Better?"

"Better enough," he said, forcing a small smile.

Around them, the cowboys traded stories. On the far side of the tent, Clayton Briggs leaned against a fence rail, easy and confident, chatting with men decades older and younger. His voice carried over the din.

"Kid's got fire," Clayton said, nodding toward Hank. "Giving me a ride for my money today."

Some of the older men grunted approval. A pair of younger hands, leaning against a tack box, snickered. "He'll blow that horse out before the weekend's done. Shame to ruin a good buckskin running him like that."

Hank heard every word. He didn't rise. He didn't even look up. The corner of his mouth twitched, just enough to show he'd taken it in. Sometimes silence was the stronger answer.

Mirabella tugged the knot tight on his bandage and sat back on her heels. "They don't see what I see," she whispered, eyes sliding toward Bob. The stallion shifted, ears pricking as though in agreement.

Hank followed her gaze. Bob stood steady, muscles loose under the sheen of his coat, eyes calm. Not a horse coming apart, not a horse being ruined. A partner.

241

Mirabella rose, brushed the dirt from her knees, and rested a hand on Bob's neck. She leaned close, whispering in Spanish, words Hank couldn't follow but understood in rhythm and tone—words meant to soothe, to promise.

She turned back to him, voice low. "You and Bob aren't alone. Not anymore."

For a long moment, Hank stared at her, the noise of the tent dimming. He thought of the pond where she, Tegan, and he had pledged to be the Three Musketeers. That circle had shattered the day Tegan fell—but here was Mirabella, standing firm, and here was Bob, holding steady.

He nodded once. He couldn't trust his voice to carry what the gesture meant.

The sun dropped lower, shadows stretching under the canvas. Around them, the rodeo pressed on, broncs waiting in their pens, the finale drawing closer. In that hushed corner, boy, girl, and horse stood entwined—not through triumph or coin, but through faith, and the quiet covenant of friendship.

The new Three Musketeers.

The arena shimmered under the floodlights, dust rising in golden clouds as the crowd pressed shoulder to shoulder on the bleachers. The smell of fried dough and manure clung to the air, and the sound of wagers passing hand-to-hand rippled through like wind in tall grass.

This was it. The last event. Bronc riding.

Hank stood at the chutes, hat brim low, ribs bound tight beneath his shirt. Every breath dragged against bruises still fresh, but he'd stopped noticing pain as something separate from himself—it was stitched into his body now, part of him, just another weight to carry.

Beside him, the bronc snorted and slammed its shoulder into the steel, wild-eyed and white-lipped, ropes creaking under the strain. The animal's muscles quivered with coiled rage, dust frothing around its hooves.

A cowboy Hank didn't know leaned against the rail, chewing a toothpick. "That's a mean one," he muttered. "Most wouldn't want him."

Hank just nodded. He didn't have the luxury of wanting.

From the stands, Marshall sat stiff-backed, jaw locked, eyes pinned to his son. Grandma Ginny's lips moved in silent prayer, fingers gripping Grandpa Joe's hand. Agustín and Don Antonio leaned against the rail in their pressed jackets, watching intently. And at the chute gate, Mirabella pressed close, her braid catching in the arena lights, her green eyes bright with fear and something fiercer.

"You don't have to—" she started.

"I do." His voice was calm. "For the farm. For Bob. For Tegan."

Mirabella swallowed, her hand brushing his sleeve. "Then do it for us too. Musketeers, remember?"

Hank gave the smallest smile. The pact had changed, but it lived on. Him. Mirabella. Bob. Carrying Tegan with them in spirit. The Three Musketeers reborn.

He tugged his glove tight, settled the rope, and nodded to the chute man.

The gate banged open.

The bronc exploded into the arena, sun fishing high, legs splaying wide as if it meant to shake the earth apart. Hank's ribs screamed with the first jolt, a searing crack through his side, but his hand stayed welded to the rope, his free arm slicing the air for balance.

The animal twisted, bucked, lunged sideways—every motion designed to fling him a rag-doll cloth. Hank's jaw locked, teeth rattling with every impact, but his legs clamped like iron.

The crowd roared.

"One!"

The bronc pitched forward, nose to dirt, hindquarters snapping high. Hank's head snapped back, his hat nearly flying, but he held.

"Two!"

It spun midair, a twisting sunfish that sent dust spraying into the lights. Hank leaned with it, ribs shrieking, his vision narrowing into a tunnel of raw grit.

"Three!"

The rope burned in his palm, sweat slicking the leather, but he dug in. His body moved in jerks and shudders, but still he was there, glued to the storm.

"Four!"

The bronc landed hard, shoulders hitting like anvils. Hank's breath tore out of him, pain splintering through his chest. For a heartbeat, blackness rimmed his vision. He heard Mirabella's voice faint in his mind—*Musketeers, remember.* He snapped himself back.

"Five!"

Clayton Briggs leaned on the rail, watching, eyes sharp. He didn't grin or smirk. He nodded once, with the faintest flicker of respect.

"Six!"

The bronc reared high, silhouetted against the lights, then crashed down. Hank's body whipped, pain biting into his bones, but his hand never let go.

"Seven!"

Every nerve screamed, his breath coming ragged. His ribs felt like they'd split apart. Still he clung, eyes blazing.

"Eight!"

The whistle cut through the din, sharp and shrill.

The crowd erupted—cheers, stomps, hats flung into the air. Hank ripped his hand free, sliding from the bronc's back as the pickup men swarmed in to settle the beast. He hit the dirt on his knees, chest heaving, shirt smeared with blood from where the bandage had rubbed raw.

He'd made it.

But the arena still held its breath.

Clayton Briggs was next. The veteran swung into the chute with effortless grace, tipping his hat toward the crowd. His bronc burst out, kicking clean, twisting sharp, his form smooth as water. Where Hank fought, Clayton flowed. Where Hank gritted, Clayton styled.

When the whistle blew, the crowd erupted again. The scoreboard lit the numbers—Clayton by a handful of style points.

The announcer's voice boomed: "Ladies and gentlemen, your all-around champion once again—Clayton Briggs! But give a hand to our runner-up, by the slimmest margin we've seen in years—Hank Miller!"

The roar that followed wasn't about pity. It was about respect.

"Closest anyone's come to beating Briggs," someone said.

"That Miller boy can ride," another muttered, awe in his tone.

Hank staggered out of the arena, one arm pressed against his ribs, sweat and blood soaking his shirt. Fire flew through him with every step. But his chin stayed high.

Mirabella was there before anyone else, slipping under the rail, catching his elbow to steady him. "Second isn't last," she whispered fiercely. "You made them believe."

Hank tipped his hat toward his family, toward the Castillas, toward the roaring crowd. His chest burned, his body battered, but pride lit his eyes.

He nodded once to Mirabella, his voice rough. "And belief is enough."

Together, they walked toward Bob's trailer under the buzzing lights, the roar of the crowd fading behind them. The Musketeers—boy, girl, and horse—were ready for what came next.

The rodeo grounds were settling into silence. Lanterns swung from poles, their glow soft against the night, casting long shadows across the trampled dirt. The smell of fried food had thinned, replaced by dust, sweat, and the faint sour note of manure. Crickets had started their chorus, a reminder that the world beyond the arena moved on even after the crowd's roar had faded.

Cowboys moved slowly now, their energy burned out, voices low as they loaded tired horses into trailers. Hooves clanged on ramps, tack jingled, the last of the noise winding down.

Hank stood near Bob's trailer, hat pulled low, still catching his breath. His ribs throbbed like live coals, but the night's pulse dulled the ache, along with the memory of cheers, the sting of loss, and the taste of grit and almost-victory.

A shadow stretched across the lantern light. Clayton Briggs stepped forward, his own hat tipped back, sweat still streaking his face. The reigning champion looked Hank over, eyes sharp but kind.

"Didn't think anyone could make me sweat, Miller." Clayton said, voice low and steady. "You did. Respect."

Hank straightened, meeting his gaze. "Means a lot, coming from you." He reached out, their hands locking in a firm shake. His grip was tired but unflinching. "I'll get you next time."

Clayton's grin flashed. "I bet you will." He tipped his hat again before turning toward the rail where his crew waited, the gesture as much blessing as farewell.

For a moment, Hank just stood there, watching the older cowboy vanish into the shadows. The handshake still tingled in his palm, a marker of respect earned the hard way.

Behind him, footsteps scuffed. Marshall approached, boots dragging in the dirt, his shoulders heavy but his presence solid as bedrock. He stopped close, laid a hand on Hank's shoulder—firm, wordless. Hank didn't need the words. He felt them all the same.

Grandma Ginny swept in next, her arms wrapping him tight despite his grunt of pain. "My brave boy," she whispered fiercely, tears wetting his shirt. She stepped back only when Grandpa Joe reached forward to clasp Hank's hand, the grip rough with callus, steady with quiet pride.

"Good work, son," Grandpa Joe said simply, his eyes shining beneath the brim of his hat.

Hank dug into his pocket and pulled out the envelope of cash, pressing it into his father's hand. "A thousand bucks," he said, his voice sharp with determination. "And there'll be more tomorrow."

Marshall looked down at the money, then back at his son. He didn't argue, didn't remind him of risks or bruises or fear. He just nodded once, eyes steady.

The lanterns hummed. Crickets filled the pause.

But the absence pressed in as hard as the ache in Hank's ribs. There were no soft steps of June's shoes, no mother's arms reaching for him, no voice whispering pride. Hank's jaw tightened, his face hardening as he glanced at the space where she should have been.

Marshall noticed. For once, he broke his silence. He pulled Hank into a rough, uncharacteristic hug. The embrace was stiff at first, but then it tightened, the father holding his battered son against him.

Marshall's voice was low, raw. "I'm proud of you, son. And I love you."

The words landed harder than the bronc's kicks, sharper than the steer's horns. Hank froze, then let himself lean for a heartbeat into the embrace. His father's pride was a salve no doctor could prescribe, no jar of Grandma Ginny's herbs could match.

When they parted, Hank's eyes burned, but his chin stayed high. Tomorrow waited—dust, blood, and another chance. Tonight, he carried victory, bruises, and belief.

The barn had gone still. Lanterns hung low, their glow soft over the rows of stalls, shadows curling where horses shifted in straw. Most of the cowboys had left for the night, their horses fed, watered, and blanketed, trailers locked tight. The dust and noise of the rodeo had faded into the hum of crickets and the steady rhythm of horses breathing in the dark.

Mirabella's boots scuffed softly over the packed dirt aisle. Bob walked beside her, lead rope slack, his head hanging low but his steps steady. His coat gleamed faintly even in the dim light, sweat rinsed and brushed away until only the clean smell of horse and liniment lingered.

She talked to him in a quiet, lilting voice, her Spanish accent softening each word. "You did well today, Bob. Better than any of them thought you could. Better even than Hank believed, maybe." She stroked the buckskin's neck, fingers moving in small, soothing circles. "Do you know, it was Tegan who gave you your name? She said it was perfect—a simple name for a horse of substance. And tonight...you lived up to it."

Bob flicked an ear, blowing out a long breath, as if he understood.

From the shadows at the far end of the barn, Hank paused. He came to check on Bob before turning in, but the sight rooted him to the spot. Mirabella—barely fourteen, her braid falling loose down her back, eyes soft as she whispered to the stallion—looked more certain than anyone he'd ever known.

For a moment, he saw it clear as day: a life ahead, training and breeding horses with her, building something of their own. Not just survival, not just saving the farm—something bigger, steadier, lasting.

He stepped forward, his limp pronounced after the day's pounding, and Mirabella turned. Her face lit with the faintest smile, a mixture of weariness and warmth.

"You should rest," she whispered, though she didn't scold.

"So should he," Hank answered, nodding at Bob. "Figured I'd keep him company for a while."

Together they led the stallion back toward the temporary stall Hank had fashioned beside the trailer—rough boards and rope, but safe enough for the night. Hank stroked Bob's neck before tying him, fingers brushing along the sweat-darkened mane.

"Thank you," Hank whispered, low so only Bob could hear. "You gave me everything you had. And tomorrow...we'll go again."

Bob shifted closer, pressing the weight of his head against Hank's chest, tired but unbroken. Hank's ribs flared with the pressure, but he didn't move away. He leaned into it, drawing strength from the horse's quiet trust.

Mirabella leaned against the rail, arms folded. The lantern behind her caught her profile, making her seem older than her years, etched with both pride and fatigue. "Clayton had three horses tonight," she said. "And you had just one."

Hank met her eyes, a tired grin tugging at the corner of his mouth.

"One's enough," she finished, her voice firm. "If it's Bob."

For a moment, silence stretched. Not empty, but full—of everything unsaid. Hank's chest tightened in a way that had nothing to do with bruised ribs. The look between them was quiet, awkward, raw, but there was no mistaking it.

He smiled. She smiled back. No grand declarations, just that shared understanding—the Three Musketeers reborn.

Bob shifted, pawed once at the straw, then sank to his knees, folding himself into rest. The lantern-glow haloed around him, dust particles floating like tiny sparks.

Hank sank onto the stall rail beside Mirabella, wincing but refusing to let pain show. She slid down to sit in the straw, her shoulder brushing his. They said nothing more, just watched Bob breathe, strong even in sleep.

Bruises screamed across Hank's battered body, yet belief burned steady inside him. Tomorrow the jackpot would decide everything—but tonight, under the lantern's glow, he had Bob, Mirabella, and the fragile strength of faith.

And that was enough.

LIGHTNING ON THE TRACK

T he kitchen carried the warm smell of bacon and biscuits, though no one seemed hungry. Sunlight slipped through the curtains, painting narrow stripes across the worn table. June sat at the end, both hands wrapped around a mug she hadn't touched.

Marshall spread jam over a biscuit; his movements were deliberate. "You ought to come today," he said, voice steady but carrying weight. "Hank needs his family in those stands."

June kept her eyes on the steam rising from her cup. "I don't know if I can," she murmured. Fear pressed at her chest—fear of watching her son battered again, fear of seeing the crowd cheer him into danger. She had hidden from it yesterday, convincing herself it would be easier not to watch. But staying home hadn't eased her worry; it had only sharpened her guilt.

Grandma Ginny laid her fork down, apron still dusted with flour from the morning's baking. "You missed him yesterday, June. He rode hard, finished second, and you weren't there to tell him you were proud. Don't let him face today the same way."

Grandpa Joe set his coffee cup aside and leaned forward, his lined face firm. "This isn't only about the purse or the race. Hank's riding for this family—for all of us. He deserves to see you there, standing with him."

June's gaze drifted past them, to the empty chairs along the table. Tegan's seat would never be filled again. Jesse's seat too, lay cold—her eldest had left without a word, leaving the family to clean up the mess he created. Only Hank remained out there at the show grounds, riding not for glory but to keep the farm alive. The ache of all that absence hollowed her chest.

The clock ticked steadily above the stove. June tightened her grip on the mug until her knuckles paled. The smell of bacon turned sharp in her nose, and the quiet felt suffocating. She had missed too much, letting her fears build walls between herself and her boy.

Her shoulders slumped, and she drew a trembling breath. "Alright," she whispered. She lifted her eyes, rimmed with tears but steady. "I'll go."

Marshall gave a slow nod, sliding his chair back. Grandma Ginny reached across and squeezed June's hand, warm and certain. Grandpa Joe leaned back, satisfied, as though her answer had been carved in stone all along.

The rodeo grounds stirred awake with the first heat of the sun. Hank splashed cold water from a tin basin onto his face, the sting sharpening his breath. His ribs throbbed when he bent to rinse again—yesterday's bronc ride still written into his body. He straightened slowly, wiped his face with a rag, and stood a moment listening to the muffled hum outside the barns.

In the stall beside him, Mirabella moved with her usual quiet precision. Bob stood gleaming under her brush, the buckskin hide lifting and settling with each long stroke. She spoke to him in Spanish, soft and steady, her braid sliding over her shoulder as she leaned in. The stallion flicked an ear but kept still, his sides dark with a sheen that caught the lantern light.

Beyond the rows of pens, the grounds grew louder. The grandstands filled with a rolling rumble of voices, boots clattering on planks, vendors hawking corn dogs and soda in singsong calls. Children shrieked in bursts of laughter, their pennants whipping bright against the breeze. The scents of manure, fried dough, and dust tangled in the morning air, heavy and familiar.

The loudspeakers cracked alive, drawing every head upward. "Ladies and gentlemen," the announcer boomed, "thanks to an anonymous donor, to-day's jackpot purse stands at forty-five hundred dollars!"

From his seat near the Millers, Don Antonio didn't react—except for the faintest twitch of a smile beneath his mustache.

Hank froze, towel hanging slack in his hand. He had been riding for the farm all along—every bruise, every breath pressed through broken ribs—but now it was possible. Yesterday's second place had brought only a thousand. Today, with the purse raised from thirty-five hundred to forty-five hundred, a win would give them enough to clear the mortgage.

Mirabella caught his eye. She didn't need to say it. The number uttered on the loudspeaker had turned chance into certainty.

At the far edge of the grounds, a motorcycle rumbled low and cut out. Jesse swung off, helmet still on, and parked in the shadows behind the bleachers. He kept close to the frame of the stands, half-hidden, careful that no familiar eyes might find him.

A knot of cowboys leaned against the rail nearby, their voices low but sharp enough to carry. "Kid Miller's the one to beat," one said. "Nearly had Briggs yesterday. Tough as rawhide even with busted ribs." Another spat into the dust. "We can't let him take it. He wins, he takes the whole pot."

Jesse's chest tightened. Pride flared first—Hank, his little brother, spoken of as a threat among men who'd been riding longer than him. But the pride soured quickly into jealousy. Hank was doing what Jesse couldn't: fighting for the farm, carrying the family's weight with a rope and a horse. Jesse had been the one with the talent, the big dreams. Now he was bussing tables at a San Francisco diner, strumming his guitar in the shadows.

He pulled off the helmet, ran a hand through his hair, and leaned back against the bleacher post. The sounds of the crowd rising above him made his gut churn. He wanted to be proud without bitterness, but the two tangled until he couldn't tell them apart.

Back by the stalls, Hank shifted to pull on his shirt. Mirabella stepped forward, smoothing the collar into place with one hand. Her palm rested briefly against his chest, warm over the ache in his ribs. He let out a slow breath, steadying himself with that small touch.

The loudspeakers snapped again. "Riders, report to the starting line. Ten minutes until the jackpot race begins!"

From the grandstands, the crowd swelled louder, a tide pulling them toward the arena. Hank closed his eyes once, braced, and opened them again. The storm was coming, and there was no turning from it.

"Ten minutes to the jackpot race!" The announcer's voice cracked again through the loudspeakers, bouncing off the tin roofs and wood rails.

Hank tightened Bob's cinch with a short pull on the latigo, ribs aching with the effort. The stallion shifted under the pressure, ears flicking, but Mirabella laid a steady hand on his neck. She moved with calm precision—bridle checked, breast collar straight, stirrup length checked and adjusted. Her focus steadied Hank more than his own breath could.

When she finished, she brushed her palm over Bob's shoulder, then turned to Hank. She hesitated just a beat, then rose on her toes and kissed him lightly on the cheek. His face flushed, but her own breath caught, as if afraid she'd overstepped. Before he could react, she turned to Bob, kissed his muzzle, whispering soft

Spanish—words meant for him, and maybe for herself too. The stallion's ears pricked, his body easing under her touch.

Across the way, Jesse lingered in the shadows near the rail, helmet hooked on his arm. He watched the three of them—the girl, the horse, his younger brother. Hank wasn't the scrawny kid who trailed after him anymore. He stood taller now, shoulders squared, his jaw hard as iron as he cinched leather and set his face for the fight ahead. Jesse's throat tightened. Hank was stepping into something real, something Jesse himself had reached for once and let slip. Pride surged, then burned into jealousy. Hank had his chance; Jesse had only a diner apron and a stack of unplayed songs.

Mirabella gave Hank's hand a quick squeeze, her eyes catching his eyes for a last moment of unspoken faith, then she turned toward the grandstands. Her braid swung against her back as she climbed to join the Millers, Don Antonio, and Agustín.

The alleyway thickened with riders crowding their horses, dust rising under hooves. A pair of cowboys edged near Hank, voices sharp with mockery. "Those ribs still holding together, Miller?" one drawled. "Better hope that stallion of yours can carry dead weight," another added with a grin.

Their laughter cut like spurs. Hank kept his jaw tight, his hands busy adjusting Bob's reins, refusing to rise to the bait. Still, the words pressed deep, gnawing doubt where the pain already lived. Bob flicked an ear back, waiting for his rider's calm, but Hank's chest tightened.

Above them, the announcer's voice roared again: "Riders to the line!" The crowd thundered in response, a tide surging toward the moment no one could stop.

The air in the chute alley trembled with noise. Riders lined up shoulder to shoulder, their mounts restless behind the taut starting rope. Bob arched his neck, hooves pawing, ears flicking at the surrounding chaos. To his left, a bay snapped at its neighbor's flank; to his right, a gray reared high, striking the air. The rope sagged and jerked as the horses fought for space, nostrils flaring, sweat and dust thick on the wind.

Hank leaned low in the saddle, ribs already aching, whispering into Bob's ear to hold steady. The crowd's roar pressed down like a storm cloud, shaking the grandstands.

The announcer's voice boomed, "Riders—ready!"

The rope dropped.

The pack exploded forward in a blur of muscle and fury. Dirt flew, sunlight flashing off sweat-slick hides. Hank urged Bob on, but the stallion was boxed tight, shoved by the press of horses on either side.

They burst onto the first turn. A rider cut too close—an elbow jabbed, then a fist slammed into Hank's ribs. Pain seared white-hot. He pitched sideways, balance slipping.

Bob felt it instantly. He slowed, head angling back as if ready to catch his rider from falling. In that heartbeat, three, four, five horses thundered past, swallowing the ground Hank had fought for. The grandstands roared for Briggs, the black gelding already driving ahead. "Briggs! Briggs! Briggs!"

Hank clung to the reins, vision swimming. Breath came ragged. He pressed his face into Bob's mane, voice a hoarse rasp. "I need you."

The words lit a fuse. Bob's stride lengthened, his body coiling and snapping like a thunderbolt loosed from the sky. He shot forward, cutting through the dust, weaving past the stragglers first, then clawing back into the heart of the race.

From the stands, Mirabella gripped the rail, knuckles white. Her lips moved in prayer and praise both. Agustín slammed his palm against the boards, shouting Hank's name over the roar. Don Antonio stood tall, composure fraying into a rare smile.

Marshall rose to his feet, hat clenched in his fist. Grandma Ginny clasped her hands tight, whispering encouragement through her tears. June pressed both hands to her mouth, fear and pride twisting inside her. Grandpa Joe leaned forward, elbows braced on his knees, eyes unblinking.

Down on the rail, Jesse's chest heaved. Pride, jealousy, guilt—every emotion ripped through him at once as he watched his brother claw back ground he had no right to gain.

Hank and Bob surged, one horse length, then another. Dust billowed in their wake, cloaking the track in a storm of earth and light.

The final stretch opened wide. Clayton Briggs led, black gelding devouring the ground, the crowd chanting his name louder. "Briggs! Briggs! Briggs!"

Bob answered with fire. Muscles bunched, hooves hammered, and suddenly the chant faltered. Spectators leaned forward, mouths open, watching the buckskin streak from the dust like lightning unchained.

One by one, the voices turned.

"Hank! Hank! Hank!" The name rolled through the stands, gathering strength until it drowned the old champion's cheer.

Neck and neck with Briggs now. Two horses stretched flat against the earth, riders bent low, crowd screaming in a single roar.

Then Bob found one last burst. He drove past, neck extended, mane whipping, body blazing with power. The wire flashed.

They crossed first.

For a moment the world held still—dust suspended in sunlight, the echo of hooves still ringing. Then the grandstand exploded. Hats flew skyward. Boots hammered the boards. The name thundered everywhere at once: "HANK! HANK! HANK!"

Mirabella collapsed against the rail, laughing and crying at once. Agustín whooped loud enough to shake the boards. Don Antonio raised his glass, pride etched on every line of his face.

Marshall tipped his hat, eyes bright. Grandma Ginny clutched June's hand, both of them weeping. Grandpa Joe slapped the rail and shouted, his voice hoarse with pride.

Across the aisle, Don Antonio caught Marshall's eye. He gave a small shrug and a slow wink. Marshall nodded once, lips twitching into a knowing smile.

And Jesse—hidden in the shadows of the bleachers—smiled through the ache. His brother had done what he never could. Lightning on the track—and the family saved.

Hank pulled Bob up from his gallop, the stallion blowing hard, sides heaving, dust and sweat streaking his hide. Bob tossed his head, then turned it back toward Hank, lips tugging playfully at his boot. Hank let out a shaky laugh, reaching down to run his hand along the stallion's damp mane. "Good boy," he whispered, patting his neck with gratitude. The horse snorted, ears flicking forward as if he understood.

The grandstand erupted, hats spinning skyward, boots hammering the planks, voices thundering Hank's name.

Marshall stood tall in the stands, tipping his hat with a rare, full smile. Pride softened his hard features.

Down on the track, Hank gathered the reins and guided Bob toward the center. The buckskin lifted his head high, ears pricked as if claiming the moment. At Hank's cue, Bob reared, hooves slicing the air, while Hank raised his hat overhead like the Lone Ranger saluting Silver. When Bob came back down, Hank leaned forward and cued a bow—forelegs folding, muscles rippling beneath the dust. The crowd roared even louder, the sound rolling like a wave.

Hank's eyes lifted first to the grandstands. He found his mother. June's face crumpled, tears streaming freely, her hands pressed over her heart. For the first time in longer than he could remember, love shone clear between them, steady as sunlight breaking through clouds. He then looked at Mirabella. She leaned over the rail, emerald eyes bright, and blew him a kiss that made his throat tighten.

June broke down altogether, sobbing openly. Marshall slipped an arm around her shoulders, pulling her close. She turned and kissed him through her tears. He met her gaze with a look that held understanding—and forgiveness.

Clayton Briggs rode up slowly, his black gelding slick with sweat. He reined in beside Hank, tipped his hat, and lifted Hank's arm high for all to see. The crowd roared again, honoring the new champion. Hank's breath caught at the gesture, respect passing between them like a torch.

At last, Hank swung down from the saddle. His ribs screamed at the stretch, but his grin broke wide as he loosened Bob's cinch. Mirabella was there in a heartbeat, slipping through the press of people to reach them. She ran a hand down Bob's damp neck, whispered something quick and low, then turned to Hank. Together, they led the stallion from the track, the crowd pressing in on every side.

Children swarmed him, eyes wide, scraps of paper and pencils thrust forward. "Sign this, Hank! Please, mister!" His hands shook as he scrawled his name, each trembling letter proof that this moment was real. The first taste of legend rested in his palm, fragile and dizzying.

Mirabella winked at him, then took Bob's reins. "Go on," she said, her smile proud. "This is yours." She led the stallion toward the trailer, leaving Hank alone in the swell of glory.

Flashbulbs popped, white sparks cutting through the dust and noise. Reporters crowded close, firing questions, cameras clicking. Hank stood in the center of it all—sweat, pain, dust, and triumph—his world forever changed.

The noise of the arena faded behind the barns, replaced by the slow creak of wood and the faint hiss of lanterns burning low. Mirabella stood in Bob's stall, sponge in hand, water dripping dark trails down his sweat-soaked coat. The buckskin sighed under her touch, lowering his head into the crook of her arm.

"You were brave today," she whispered in Spanish, her voice soft but thick with emotion. *"I wish you'd lived to see it, Tegan."* She set the sponge aside and pressed her forehead against his, closing her eyes. "Tegan is proud of you. We both are."

Bob shifted, muzzle brushing against her shoulder, then let out a soft knicker that shivered through the quiet. The sound broke something inside her, and tears slid down her cheeks unchecked.

A scuff of boots on gravel broke the moment. Mirabella lifted her head quickly, brushing at her face. Jesse stood in the shadows of the doorway, helmet dangling at his side, eyes glistening. He had heard every word.

He stepped inside slowly, gaze locked on Bob with his voice unsteady. "Tegan," he said, as if testing the name aloud. His throat worked, and his eyes shone wet. "I left... and Hank carried her better than I ever could." His breath hitched. "That horse—he's her dream. Their dream. All of ours."

Mirabella studied him, her expression softening. She understood then the weight he carried—not only the shame of leaving but the gnawing knowledge that his younger brother had honored the family in ways he never did.

She reached for the brush, then stopped, fingers tightening around the handle. "Help me?" she said, barely above a whisper. It sounded less like an offer and more like a hope.

Jesse hesitated, then took it. He ran the bristles down Bob's flank, slow and trembling, tears slipping free though he tried to hide them. For a moment, it felt like he belonged again, his hand moving in rhythm with hers.

"You should come to the Estancia," Mirabella murmured. "There's room for you still. Tonight is Hank's night, but it doesn't mean you have no place."

Jesse shook his head, eyes still fixed on the stallion. "I'd ruin it for him. Got a gig anyway." The lie cracked in his throat. They both knew it.

He set the brush aside, breathing hard, and turned toward her. "Don't tell him I was here. Please."

"I can't promise that," Mirabella replied. Her gaze met his, unwavering emerald eyes searching his face.

His composure faltered. "You don't know how dark it gets," he whispered.

"I do," she answered softly. "But you can change if you want to."

Jesse's lips trembled, voice raw. "Maybe someday."

He turned and walked out, boots scraping against the dirt. A moment later his motorcycle roared to life, the sound tearing through the quiet before it dwindled into the distance.

Mirabella stayed in the stall, resting her hand against Bob's neck. The stallion shifted, eyes half-lidded, breathing slow. Lantern light flickered against the dust rising in the warm air, and Jesse's shadow lingered long after he was gone.

BREAD, WINE AND PROMISES

T he night sky spread wide above Estancia Castilla, lanterns glowing warm along the courtyard walls and casting long fingers of light across the fields. Hank walked beside Mirabella, Bob's lead rope loose in his hand. The buckskin ambled quietly, steam rising faint from his coat with each slow breath. After the roar of the crowd and the blinding flash of cameras, the hush felt almost holy.

They slipped through the whitewashed gate into the pasture. Bob lowered his head immediately, teeth pulling at the grass still damp from the evening dew. Hank leaned against the top rail, ribs aching with every shift of his body, but a smile he couldn't hold back softened the ache. Mirabella stood close, her braid brushing his arm, the air carrying lavender from the garden and the faint curl of olive wood smoke from the courtyard fire.

"Thank you, boy," Hank murmured, running his hand through Bob's damp mane. The stallion flicked an ear and nickered softly, as if he understood.

Mirabella's voice came quietly beside him. "You and Bob are legends now. But more important than winning is your bond with him. You took a scared, untouchable horse and turned him into a champion."

Hank glanced from Bob to her, the lantern light catching in her emerald eyes. "Couldn't have done it without you," he said. He hesitated, then asked the question that had been pressing at him all night. "When are you going back to Argentina?"

She lowered her gaze, brushing her hand along the rail. "Next week." A pause, heavy as the dark between stars. "I want to go back home. I miss my family." Her eyes lifted again, finding his eyes. "But I also want to stay... I'll miss my new family." She glanced at Bob, then at Hank. "I don't want to leave him, but I know he's in excellent hands." The words faltered there, too shy to admit the truth that trembled beneath them—that she didn't want to leave him.

Silence stretched. Bob chewed steadily, grass tearing in rhythmic snaps. Mirabella finally drew a slow breath. "There's something else."

Hank turned, his smile fading.

"Jesse was at the race," she said. "He stayed hidden. He didn't want to spoil your day."

Hank went still, the words hitting harder than any punch to his ribs. He looked back out over the pasture, jaw tight. "I haven't read his letter," he admitted after a long moment. "Maybe I never will. I want to look forward, not back."

Mirabella's voice was soft, but steady. "To move forward, you must face the past. Jesse should be in your life in some way."

Hank's jaw worked. He let the silence stretch, then whispered, "I'm not ready."

Mirabella's eyes softened. She didn't argue. Instead, she reached across the rail and let her fingers brush his hand, the gesture light as a breath. In the lantern glow, her gaze held steady, carrying both understanding and patience.

Bob lifted his head from the grass and snorted softly, ears flicking toward them before lowering to graze again. Hank watched the stallion in the moonlight, Mirabella's touch still warm against his skin, her words and his own admission lingering heavier than the night air.

Lanterns swayed gently in the branches of the olive trees, their glow spilling across long wooden tables set in rows through the courtyard. Platters of roasted lamb steamed beside bowls of olives and baskets of warm bread. Pitchers of deep red wine caught the light each time they were lifted and poured. Music spilled into the night air—fiddle, guitar, and the sharp beat of a drum echoing off whitewashed walls.

Don Antonio had turned the evening into a fiesta. The vaqueros sat together at one table, laughing loudly and clapping in rhythm, but it was the Millers who held the place of honor in the center. Marshall and June sat at Don Antonio's right, Hank and Mirabella side by side. Grandma Ginny, cheeks rosy in the lamplight, kept the bread basket moving and scolded Hank gently whenever he tried to wave away more food.

When the meal settled, Grandpa Joe produced his old camera, the polished brass gleaming in the lantern light. "A night like this ought to be remembered," he said, shuffling people together. He snapped pictures of the long tables, of Don Antonio with a glass raised, of the Millers caught laughing in the glow. He even leaned across to catch Hank with Mirabella at his side, the boy flushed with attention but smiling despite himself.

Don Antonio rose at last, a glass of wine lifted high. His commanding presence drew silence with ease. "Tonight," he said, voice rolling across the courtyard, "we honor courage. We honor partnership. Hank Miller and his stallion, Bob—together they gave us a race for the ages. The way of the vaquero is not only strength—it is bond. Today, Hank showed us both." Cheers erupted, cups lifted high.

Don Antonio let the sound crest and fall before lifting his glass a little higher. "And we remember Tegan, whose light still guides us. It was she who gave this horse his name. She saw his heart before any of us. Her spirit still rides with them still."

For a breath, the courtyard hushed. Even the fiddler lowered his bow. June pressed a hand to her lips, eyes wet. Hank bowed his head, heat stinging behind his eyes. Mirabella slid her hand into his under the table, her grip firm, anchoring.

Don Antonio's voice carried steadily through the silence. "To Hank. To Bob. To Tegan."

Glasses clinked all around. The silence broke, and the music leapt back, faster and louder, grief folded into joy.

Marshall pushed back his chair, stood, and raised his own glass. His hand trembled slightly, but his voice held. "My boy has worked harder than most men twice his age. He's carried the weight I should've carried for him. Today he showed not only grit, but heart. I'm proud of him." He cleared his throat, then added, half-smiling, "Tomorrow, son, you're coming with me to the bank. We've got business to settle."

The courtyard erupted again. Tables pounded, wine sloshed over rims. Hank flushed hot. He wasn't used to this—the cheering, the spotlight. That had always been Jesse's gift, or Tegan's light. He'd been comfortable in the shadows. Now, every eye was fixed on him, and it was both thrilling and unsettling.

The music surged. Agustín leapt up, pulling Mirabella into the circle. Grandma Ginny clapped along, apron fluttering. One of the Castilla women coaxed June forward, her steps stiff at first but loosening as laughter took her. Marshall even tapped his boot against the stone floor, a grin tugging at his mouth. Grandpa Joe crouched at the edge with his camera, snapping picture after picture as the circle spun.

Mirabella's braid whipped as she twirled, her emerald eyes flashing toward Hank. Then she broke from Agustín and reached for Hank's hand. "Come," she urged.

"My ribs—" he started, but her smile overruled the protest. She tugged him into the circle, his boots heavy, and steps awkward, the crowd laughing and cheering louder at his stiffness. But as Mirabella guided him, her hand warm in his, Hank found a rhythm, halting at first, then freer. The ache in his side flared, but the surrounding joy burned brighter.

For the first time since Tegan's death, the Miller family laughed together, their grief softened by music and light. Grandpa Joe captured the moment—their faces bright, the circle wide—as if to keep it safe for the years to come.

The Estancia Castilla pulsed with life, lanterns glowing, music rising, sorrow loosening its hold for one night.

The courtyard rang with music and laughter, lantern light spilling like liquid gold across the stones. June slipped away into the garden, where rosemary hedges and cypress trees kept the shadows deep. She pressed her hands together, listening to the voices rise behind her. It had been so long since she'd heard her family laugh like that. Too long. And she hadn't earned the sound.

She didn't hear Hank approach until he was standing beside her, the faint hitch in his step giving him away. He leaned against the low garden wall, posture stiff, face unreadable in the half-light.

"Thanks for coming today," he whispered. His voice carried the weight of a man, though his eyes were still young.

June turned, her breath catching at the sight of him in the lantern glow. "I was afraid," she admitted, voice trembling. "Afraid to watch you hurt, afraid of losing you like we lost her. So I stayed away, as if that would protect me." She shook her head, tears welling. "But it didn't protect anything. It only left you alone."

Hank didn't answer, only listened, his hand resting flat on the stone wall, steadying himself against the ache in his ribs.

Her tears slipped free. "I've been so caught up in my sorrow, I forgot to be your mother. I missed too much. I missed you. And yet, you've carried us all. I am so proud of you, Hank. I love you. I should have said it more."

He let her words hang, then spoke with quiet purpose. "Grandpa Joe and I have been working on something. A silver locket. I want to give it to Mirabella before she leaves next week, with a picture of Tegan on one side, Bob on the other. That way she can take them with her to Argentina."

June's tears deepened, shame mingling with awe. "I didn't even think of her birthday," she whispered. "I was too lost in myself. I should've thought of it, Hank. But... if you'll let me, I'd be honored to help you choose the photos."

He nodded once, a simple acceptance.

June studied him through her tears, the way his voice softened when he spoke Mirabella's name, the way his gaze turned steady at the thought of giving her something so meaningful. She didn't ask, but she knew—the feelings he carried for Mirabella were real, deep-rooted in a way that was no boyish crush.

Her chest ached, but differently now. She reached for him, gathering him into her arms. His ribs made him flinch, but he didn't pull away. His arms circled her back–awkward, strong, certain.

From the courtyard came another swell of music, laughter carrying on the night breeze.

When she let go, June wiped her cheeks with her sleeve, ashamed yet lighter. "Thank you," she whispered.

Hank only nodded, his face calm, compassionate. Then he turned back toward the lantern glow, leaving June in the garden, hope flickering where regret had ruled for far too long.

Dawn spread pale light across the Miller farm, gilding the pastures in silver mist. Hank and Marshall trudged in from the barn, boots heavy with straw and mud, the smell of milk and hay clinging to their clothes. They had milked the cows, fed the chickens, watered the horses—and even slopped the pigs, who had greeted them with squeals and snorts, jostling each other at the trough. Ordinary chores for an ordinary morning, though nothing about the day felt ordinary.

When they stepped into the kitchen, the air was thick with the smell of blueberries and sausage. The table displayed Hank's favorites: sausages sizzling on a platter, eggs fluffed in a bowl, and biscuits steaming in a towel-lined basket. At the stove, June flipped a pancake shaped like a lopsided steer. Another browned in the pan, a cowboy hat in blueberries. She turned, cheeks flushed, hair loose around her face.

"Surprise," she whispered. "Breakfast fit for a champion."

And from the radio perched on the counter, country music twanged low—a song about grit and dust and holding on. June had turned it on in Hank's honor. Music had always been Jesse's domain, but today it played for Hank.

She slid a plate piled with the special pancakes into Hank's hands. He took it, staring down at the strange shapes. His throat tightened. He remembered mornings when Tegan used to slide her extra sausage onto his plate without a word, knowing he was hungry but too stubborn to ask. She had always thought of others first. And now, standing in the kitchen, Hank saw it—that same thread ran through their mother. For years he had put her on a pedestal as some untouchable musician, or else pushed her away for not being there. But here she was, an apron dusted with flour, cooking for him. Not unreachable. Just human. Just his mother.

Grandma Ginny called everyone to the table, bowing her head as they settled in. Her voice was steady, rich with gratitude. "Lord, we thank You for watching over Hank during the rodeo and the race. We thank You for Bob, for this family gathered here, and for the bounty of food before us. May we never forget where our blessings come from. Amen."

"Amen," the family echoed, hands loosening as they passed the plates.

The door creaked open, and Grandpa Joe stepped in, his boots carrying the dust of town. In his hands was the morning newspaper, folded crisp. "Hot off the press," he said, laying it flat in the center of the table.

The family crowded in close. Across the front page stretched a photograph—Hank and Bob mid-stride, dust flying, man and horse locked in perfect motion. The headline screamed his victory.

June lifted the paper, holding it with trembling fingers. Her eyes filled, tears sliding silently down her cheeks. "Look at you," she whispered.

"I'm building a frame for this one," Grandpa Joe said firmly. "Something worthy of the moment."

Hank flushed, pushing back in his chair. "It's too much."

Marshall's gaze cut to him, calm and steady. "This is just the start," he said. "You've got more in you."

The kitchen fell quiet for a beat, the weight of his words settling over the table. Hank stared at the headline, at Bob's stretched stride frozen in time, and tried to see himself the way the world suddenly saw him.

Monday morning broke clear, sunlight slanting across the valley. Marshall eased open the barn doors, and there sat Bess, his 1972 Chevy C20, red and white two-tone paint shining like enamel under the morning sun. He kept her polished as if time could never touch her. Gravel crunched beneath their boots as he and Hank crossed the yard.

The truck's door groaned as Hank climbed in beside his father. The bench seat was smooth and firm, smelling of Armor All and the faint tang of oil. Marshall turned the key. Bess rumbled to life, steady and strong, exhaust puffing white in the morning chill.

They rolled down the gravel drive; the tires threw small stones into the ditch. Dust lifted in their wake, hanging like a pale ribbon over the farm road. Neither spoke at first. Hank fidgeted with his hat in his lap, ribs aching each time the truck bounced over a rut. The silence wasn't empty—it carried the weight of all they'd been through.

Whitaker Falls Bank sat squat and solid at the corner of Main, its brick faded but dignified, the glass door etched with the town's crest. Inside, the air smelled faintly of lemon polish and ink, just as it had when Hank was a boy waiting on the lobby chairs while Marshall spoke business. The wooden counters gleamed, the floors worn by generations of boots.

"Marshall," Douglas called warmly from behind the desk. His tie was crooked, his hair thinner than Hank remembered, but his grin was easy. "Good to see you. And this must be the young man of the hour."

Marshall tipped his hat. "Morning, Douglas. We've come to settle some business."

"Business, is it? Or a celebration?" Douglas chuckled as he ushered them into his office. "Either way, the town's still buzzing about that race."

Marshall set the envelope on the desk, thick with winnings. "Let's see the Millers free and clear."

Douglas sorted the bills with care, then slid the papers across the oak desk. "Well, Marshall, it's done. The mortgage is cleared. The Miller farm stands on its own again."

Relief passed across Marshall's face, quiet but certain.

Douglas tapped the small remaining stack of bills. "And you've even got a little extra. Might be time for this young man to start a savings account."

Marshall glanced at Hank. "That's yours. You're opening an account today."

Hank bent to sign the forms, his hand trembling a little as he scrawled his name. When he straightened, Douglas extended his hand across the desk. Hank took it, the man's grip firm.

"I'll look forward to doing more business with you in the future," Douglas said.

Hank blinked, then nodded, a strange heat rising in his chest. The handshake carried more weight than the paper—like a door to something he couldn't yet see but knew he would build.

Back in Bess, Marshall steered them toward the ridge. Gravel crunched beneath the tires, and the valley stretched wide below. He cut the engine, and for a moment only the tick of cooling metal filled the cab. They exited the cab and walked out onto the ridge overlooking the valley.

He unscrewed the dented thermos, poured two cups, and handed one to Hank. The steam curled between them.

Hank looked out over the valley. "Last time you brought me here," he said slowly, "you'd bailed me out of jail. Jesse was left to sleep it off."

Marshall gave a curt nod. "Different day. Different man beside me."

They sat for quite a moment, coffee warming their hands.

"You've proven yourself," Marshall said, voice low but steady. "Time I treated you like a partner. The Miller farm has been in our family for generations. There's no one I'd trust more with its future. You'll take it farther than me or Grandpa Joe ever could."

Hank's throat tightened. "What about Jesse? I thought the farm always went to the eldest."

Marshall sighed, his shoulders heavy. "Farm life was never for Jesse. I made the mistake of trying to force it on him. Should've let him follow his music sooner. Maybe Tegan would still be here if I had. That's a mistake I'll carry to my grave."

Hank turned. For the first time, he saw not only the strength in his father's face, but the pain etched deep, borne alone for too long. He made a promise to himself then—he would never let his father carry it all again.

After a silence, Hank spoke, voice quiet. "Mirabella told me Jesse was at the race. He hid in the stands. I don't know what to do, Pa. I love him... but I don't know if I want him in my life. Not like this."

Marshall looked out over the valley. "Jesse's his own man. You can't ride his trail for him. But he's blood. Someday you'll have to decide how far to let him back in. Don't rush it. You'll know when it's time."

Hank nodded, torn but steadier for having said it aloud. His eyes swept the land below. "I want to build something here. A breeding and training facility. With Bob at the heart of it. For Tegan."

Marshall didn't speak, so Hank kept going, the words dragging truth behind them.

"I thought I was honoring her when I started training Bob. But the truth is, I was trying to *fix* it. All of it. I rushed him. Got myself thrown. And still I pushed, like if I could just make him into something perfect, maybe I could outrun the way she died."

He looked out over the valley, jaw tight.

"But Bob's not a machine. And neither was Tegan. She always said horses were partners, not projects. I forgot about that. I forgot *her* in the way I tried to keep her alive."

The wind stirred the grass below them. Hank exhaled.

"Now I want to do it differently. Train with patience. Build something real. Not out of grief... but out of *grace*. That's what Tegan would've done. She believed in second chances—gave Bob one when no one else would. She deserved one, too."

His voice dropped, more vulnerable now. "And Mirabella... I don't want her to go back to Argentina. We're young, but—I see my future with her."

Marshall turned then, and for the first time that morning, a smile broke across his face. Not wide, but warm. "She's worth it, Hank. Worth waiting for. Worth fighting for. Treat her with respect and make sure her dreams are the same as yours. That's the only way a life together will stand."

Hank met his father's eyes, the weight of the advice sinking deep.

Marshall lifted his cup. "Then build it, son. Build all of it."

They stood side by side leaning against Bess's hood, coffee warming their hands, the valley stretching endlessly beneath the morning sun—past, present, and future bound between them, no longer untamed, but full of promise.

PETALS ON THE WATER

I t had been a week since the rodeo and the race. The days had drifted, with a quiet that settled after storms, though bruises lingered and chores never ceased.

At dawn, the first light slanted through the narrow window of Grandpa Joe's workshop, laying long streaks across the scarred oak bench. Sawdust drifted in the air like pollen, catching in the golden beams. The place smelled of linseed oil, oak curls, and iron filings — the scents that had carried Hank through months of learning patience beneath his grandfather's steady eye.

He bent low over the bench, ribs still stiff, hands steady despite the ache. With tweezers, he guided the photographs into place inside the silver heart locket. On one side, Tegan's smile lit up the tiny frame, her hair loose and wild, eyes caught in mid-laughter. On the other, Bob stood at rest in the pasture, golden coat bright against the grass, his ears pricked as if listening.

The clasp clicked shut with finality. Across the front, engraved in curling script, gleamed a single word: *Mia*. Tegan's nickname for Mirabella, simple yet tender, pressed into the silver as if to last beyond them all.

Grandpa Joe leaned on his cane, studying Hank without a word. When they finished the work, he gave a single nod — the same quiet sign he had given the day they finished shaping Bob's bit together. The memory hung there, heavy with meaning. Hank's hands had grown sure since then, his fabrication work now honed to a craftsman's polish under Grandpa Joe's watchful eyes.

Hank exhaled slowly, setting the tweezers down. His mother stepped forward, carrying an envelope of photographs. She had spent the last two evenings bent over the kitchen table, sorting through dozens of prints. Now she touched the locket lightly, her voice low.

"These were the right ones," June said. "She'll carry both with her. Tegan, and Bob."

Her hand brushed Hank's shoulder, warm, steadying. Her smile wavered at the edges, caught between pride and sorrow. "It's beautiful."

She reached for the locket, careful as if it were glass. "I'll wrap it in tissue and ribbon before you give it to her."

From outside came the crunch of tires on gravel, the sound of an engine drawing close. June glanced toward the window, the faintest curve of a knowing smile on her lips.

"That'll be Agustín," she whispered. "He's bringing Mirabella."

The sound of the car faded down the lane. Dust swirled in the first light of morning, drifting across the porch and the yard. Outside, the car door slammed shut, followed by the familiar sound of boots on gravel. Mirabella had arrived.

Inside the workshop, the silver locket lay wrapped in tissue and ribbon, waiting.

Not long after, before the breakfast table filled, Grandma Ginny beckoned Mirabella into the herb garden. She did it with a wave of her hand and a look that made it clear she would brook no argument. The garden was her domain — rows of rosemary and lavender, beds of marigolds burning orange, and sage bushes spilling over their borders. Bees moved lazily from bloom to bloom, their hum a kind of hymn that rose and fell with the breeze.

Grandma Ginny's motives were layered. She wanted to give Hank, June, and Grandpa Joe time to finish their work inside, but she also wanted a moment with the girl who had become woven into their family's days. Tegan had taken after Grandma Ginny more than anyone — the spark in her step, the wildness tempered by loyalty — and so it felt natural that Mirabella, with her quiet fire, had found a place in the old woman's heart as well.

She moved to the garden bench and lifted a small jar, pressing it into Mirabella's hands. The salve inside carried the sharp-sweet tang of comfrey and calendula.

"You remember this," Grandma Ginny said. "The same salve you and Tegan rubbed on Bob after that poor horse was beaten by the estancia hand. Hank used it too. It heals more than skin. Keep it close."

Mirabella closed her fingers around the jar, her eyes shadowed with the memory of Bob's trembling body and the way Tegan had coaxed him calm. She nodded. "Thank you."

Grandma Ginny bent again, this time snapping sprigs of rosemary and lavender. She tucked them carefully into Mirabella's satchel, her hands steady despite their age.

"For remembrance and safe travels," she said. "Wherever you go, carry a piece of this valley with you."

Mirabella's throat tightened. She leaned forward and hugged her. Grandma Ginny's frame was small but solid, smelling of sun-warmed herbs, wood smoke, and earth.

When they stepped apart, Grandma Ginny reached into her apron pocket and drew out a slim bundle wrapped in faded ribbon — an antique pen and a small stack of paper, yellowed at the edges.

"Write to me about your home from time to time," she said, pressing it into Mirabella's palm.

Mirabella smiled through misted eyes. "I would love to. Would you write to me and let me know about the Miller farm?"

Grandma Ginny's eyes twinkled, her mouth curving into a mischievous grin. She knew exactly what the girl was asking, even if Mirabella wouldn't dare to speak it plainly. "Of course," she said.

Mirabella laughed softly, fingers tightening around the bundle as if it might slip away. The bees droned on; the herbs swayed in the breeze, and the moment settled deep into both of them, fragrant and unspoken.

Grandma Ginny and Mirabella walked into the kitchen filled with morning light, curtains drawn back to let the sun spill across the oak table Grandpa Joe had built. The table nearly disappeared beneath platters and bowls — golden empanadas still steaming, flaky media lunas dusted with sugar, thick biscuits rising high as bricks, scrambled eggs flecked with fresh parsley and thyme. The smells of butter, chorizo, and brewed coffee mingled in the air, a union of Argentina and America laid out in food.

Mirabella sat straight-backed at the table, though her braid slipped loose over her shoulder. She had chosen her clothes carefully, yet the softness of her hair and the brightness in her eyes made her look both elegant and fragile, caught between girlhood and something more.

Grandma Ginny raised her voice, gentle but firm. "Joe, would you say grace this morning?"

Grandpa Joe folded his hands. His voice, slow and resonant, filled the kitchen. "Lord, we thank You for the bounty before us — for hands that worked the fields and hands that shaped the meal. We thank You for Mirabella, who has brightened our home in days that felt dark. Safeguard her travels to her family, keep her steady in Your care, and let her carry a piece of this valley with her always — and guide her back to us again, when the time is right. Amen."

As the blessing washed over him, Hank's gaze strayed to Mirabella. Her eyes were closed, lashes brushing her cheeks, her braid resting across her shoulder. In that moment, she looked as though she belonged here — not as a guest, but as part of them. Hank's chest tightened with a fierce, wordless vow: he would make it happen. Somehow, someday, there will be more breakfasts like this one.

A chorus of amens followed. They passed the plates, laughter spilling as they traded stories of the rodeo and the race. Hank told how Bob had crow-hopped in the chute before settling like he'd been waiting his whole life for that moment. Mirabella laughed, cheeks flushed, as Marshall teased Hank about nearly getting dumped in front of the grandstand. Even Grandma Ginny chuckled, her eyes bright. For a while, the table felt whole, the burdens lifted.

The laughter softened into smiles, conversation quieting like a creek easing past stones. June rose silently and stepped into the next room.

When she returned, she carried a parcel wrapped in ribbon. Her hands lingered on it for a moment before she set it in front of Mirabella.

Mirabella untied the bow, careful not to tear the paper. Inside lay a stack of sheet music, the pages softened at the edges, notes pressed into the yellowed paper like veins in leaves. Her breath caught. Fingers trembling, she looked up at June, wordless.

June's voice wavered but did not break. "I always thought these would be Jesse's. But now... I see they're meant for you."

The room stilled. Hank stared at his mother, stunned. The shift in her heart was plain — she had given Mirabella not only music, but a piece of herself, the quiet acceptance of who would carry that legacy forward.

She bowed her head slightly, as though the weight of the gift asked for reverence.

Marshall cleared his throat, leaning back in his chair. A faint smile touched his face, rare as rain in a drought. "You'll always be a part of this family," he said.

Grandma Ginny murmured a blessing, her voice like a prayer wrapping the moment in silk.

Mirabella lowered her gaze to the sheet music, then lifted it again. Across the table, her eyes found Hank's. They did not speak, but something passed between them — quiet, steady, undeniable.

The clatter of dishes drifted from the kitchen as June and Grandma Ginny cleared the table. Grandpa Joe lingered with his coffee, humming under his breath, while Hank slipped out the back door to ready the Apache for the drive.

Mirabella stepped onto the porch, the morning air cool against her cheeks after the warmth of the crowded kitchen. She paused at the top step, the sheet music pressed lightly to her side like a secret. The hum of bees from Grandma Ginny's garden still carried on the breeze, mingling with the faint creak of leather from Hank adjusting tack in the truck bed.

Marshall stood near the railing, thermos in hand, his boots set firm on the porch boards. He watched her for a moment, his gaze steady but not unkind.

"Thank you," he said at last, his voice low, even. "For being the sister Tegan always wanted. She loved you, Mirabella."

Her hand rose instinctively to her chest, pressing over her heart. The composure she had carried through breakfast trembled now, her voice a whisper. "I loved her too."

Marshall shifted his thermos to his left hand and stepped closer. He wrapped his arm around her back and gave her shoulder a firm squeeze, nothing more. No extra words, no ceremony. His blessing spoke the only way he knew how.

Mirabella held the sheet music tighter, her boots warm on the porch boards, and let the silence stand between them, heavy with meaning.

Marshall's words lingered in the quiet like the last echo of a hymn. Mirabella stood still on the porch, one hand pressed to her chest, the ribboned parcel clutched in the other.

His blessing had been simple, gruff, but it opened something inside her. She remembered an afternoon not long after she first arrived, standing by Valeroso's stall as she was showing Tegan her beautiful grey PRE stallion.

Mirabella had lowered her voice. "What's Hank like? Truly?"

Tegan had tilted her head, thoughtful. "He feels things real deep, but doesn't talk about it. He acts like he doesn't care... but he always shows up. That's how you know he does."

Now, listening to Marshall speak of her as the sister Tegan always wanted, Mirabella understood more. She saw Hank in those words — not the boy who hid behind silence, but the one who carried loyalty like marrow in his bones. The one who would always show up.

She drew a breath, steadying herself, and pressed the sheet music tighter to her chest.

In the yard, Hank cinched the spare saddle and checked the Apache's bed—lariat, two lead lines, a tow strap—each coiled tight. He felt the presence before he saw it — the slow tap of a cane against packed dirt.

Grandpa Joe shuffled up beside him, eyes sharp under the brim of his hat. He waited until Hank wiped his hands on his jeans and turned toward him.

"You built her something with your hands," Grandpa Joe said, his gaze dipping to the locket Hank still carried in his palm. The tissue wrapping rustled softly as Hank closed his fist around it.

"That means more than words," Grandpa Joe went on, leaning a little heavier on his cane. "Women remember when a man makes something last."

Heat crept into Hank's cheeks. He ducked his head, not trusting himself to answer.

Grandpa Joe's eyes twinkled, sly as a boy's despite his years. "Don't worry," he added. "That one'll remember."

Hank swallowed hard, the locket's weight pressing into his palm, and for a moment, even the ache in his ribs seemed far away.

The Apache idled by the porch, its engine humming steadily as Hank stepped out to open the passenger door. Mirabella still stood where Marshall had left her, the ribboned parcel pressed against her chest. She turned when Hank met her eyes.

"Before we go to the estancia," she whispered, "will you take me to Tegan's grave? I need to see her one more time."

Hank only nodded.

They drove in silence up the lane and parked near the rise where the family plot lay. Dew clung to the grass, soaking the cuffs of their boots as they walked side by side through the hush. The air smelled of earth and lavender, sharp from the sprigs Mirabella carried in her satchel.

The headstone rose plain and unadorned against the morning sky, yesterday's flowers faded at its base. Mirabella knelt, laying down a fresh bundle from Grandma Ginny's garden — marigolds bright as fire, lavender cool as dusk, rosemary bound in twine. Her hand lingered on the stone, her fingers tracing the carved letters.

Her voice wavered, yet it carried. "I wanted to bring you to Estancia Castilla. To show you the horses, the olive trees, my family's home. To keep teaching you dressage, and Spanish, and the old dances. We were only beginning, Tegan." Her braid slipped forward, brushing her shoulder. "I would have done all the things an older sister should."

Hank lowered beside her, palm pressed flat to the stone's cool surface. His words came out roughly but with certainty. "We're still the Three Musketeers. That doesn't end here."

Mirabella's lips trembled. She straightened her shoulders, her voice quiet but fierce. "Then I'll carry your dream, Tegan. All of it. *I'm going to Argentina. Then I'll travel the whole world. I'll learn ten languages. I'll sing, dance, and become the best cowgirl the world's ever seen.*" A tear streaked down her cheek, but her chin lifted with resolve. "I promise I'll make it so. For both of us."

Her hand sought Hank's, their fingers threading together against the stone. Neither moved to let go.

Hank swallowed hard, his chest aching in more ways than one. He didn't speak the thought aloud, but it burned steady in him: if Mirabella vowed to carry Tegan's dream into the world, then he would vow to keep her tethered here, to this valley, to him. He would tend the land, build a life worthy of her return, and lay flowers on this grave as long as he drew breath.

It felt almost like a ceremony — a vow spoken to the dead but binding the living. The weight of it settled between them, not as a burden but as a bond.

A breeze swept over the hill, scattering petals across the soil. They danced and spun, laughter caught in the wind — fleeting but alive, as if Tegan herself had heard and answered.

Mirabella tightened her grip on Hank's hand. He met her gaze, and for a moment, with the stone between them and the valley opening wide around them, it was as if they had spoken vows meant for a lifetime.

The Apache rattled down the familiar road, its tires kicking up soft clouds of dust that hung in the warming air. Hank drove without hurry, letting the hum of the engine carry the silence. The vows they had spoken at Tegan's grave still lingered, but neither needed to fill the space with words.

The whitewashed walls of Estancia Castilla came into view, the olive groves glinting in the sun. Hank turned the truck onto the gravel drive and brought it to a slow stop.

Mirabella gathered the satchel at her feet, the ribboned parcel of sheet music, and the small bundle Grandma Ginny had pressed into her hands. She looked once toward the pasture where Bob grazed, golden against the grass, then back at the house.

"I should put these away first," she said. "They'll keep better inside."

Hank lifted his chin. "Go on. I'll meet you by the pasture."

She slipped through the estancia's heavy wooden door; her figure vanishing into the cool shadow of the entry hall.

Left alone, Hank moved toward the stables. The air was thick with the smell of hay and horse sweat, flies buzzing lazily in the warm light. He chose a sturdy

Castilla gelding, brushing dust from its flank before swinging a saddle into place. The gelding flicked an ear, patient beneath Hank's hands as he tightened the cinch and checked the bridle. The familiar rhythm steadied him, giving his thoughts somewhere to rest.

By the time Mirabella returned, her arms were empty, her step lighter. She didn't pause at the truck or the stable but walked straight toward the pasture fence, braid swaying against her back.

"Bob!" Her voice rang clear across the fields.

The buckskin raised his head, ears pricked, and for a moment he stood motionless, as though testing the call. Then he broke into a gallop, mane streaming like fire in the sunlight, hooves pounding the ground in a thunder Hank could feel through the soles of his boots.

Mirabella laughed, her voice catching between joy and tears. She pressed her cheek against Bob's forehead when he reached her, arms tight around his neck. Bob blew warm breath against her braid, nickering low as if he had been waiting only for her.

Hank swung up onto the gelding's back, guiding it out into the pasture. He watched Mirabella vault onto Bob with the ease of a vaquera, settling bareback against his broad back, her hands twined lightly in his dark mane.

Their eyes met across the pasture. No words passed, only an understanding as sure as the rhythm of hooves beneath them. Together they turned their mounts toward the pond, riding side by side as the valley opened wide before them.

The ride to the pond stretched quiet and steady. Hank let Mirabella guide Bob ahead, the buckskin's stride long and fluid, while his own gelding matched pace beside them. Dust rose softly around their boots, sunlight slipping through the oaks to dapple the trail.

As they neared the water, Hank's eyes went to Bob. The stallion's ears flicked between them, his body alive with fire under Hank's training yet softened under Mirabella's touch. Hank felt a swell of something he couldn't name. Bob had given him grit, the fight to stand when the world wanted him broken. Mirabella had given Bob calm, the gentleness he hadn't known he needed. The horse belonged to them both, two halves of the same trust.

They dismounted at the bank. The pond glimmered in the morning light, reeds whispering at its edge, the same place where their friendship had begun in awkward conversation. Now it held more: grief, survival, and a bond stronger than either expected.

Hank reached into his pocket and unwrapped the tissue. The silver heart locket glinted in his palm. "For you," he said.

Mirabella took it reverently. Her breath caught as she opened the clasp, seeing Tegan's smile on one side, Bob in the pasture on the other. Her thumb brushed the engraving on the front. "Mia," she whispered, the name like a prayer.

Her eyes lifted to his. "Help me put it on?"

Hank stepped behind her. His fingers fumbled with the clasp, brushing her braid. He managed to fasten it, the chain catching sunlight as it settled against her collarbone.

She touched the locket, voice trembling. "Thank you, Hank. This means more than I can ever say."

"I just wanted you to carry them with you," he whispered. "So you don't forget."

She shook her head. "I won't. I couldn't."

They sank onto the grass, shoulders brushing as they faced the water. Silence stretched, full and steady.

Mirabella broke it first. "Grandma Ginny gave me paper and a pen. She wants me to write to her about Argentina. I told her I would." A small smile touched her lips. "She promised she'd write me back with news of the farm."

Hank smirked. "You mean news about me."

Her mouth curved, teasing through the sadness. "Of course. Someone has to keep track of you when you become a famous cowboy."

Hank chuckled under his breath, shaking his head. "Famous, huh? Not likely." His smile faded, thought creeping back in. "Truth is... there are still things I've got to face before I can think about any of that." He picked at a blade of grass, eyes fixed on the rippling water. "You once told me I should try with Jesse. Have some kind of relationship."

Mirabella's hand brushed his, not quite clasping. "You'll know when it's time. And when you do, you won't be facing it alone."

Something loosened in his chest. He nodded. "Someday. Not yet. But someday."

Mirabella leaned closer, her head resting lightly on his shoulder. Hank froze for a breath, then let himself breathe into it. She smelled of lavender and dust, of the valley itself.

"Promise me you'll come to Argentina," she breathed. "See my horses. Hear me play."

He turned his head slightly, speaking into the crown of her hair. "I'll save enough. I'll come. No matter how long it takes."

Their eyes held, the moment charged but restrained, as if they both understood what waited in the years ahead. They sat that way; the locket gleaming at her throat, the pond glimmering before them.

Mirabella's gaze drifted to the reeds and back again. "Do you remember? Here, under the tree." Her hand brushed the grass. "Tegan made us promise — best friends forever."

Hank's throat tightened. He saw it clearly: Tegan's small hands clasping theirs, the triangle they had made together.

"Forever," he murmured, the word carrying the weight of both past and future.

Mirabella lifted her head just enough to meet his eyes. "Forever," she echoed.

Not lovers, not yet. But bound by vows — hers to carry Tegan's dream into the world, his to keep her tethered to this valley. The pond bore witness to it all, as it had before.

The sun climbed higher, warming the meadow. Mirabella rose, brushing grass from her skirt, her hand lingering on the locket at her throat. Somewhere far off, a screen door creaked. Mirabella glanced toward the distant shape of the estancia, a flicker of decision in her eyes.

"I have to get back. Agustín will be waiting."

Hank stood too, his boots heavy in the damp earth. He met her eyes, and she saw it plain — he couldn't follow. Watching her leave would be harder than holding onto this moment.

She gave a small nod, understanding, and managed a whisper. "Goodbye, Hank."

With one fluid motion, she swung onto Bob's back. The buckskin broke into a gallop, carrying her across the meadow. Sunlight poured over her, the braid trailing down her back as she rode toward the whitewashed walls of the estancia.

Hank stayed behind at the pond, the ribbon that had once bound the locket curling in his palm. The reeds whispered, the water rippled, but he did not move.

He bowed his head and whispered to the quiet, "One's enough, if it's Bob."

A PLACE AT THE TABLE

T he sun had barely crested the hills when Hank pulled the Apache into the gravel lot at Estancia Castilla. Dust clung to the truck's fenders, to his boots, to the cuffs of his jeans. He swung down stiffly, shoulders heavy from a night spent too restless for proper sleep. The valley smelled of dew and olive smoke, sharp on the morning air.

Inside the barn, the air was cooler, quiet but not empty. Hank stepped into the tack room first, and the ache hit him square.

Everything bore her hand. Bridles gleamed on the racks, each one polished and tagged with her neat script. Saddles sat spotless, their leather supple from conditioning, not a speck of dust on the stitching. In the corner, her tall dressage boots stood side by side with her field boots, both polished to a high gloss. On the tack trunk, a dark ribbon lay coiled loosely, as if she had set it down in haste and forgotten it.

Hank reached for the ribbon, folded it carefully, and slipped it into his pocket. The weight was small but steady, something of hers he could keep close.

He moved down the aisle until he reached Valeroso. The gray stallion lifted his head at the sound, ears flicking forward. Her last scrubbing still made his coat shine, and she had raked the stall clean, hanging the buckets at the height she always preferred.

Hank leaned against the stall door. "She'll be back," he said, voice low.

Valeroso nickered, stretching his neck. Hank pulled a sugar cube from his pocket and offered it on his palm. The stallion's lips brushed against his skin, warm and soft.

"I know," Hank murmured. "You miss her too." He stroked the horse's forehead. "She'd stand here talking to you in Spanish, like you understood every word. Maybe you did. She called you her professor. Said you were teaching her as much as she was teaching you."

The stallion blew softly, as if answering.

"She's got her dreams," Hank went on, his voice rough but steady. "Argentina, the horses, her music. She'll chase them. But she'll come back. To you. To this place."

Valeroso tossed his head, as if he agreed, and Hank let a small smile break across his tired face. "Until then, we'll keep you ready."

A voice behind him, clipped and precise: "You must be Hank."

Hank turned. Mirabella's dressage coach stood in the aisle, tall and angular, a tack bag slung over his shoulder. His German accent clipped the edges of his words, his English colored with an academic polish.

"That's me," Hank said.

"I am here for Valeroso," the man replied, stepping closer. "Fräulein Mirabella was... very exacting with his work."

Hank gestured toward the brushes and wraps. "I can help get him ready."

One brow arched. "You would?"

Hank stepped into the stall. He ran his hand down Valeroso's leg, crouched, and began unrolling the standing wraps. Each layer came away smooth and even, no tugging, no haste. He folded them neatly, stacking them at the door. Then he reached for a set of polo wraps, rolling them tight in his hands before winding them back on with precision—flat, even pressure, never a wrinkle to pinch tendon or skin. When he finished, the white cloth looked like it had grown onto the horse's legs. He pulled on the bell boots, checking the fit so they covered the bulbs of the heels without rubbing.

The coach leaned against the doorframe, arms folded, watching intently. "Curious," he murmured. "You are meticulous. Not careless like most cowboys."

Hank glanced up, brushing dust from his palms. "Attention to detail saves time in the long run. She—Mirabella—taught me that."

The German nodded once, approving. "Ja. And I see how you handle him. Calm, but not timid. That balance is rare." His gaze sharpened. "I recognize you now. You are the boy who beat Clayton Briggs."

Hank gave a single nod. "That was me. Bob's mine and Mirabella's. Buckskin Quarter Horse stallion. She trained him in dressage."

The coach's brows lifted. "A Quarter Horse in dressage? Unconventional. But yes—I recall. He had remarkable balance. That is not an accident. That is training, and a rider with an eye." He studied Hank for a long moment. "If you wish, I will continue to train you. Pick up where she left off."

Hank's hand went to his pocket, feeling the folded ribbon there. The fabric pressed against his fingers, and with it, the thought of Mirabella's steady gaze. Accepting the offer felt like accepting a tether to her, a way to keep her near though she was far.

"I'd like that," Hank said. His voice was quiet, but certain.

The coach gave a curt nod, satisfaction flickering in his eyes. "Then we begin next week. I think you will do well."

Valeroso blew through his nostrils, stamping once as though sealing the promise. He stood a little taller, his stance steadier than when he'd arrived.

When Valeroso was settled back into his stall, Hank left the barn, the German's words still turning in his head: *We begin next week.* It gave him something to hold on to, but today's work waited elsewhere.

By midday he was out on the range, the sun glaring white off stone and grass. The herd stretched long across the slope, bawling low, tails swishing against flies. Hank swung into his gelding's saddle and rode forward.

The vaqueros fell into line the moment he lifted a hand. They had always respected him — his horsemanship, his grit — but since the rodeo and the race, something had shifted. Now they watched him like soldiers eyeing their commander, eager to catch his signals, eager not to fail him.

Hank didn't think about it much. He saw what needed to be done. "Keep them wide through the draw," he called. "Hold the pace steady."

The men fanned out in practiced arcs. A calf broke rank, and two riders wheeled without hesitation, guiding it back in as though they had read Hank's mind. The herd flowed clean, dust rising in slow curtains.

Don Antonio rode among them, not apart but in the line, his horse moving at Hank's pace. He said nothing, though his sharp eyes tracked not just the cattle, but the men — how they leaned toward Hank, how they gauged every small motion of his hand.

They see him as more than a boy now, Don Antonio thought. *He carries himself like a man who knows where the herd should go — and others follow.* Pride touched him, quiet but fierce. He had watched Hank grow from a wiry youth into some-one who might one day shoulder more than his own family's land.

At a choke point near the creek bed, the herd threatened to bunch. Hank guided his mount forward, angled to open space, then signaled with a lift of his chin. Two riders pressed at the flank, and the cattle spilled through smoothly, no break in the rhythm.

Don Antonio tipped two fingers off his reins. "Good call."

Hank only nodded, his eyes still on the moving line.

As they turned the herd toward water, the bawling echoing across the flats, Don Antonio eased his horse alongside. He didn't look over, but his voice carried low and certain.

"Come to the office after work."

The words held the weight of an order, but pride sat tucked behind them. Don Antonio had seen how the men looked at Hank — and, for the first time, he admitted he saw it too.

Late afternoon pressed heavy over the estancia. The grit of the range still clung to him as he stepped into the cool shadow of the main house. Don Antonio led the way down the tiled corridor, footfalls sharp on the tile.

They entered the office where Agustín waited, sleeves rolled, spectacles pushed low on his nose. Ledgers, pasture maps, and stud books lay scattered across the desk. He looked up and smiled when Hank came in.

"Here he is," Don Antonio said, his voice carrying more weight than usual. He paused, studying Hank a moment longer than necessary, then added, "The boy who rode the herd like a captain today."

Agustín's brows lifted. He already knew Hank's skill with cattle, but Don Antonio's words told him something had shifted.

Hank stood straight, trying not to fidget under the scrutiny. "You wanted me?"

"Yes," Agustín said, gesturing him closer. "We are reviewing stock rotations, pasture yields, and margins. Since you've had charge of the cattle this season, I'd like your perspective."

Hank leaned over the maps, tracing lines with his calloused finger, speaking plainly of where the grass was thinning, where calves had come on strong. Don Antonio nodded occasionally, saying little.

When the conversation dipped, Hank hesitated, then cleared his throat. "There's something else I've been thinking about."

Agustín looked up, curious. "Go on."

Hank drew a breath. "We've got cattle, yes. But there's room here for more. Horses. A breeding and training program. Not just ranch mounts but something broader. Stock that works cattle, yes, but with balance enough for dressage. Even jumping. A line that can serve the valley and the show ring."

Agustín leaned back in his chair, folding his arms. "Ambitious." A flicker of interest sparked in his eyes. "Keep going."

Hank bent closer over the desk, pointing at an unused paddock on the map. "Facilities could go here—stalls, a ring. Training cycles for young colts, starting them slow, building them right. We could bring in outside horses for breaking and schooling. That's revenue—steady, not tied only to beef or olive oil prices."

He warmed as he spoke; the idea shaped itself with each word. "Mirabella's taught me plenty about balance. Bob's proof of it—cow horse, but soft and supple enough to ride patterns. With the right breeding, the right work, we could raise horses that do it all. Ranch work. Dressage. Maybe even show jumping one day. Horses that carry strength and cow sense, but also scope enough to clear rails. A real working sport horse."

Don Antonio sat silent, expression reserved, but his gaze was sharp. Agustín, though, leaned forward, the corners of his mouth lifting.

"I had thought of you as a foreman," he intoned. "A talented one. But I did not realize you had such an eye for business—and for possibility."

Hank shifted, embarrassed by the heat rising in his neck. "It's only an idea. But I believe it could work."

Agustín tapped the map with one finger. "I believe so too. And I think it is worth developing—together." He paused, his gaze steady. "One day, I would like to take you to Argentina. To see the horses there. To judge if the mares would suit—bloodlines with fire and scope, matched to your stallion's grit. Bob could be the start of something greater."

The thought struck Hank with force, almost more than he could hold. Bob, a horse he had once fought to gentle, now stood at the foundation of a breeding program that might outlast them all.

For a long moment, the only sound was the rustle of pages as Don Antonio closed a ledger. The man gave no praise, but the faintest of nods passed between him and Agustín. To Hank, it felt like a door opening.

The talk of Argentina lingered in the air, heavy with promise. Hank shifted his weight, his hand brushing the map where his finger had traced the paddocks. The thought of Bob standing at the head of a line of foals—bloodlines that stretched across oceans—still pulsed inside him.

Agustín leaned back in his chair, studying him. "You speak as if the future is already in your hands," he said. His tone wasn't mocking, but measured, like a teacher testing a pupil.

Hank straightened. "No. Only in my head. But it could be."

He hesitated, then added voice lower, "I don't have the kind of brains you and Don Antonio do. I couldn't make it through Harvard or run an estate like this. But I do want to learn. The business side. How to build something that lasts. I know what I want the ranch to be—I just need to know how to make it real." His gaze flicked to the map again. "If I can do that, maybe I'll be worthy of it someday."

Don Antonio gave the faintest grunt of approval, though his face remained unreadable.

Agustín folded his hands. "Let me ask you something more difficult. What place do Mirabella's dreams have in this future you speak of?"

The question hit like a stone dropped into still water. Hank thought of her at the pond, head resting on his shoulder, her voice steady: *Promise me you'll come to Argentina. See my horses. Hear me play.*

"She has her path," Hank said slowly. "Argentina, competing all over the world, her music. I won't get in the way of that." His jaw tightened. "My father tried to steer Jesse. Forced him toward what he wanted, not what Jesse wanted. And it ruined things. I won't do that to her."

Agustín studied him in silence for a long moment, then nodded once. "Good. Because I will not allow anyone to stand in the way of her dreams."

Hank met his gaze evenly. "Neither will I."

Something shifted in Agustín's expression—an easing, almost a smile. Don Antonio, silent until now, let his eyes linger on Hank, as though measuring the boy against the man he was becoming.

Agustín leaned forward, his voice softer. "You should know I still speak with Jesse."

Hank's shoulders stiffened.

"He is not in a good place," Agustín continued. "I tell you this not to burden you, but because I believe he still needs his brother. He may not admit it, but he does."

Hank's voice came low. "I haven't been there for him. Not since Tegan."

Agustín tilted his head, thoughtful. "Grief makes us all exiles. But one day you must decide whether to stay away or return." He slid a slip of paper from the corner of the desk, pressing it under his palm. "When you are ready, I know he would love to hear from you."

Hank swallowed hard, words catching in his throat. "Thank you—for not giving up on him." Hank accepted the contact information and placed it in his back pocket.

Agustín gave the faintest smile. "Families are worth the fight. You, of all people, should understand that now."

The light from the window slanted across the maps, dust motes drifting between them. Hank sat with the weight of it—Mirabella's dreams, Jesse's absence, and his own first step into something larger than himself.

For the first time, he felt not only like a hand at the estancia, but like a man being measured for the future.

By the time Hank eased the Apache into the Miller farmyard, the sky had gone soft with evening. The porch light glowed warm, and the house carried its familiar sounds: June moving in the kitchen, pans clinking, the faint murmur of Marshall's chair creaking on the porch.

Hank climbed the stairs two at a time, dust still on his boots. In his room, he lit the dented reading lamp on his desk, its yellow glow pushing back the shadows.

The 1967 Mustang Fastback sat finished now, its sleek lines gleaming under the light. The miniature jars of paint were closed, brushes cleaned and set aside. It stood steady on the scarred oak surface, no longer half-done, but whole—an unspoken marker of how much had changed since that first night he left it unfinished.

Hank settled into the chair, staring at the envelope that had been waiting for weeks. Jesse's handwriting curled across it, careless but familiar.

His thumb slipped under the flap. The paper tore with a soft rip, and the letter slid free.

He unfolded it slowly.

Hank,

I don't know how to start this, so I'll start plain: I failed you. I failed Tegan. I wasn't the brother I should have been. I was the one who ran, who broke things, and you were the one who always picked up the pieces. I don't deserve your forgiveness, but I hope one day you might give it anyway.

You always carried more weight than I did. You shouldered it quietly, where I was loud. I chased songs and lights while you stayed behind to keep the fences mended and the cattle fed. I see now that you were braver than me. You fought the fight I ran from.

I wish I could tell Tegan how sorry I am. She deserved an older brother who showed up, who kept his promises. All she got was me, full of excuses and empty chords. I'll carry that regret as long as I breathe.

And you—little brother—God, I hope you know I loved you, even when I didn't show it. I see now that love isn't words; it's staying. You stayed. I left. I can't change that.

I won't ask for much. Only that you keep a corner of your heart open in case the day comes when I can be more than the mess I've been. If that day never comes, I understand.

Your brother,

Jesse

A smaller fold of paper slipped loose from the envelope and landed on the desk. Hank picked it up and opened it.

A sketch stared back at him—himself astride Bob, drawn in Jesse's quick, fluid hand. The lines were raw but full of life, catching the arch of Bob's neck, the lean of Hank's body in the saddle. The strange part was that Jesse had drawn it before Hank had truly chosen Bob, before he had claimed him as his own.

Jesse had always had that gift. He could see people clearer than they saw themselves. He could catch the song inside them and set it down—on paper, in melody, in a sketch like this. But when it came to himself, he was blind until now.

Hank sat back in the chair, the letter trembling slightly in his hand; the sketch spread open on the desk beside the Mustang. The house murmured around him—June's voice faint in the kitchen, the steady scrape of Marshall's chair on the porch—but he heard only Jesse's words, lingering like the last note of a song that would not fade.

The night settled quietly over the farm; the sky washed in pale starlight. Hank stepped out onto the porch, Jesse's letter folded in his hand. Marshall sat rooted in his usual chair, pipe ember glowing faint in the dark.

Without a word, Hank held out the letter. Marshall hesitated, then took it, the paper crackling between his fingers. He bent over it, reading slowly. The porch creaked under the weight of silence. Hank kept his eyes on the yard, the outline of the barn steady against the night.

When Marshall finished, his jaw flickered. His eyes shone, but he didn't wipe them. He folded the letter carefully, as if it might break, and handed it back.

"Thank you for sharing it," he said, voice rougher than usual.

Hank tucked the letter against his chest.

Marshall studied him, then asked, "Do you know how to reach him?"

"Agustín gave me his info," Hank said. "I might write."

Marshall nodded slowly. "That's a good idea." He paused, gaze lifting toward the fields. "Maybe I should write to him too."

The thought struck Hank with unexpected warmth. For the first time, he felt his father and brother standing with him in the same space—different but not divided.

Mirabella's words rose in his memory, steady and certain: *To move forward, you must face the past. Jesse should be in your life in some way.*

Hank drew a long breath, and it no longer hurt to let it out. Marshall leaned back in his chair, shoulders easing, as if some of the weight had shifted from both of them.

The porch had gone still, with only cicadas droning in the dark. Hank sat beside Marshall, Jesse's letter folded safe in his pocket. No words passed between them, yet the quiet carried a different shape now—open, steady. They sat, not as father and son locked by grief, but as men who had moved through it together and come out ready to face whatever waited ahead.

Then the telephone rang inside the house, sharp and insistent. The sound cut through the night like a bell, too loud for the quiet porch. To Hank, it felt less like a summons and more like a threshold—pulling him from the weight of the past and toward something waiting ahead.

Marshall rose, pipe tucked into his pocket. "Go on," he said. "Answer it. I'll check the stock before turning in."

Hank pushed open the screen door, the ringing carrying him into the kitchen. June stood by the counter with the receiver against her apron. She looked up as he entered.

"It's Clayton," she said, eyes widening slightly. "For you."

Hank crossed the room and took the phone. "Mr. Briggs," he said, steady but respectful.

Clayton's voice came warm, gravelly from years of dust and smoke. "Miller. Hope I'm not catching you too late. I wanted to tell you—I watched you at the rodeo. That buckskin of yours is a fine animal. You sat him with the kind of feel I don't see often, not at your age."

"Thank you, sir," Hank said, pulse quickening.

"I've got a couple of young colts that could use that kind of hand," Clayton went on. "Thought I'd ask if you'd consider starting them."

Hank drew a breath. "I'm beginning a breeding and training program with the Castillas at their estancia. If you'd like, you can bring the colts there. I'll work out the details with Agustín and call you tomorrow."

On the other end, a pause. Then Clayton's reply, firm and genuine: "Sounds like you're on to something. I'll look forward to your call." The line clicked dead.

Hank replaced the receiver, the silence of the kitchen rushing in. June watched him closely, her hands still on her apron.

"Breeding and training program?" She asked, with a note of surprise in her voice.

Hank nodded, feeling the truth of it settle in his chest. "It's an idea I've been working on with Agustín. Nothing is set in stone yet, but... it could be something real."

June's expression softened, pride and wonder mingling. "You're just like your Grandpa Joe," she said. "Making your own way from nothing. Self-made."

Hank's throat tightened, but he managed a small smile. "Thanks, Mom. I'm gonna turn in. Early start."

She watched him head down the hall, her heart full, the echo of the ringing phone still hanging in the air like the sound of a door opening to the future.

The house settled into its nighttime hush by the time Hank sat at his desk. The dented lamp cast a cone of yellow over the scarred oak, throwing shadows across the finished Mustang and Jesse's sketch of him astride Bob. He pulled a fresh sheet of paper from the drawer and stared at it for a long moment, the pen heavy in his hand.

At last, he began.

Jesse,

I've been angry for a long time. I thought if I stayed angry, it would hurt less. But it doesn't. I'm ready to forgive you. I can't say I understand why you left, but I don't want to carry the weight anymore. I want to be brothers again, if you'll have me.

Thanksgiving is coming. Come home. We'll set a place for you. No conditions, no questions. Just family.

—Hank

He sat back, the words plain on the page. Not fancy, not dressed up. Just true.

A soft knock came on the door. "Hank?"

"Come in," he said.

June stepped into the lamplight. Her eyes flicked to the page, but she didn't pry.

"I'm writing to Jesse," Hank said, his voice steady. "I'm ready to forgive him, Mom. Thinking of inviting him to Thanksgiving."

Her face softened. She crossed the room, resting a hand on his shoulder. "Tell him I love him. Invite him. There will always be a place for him at the table. But don't be surprised if he doesn't come."

Hank nodded, swallowing hard.

She bent, kissed the crown of his head, then slipped out, leaving him with the letter and the steady glow of the lamp.

Hank lowered the pen again, the scratch of ink on paper carrying him forward. For the first time, it felt like the past might loosen its grip.

A week later, the diner's neon sign buzzed against the night, its pink glow stuttering on the brick wall. Jesse leaned there in his shirtsleeves, cigarette burning low between his fingers, the smoke curling up into the damp air. He took a drag, exhaled slowly, and unfolded the letter once more.

Reading and rereading the paper creased and softened it at the folds. His eyes slid down the lines he could already recite, catching again on the words near the bottom: *Come home. Thanksgiving. We'll set a place for you.*

His chest tightened. He had told himself he didn't deserve a seat at that table, but the invitation clung stubbornly as a melody he couldn't forget.

The door creaked open behind him. A waitress stepped out, apron loose, a cigarette in her own hand. She caught sight of the letter and grinned. "Secret girlfriend?" she teased, smoke curling from her lips.

Jesse shook his head, folding the page carefully. He slid it into his breast pocket, close against his heart. "Nothing like that."

He flicked the ash from his cigarette, ground the butt under his heel, and tapped his breast pocket. He didn't move, didn't speak. Just stood there a little longer, the words tucked close against his chest, like warmth he wasn't sure he deserved.

THE WORK AHEAD

T he valley carried the hush of late autumn. Morning frost clung in the shaded corners, melting quickly once the sun rose over the ridges. The oaks along the creek stood bare, their branches etched against a sky washed clear by the season's first rains. Smoke curled from the farmhouse chimney, sharp with oak and eucalyptus, drifting low across the yard.

Hank stepped off the porch, boots pressing into ground firm from the night's chill. His breath hung white in the air before fading, a reminder of how close Thanksgiving had come. Two months had slipped past since the rodeo, the days folding into work at the estancia and quiet evenings at home.

Today was his day off, a day to turn his hands toward the farm itself — fences to mend, barn boards to repair, a new table order to cut with Grandpa Joe. Work steady and simple, the kind that stitched a place back together.

A meadowlark sang from the fencepost, its notes lifting into the still morning. Hank paused, letting the sound settle over him. It no longer stung like it once had. Tegan's presence came now not as a hollow ache but as something gentler, like a guardian angel close at his ear. He let the song carry him forward, warm in the cool air, ready for the work ahead.

The sun had risen higher by the time Hank joined Grandpa Joe and Marshall in the pasture. Frost melted off the wire, leaving beads of water that caught the light. The air smelled of cedar posts and churned earth. They worked in rhythm — Grandpa Joe laying out tools, Hank hauling timbers, Marshall driving nails with slow, deliberate strokes.

The fence had sagged where a steer had leaned too hard. Hank braced the old rails while Marshall pried the nails loose, their movements wordless but steady.

Once, this kind of work had carried a strain between them: Marshall correcting every motion, Hank stiff under the weight of it. But that edge had dulled. Now, the silence between them held no judgment, only focus.

When the rails stood straight again, Hank wiped his palms on his jeans. "I've been thinking," he said, glancing between them. "Instead of keeping the cattle fixed in the same pasture, we could rotate them — like Jesse used to talk about. Let the ground rest, bring in chickens and pigs after, then seed grass behind them. It'd keep the soil stronger."

Grandpa Joe leaned on his cane, the sun cutting across the lines of his face. He gave a single nod. "It's sound. Land'll thank you for it."

Marshall paused, hammer resting against his thigh. For years he had seen Hank as a boy to be shaped, a son to be held tight while Jesse slipped through his grip. But tragedy and hard labor had stripped that away. Standing here, he no longer saw a child in need of molding, but a man with ideas worth trusting.

He met Hank's eye and said, "Let's try it your way."

The words were plain, but they landed heavier than any post they'd set in the ground.

They moved on to the barn, the siding rough beneath their gloves. Sawdust rose as they cut boards for repairing the wall, the saw's buzz steady as a hymn. Hank marked lengths with a carpenter's pencil, marking his cuts clean. As he bent to draw a line, Marshall reached out without a word, catching the far end of the plank to hold it steady.

Once, Hank would have bristled at the gesture, thinking it a correction. Now he saw it for what it was: partnership. A father choosing to lean on his son, man to man.

By midday, the fence stood tall; the barn was fully patched, and a neat stack of lumber waited for Grandpa Joe's next table order. The three of them leaned back from work, sweat drying in the autumn air. For the first time in a long while, the labor felt less like survival and more like building a future — together.

The light slanted low through the front windows, filling the room with the warm gold of late afternoon. June sat at the piano, shoulders relaxed, fingers searching for a melody. The tune shifted and wavered, phrases curling into something half-remembered — echoes of the silly songs Tegan used to sing in the kitchen while they prepared meals together.

Marshall stepped into the doorway, boots still dusty from the fence line. He paused there, silent, listening. For a long moment he stood as he always had — on the edge, watching, unsure of how to bridge the space between them. But this time, instead of holding back, he crossed the room and lowered himself onto the bench beside her.

Her fingers faltered, but the music didn't stop.

"I missed hearing you play," he said, voice low with years of quiet. After a beat, he added, softer still: "I missed you."

He leaned in and pressed a kiss to her cheek, awkward and tender.

June's eyes brightened with sudden tears, but her hands kept moving over the keys. The melody steadied, filled the house, and wrapped around them both. Marshall stayed where he was, shoulder against hers, the music bridging what words couldn't. For the first time since loss had hollowed their home, it felt as though the silence had finally broken.

Out in the garden, Grandma Ginny bent over her herbs, trimming sprigs of rosemary and lavender against the cool air. She hummed without thinking, the very tune drifting from the piano inside — the same one Tegan used to hum while skipping barefoot through the rows. The sound carried between house and garden, stitching past to present, loss to renewal, in a single unbroken thread.

Marshall didn't move away. June leaned into the keys, her shoulders brushing his sleeve, her music finding a steadier rhythm as though his presence grounded it. The notes lifted into the rafters, soft and unhurried, filling corners of the house that had stayed too quiet for too long.

From the garden, the same tune drifted faintly back through the open windows, Grandma Ginny's hum joining the piano's voice. For a heartbeat, the house and the land breathed in unison — music and memory, melody and hum — all woven through with Tegan's thread.

Marshall closed his eyes, listening. June pressed a hand briefly against his, never breaking the flow of the song.

Outside, Grandma Ginny straightened, herbs gathered in her apron. She paused, head tilted, realizing she and June had fallen into harmony without meaning to. The sound made her smile, weary but full, as if her granddaughter's spirit had slipped quietly between them, reminding them what had always bound them together.

The light thinned, shadows stretching long across the garden and into the rooms of the farmhouse. The music carried on until the last phrase faded into silence, leaving the air warm, expectant — as though something had shifted, and the house knew it.

The screen door eased shut behind Grandma Ginny as she stepped into the late-afternoon light. The air carried a crisp edge; wood smoke drifted faint from the chimney, the scent of rosemary trailing her hands. Down the lane, the mailbox sat waiting, its metal cool beneath her touch. Inside lay a single envelope, pale and delicate, marked with Argentine stamps.

The handwriting was Mirabella's — rounded and careful, but practiced, the strokes confident. Grandma Ginny's heart tugged. She carried it back to her bench beneath the old oak, where the garden's lavender bent in the breeze, and broke the seal.

Dearest Grandma Ginny,

I started this letter three times already, trying to sound grown-up, but it turns out I just miss you, so I'll write it like we're sitting in the garden together.

It fills me with joy to be home again with my family in Argentina. My father's voice carries across the courtyard each morning, my mother hums softly while she tends the roses, and my brothers ride out with the cattle at dawn. After so many months away, these familiar sounds and faces feel like the embrace of the land itself.

Soon, I will leave again, this time for Vienna. I have been invited to study at the Spanish Riding School. The thought both thrills and humbles me — to step into that ancient hall and learn where so many masters have ridden. I am still only a girl, yet every day I feel closer to the dream I have carried since childhood: to ride in a Grand Prix.

Life here has been bright with festivals. At harvest, the entire village gathered under strings of lanterns. Tables groaned with empanadas and roasted meats, the air sweet with oil and lavender pressed from the groves. The guitars played until dawn, accompanied by the deep pulse of the bombo drum. The women twirled in bright skirts, lace shawls glimmering in the lamplight, while the men stamped and turned with proud precision. I danced until my hair clung damp to my cheeks, until laughter spilled out of me like a song. I thought of you in that moment — how much you would have loved the rhythms, the laughter, the joy. It felt as though you were there beside me, your hands clapping to the beat.

Please give my greetings to all the family — to Marshall, June, and Grandpa Joe. Tell Hank that I think often of Bob and Valeroso, and I trust they are under his watchful eye. I wear the locket every day, and with Tegan beside me, I never ride alone.

With all my affection,
Mirabella

Grandma Ginny folded the letter slowly, her thumb pressed against the crease as though reluctant to close it. Her eyes blurred with tears, but her lips curved in a smile. Mirabella's words were more than a letter — they were a song across the ocean, carrying Tegan's spirit within them, alive in memory and promise.

She sat back against the bench, the garden warm around her, lavender stirring in the breeze. For a moment, she could almost hear Tegan's laughter weaving through the rosemary stalks, as if the valley itself were answering Mirabella's call.

The long oak table carried the weight of a midday feast. A pot of stew steamed at the center, thick with carrots, onions, potatoes, and beef that had simmered down to tender shreds. The fragrance of thyme and bay leaf drifted up with the steam. Loaves of fresh bread sat beside it, crusts browned and crackling. Hank and Grandma Ginny had tested a new recipe that morning — fresh rosemary kneaded into the dough, a hint of olive oil giving it a sheen.

Bowls were filled, spoons dipped. For a while, the only sounds were the scrape of cutlery and the soft clink of plates. The house smelled alive again, rich with herbs, meat, and warmth.

Marshall tore into a second hunk of bread, butter melting into the crust. June arched an eyebrow at him. "You planning on leaving any for the rest of us?"

Marshall looked up, surprised, then gave the faintest shrug. "It's good bread."

"Good?" Grandma Ginny huffed. "That recipe is better than good." She tipped her chin toward Hank. "This one helped me perfect it."

Hank grinned, tearing his own piece. "We'll make more, don't worry. Plenty of rosemary left."

Laughter rippled lightly around the table before giving way to the steady rhythm of eating again.

When the bowls were nearly empty, Grandma Ginny unfolded an envelope from her apron pocket, smoothing the paper flat. "I've got a letter," she said, and the table hushed.

Her voice carried steadily as she read Mirabella's words — about her joy at being home in Argentina, about the festivals and dancing, about her dream drawing closer as she prepared for Vienna. When Grandma Ginny reached the line about the locket, Hank lowered his head, a smile tugging at his mouth. It was enough to know Mirabella carried a piece of this valley with her.

When the letter ended, the silence lingered warm, full of unspoken thoughts. Hank set his spoon aside. "I've got news too," he said.

He looked around the table, steady and unashamed. "Clayton Briggs asked me to start a couple colts for him. I'm working it out with Agustín at the estancia. We're planning an equestrian facility there — breeding, training, the whole works. And next weekend, I'm entering the rodeo. Bob's ready. I think I can beat Clayton Briggs."

A spark flickered in June's eyes. She reached across the table, her hand covering his. "We know you can, Hank."

Marshall gave a single nod, chewing slowly, but there was no mistaking the pride in his eyes.

Hank leaned back, a grin breaking through. "Bob's been full of mischief lately. Keeps working the latches, letting himself out. Last time I pulled up, he trotted out of the pasture like he'd been waiting. I've never had a horse like him. It's like he can read my thoughts. He's... special."

Grandpa Joe chuckled, slapping the table with his palm. "That horse has more tricks than a card shark. You better hope he doesn't figure out doorknobs."

That brought laughter from everyone, real and unguarded. Marshall's deep chuckle mixed with June's bright laugh, Grandma Ginny shaking her head as if she could see Bob's antics herself. For the first time in too long, the table sounded like home.

When it settled, Grandma Ginny gave Hank a sly wink. "You should write Mirabella yourself."

He flushed, shaking his head. "I don't have the gift of words."

Grandpa Joe leaned back in his chair. "Then lend your hands. Help me with this table order when you get back."

Marshall cleared his throat, his voice low but sure. "If this is the road you're taking, I stand behind it."

The words landed quietly but certain, filling the table with a new stillness — not the hush of grief, but the recognition of a family moving forward together.

The sun had slipped low by the time Hank drove the Apache into the yard at Estancia Castilla, the truck's exhaust echoing against the whitewashed walls. The air smelled of hay and wood smoke, the last rays of daylight turning the fields copper.

From the pasture, a head lifted — golden hide catching the light. Bob pricked his ears, nostrils flaring at the sound of the truck. He tossed his head once, then went to work on the latch. With a practiced nudge of his nose, the gate clanged open. The stallion trotted out, tail flagged, hooves drumming the hard earth as he came straight for Hank.

Hank swung down from the cab, laughing as the horse closed the distance. "You've become a regular Houdini, Bob."

The buckskin halted in front of him, blowing warm breath across his chest. Hank rubbed the star on his forehead, the familiar strength steady under his hand. Bob's dark eyes gleamed with mischief, as though he knew exactly what he had done.

From across the pasture, another rhythm joined — the beat of hooves against soil. Agustín cantered up on a dark bay, slowing as he reached the yard. His laughter carried ahead of him. "He's a legend with the vaqueros now. They swear he opens gates better than the ranch hands."

Hank glanced down at Bob, still snorting like a triumphant thief. He shrugged, a twinkle in his eye. "Guess he figured it out on his own."

Agustín swung out of the saddle, grinning. "If you didn't teach him, you must have encouraged him. He has the look of a horse who knows his rider will forgive him anything."

Hank only smiled, patting Bob's neck. "Maybe so."

The stallion leaned into the touch, ears flicking as though listening. Hank's grin lingered. Whatever tricks the horse picked up, one thing was certain — they were his tricks now, and Hank wouldn't have it any other way.

Hank and Agustín rode side by side, Bob's stride strong and loose beside Agustín's bay. The sun hung low, copper light pouring across the fields. Ahead, the pond glimmered, reeds whispering as a breeze slid across the water.

Agustín drew a leather tube from his saddlebag and unrolled a crackling sheaf against his thigh. "First drafts," he said. Squares and lines marked barns, paddocks, and an arena bold in the center. "Foaling barns here. Training facilities there. Enough to carry a new program forward."

Hank leaned down from Bob's back, eyes narrowing as he studied the sketch. "It's good," he drawled. "But look here." He traced the line with his finger. "These paddocks are too tight. Horses need more. They should graze, stretch, feel the wind, not just circle in a pen. Barn life and pasture life together — that's how you keep them whole."

Agustín's mouth twitched, amused. "So how would you lay it out?"

"Wide paddocks with run-outs to pasture," Hank said. His voice quickened, the ideas tumbling over each other. "Foals raised with grass under their hooves, but brought in to school early. Dressage for balance, jumping for scope, cattle to sharpen instinct. Natural horsemanship woven with classical technique. That's how you build horses that don't just perform, but partner."

His eyes lit, the words carrying more heat. "We could make this a place riders would come to from all over the world. Not just to see horses worked, but to learn how to work with them. A place where people and horses find each other through nature first, training second. A world-class facility — built right here."

Agustín studied him, the rolled plans forgotten in his hand. Hank wasn't speaking like a boy dreaming. He was speaking like someone who had lived the truth of what he described, every callus, every bruise, every hard-earned lesson pressed into his words.

Hank let out a breath, softer now. "Mirabella wrote to Grandma Ginny. She's leaving for Vienna — to the Spanish Riding School." His grin flickered quickly. "She's fourteen, and already halfway to the top of the world. I'm proud of her. More than proud. I'm glad she's chasing it. And I'll be ready for her when she comes back. Bob. Valeroso — they'll be sharper, straighter, up to her standards."

Agustín's brows lifted, and for a moment he said nothing. Hank's voice had steadied, carrying not envy or fear, but a surety born of loss and of loyalty.

"I've learned something from both Jesse and Bob," Hank went on. "If you want a true partnership, you have to listen. Make room for your partner's dreams in your own life. That's trust. That's how you keep it strong."

The words settled between them, quiet as the pond at their feet.

Agustín rolled the plans with slow precision, his gaze lingering on Hank. In him he saw not only a foreman, not merely a boy brimming with promise — but a presence steady as the valley itself, surprising as spring rain on parched earth. Not a brother replaced, but a brother found, carried into his future like kin he hadn't expected yet already trusted.

He looped the plans into the saddlebag and shifted the reins in his hand. "Come to dinner," he said at last. "Don Antonio will want to hear of Mirabella's letter. And after, I would like us to speak more of your vision — the three of us together."

Hank ran a hand down Bob's neck, the stallion blowing softly. "I'll stay a little longer. Be in after."

Agustín gave him a nod and turned his horse toward the estancia, leaving Hank by the water's edge, the weight of vision and promise full in his chest.

The sky was already deepening when Agustín's bay gelding disappeared into the distance, his silhouette swallowed by the glow of lanterns kindling at the estancia. Hank sat astride Bob a moment longer, the stallion's ears flicking toward the pond.

He swung down and slipped the halter loose. Bob shook his neck once, mane catching the last of the light, but he didn't wander. He stayed fixed on Hank, muscles taut, waiting. No rope, no lead — only the quiet bond between them.

Hank stepped out onto the open ground by the pond. Bob followed, shadowing him close. Hank quickened his stride, and the stallion matched him, hooves thudding in rhythm. When Hank slowed to a jog in a circle, Bob mirrored him step for step, ears pricked, eyes alive.

Hank dropped suddenly into a crouch. Bob snorted, lowered his head, and came to him, blowing warm breath over his hair. Hank laughed, the sound breaking into the cool air. He sprang up again, clapping once. Bob surged forward, breaking into a gallop, mane streaming, pond water rippling at the edge of his stride. He curved wide, then spun back, sliding to a halt in a storm of leaves that curled golden in the fading light.

"Good boy," Hank murmured. He turned on his heel, and Bob wheeled with him, rearing high, forelegs slicing the dusk, then dropping into a playful trot at his side. Hank lifted his hand, and Bob lowered his forehead until it pressed into his palm.

They stood like that, man and horse breathing in unison, until the stallion dropped his head and grazed, pressing his shoulder gently into Hank's chest. Hank leaned into him, steadying himself on that weight. He watched the pond ripple in the dusk and felt something settle — not just peace, but a kind of knowing.

"Someday," he murmured, brushing his hand along Bob's neck, "I'll teach this to someone else — the way we're doing it now. Not with ropes, not with reins. Just trust."

The pond mirrored the branches overhead, rippling faint with the breeze. Hank spoke into the stillness, his voice low but unwavering.

"One day, I'll build a place here. Valley Vista Ranch. A place where horses can heal, and people too. Where real bonds are made through trust and skill. You'll be the start of it, Bob. And Mirabella will be part of it."

His voice dropped further, steadier still. "And you too, Tegan. Always you. I'll carry your dream into this place. You'll never be left behind."

Bob lifted his head at the sound of his name, ears twitching. He nickered softly, pressing closer, as though the promise belonged to him too.

The reeds stirred. For a heartbeat, Hank swore he heard Tegan's laughter dancing in the wind — not haunting, but guiding, woven into the land itself. He smiled faintly, sure she was with them still: in the horse beside him, in the dreams rising like fence posts yet to be set, in the path he was ready to walk.

He rested a hand on Bob's warm neck, eyes on the horizon where the sun bled into shadow. The pond held their reflection — boy and stallion moving in liberty-born harmony, the foundation of something larger than either of them alone.

The journey had been hard. The losses were real. But here, at the water's edge, Hank felt it settle clear inside him: it had been worth it, and it had only begun.

ABOUT THE AUTHOR

Maria V. Badin is an equestrian, writer, and lifelong advocate for living close to the land. With decades of experience in show jumping, eventing, and dressage, she brings authenticity, depth, and emotional truth to her storytelling. *An Untamed Valley* is the second book in the *Stable Life Series* and the prequel to her debut novel, *A Stable Life*. It centers on Hank Miller and traces the origins of Valley Vista Ranch, exploring the bonds, fractures, and hard-earned legacy that shape its future.

Based in California, Maria lives on her ranch with her husband, her horses True, Bubbles, and High Duty, her dog Bentley, and her cats Turbo and Indy. Her work celebrates grit, grace, and the unbreakable bond between horse and rider.

You can follow her online: **@badinmaria**

Also by

Maria V. Badin

Adult Novels

A Stable Life

Children's Novels

Andi the Andalusian
Leo and Izzy The Crown Bearers—Coming Soon